MW00685171

WINTER

ETERNAL

WINTER ETERNAL

E. Thomas Joseph

PRODIGY GOLD BOOKS

PHILADELPHIA * LOS ANGELES

WINTER ETERNAL

A Prodigy Gold Book

Prodigy Gold E-book edition / May 2018

Prodigy Gold Paperback edition / May 2018

Copyright (c) 2018 by E. Thomas Joseph

Library of Congress Catalog Card Number: 2018931000

Website: http://www.prodigygoldbooks.com

This novel is a work of fiction. Any references to real people, event, business, organization, or locales are intended only to give the fiction a sense of reality and authenticity. Names, characters, place, and incidents are the product of the author's imagination or used fictitiously. Any resemblance to actual persons, living or dead, events, or locales, is entirely coincidental.

All rights reserved. No parts of this book may be used or reproduced in any manner whatsoever without written permission from the author, except in case of brief quotations embodied in critical articles and reviews.

ISBN 978-1-939665-51-5

Published simultaneously in the US and Canada

PRINTED IN THE UNITED STATES OF AMERICA

For

Melissa, Developmental and Copy Editor

Rahiem, Line Editor

Laura, Proofreader

Map of the Progress of his
MAJESTY'S ARMIES in NEW YORK,
During the late CAMPAIGN Illustrating the Accounts
Publish'd in the London Gazette.

N E W

J E R S E Y

STATEN ISLAND

Amboy

LONG ISLAND SOUND

SUFFOLK

HAMSTED PLAINS

L O N G   I S L A N D

Hamsted

JAMAICA
BAY

HAMSTED BAY

Beach

Beach

Scale of Statute Miles.

WINTER

ETERNAL

"And my companions suffer from a disease of the heart which can be cured only with gold."—Hernan Cortes

Prologue

November 1755.

The northeastern wilderness had already begun its winter rest. A thin layer of wet snow gave way to patches of brown-green grass. Fallen leaves, dull, russet, and drained of all autumnal brilliance wisped about aimlessly. Each of the many rigid, tangled tree limbs reached for the dark gray sky to appear as shattered glass over the backdrop of the colorless heavens. Steadily, tiny flakes of snow were blown sidelong with the passing wind, as it hummed and fought its way through the thicket of branches. A creek lay to the west and flowed gently from the northwest, a shallow tributary of the Mohawk River. Under a thin blanket of mist, its gray water gently cast small ripples on the shore. Along the western horizon, the rolling Catskills were stripped of life and color, white and gray with snow, they bristled with leafless trees watching over the landscape. The creek flowed slowly in a shallow valley; an embankment supported a trail, several yards in width, which ran parallel to the water on the west and a dense forest of evergreens, oaks, elms, and maples, to the east.

A wandering buck lingered casually and approached along the partially frozen, muddied trail for a drink. The handsome beast trotted toward the bank, where he stood amongst the large stones and hardened soil along the river, his antlers tall and proud. He was thinner than he should be, aged to have seen most of his years already passed. His hide was patchy, dull brown and gray, and his eyes were expressionless black pearls. For years he and his kind had roamed the temperate countryside. Never had they laid claim to the land, spoiled nor polluted any of its beauty. For all his magnificence, he was a silent, peaceful creature, a grazer, and wanderer. He looked around as if fondly taking in the natural beauty of his surroundings. He drank from the river, before roaming deeper into darkness.

A faint clap began to draw near. He lifted his head eastward, facing the direction of the rumbling. Without hesitation, he raced into the forest, sprinting along the river way to the west. With each stride, his gallop grew softer, replaced by a rolling, thundering rumble that became louder as it neared.

Three riders, each astride impressive stallions, traveling from the south, revealed themselves and clamored along the same trail with a quickened gallop. Snowflakes melted upon their cheeks, but they remained focused as they moved forward. The warm mist of the horses' breath billowed alongside as the column hurriedly marched along. All the steeds were clad with forest green blankets adorned with gold and white embroidery, various straps, harnesses, pouches, and canisters that rattled as they galloped forward. Each rider had a haversack draped across the saddle and mounted on the left shoulder, a long "dragon" flintlock musket, and accompanying pistol. The riders sat tall and assured, appearing taller still in part for their signature black Tarleton helmets. A black plume of feathers ran along the top, from front to back, then continued as a tail for some ten to twelve inches behind the soldiers' backs. The middle horseman had a distinctive peak, ornamented with white goose feathers. They each wore heavy crimson waistcoats with a large, horizontal white striped placket from collar to bottom. Green and gold inlays marked the shoulders, collars, and cufflinks, a white leather belt, clipped with a gold clasp, and coattails behind. The harnesses around their chests met at a gilded plaque with "IV" etched into its surface. Below the inscription, a rare black beryl and ruby gemstone *cross sword and crown* insignia were embedded. Sturdy white pantaloons were embellished with a forest green stripe running vertically on the leg. Heavy, black leather boots with silver-plated spurs, buttoned and laced, sealed with rugged white canvas sleeves along the calf. Along their left hip was the polished brass handles atop long sabers, which rested in their scabbards. Tassels hung from the mouth of each scabbard, the middle rider's being braided white rope, the flanking riders' black. These were the unmistakable and unique markings of the enigmatic

Fourth Order of Aquitaine Light Horse Guards of the Royal Dragoons.

The Fourth Dragoons had earned a reputation for tenacity and ruthlessness through several conflicts for the King and Country. As such, they enjoyed preferred status amongst the Ministry and were never wasted on open combat or trivial operations. Equally formidable on a horse, dismounted as a musketeer, or as a piquet warrior, the Fourth Royal Order was not often seen entering or leaving a battlefield, yet their paths could be traced along wakes of desolation. Rumors of their nature and origins had spread like wildfire within the Empire's army. The most sensible gossip suggested each of these dragoons was nothing short of the most skilled and disciplined soldier, personally selected by the king himself. Reasonable men had insisted their existence to be nothing more than myth, legend, or some manner of exaggeration intent to inspire terror and submission before His Majesty's enemies. And credence could be rightfully granted to such speculations, given the unusually ambiguous accounts of their formal obligations and whereabouts in wartime operations. Others called the Dragoons the "specters," shadowy, supernatural archangels of the Almighty—the deadly protectors of the faith. Their mystery and intrigue had only grown as haunting tales of ghosts and demons amongst the king's men. The Ministry did nothing to disclaim such myths, nor did it discourage their propagation.

The three horsemen proceeded some two hundred yards along the trail as it climbed a small knoll through a gap between two large rock formations. Trotting briskly, they headed toward a thin tower of blackish smoke that bent and rose toward the sky. The lead rider remained no more than a pace ahead of the others. Until he pulled back on the reins and slowed to a near stop when they reached a clearing at the apex of the hill, where a gathering of structures and figures appeared. They were mostly surrounded by a treeless stretch of ground, which revealed furloughs, gardened patches, and tree stumps. At the far end of what would seem to be an archaic village was an unfinished wall of oak logs roughly twelve-foot-high, mounted side by side, each with pointed tips carved atop. The partition began at the northern corner of the encampment, snaked toward the west, then back toward the south, where it ended unfinished near a pile of logs that lay on the ground. The barricade resembled a crescent moon that partially encircled the encampment. Twenty-plus paces behind the incomplete bulwark was an abrupt cliff, dropping some fifty feet or so toward the river valley. From the edge of the precipice, one could see the creek winding amongst the trees.

Three longhouses, mud-clay structures, with curved roofs, wooden supports, and narrow arched entrances were positioned almost congruent to one another. The largest was positioned farthest north and was approximately six feet tall and thirty feet long. It stretched east to west, as did its two, slightly less impressive, counterparts. Various symbols appeared painted along the structures: a black turtle, deer, bear, and a red painted bird among other such animals. A fourth, smaller structure of similar design rested apart from the others to the east. A lone white maple towered in the near center of the village, and pottery, baskets, blankets, and tools of assorted manner lay about without apparent organization. Several large animal skins, resembling those of bears and deer, were stretched flat and bound to frames made from thick tree branches and rested amongst the buildings' walls. Smoke rose from a dying fire, and the snow continued to lightly fall as three canines angrily barked toward the oncoming horsemen.

A score or more of men, women, and children sat, side by side, in a circular pattern. Most had their arms wrapped around both knees, and all were silent and still. They were a clan of the woodland Iroquois, a people who had lived in these lands for centuries. The Iroquois were mostly nomads who roamed the countryside. After settling, an Iroquois tribe could count on surviving two or three generations before needing to wander again in search of food. This tribe had settled along the creek in the past summer, after being driven out of their eastern home by American settlers. Their manner of dress consisted of deerskin or rough leather blankets, skirts, smocks, sashes, and moccasins. All were embellished with regalia of beads, fringes, jewelry and stitching of varying sort. Some wore differing types of feathered headdresses or bands.

Clad in similar garb to the riders, with cardinal-red waistcoats, nine soldiers stood, spaced several feet apart, in what appeared to be a formal column, alongside the huddled Iroquois. Their appearance seemed more functional than their mounted counterparts. Each had a circular canteen strewn along his back, leather pouches along his waist sides, and a short, cylindrical container strapped to his belt along the small of his back. Each of the soldiers dared not flinch or utter a sound. They were steadfastly focused, dutifully resting long, bayoneted muskets, butts at their feet, up to and over their left shoulders with the muzzles facing skyward.

Lieutenant Colonel Emrick Bowman, flanked by two lesser officers, arrived from the southeast, along the riverbank trail. A broad and tall man, he stood just over six feet, with a chiseled chin, dark eyes, and narrow brow. He was cold in nature and showed little compassion or empathy, wasting few words. The Bowman family were of high noble order. Their legacy of military worth traced back to the waning days of the Holy Roman Empire, their name one of prestige and honor. Lord Leonard Bowman enlisted his son in the imperial war academy, where young Emrick quickly demonstrated exceptional ruthlessness in combat. He appeared set on a path for generalship, yet for peculiar circumstance, was unseen and unaccounted for, for some time. Who he was, or who he had become remained mostly unknown, other than the suggestion of a few cryptic clues here and there. What was assured, however, was that Colonel Bowman had hardened as the witness to more than any man's share of bloodshed and death over the course of his forty-seven years. Since his days as a fledgling officer, Bowman had earned his customary perception, fervently promoted by his father, for tenacity and cruelty. During the Jacobite uprising, Lieutenant Bowman had been believed to have inflicted death upon more Scots than some entire royal regiments. It was a common belief he was eager to uphold his standing among the ruthless, and as such, he had a loose interpretation of the code of honorable gentleman's warfare.

His warhorse, Shadow, stepped slowly and cautiously toward the center of the village, where another mounted soldier stood motionless with three Iroquois figures, also standing in place. The mount was gray with patches of white, had dark black eyes, and has been the lieutenant colonel's valued companion for nearly three years. While holding the reins with his left hand, the colonel raised his right, lazily, to instruct his subordinates on either side to remain in place.

"I'm forever impressed by their ingenuity," he said as he surveyed the village slowly from left to right.

"And their craftiness," replied Ensign Davies, who was positioned to Bowman's left.

The colonel offered Davies a cold look in return. "You there… girl!" he bellowed to the nearest native, a very young woman who was sitting on the ground with legs folded up and arms wrapped protectively around them. He lifted his head slightly as if to point her in a direction. "Fetch me the small clay jar over there, the middle one with the handle. Bring it to me. Go on…"

Visibly nervous but remaining on the ground, she looked about in a confused state and with dread on her face. The young native could have been no older than ten or eleven years of age. She had dark, smooth hair that framed her teary and terrified walnut eyes. Urgently, she looked toward others huddled around her, desperately seeking guidance or assurance, yet only one reacted. A native woman, perhaps twice her age, finally put her arms around her shoulder, and in a quite exasperated tone, began to murmur and plead to the colonel in her native language.

Partially frustrated, Bowman clarified his command sarcastically, "Right, fascinating, really…now bring me the jar from over there." He sighed, then paused for a moment. Still, she sat, her eyes welling, and her companion continued to fearfully grovel indistinguishably. He slowly shook his head with impatience and, with a blend of calm sarcasm and austerity, remarked to another native, standing to his left, "When you get a moment, could I trouble you do your job and please tell her to fetch me the fucking the jar?"

Without taking a stride, Otaktay looked at her and barked Bowman's instructions at her in her familiar Iroquoian tongue. Confused and sobbing, she took no immediate action until he repeated the command more directly. Frantically, she hurried toward the jar, which had rested along the base of the nearest longhouse, and reached up to hand it to the colonel. The colonel received it, smiled wryly, and bowed his head in subtle mockery. He accepted the mud-clay jar and said a patronizing "thank you," then waved her away. Without hesitation, she scurried back into the arms of the mother figure, who rubbed her shoulders reassuringly.

"I expect there will be no need to tell you to do your job," he said to his translator, who proceeded to grunt some sort of moan in displeasure. The exchange between Bowman and the young native was precipitated by two ambitions. The colonel genuinely wanted her to retrieve the jar, but, more importantly, he wanted to see if she, or any of the natives, could speak English.

The pottery was mostly functional and decorated with impressively etched designs and line patterns. One by one, Colonel Bowman removed various items from within, briefly examined it, then dropped it to the ground. A small stone chisel, two carved adzes, assorted arrowheads, and whittled wood carvings each carelessly dropped after his quick inspections. An interesting item caught his attention, and he held it for several seconds while gazing at it more intently than all the others. Bowman had a personal custom, collecting keepsakes of his adventures and ordeals. He was fond of the Iroquoian artifact, and it would make for a nice addition to his already impressive collection of trophies.

Bowman held an antler carving, from perhaps a deer or a moose. The small figurine was the size a pear and featured a man's head bound back to back with that of an eagle. Feeling content, he unbuckled one of the pouches worn at his waist, emptied several musket balls from it to the ground, and replaced them with the statuette. He extended the jar to Otaktay, no longer interested in searching whatever contents may remain. "What do I do with it?" asked the native translator, through a broken accent and with a confused look on his face.

"I don't care," replied Bowman. And with that, the brutish native flung the ceramic jar into the huddled crowd of his kind. Several of them scampered, to narrowly avoid being struck. This, of course, made Otaktay giggle with sinister glee.

The colonel commanded his horse forward by flicking his tongue to his upper teeth in a distinct *tick-tick*, while gently lashing the reins. Bowman, and Otaktay, who followed on foot, approached a small band of natives, who stood ten or so paces in front of them. The colonel pulled the reins to a halt, and Shadow grunted and shook his head powerfully from side to side. The horse then blasted a large gust of air from his nostrils, and the cold mist could easily have been mistaken for the smoke of cannon fire. His chest bore the scrapes and scars earned in battle as proudly as his rider's many medals and decorations. Bowman patted his horse on the back of his neck to calm the animal. It was Bowman's belief that Shadow had a disdain for the Indians that equaled his own. "He hates being among these Indian animals, as do I. Whom do I address?" he barked to nobody in particular, while gazing into the woodlands.

Otaktay lightly shoved the older of the two native men. "This one, the elder of the counsel." Otaktay was unique among the native complement; a scout and a translator, he had been very well compensated by royal offices for his services to His Majesty. He was of broad and muscular build, his face marked with dark red and black paint, head fully shaven aside a long Mohawk, which continued nearly three feet in braids behind his back. The Dragoons mockingly call him "Pineapple" because of what they believed to be the unique style in which he wore his hair. Otaktay was a trusted companion, equally reliable and merciless as his European brethren, and upon proving his merit, had been adopted almost as one of their own. Officially, Otaktay was to be treated as any native scout within the hire of the Empire. Over the many months of service, the admiration for his white colleagues had hastened his assimilation. Often, he attempted to speak the King's English, though he still tended to misuse colloquialisms comically. He wore the same red coat as the British comrades, with deerskin pants and moccasins, a leather belt with a stone dagger holstered, and a large, stone talisman with a winged hawk carved into its face.

Bowman, disinterested, still glancing into the distance, lazily waved the man Otaktay labeled as the elder forward. The translator snarled a few words in his native tongue, and the two men stepped toward the still-mounted colonel. With a casual tone, and with eyes adrift, observing the natural magnificence in which he was surrounded, Bowman assured the native before him, "We are not here to bring harm, though the manner in which you address my inquiries may change this. Reliable word has reached my ears suggesting you and your ilk are the friends of our enemies. Should this be true, of course, you will be treated as our enemy."

Otaktay repeated Bowman's warning to Shappa, the village elder, in his Iroquoian tongue. Nervous and pleading, Shappa replied in his native language. The translator relayed his message to the colonel: "He say they have no wish to fight in your wars, seek only to harvest before the winter. They are not friends with French. Not your enemy, he say."

Bowman nodded slowly, revealing no emotion about his face, then paused and coldly responded, "Then he will not mind if we search the village."

Shappa became the tribal elder at a young age, after his father, a brave warrior chief, was killed hunting big game. Though he is quite old, Shappa was in good health, yet seemed meek and unassuming, with long gray hair, dark calloused skin, and sad, deep-brown eyes. He stood only about five and a half feet and appeared shorter still given his failing posture. "I beg him…we have no wish to assist the French enemy. We are people of peace. We seek only peace. We seek no war with his kind."

Now less disinterested and as animated as Bowman will maintain, "It seems you speak English, then. You attempt to deceive me?"

"I do not know. I beg for his pity. I am not skilled in his words. We do not wish to help his enemy, we have no gain to do so—"

The soldier raised his hand in a manner to direct Shappa to stop speaking as he interrupted. "I understand. I believe you do not wish to help our enemies. However, *you* must understand, it does not matter if you did not wish to help the French, it only matters if you have." The Lieutenant Colonel waved forward the five horsemen positioned throughout the village. One of the soldiers had his face covered entirely with a dark gray hood. He sat tall and sturdily clasped his saddle's horn, yet his horse was harnessed with a short rope to one of his Redcoat companions. His three cohorts dismounted, two drew pistols from their saddled holsters, one, a massive Blunderbuss musket. With his face hidden under the shadows of a shroud, Lieutenant Wilkinson remained mounted and still, while Lieutenant Shaw stood near, clasping the reins of his and Wilkinson's warhorses.

Lieutenant Stone and Ensigns Davies and Richardson walked toward the western entrance of the nearest longhouse. They approached with weapons ready, cautiously, though without hesitation. The Fourth Order Guards were quite unique amongst the king's forces. None were more qualified than these, the highest levels of scrutiny and exhibitions of gallantry, loyalty, and ferocity. The troops today, as with most days, were eager for strife and bloodshed. The war had grown tedious and dull. Winter was quickly moving in, and the members of the Fourth Order were beginning to feel jaded and not sharp.

Stone had been born without a drop of royal blood. Shaw and the other three Ensigns, Gregory Wilkinson, Jacob Richardson, and Todd Davies were all, by chance, of the lesser nobility. Traditionally, their commissions would have been accepted by the Ministry regardless, though the circumstances regarding this unit were not commonly known. Every man offered a unique talent, which, bound together, formed an unrelenting fighting force. The four had remained bound and driven by a pledge to remain loyal to the traditions of the Aquitaine Order and defend the institutions of the Royal Empire. Though they were to maintain their name, each had cleansed all associations to family and all such obligations, purified to uphold the oath of the Order.

With the butt of his large Blunderbuss, Richardson chopped away either side of the narrow, arched entrance and forced his way into the mud hut. Davies followed while Stone and Shaw remained at the entrance. As he approached the longhouse entryway, Lieutenant Shaw became intrigued by the pair of dried carp draped across a knotted line strung over the charred remains of timber. One of the smoked fish dangled head low, and the other tail low. Prompted by his curiosity, Shaw drifted a few feet in their direction. "This is interesting," he grumbled to Davies, who was just within earshot.

His understanding of the Native Americans suggested they were hardly more developed than the animals the Brits kept as house pets. Driven by curiosity, he reached for the nearest of the dried fish, tugged it off the line, and surveyed the village and its inhabitants as he held the lifeless fish in his hand. "Perhaps Otaktay is not as outstanding as we believe. They may be closer to human than I thought."

Davies shook his head coldly. "I'm surprised you are so moved by them. Men die young when they rely only on what their eyes reveal to them. What do you see, primitive people who worship fire, dance like children, and sleep in mud huts? The Indians are clever enemies. Hunters hollow out pumpkins and place them over their heads when they fully submerge themselves in the river. When the deer gather to drink at the waterline, they seed only a floating pumpkin, until the hunter creeps closer and runs his spear through his hide. They win when we underestimate their cunning."

Shaw simply sighed with confirmation. The instance offered a new perspective, allowing him to come within a fraction of empathizing with the tribesmen and their brood as persons. He was immediately unsure whether to trust the wisdom of his judgments and began to consider philosophical perspectives. For a moment or so he lost himself in the thought until Stone nudged him back to attention and shrugged as if to inquire what the hell he was doing. "Right…" mumbled Shaw as he was moved from his trance. He then quickly flung the dead carp off to the side of the longhouse.

Davies met Richardson inside the hut, and the pair proceeded to pillage. They shattered and emptied clay pots, rummaged through baskets and bags, searched under blankets, and without concern, smashed all the ceramic objects within their sight. From outside, the thumping rumbles of cluttering movement suggested the soldiers were showing little care or consideration. The two lieutenants emerged from the structure. Richardson was clutching two five-gallon wooden kegs, and Davies carried one more of the same. They brought them to Bowman, where they carelessly dropped them. Grayish-white powder puffed through the wind and flakes of snow. Davies informed the colonel, "These were hidden in trenches and covered over with their animal skins. Sneaky little shits they are."

Moments later, Stone, with an armful of long muskets, approached. The weapons were tossed to the ground by Richardson. They appeared to resemble early Charleville muskets, the very same guns in common use by the French expeditionary forces in North America. Davies picked up one of the five guns, intent on giving a closer inspection. Prompted by the Louis XVI proof marks, he confirmed, "Yep, these are French," then threw the weapon to the ground.

"I do not know of these weapons. French warriors take away many of our folk and threaten our young. We have not wished to help—please, we have never wished to," pleaded Shappa, desperate, voice trembling and eyes welling with tears. "I do not know these weapons…have not seen. The French warriors…fire guns kill our kind, our blood runs as yours. We are not a friend of those French. We are only of peace. We seek only to harvest now before the winter, and we share with you all we have. Please, we do not help your enemy. I do not know of these guns."

Some of the uniformed soldiers glanced toward the exchange, meaning to remain disciplined, yet intent to listen. Each began to conclude some manner of a deadly outcome in which he would assuredly play a part. They had not been under the command of Bowman for very long, yet long enough to understand his determination and cold heart.

The colonel remained undeterred. His intentions had been presumed before he entered the village. Understanding the contingent of his underlings were drawn to the interaction, he sought to badger and belittle. "You will share with us?" he asked. "Why would we agree to share when we can simply take all there is to be had? My enemy's weapons are piled at your feet. I don't give a shit about what you can share. The insult upon my reasoning by itself is worthy of punishment, and yet you plead for my leniency. I don't think you understand what is happening here."

Appearing from the near western corner of the village, a small native boy, ten or twelve years old, hurriedly ran toward Shappa. He breathed heavily and pulled on his pant leg, and Shappa looked down at the child. The elder's face dimly glowed, and the semblance of a smile began to emerge. Delighted to see the Kanuna, Shappa momentarily escaped the tension of Bowman's interrogation. His affection for the boy was enough to temporarily free him from the fear presented by the British intruders. He leaned into him, and Kanuna mentioned a few words to Shappa in his native language. He stood upright, and affectionately rested his hand on the back of Kanuna's head. "I understand you do not understand."

"I beg your fucking pardon?" griped Bowman.

"I mean not to insult. You do not know what has brought you here. It is not French guns. It has chosen you. We hold something of great wonder and value—he has never seen and will never. We must give it to him. It has given to us and now it will give to him," he replied. "It is why you are with us today."

Bowman refused to reveal a thought and was not entirely sure what Shappa was referring to, though he had an inkling. Following his instincts, Bowman sought to dig deeper. "I have no time or concern for this Indian nonsense."

"We believe you will have time for this, you will have much time for this," replied Shappa. "I stand without fear. It did not call you to slaughter us as animals. It has brought you here for a reason, we know this. Please, after, he can be on and go about. Murder us now he will never see its wonder. It is of interest to him—it is worthy. We know it is why he is here, with us today."

Intrigued, Bowman paused and turned slightly toward Stone, who was standing just to his left. The two locked eyes for a moment, seemingly communicating through some non-verbal language, and in mutual understanding. Stone tilted his head slightly and shrugged as if to suggest his endorsement. "Bring Wilkinson here," he ordered.

Stone turned toward Shaw and gestured him forward by leaning his head toward the colonel's position.

"Let's go," uttered Shaw, and he advanced, tugging the line. Wilkinson's stallion trotted behind, and the lieutenant caught himself, nearly falling off balance. Bowman dismounted, again stroked the hind neck of his four-legged companion, and handed the reins to Richardson. He slowly and casually removed his riding gloves, finger by finger, as he looked about. For a moment, his eyes became fixed on the shivering natives who were still huddled on the ground. The cold soldier was indifferent to their fears, and by now, he had accepted they would not see tomorrow's sunrise. Bowman had become supremely effective at what he did, relying in large part on the cold indifference he'd built around himself.

"You have something important you say?" he said with less than mild interest.

"Important, yes. I think he knows this, please. I speak truth. I do not know of these weapons. Please, I beg him."

Bowman turned back toward Wilkinson. "What do you think?"

Slowly and deliberately, he nodded his cloaked and shadow-covered head. "He is not afraid. I believe he speaks the truth. I trust him."

"Fine," muttered the colonel.

"Follow," instructed Shappa.

"Follow? No, I'm not going to follow. You bring the item to me here."

"Please, it cannot. A short…few steps. These, all of them wait behind and he will return. I share my trust and the safety of my people. It cannot bring to him, he will understand. If he does not return, all of us will die. I know this, as does he."

Assured that Shappa realized any attempts at trickery or deception would certainly bring about the execution of some, if not all, of his clan, Bowman agreed to escort him. "My scout and I will go with you, and, to be clear, should any harm befall me or any of my companions, yours will be shown no mercy. My Mohawk companion has an odd craving to drink the blood of his brood. It's been some time, and I imagine he is quite thirsty."

Shappa reassured Bowman of his word. "No harm to no one, I share my trust."

Otaktay knelt to one knee as he removed a pouch worn across his back. He fumbled about for a few seconds, then stood with a decorated spiked tomahawk clutched in his right hand. The weapon was nearly three feet long, a sharpened, polished bronze blade attached to a thick oak branch. The rugged Iroquoian warrior staggered toward Bowman, where he stopped and stood tall by his side. Silently, the colonel turned his neck toward Shappa and looked down at the diminutive native to make eye contact. For a moment, the large, kindhearted eyes of the elder and the soulless ones of the colonel remained fixed on one another. Without yielding a glimpse of emotion, Bowman's eyes glanced toward Otaktay, and the three men began to march toward the eastern corner of the village.

A narrow trail of flattened grass and patches of frozen mud descended slightly down the knoll as it snaked away from the center of the village. Shappa moved slowly, his old bones unable to reach a brisk pace. He was hunched over and relied on the aid of a walking stick fashioned from a branch in order to move forward. The translator and the colonel followed. As they progressed, the trail continued along a terraced footpath aside the village hill. Two or three dozen paces farther, the path gave way to a clearing of flat ground. The upper portion of a domed mud-clay structure, similar in style to those of the village longhouses, appeared. It was nestled snugly, four feet or so inside a man-made ravine surrounded by several large stones. Faint traces of smoke rose from a rounded, clay conduit at just about its peak, and a narrow stone stairway ended at the arched entranceway, which was covered by a deerskin flap. To the right of the entrance, the black silhouette of a large, black buck had been painted, and one of a crescent moon, over the entrance.

"Ohskennon'ton," Otaktay muttered under his breath.

"He is great Kenraken Whitetail," Shappa added. "He served the Kahontsi Ehnita, the keeper of life, sharing force to our people. Kenraken is the moon eye, watches over us at night. It has seen his coming."

Shappa lifted the deerskin and waved the other two in, and each bent to fit through the slight entryway. Upon entrance, the translator and the colonel straightened their backs and were immediately overcome by a heated sensation throughout their bodies. For an instant, their ears rang and their vision blurred, eventually clearing, but with a red hue. In a reflex motion, Otaktay dropped his hatchet, and its blade clanged against the hard, stone floor. Both men rubbed their eyes softly and staggered to maintain their balance. There was no urgency or threat, and they felt strangely relaxed, given the highly unusual occurrence. A gentle fire struggled for life in a pit near the middle of the circular space. It cast light when Shappa closed the entrance flap, and the sullen darkness seemed to fully correct their vision. Inside, the walls were reddish clay, and a few beams of the subdued sunlight penetrated the hut.

"What is this, Indian wizardry?" Bowman asked, his tone far less authoritative than earlier. His inquiry was not a demand for an explanation, but an expression of concern. "Tell me what you are doing to us."

A decrepit, feeble man rested in a bed of hay straw, quilts, and soft bearskin blankets at the far end of the chamber. Shappa announced his presence: "We do nothing…please. This is Red Sky, my grandfather's grandfather. Red Sky has been warned of his arrival and warns of many others. He waited for him to arrive, did not know it would be on this day, but knew it would be someday."

"This is lunacy," snapped Bowman. "I cannot be bothered with this Timber Nigger nonsense—"

"Lunacy," groaned Red Sky. "An interesting choice in words." While he was mostly covered in bearskin blankets, he appeared to be of unnaturally frail frame and stature. His right arm dangled at his side, fallen as such, and the back of his hand lay on the cold floor lifelessly. Thick folds of fleshy skin rested on the floor at his wrist, as though it had slowly seeped into the ground. The nails of each finger had grown long and were bent like the talons of a wretched vulture. Long, stringy white hair, twisted cobwebs, perhaps five feet in length, fell from his head to the ground. His face was disfigured by a pear-size lump, which had grown just below his left eye. The large protrusion had forced the dry white sphere almost entirely out of his skull cavity, where it permanently peered sharply to his left. The white of his eye was dried like the skin of an old melon, and the iris black and lifeless. He struggled with every deliberate breath, each one announced with a most unpleasant wheeze.

"I am Hiamovi Red Sky." His words were tired, halting and gravelly in sound, though his simple introduction seemed to cast a spell.

"Rahronkas…Ratkahthos." Otaktay bowed his head and then sat on the floor at the foot of the bed. Colonel Bowman noted Otaktay's uncharacteristic obedience and stood at ease, removed his helmet, and held it at the waist, hand over hand.

Bowman repeated a script he had well-rehearsed, yet, unnerved, he struggled to maintain formal composure. "I am Lieutenant Colonel Emrick Bowman, commanding officer of the Fourth Royal

Dragoons of Our Majesty's Army. Our company has found French contraband in your possession—"

Hiamovi seems entirely disinterested and interrupts, "Sit low, please. My ears are weak, and far-traveled words do not reach them." Bowman paused for a moment, mildly concerned about following an order in Otaktay's presence, even such an insignificant request for courtesy. Not since childhood had he conducted a verbal exchange in such an undignified manner, sitting on a dust-covered floor of uneven rocks. He placed his helmet gently on the floor, tilted his saber back, and sat. The disciplined soldier held his hand up in a halting motion in front of Hiamovi and needlessly fiddled with the position of his helmet on the ground. The gesture was a frivolous attempt to establish authority.

Hiamovi was unconcerned in the insignificant contest for dominance and continued, "I trust Shappa more than any, and am filled with as much sorrow as relief as you sit before me."

Bowman rubbed his brow and left eye with the palm of his hand. Another wave of tingling warmth was felt within him. He clenched his jaw, scrunched his face, and closed his eyes.

"Yes"—*cough*—"the Moon Eye has seen it." Hiamovi closed his eye and paused for a moment, working to breathe long, slow gasps, then continued. "My people and our kin have been blessed with the gifts of Nature. She has nurtured us with her warmth and rain, glimmering waters, green leaves. We have walked with her mighty beasts, and gentle creatures, beneath soaring birds, and there remained always abundance." He paused, struggled with his breath. "The twilight of our time has begun, lands infested by the infectious plague of your brood, the scourge of your will; your quest for dominion require you to slaughter with no regard. You are cursed by your poisoned nature to claim the creations and greet them to their end; it compels you to abandon humanity and to embrace butchery."

Unimpressed, Bowman responded, "Humanity is to believe nature has endowed us with the might to flourish, to believe we are not unlike the beasts you profess to admire. We are the conception of nature; we are jaguars and you are fawns."

Red Sky closed his eye and rested his head back on the bed, struggling once again to capture the air in his lungs. "I have seen stars dance across the sky, the sun hide behind the moon, the earth swallow mountains. Yet, never have I seen a limit to the malice, discontent, and foolishness of your kind."

Otaktay looked at his leader, curious to hear his response. He had not often witnessed his commander insulted.

Bowman allowed himself a sigh of laughter. "This is what you wish to share, judgments and insults?"

"Observations, not insults. Should you accept them to be, I cannot say." Speaking slower yet, Hiamovi replied, "These things I do not understand. You are here, so you must be meant to be here. You are meant to be blessed with the weapons of carnage and the tenacity to use them. I will trust it is Her way. The yellow toad knows no restraint; he eats until his death. It is his spirit. He will always be at the mercy of abundance. He survives because of all his kind... consume until their deaths. They all hunt always"—*cough*—"the same prey, making certain it will never flourish and their gluttony both protects and endangers them. They are cursed by nature, which compels them...it ensnares them into a trap from which they will never escape. That, too, is nature. This war, your war, you slaughter one another to be free to slaughter us. I no longer question such things."

The colonel was at a loss. He felt no inclination to continue his attempts at agitation or hostility. All four of the men remained silent, and the fire flickered, causing their shadows to dance. Tension had turned to sorrow. Bowman did not see humanity in his enemies, and that is what enabled his ambition. He harbored no specific ill will for the Natives, nor did he care one way or the other if they suffered. From his perspective, they were simply trees that needed to be cleared so the Empire could reap the seeds it intended to sow. Despite the strange energy within him, Bowman was beginning to tire of this discussion, and Hiamovi was simply tired.

Hiamovi rested and then pointed toward an artifact that hung on the clay wall before him. The item was an amulet of sorts, its most striking feature being a jagged triangular shard with two or three stone beads and two long, sharpened stones on either side. A thick, soft leather lace ran through the pieces and was bound by a knot.

In anticipation of the gesture, Shappa approached the object, removed it from the small spike it was hanging on, and lightly rested the shard in his opened palm. With the stone beads dangling, he gently presented it to Bowman, who received it with the same care it was given with. The metallic item was oddly cool to the touch, but the trooper felt a continued warming sensation radiate within him.

Hiamovi offered Shappa a warm smile, then continued, "We share an enemy. The relentless killer who slays all. I have fought this hunter for too many years, seen it take more of my brothers and sisters than I care to consider. The Moon Eye has brought you here, and I am ready to face time, the hunter of the hunters, the killer of all. Time is merciless and will always catch his prey. Time will destroy you and your kind as indiscriminately as it will destroy us. Your fierce determination and fire guns cannot save you from its grasp. You are here as a blessing. Now I can rest...The Kahontsi Ehnita, the giver of life, the moon is the watchful eye and the Kahontsi Ehnita has given me the years of many lives. Now it calls you to serve. It offers to the holder years beyond his years. You need to take it."

Bowman had heard tales of Indian witchcraft and had always dismissed them as the superstitions of the simple-minded. Here, he was not nearly as dismissive, yet was captured by the magnitude of what had been presented to him. The energy within him seemed to confirm the object's significance. "The tales are true. Why are you giving this to me? Why am I worthy to possess such an item? Am I to believe you present me with this gift so I will spare you and your people, or is this mischievous Indian sorcery?"

Shappa became rather perplexed at this. He had anticipated Bowman snatching the amulet from him without hesitation or thought. He looked to Hiamovi, hoping for an explanation.

"You believe I would share with you my intent to trick you? Why should you trust us, when you aim to kill us? It is too late," muttered Hiamovi. "I have stolen too many days. I am needed no longer, and I have no desire to see our further devastation. Mischief is meaningless. You will depart to the west, and others will come from the east. Your decision matters little. The Moon's Eye is yours to serve, Colonel Bowman—it has chosen you. I do not question such things."

Bowman's charge was not based on superstitious speculations, and as it seemed, not in vain. The colonel was intrigued, yet looked steadfast in his decision. He had made his conclusion and was not compelled to waver under the influence of a frail, old Indian.

"Keep it with your people, Shappa, or another," Bowman said. Otaktay's eyes bolted toward the colonel in shock. "Assuming it is as you describe, it is not an item I wish to be in the procession of for my king."

A glimpse of life seemed to have found Hiamovi. "You reveal your humanity. It is clear why this has all been and why you are here. It is that your arrival is serendipitous." He grasped Bowman's hand and gently closed it around the amulet. "It is not mine to do with what I choose. It has chosen you. This conversation no longer has purpose, Colonel."

Bowman looked at the relic in his hand and remained unsure. He felt its significance, yet continued to question Hiamovi's insistence he accept it. Now, presented with a gift of such magnitude, he was torn between his convictions and principles as a soldier in the king's army and an unfamiliar instinct to abandon all he thought he had held true. Bowman has remained loyal to lineage and its way for his entire life. He had mocked the customs and convictions of the natives, dismissed them as ridiculous peculiarities of uncivilized people. Now, he felt compelled to honor what he had ridiculed and to compromise his virtues for personal gain, for an everlasting life.

Masking his irresolution with bravado, Bowman sought to appear as though he was somehow still in control. "I am of kingly character, a man of great accomplishment, so why should I fear the burden you claim? You are frail, a relic of a time that will soon be forgotten. Your tribesmen still wait in terror, their fortunes tied to the whims of my mercy. I have decided I am going to take this from you, not as a gift, but as a spoil of my conquest."

Bowman stood, placed his helmet back atop his head, and hovered over Hiamovi. "We are going to rest here; we are going to feast on your hunt and take up quarters within your house. I'm yet unsure of your fate and will have decided by morning, thus be assured, tomorrow, we will ride and continue our charge. One way or another, none within this village will ever see us again."

Otaktay quickly glanced at Colonel Bowman. The barbaric Iroquois warrior normally delighted in the prospect of bloodshed, yet he felt pity toward Hiamovi, Shappa, and the others. He suspected Bowman intended to slaughter the village, yet he feared to express this, lest he finds himself within the carnage.

Bowman continued, "I hold you in such little regard, I will make no considerable preparations for mischief or attempts to kill us as we sleep."

"The server will never find harm from our hands," replied Hiamovi. He had no interest in playing Bowman's game. "And his hands will never bring us harm."

"You have faith in my sympathy, then?"

"No," answered Hiamovi, "faith is to believe without reason...I have reason to believe you will show us no harm."

Bowman did his best to remain unmoved and ordered Otaktay to follow him as he hurried out of the hut. At a quickened pace, the two men walked back along the trail to the upper village, where the rest of the contingent of soldiers and huddled natives waited. In stride, Bowman carelessly shoved the talisman behind his coat at his waist; the warming sensation radiating from it intensified within him. Otaktay remained fixed on the object and noted where the colonel put it.

Corporal Langley approached Bowman as he reached the near center of the village. Langley was a nameless pawn as far as the colonel was concerned. In truth, he had been known to be of lesser disposition, yet was a more than a capable soldier. He held a paper manifest with notes and indistinguishable scribbles. At a few paces ahead of the colonel, although not as encumbered, the corporal began to slow his pace and seemed to lose a bit of balance as he neared. He had a slightly dazed look on his face, as he was struggling to refocus on his whereabouts. Despite Langley's somewhat unusual behavior, Bowman did not flinch. The colonel then took care to better secure the amulet and pulled his coat farther down, ensuring Langley would not see it.

The corporal regained a sense of his calm and did his best to hide his discomfort, as he was quite eager to win the good grace of his superior. "Sir, we count twenty-seven, six children and eleven lady folk. I need," he began, and then breathed to further collect himself before he started again. "I request, respectfully request, a few minutes with the Pineapple so we can find out exactly who was here and where they went. Early reports detailed Dumont has been recruiting Indians along these parts." It was not even thirty degrees, yet Langley brushed beads of sweat from his brow. "Sir, I…believe Capitaine Dumont or another French regiment traded stores and weapons to the Indians in exchange for the services of scouts. I have inventoried the munitions thus far and will continue to investigate."

Bowman remained mostly indifferent to what Langley was telling him and paid little attention to his proclamations and assumptions. The colonel's mind was still on the Moon Relic and the burden it presented to him. He took care to secure it within his coat, out of the view of Corporal Langley and any other curious eyes.

"Fine, yes, take Otaktay to get what you need," replied Bowman. "And do not assume yourself to be in such standing as to belittle our tracker with childish nicknames, Soldier."

Langley remained silent for a few seconds, unsure how to respond.

"Yes, sir. Of course, I apologize for offering disrespect." He again stood silently, awaiting further instruction. Typically, Bowman would require thorough interrogation and inspection, so his brevity and ambiguity seemed out of place. After another moment of tense stillness, Langley excused himself, with a humble, "I will see to it, Colonel."

Bowman advised Lieutenant Stone of his intentions to remain until dawn, and the company of the Fourth Order prepared sleeping schedules in semi-hourly shifts. The arrangement called for the regular army enlisted to sleep in the easternmost longhouse, the Fourth Order in the westernmost, while the natives would be crowded into the securest area of the village. A lieutenant and two troops would alternate shifts throughout the night and guard the entrance of the western longhouse. Kahente, a five-year-old Iroquois girl, would stay within the alternating company of three, as were three pistols and three muskets. Otaktay made it clear to the Iroquois that her plight would be based on the actions of all her village mates, giving them ample reason to cooperate.

The river valley's autumnal gloaming yielded to twilight, which then yielded to nightfall. The temperature fell, though not as much as to be expected given the cold day that preceded it, and the surrounding forest remained dark, ominous and silent. Corporal Bragg and Private Williams sat adjacent to the assembly of natives, between them and the nearest entrance to the eastern longhouse. A small fire crackled and glowed in front of them. Bragg sat with his arms rested on his bent knees as he puffed on a wooden pipe of stale tobacco and tinkered with a few twigs and small stones about him, occasionally flicking one into the flames. Williams diligently cleaned his carbine pistol. Young Kahente nestled alongside the fire. She kept her eyes closed and remained as silent and still as she could. Bragg had quickly grown rather bored and began to fling pebbles and such in her direction, aiming for her head. He was flabby and hardly fit to be a king's soldier. It was a wonder he made it into the army, to America, and that he could fit into his madder red coat. A few of his attempts hit their mark and would lightly bounce off her face, and without fail, he would giggle childishly every time, delighted. As would be expected, she was not able to sleep, but she kept her eyes closed as they filled with tears, and she did her best not to twitch or tremble, even when a larger projectile hit her face.

"I would rather you stop doing that," said Private Williams.

"Nah, I don't think I will," replied Bragg. "I am bored to fuck. This is all we do—sit, wait, and sit." He looked about the ground for pebbles and saw the carp Shaw had discarded earlier lying a few feet from him. Clumsily, he crawled on his knees, snatched it from the ground, then sat back up, leaving it lying in his lap. "Why is there a dead fish on the ground? What the hell ritual do these savages perform? Strange. You want to see me slap her with it?"

"I don't, and I do not want to see you in front of a firing squad," said Williams. "Or strung up by your neck. Does the colonel strike you as one who will tolerate inappropriate behavior in any way?"

"This bloke? No, he strikes me as one who would prefer we treat Indians like Indians. Regardless, I'd rather shoot toads than sit in the dirt to babysit little Indian whores like this one—yeah, you native wench. She likes me throwing shit at her, think it's some Indian sex thing. They like being hit around. I heard it makes them horny. This one, she's loving me right now. Think she wants to suck my cock or fuck me…or both. I think she wants me to fuck her. Right?"

"I'm not getting that," said Williams. "Because you are hitting her in the face with rocks and threatening to slap her with a dead fish?"

"Partially that," replied Bragg. "Look, her eyes are telling me she wants me to get up, go over there, and push my cock into her ass. I don't want to be rude." Corporal Bragg rose to his feet and arched his back. "I love the young ones, tight young asshole only had shit gone through it. Then, she looks unfucked, and it would mean something to me to know I have an Indian bastard running around this fucking place. Fuck this, fucking Indian bitch. You want to fuck her too?"

Williams silently shook his head in disapproval. "Not a good idea. Do you know Colonel Bowman? He doesn't put up with horseshit and will never turn a blind eye to rape, even with Indians. Why don't you just go stroke your dick?"

"This guy?" asked Bragg. "Do *you* know who they are? They are not regular Kingsmen, they are ruthless. These bloody fuckers are brutal. I think he would encourage it. I'm surprised he hasn't ordered us to do it already. She's an Indian. I'm sorry, but you are very wrong, my friend."

"Exactly, they are ruthless. If Colonel Bowman wanted us to rape them, we would have already raped them. Do what you will, but know I will be nothing but honest and forthcoming in the likely event of inquiries and disciplinary measures. I'm not going to stand next to you in front of a firing line so you can get off."

Bragg was still for a moment as he processed all potential outcomes. His inkling was to trust Williams's assessment, yet his urge to fornicate had taken control of his weak will. "You're probably right, but nature is calling me…"

He staggered over toward Kahente, snatched her up by the hair behind her neck. "Let's go, bitch, you're going to get what you asked for." She cried and desperately clutched at the ground as he dragged her forcefully toward the darkness of the trees. None of the huddled masses of natives did more than flinch, almost paralyzed with fear.

Williams looked about in all directions, as though he expected the commotion to catch one of the officer's attention. "Son of a bitch," he mumbled to himself. He knew at that moment he was as guilty as Bragg, and for an instant, considered stopping him, but seconds later joined him instead.

*　*　*

Outside of the village, Bowman sat atop a small grassy hill that overlooked the creek. It was nearly covered in a thin layer of soft snow, and the air was crisp all around. His breath billowed from his nose and mouth as it hit the bitter night air, and yet he wore only a rather thin linen shirt with no cover or coat. The colonel remained fixed on the blackened sky, as stars poked through the traces of the gray clouds that remained. The gibbous moon was bright and cast a soft glow upon the countryside. Bowman held Hiamovi's artifact in the palm of his hand, the beads and lace dangling low, as he only clutched the centerpiece.

The most significant piece of the talisman was the large ornament that hung between the beads and stone. It was a metal or metal-like shard with sharp-toothed and gnarled edges. The lace ran through a small, jagged hole that appeared to have been punctured along the top. It was very thin, yet remarkably strong, unbendable by human hands. The forward surface looked to be painted a flat white, and the paint had chips, along with many scrapes and scratches. The back side was silver-gray and polished or galvanized. The lower third of the piece featured what appeared to be rivets of some sort, as if it was made of two pieces bound together.

Bowman continued to feel the unnatural warmth inside of him as he held it. For perhaps the first time in his life, he was at a loss and could seek no counsel here. He felt in some way moved by what he held in his hand, and he believed Hiamovi about its importance and felt compelled to keep it. This had been trusted to him as a man of stout heart and noble character. Hiamovi was wise. He knew those who sought power were the ones most corrupted by it. He did not offer it to the French, nor to one of his kin. The company of Dragoons could easily still destroy the entire village, and he could keep Hiamovi's gift. Bowman's arrival was not merely a chance encounter; this was a passing of one people and the rise of another.

Perhaps the Indians were attempting to poison his mind. He could fathom no other reason to offer it so freely. This must be deception, venomous Indian magic devilry. Yet, wielded properly, this could be a powerful weapon to defend his king and countrymen. With it, artificial life, he would be able to fight many battles and slay many enemies, the Indians and French alike. He would be hailed as a champion, his name living in myth and song. His legacy would live among the most honored of his kind. He could begin a new chapter in the story of Aquitaine Order.

In 1221 the reign of King Henry III, Duke of Aquitaine, son of King John, was enmeshed in the First Baron's War. The fourteen-year-old king was besieged within the Royal castle of Rochester, one of the last fortresses to fall to the barons and their insidious rebel armies. After weeks of hopeless entrapment, the wells had dried, become wrought with disease and sewage, the air was overwhelmed with the stench of rot and death, and the meat had spoiled. The bread was meager and stale, and those within the court had been forced to feast on the remains of the ones who succumbed to starvation or disease. The young, particularly the infants, were the first to fall. Then, others volunteered their bodies. The meat was labeled, thus family would not consume family, though many opted to remain blind, to be guided by the Lord's good grace.

The barons' patience expired, and their insurmountable forces were prepared to storm the castle. Per legend, a martyr's flesh rested within the belly of the king and spoke to him in a dream. King Henry was inspired by a vision, an omen of some divine province. The king called for his most worthy and valiant knight, Leofric, to gather his band of five warlords and all the firstborn sons within the castle walls. Henry presented each with a ruby pendant from the regal necklace, which had been worn by the many kings before him. Six rubies for six soldiers. He pledged to them, through these pendants, the Almighty would quicken their swords, harden their shields, and bolster their resolve.

Not long before the sun had set, the mighty Leofric finally fell to the onslaught of the barons. The first blow fractured the jawbone on his right side. A left-handed strike from a heavy, dull sword. With his face partially collapsed inward, he continued the fight. A second strike came from behind, a small blade in a down-up motion toward the back of his skull. The jolt opened a gaping crevice in the back of his head, above his neck, and forced skull fragments into his brain. Still, Leofric continued the fight and refused to yield to the mercy of his enemies. When his right ankle was cut from under him, he crashed to the hard ground and desperately swung his blade about. A final strike bisected his skull and caused a massive cleft from his right eye to the base of his jaw, to the left. The heavy, cold blade was twisted and thrust about to nearly sever his head into two halves. Soldiers of the barons' army kept the sword staked in Leofric's skull as some banner noting their conquest. His lifeless body remained on the field through the night, pierced with arrows and broken bones. He was the last to be defeated. Fifteen of King Henry III's divine crusaders had slain eighty men of the barons' army and broken the siege. The king, the women, and the younger sons escaped.

King Henry's fabled heroism inspired his great-grandson's, great-grandson's great-nephew, King Charles I, to commission a select regiment in his honor. In 1648, during the First English Civil War, Charles assembled six of the most highly regarded warriors within the kingdom. They had become the First Order of the Aquitaine Light Horse Guards of the Royal Dragoons. The First Aquitaine Guards made quick work of Parliamentary militia bands, helping to secure victory in the Civil War, while re-establishing order and supremacy to the Throne. The line of Aquitaine Guards had evolved, though remained unbroken. And now Emrick Bowman would be hailed in song with Henry III and Leofric.

The morning sun threatened to peek over the eastern horizon, and the forest began to awaken. First Lieutenant Stone and Second Lieutenants Shaw and Richardson stood just outside the longhouse's southern entrance. They each looked toward one another until Stone leisurely nodded his head. At the nod, Richardson ignited a long hemp fuse protruding from a wooden powder keg Shaw held in his hands. After two or three seconds, he shoved it to the ground, rolling it into the longhouse entrance. At the northern entrance, Davies lit the fuse from another keg to do the same. At the southeastern trail, which led to the village, Bowman sat atop Shadow, motionless and silent. He was mostly a black figure as the faint glimpses of sunlight rose behind him. He watched his most trusted officers initiate the massacre and appeared entirely indifferent.

From within the longhouse, the sound of panicked scurrying and rustling began to grow. The five men, positioned on both ends of the structure, stepped back several feet, then covered their faces with their forearms. Instantly, a thunderous blast erupted, followed nearly simultaneously by another. Clay shrapnel, wood splinters, bits of flesh, and debris of all manner were thrown in all directions from within the longhouse. Occasional pops and thuds burst as flames found pockets of gunpowder.

Several figures emerged from the thick black veil of smoke, stumbling, and writhing frantically. One was Corporal Bragg; he was desperately clutching his right arm, which was severed just above his elbow. His shirt was in tatters, face mostly covered in smoldered black filth, peppered with cuts and scrapes, his eyes wide and full of horror and his mouth wide open yet silent. He staggered in the direction of Lieutenant Stone, who lifted his carbine pistol, waited for a second or two until the corporal was nearly on him, and fired it into him, just below the ribs. The ball blasted through his back shoulder, shattering his bones. The corporal collapsed onto the ground, and while bleeding profusely from his right arm, his entire body twitched and jerked violently until it finally lay lifeless. Stone flung the pistol several yards, took a few steps back, and grabbed another from one of the five or six loaded pistols lying on the ground awaiting use.

Numerous faces began to emerge from the western longhouse. The Iroquois poured out of the hut, distressed, confused, and horrified. They watched as the five British officers each grabbed two pistols from the lines on the ground, then ominously stirred amongst the carnage, occasionally firing one into any soldier who still had glimpses of life within him. Each was silent and moved with deliberation amongst the streams of smoke that slowly rose from the wreckage. The mutilation was inhuman; traces of limbs and mangled flesh were strewn about the debris. Within the devastation were remnants of hard bodies and horrifically disfigured faces. One, unrecognizable soldier's torso was torn open, his right arm completely removed, and most of his ribs exposed. Some of the

Iroquois onlookers turned away in horror, others gasped, and others remained motionless in stunned confusion.

Satisfied none had survived the blast, Stone waved the others to follow him toward their horses, which had been tied to ground spikes some forty yards behind the village center. From his position, Bowman kicked his steed, and he began to slowly gallop toward the Iroquois onlookers. From within the assembly, Shappa stepped forward, preparing to greet the colonel before he reached the others. He was as distressed as any, yet maintained composure and calm, putting his left hand up in a gesture for all of them to remain where they were. The elder native knew that if the British soldiers had meant to decimate the village and all its inhabitants, none of them would be alive at this moment. In Iroquoian, he commanded the children be brought into the standing longhouse. Their not-yet-developed minds should not be exposed to such an atrocity.

Bowman met Shappa about twenty feet or so ahead of the rest of the group. As he always did, the colonel sat tall upon his mount as the distinctive white feathers upon his helmet fluttered. He wore his deep crimson uniform with all the formalities and reverence he felt it deserved, not a lace undone nor a button unbuttoned. Beams of the early morning sun gleamed from behind and glared from the metal adornments. When he neared, he pulled on the reins, and Shadow came to an immediate halt with a grunt and neigh.

"The French are fleeing north, to Quebec, up the Hudson," he said to Shappa. "They are on the run; their days here are nearly complete. They will trouble you no more, yet my people will. British regiments will approach the village as the army marches north. They will hassle you as we have, and they will ask about me. When they do, give them this." Bowman extended a leather-bound booklet he had packed into a saddle bag. Shappa was a bit perplexed, yet reached to accept it.

"This is my journal. The last entry recounts the bravery displayed by you and your brethren as you helped us resist an unrelenting French incursion until the last of us had given his life." He remained very formal and emotionless as he continued. "I lament the burden of leaving you with this…such as it is." He waved his hand, gesturing around the village. "I have left you with modest stores, but regretfully, it is all we can spare. It is mostly rations, beans and salted meats. The French gave you muskets and powder, yet no balls or powder horns. We left you such."

"We are grateful, all of us. Why does he do this?" asked Shappa.

Bowman looked at him for a moment, pondered the question himself, yet found no answer. It was as if he was as unsure of his own actions as Shappa was.

"I'm not sure," he replied. "I don't know if you would understand, and I mean this not as an insult, but as a matter of…decency, I suppose. Kings and princes are more dangerous than any other element of society. For my part, I have sworn to protect my kingdom, and I will. Your destruction does nothing to this end."

"I do see. We are no different in death. I expect one day our spirits will call each other friend," said Shappa.

Bowman grinned with agreement, then turned his head away from Shappa, peering into the trees for a moment before lashing the reins. At the usual *tick-tick*, Shadow galloped away, past the villages and toward his lieutenants.

Shappa stood silently as he watched him ride toward the others, who were all dutifully waiting on horseback near the northwestern corner of the village. Kanuna burst from the longhouse and raced toward Shappa. He draped his small arms around Shappa's legs, and the elder native looked down on him and smiled. Shappa's eyes glowed with joy at seeing his young grandnephew. Kanuna leaned into Shappa's hip, who rested his arm, gently and affectionately, on Kunana's far shoulder. Together, they stood side by side as they watched Bowman and the others trot off. They rode through a small pass in the northern woods that led to a grassy clearing beyond. Each hoof crunched into the snow, and the trees began to surround them as they continued.

Shappa watched, silently and solemnly, as the six riders disappeared into the forest before whispering to himself, "Skennen'ko wa atenro." He and his nephew were the last to set eyes on the Fourth Order of the Aquitaine Light Horse Guards of the Royal Dragoons.

* * *

"I have always observed that to succeed in the world one should seem a fool, but be wise"—Charles de Montesquieu

The reign of King George II is wrought with strife and uncertainty. His Excellency the King's ill mind seems to have been divorced from reason. Faced with the Empire's dire future, the Crown offers bewildered ramblings, threats to eat his generals and frequent and expensive festivals celebrating the consummation of new mistresses. His Majesty's war in America turned to a costly and imprudent venture and the growing rift between the Whigs and Tories has widened to a canyon. Some argue the unreasonable compunction to cling to impractical tradition will see the empire to its end. Conservatives believe the dynastic institutions of monarchy and nobility are the depths of the Kingdom and without them countrymen are no more British than the barbarous pirates they fight on the high seas. Each of His Excellency's vexing displays require the wardens of hierarchal tradition to harden their idealism. Continued allegiance to the Throne involves further investment of intellectually currency. The most loyal of the Tories have nearly driven themselves to blindness in their efforts not to see truth.

In the New World, the colonists are suddenly emboldened by their contributions toward the triumph of the mighty French Army. For the first time in their history, thirteen have joined as one, as victors in the war against a common enemy. The flickering flames of festering grievances against London are been fanned by their conquest and the maddened state of the king invites them to act upon their indignation. Consequently, the Monarchy no longer chooses to neglect the direction the colonies and the conditions of their mercantile relationship. Though their differences are many, the American colonists are equally bound by the yoke of tyranny. The valued protectorates are slipping through the tightened grasp of the Empire. Soldiers returned home from the New World with fantastic accounts of Native American wizardry. Unbeholden to reason, George II was moved to upon the whispers which have reached his ear. And now his son, George III seems to have inherited not only the Throne, but his father's sense of madness. With the colonies in revolt, he is driven to chase the same tales. The great empire stands in the shadow of dawn's light and the madness of the King has driven him to spend the Crown's resources chasing the tales of a relic with the medicinal power to defeat death.

"I wish nothing but good; therefore, everyone who does not agree with me is a traitor and a scoundrel."—King George III

One

August 1777.

It was near total darkness; orders had been issued strictly forbidding fires or lanterns outside of any exposed buildings within the garrison. Occasional flashes from outside the fortress walls offered split-second glimpses of light and intermittent, distant blasts and rumbles. Captain Isaac Pearson sat with his back against a thick, shallow stone wall, a position the typically pampered officer was not accustomed to. In a pathetic attempt at comfort, he rested a canvas sack on the cold, rigid stone base of the elevated bastion. The captain took rest between two large, iron cannons, which were projected through battlements, northward. A line of Redcoats stretched to his left and right. Each man sat in a similar fashion, and the row of cannons continued some distance in both directions. They seemed strangely comfortable lying on the dirt-caked surface, yet uneasy with the unending blasts. Pearson was most comfortable when he was secluded. He was not altogether worried about the cannon fire, but his fickle nose could not help but pick up the stench of dried sweat and partially shit-soiled uniforms wafting from his comrades.

The captain appeared as though he was a soldier from another army. Pearson had an unusual, impermeable air about him. Though it was not clear to the rank and file, in general terms, those who considered him to be a stranger had no desire to consider him otherwise. Here, he paid no mind to those around him, and in turn, they paid none to him. His face was cleanly shaven, his skin soft, and his madder red coat appeared to be tailored, pressed, and more brilliant in color than any in the British Army. Unlike his brothers-in-arms, he refused to accept such discomfort and continually shifted his weight and maneuvered about, yet managed only to look unbearably prickly.

His meticulously clean "Brown Bess" musket leaned against the wall by his side, the barrel extended upward and well beyond the height of the broad stone barrier. A raggedy copy of *King Lear* rested on the ground by his hip. Though he could hardly see, he refused to surrender to the darkness. Like his determination to find comfort, he continued to read, as best as he could, yet without result. By this time, reading one of his favorite Shakespearean plays in the night's darkness had offered more of a headache than enjoyment, thus he finally succumbed to the night's insistence and stashed the text within his gear.

Methodically and attentively, the officer wiped musket balls to a near shine, then arranged each one diligently in line, next to his immaculately shined piston ramrod and equally clean bayonet, which he placed on a handkerchief on the ground beside him. On his lap rested a French Duval flintlock pistol. Pearson's father had presented the weapon to him as a gift, celebrating his son's commission in His Excellency's Army. The weapon had three notches crudely scratched into the wood along the right of the barrel. Pearson often wondered whom those marks could have represented, and if any were scored by his father, Robert Pearson, the normally stately gentleman. Isaac had never asked his father about it, and his father had never mentioned it. Captain Pearson had decided to wishfully assume his father kept the pistol as a trophy, taken from a French officer he killed in the Seven Year's War. If anything, the scenario would have suggested Robert was, in fact, a human being.

The long voyage from the Old World to the New was as unbearable as the captain dared to imagine. Pearson lived the pampered life of privilege at home in Cambridge. Hitherto, the most unspeakable hardship he had endured was having to eat venison with a non-complementary wine. Captain Pearson had never traveled by sea in his life, and the conditions aboard the HMS *Essex* were as far from his expectation of comfort as America was from Cambridge. Pearson always kept the Duval pistol near and as immaculate as a surgeon's instrument. While battling scurvy, crowded amongst filthy, sweaty, boorish Kingsmen, between bouts of vomiting his maggoty meals and breathing the stench of the shit-filled buckets, the weapon was never far and never with a single blemish. The pistol would not be alone, wherever he was, so, too, was his father's gift.

Pearson's pristine, tri-cornered hat, the very one issued before deployment, rested on his folded left knee with neither a wrinkle nor a mark upon it. Despite the sporadic thunder of cannon fire and flashes in the night, he remained cool and as focused on the menial task as if it were a matter of some importance. Ticonderoga was under siege by an American army, eager to drive out the Brits, yet Captain Pearson could hardly seem bothered to care.

Within the shadows, a figure ascended from the ramp of the lower parade ground, at the center of the fort, and hurried toward Pearson. A rather clumsy Redcoat soldier revealed himself from that darkness as the distant guns lit the sky, and stumbled just before the captain. Winded and gasping for breath, he braced his hands on his knees. He stayed hunched over, low, below the height of the wall, and flinched with each of the remote rumbles. The private could not have been much more than sixteen years old, with his baby face and wiry frame. He suspected the aristocratic officer was the man he was looking for and nervously addressed Pearson through panting breaths. "Captain Pearson, sir? Colonel Bell needs to see you right away, sir."

Pearson furrowed his eyebrows in confusion, paused, then replied, "He asked to see me?"

"Yes, sir, Captain Pearson he required. 'Find that Captain Pearson prick and bring him here,' he said. Said he needs to see you right away, sir, in his quarters. You are the prick he was looking for, sir?"

"I beg your pardon, Soldier?" replied Pearson in his typically cold manner.

"Well, I-I, sir, you are the captain? I didn't mean that—I was only…rather, the colonel said to look for a prick. Back there, they told me you are you, and so I—please, this way, sir."

The captain refused to let the young soldier off the hook for an obvious mistake in nerves. He sighed in annoyance, placed each of the lead balls in his pouch one at a time, and in no rush, blew off the one blade of grass that had somehow found its way onto his hat. He stood tall, unafraid of the far-off blasts, placed the pistol into a holster that hung low on his right hip, his bayonet in its scabbard on his left hip, brushed himself over, straightened his coat by pulling it down firmly, placed his hat on his head, adjusted it for a few seconds, grabbed his musket, looked directly into the eyes of the young soldier, and finally said, "Alright, let's go."

The two men descended the bastion ramp toward the enclosed parade ground. They moved slowly and cautiously in the darkness. Pearson appeared much less hurried than the private, who had to pause from time to time, allowing the captain to catch up to him. Despite his best efforts to appear composed, more than a few times, the young private frantically stumbled in his steps. Either naturally clumsy or overcome by nerves, it mattered little to the characteristically haughty captain, who shook his head in silent condemnation. At the base, some fifteen to twenty feet below the southeastern bastion was a large field of hardened clay and patches of grass. More than a few dozen soldiers appeared in the moonlight shadows. The cannon blast flickers offered quick glimpses of their surroundings. Some paced mindlessly, with muskets in hand. Others sat against long, narrow stone buildings within the fortress walls. A few appeared bored, yet most were restless in some manner or another. Some were mostly still, others scribbled into journals, chomped on salted meats or cold, cooked pigeon, while others, presumably in violation of orders, slogged some sort of illicit beverage down their throats. It was acceptable and without ridicule or scorn, within the ranks of common soldiers, to rub their dicks raw, as they saw fit. Pearson made sure to keep his eyes only where they needed to be, affording no chance he could bear witness to such action. He was uncomfortable to be amongst all of them even to this extent. None were the crème de la crème he was used to consorting with. As the number of troopers around him seemed to grow, so, too, did the quickening of his pace.

Fort Ticonderoga lay on a western bank that jutted into a narrow stretch of Lake Champlain. The fortress had heavy stone walls built in a star-shaped configuration, tall bastions at all corners, two outer fortresses, and three layers of buttresses or redoubts. Nearly fifty-five heavy cannons, twenty-plus light cannons, and twenty mortars defended the southern battery aimed at the lake. Ticonderoga was a crucial strategic stronghold for the British, who hoped to secure the

Hudson River and northern waterways. The importance on Fort Carillon, as it was called years before, was not lost on the British when they seized it from their enemy, during their war with France a decade prior. On this day, in a different war with a different enemy, the importance of Ticonderoga remained the same.

Captain Pearson and his uneasy escort approached the far northern doorway of the officers' barracks, which lay near the northern wall of the lower parade ground. Pearson paused for a moment just ahead of the door, peering at the enlisted soldier silently and grimly. After a second or two of uncertainty, the private reminded Pearson, "Sir, Lord Bell does not allow nobody with muskets into his quarters. The colonel believes it bad manners to carry them into his office."

"Does not allow *any*body," corrected the captain.

"Beg pardon, sir?"

"Lord Bell does not allow *any*body to carry a musket into his quarters," he continued. "You stated 'he does not allow *nobody* to enter with a musket,' which means he will not refuse anyone with a musket to enter his quarters, and *Lord* Bell is not a lord, Private. He is a commoner, such as yourself."

Confused and afraid to ask for confirmation or to somehow seem insolent, the nervous private clarified, "Of course, my regrets, sir... Um, I'm sorry, sir, but you cannot have a musket. This is not my wish, but is the command of Lord...um...Colonel, who I really do not want to disobey."

Pearson attempted to explain, "Yes, I get that, and I am not suggesting the 'no-musket policy' was your mandate. Of course, we are within the wilderness of North America, surrounded by nit-witted colonists, yet I will not allow you to speak as they do in my presence. Present yourself with the dignity of the Empire, Soldier. This starts by properly speaking the King's English. And if you feel you are incapable of doing this within my earshot, do not speak at all."

The private was wholly unsure how to reply, or even if he should reply. He chose his words deliberately. "Of course, sir. My apologies, sir. That is not...not...unhelpful advice, and I thank you, Captain. Please, this way. The colonel's office, sir." The dutiful soldier was eager to press on and pulled the thick wooden door open and stepped aside, allowing the captain to enter.

Pearson rolled his eyes silently, content to move this along. "Hold this," he ordered before he proceeded. He carefully extended his musket toward the private with the muzzle pointing straight up. The boyish soldier looked unsure; he was still holding the heavy oak door open with one hand, while holding his own musket with the other. He looked around, to his left and right, and knelt to place his musket on the ground, all the while holding open the door. Pearson hardly acknowledged the private's struggles and offered no assistance nor made any effort to quicken his pace.

"Be careful with it, Private, and don't let it touch the ground," instructed Pearson as he handed him his weapon. "And take this too," he continued and slowly removed his bayonet from its scabbard. Clutching it with three fingers at the base, allowing the blade to dangle, he handed it over to the unnerved soldier. "This is sharp, so be careful with the blade."

For a moment, the private felt encouraged the highbrow captain offered a glimmer of concern for his well-being until he continued speaking.

"I don't want any nicks on it," advised Pearson. "I am a soldier, not a savage. Should the unlikely and horribly unfortunate situation find me, and I am given no choice but to run it through the belly of a Continental, I do not wish to tear apart his insides. Evidently, I'm a prick, though I am certainly not an ogre. In fact, here," he said as he reached into a belt pouch for a linen handkerchief. "Wrap it in this and rest it on the ground behind you, and make sure you, nor *any*body else, makes the mistake of stepping on it."

"Of course, sir," replied the slightly dejected private. Pearson paused for a moment and tugged on each of his cuffs to straighten the sleeves from wrinkles. "And you needn't be so concerned," he said without turning toward the private. "The Americans are only trying to discomfort us with this pointless cannon fire. It's nothing more than harmless three-pounders, too far even to reach these walls, let alone to cause any damage."

"I see, sir, that is good to know. Comforting. It's still hard to sleep, though,…sir."

"This is true. It is nearly impossible to sleep, just as it is for the Americans," said Pearson wryly as a glimmer of a crooked smile could not be hidden from his expression.

"Thank you, sir," replied the private.

Pearson entered the office of the fort's commander, Colonel Oliver Bell. Inside, he and his executive officer, Major Andre Morris, stood beside a wooden table, looking down on the various documents scattered across it. The room was rather small, almost confining, with unfinished brick, windowless walls. The floor was made of splintered wooden planks that were nearly covered with dry dirt. Devoid of decoration or style, the room was more of a dungeon than the quarters of a British Officer. A lone metal chandelier hung from a chain overhead, and several thick, flickering candles cast a soft light. The brims of their hats covered both soldiers' faces nearly in total shadows. Pearson nearly gagged as he was taken by the foul stench of rotted meat, human shit, dried sweat, or some such unpleasantness.

At once, the captain felt immediately submissive in the presence of the men before him. Each man adorned the regalia and decorations expected of respected, seasoned officers in His Majesty's Army. Pearson was as humbled by the displays of their worth as they appeared indifferent to them. Their crimson jackets were dulled with dust. None of the dark blue and white plackets or gold epaulets on either shoulder were shined nor cleaned with any care. Morris was a particularly dominating figure. He stood with a commanding confidence and without expression on his face. His madder red coat was snug on his muscular frame. The two appeared to be in mid-discussion of some concern as Pearson entered, and from what he could quickly gather, Morris seemed not the least bit passive to his superior.

"Thank you, Private!" shouted the major upon seeing the captain standing before them in the doorway. "You can leave us now." The young soldier bowed his head quickly, and without uttering a sound, clanged the heavy door closed behind him. Pearson glanced toward the young soldier as he slinked his way outside and felt a sense of further deflation as he was now, clearly, the least commanding of all figures within the hall.

Though not required to by proper manners, the captain removed his hat respectfully and placed it under his right arm. "Good evening, sirs. You wished to see me?" he asked.

Uninterested in pleasantries, Bell abruptly explained his intentions, while remaining fixed on the assorted maps on the table. "We did, Captain," he replied as he snarled and spit. Dribbles of saliva landed on the map, and some were wiped from his chin with his sleeve. It was not easy for Pearson to hide his cringe.

"How are things out there?" asked Bell.

Pearson paused for a moment and replied, "Quiet, Colonel, figuratively speaking, of course. Tense, though, I would say."

"You would say? Just fucking say it then," mumbled Bell, before he abruptly shifted the conversation. "I need you to get a communiqué to General Howe."

Pearson was taken back as he processed Bell's curt assertion. "I beg your pardon, sir? General Howe?"

"Yes, General William Howe—soft belly, dainty and delicate gentlemanly lubberwort who, as it happens, oversees everything on this fucking continent. I assume you've heard of him?" Bell was a highly-regarded military officer for the Empire and not one who was accustomed to questions from subordinates. Clearly annoyed, he wasted little time explaining details to Pearson and made no effort to hide his impatience or contempt for the man he believed to be hardly worthy of his time, company, or respect.

"Schuyler has fallen to the Americans. Herkimer was unable to hold off his own goddamn brother at Oriskany. The house is beginning to crumble upon us, from the Saint Lawrence to the Atlantic. Out there, I suspect it's General Gates, the fatherless fuck, giving this shit to us. He's clever. And if I am right, it means the rebels managed to slow Burgoyne's support from the south, drive him into Quebec, and overrun what was left of our northern force. *Gentleman Johnny* underestimated the colonials, the fucking idiot. If I didn't think it'd cost us the war, I'd find it amusing. Julius Caesar Dardanius…In any event, I don't expect to see his army arrive anytime soon, if at all, and this leaves us one button left from getting fucked. The only reason the Americans are not advancing past the stockade is because they don't know how dire our circumstances are, and, as it seems, they fear the lethality of our heavy guns. As you know more than most here, stores, powder, and balls are in critical supply. There is simply no way we can hold off a sizable rebel force, if, or when, they decided to advance. We control the Gibraltar of North America. I gather the Americans are willing to pay a heavy price to take it back from us. Firing occasional blasts of glass and rocks, is enough to scare them from advancing, and the dumb-fuck farmers are pissing themselves. Eventually, soon, they will learn otherwise. They will catch on to our trick or our powder stores will run out…and that is when you become expendable."

"We cannot hold through a long siege, perhaps a month or two, maybe a bit beyond, but not through winter," added Morris.

Pearson was entirely unsure why his superior officers were bestowing such matters on him, yet continued as though it mattered for him to be aware. "I see," he said. "Clearly, none of this sounds promising."

"Well, you don't say. Thank you, Professor," the colonel replied derisively as he threw a frigid glare toward the major. "I can't imagine Sir William is in any great fucking rush to send stores and ammunition upriver by chance. That is why you are going to New York to relay my contention and requests, Captain Pearson."

"New York? Humbly, Colonel, would Albany not be wiser?" asked Pearson in an uncharacteristically frantic manner. The soft light fell on the colonel's mostly unshaven and gruff face. He was aged beyond his years. The wrinkles about his face, strands of gray weaved between his dark brown hair, and sunken, dark eyes, were scars from his innumerable experiences and current stresses. Briefly, Bell glanced at the major, who subtly shook his head in mild displeasure. The monotonous cannon fire continued to rumble in the distance, although at an increasingly slower pace, the only sound attempting to break the silent tension.

Morris broke the silence with a sarcastic reply, "Thank you, Captain, we have not considered Albany. Good thing we summoned you here."

Colonel Bell paused and rubbed his hand through his stringy, gray-brown hair, then strode a few feet to his desk. He moved slowly, with a bend to his back and a slight tilt to his step. The officer's desk leaned slightly, had a missing drawer, and the surface was scratched and chipped. It was cluttered with booklets, quills, and assorted objects of varying purpose, the most notable being a small bust of an indiscriminate military figure that had been knocked over at some point. Bell was far from the most orderly of the officer corps, yet was one of the most experienced and reliable.

He shifted a few things around the desktop and then opened a drawer, then another, until he found what he was looking for. As he walked back to the table, he unrolled a dried parchment scroll, untied the band, laid it flat on the wood surface, and rested small stones on either side.

"Hold this, will you," demanded Bell as he carelessly passed Pearson his old officer's pistol, which was resting on the table. Pearson accepted it clumsily, not expecting it to be thrust into his chest as it was. "Don't drop the fucking thing, Captain. I could have tossed it on the floor if that is what I wanted." The colonel governed himself in the interest of wasting no time, and in a mildly dismissive manner, explained, "As of the last report, St. Ledger doesn't think the Hessians, and what's left of his army, can hold Albany if the rebels attack with force. I don't think the colonials can muster such an attack, but St. Ledger does. With that, it would serve no purpose to trouble him with requests, and that is why you are going to New York Island."

"Colonel, I am flattered by your confidence I am worthy of such an assignment, but, I have no skills as a scout…or, or a surveyor. Surely there are men more qualified than I," replied Pearson. "I am fearfully unfamiliar with this country, and clearly it is an imperative message you wish to relay to the general. I cannot help to think there are better trackers among us. My bona fides is commanding artillery —"

"Dammit, Pearson, we don't have the luxury of only doing what we see fit to do," replied Morris. "I figured you to be soft, but it seems you are more of a dandy prat than your reputation suggests. Do you think you stand before us for flattery? We are not interested in your concerns or personal assessments on the right course of action. Every man out there would rather find themselves in more opportune circumstances befitting their wants or needs. Maybe I'm a fool to assume a man who lectures others for a living is smart enough to assess the dire straits in which we currently find ourselves. You know our ranks have worn thin here. The shallow waters reveal the rocks. We do not at all disagree you are not an ideal candidate for this —do you know where we are, what we are up against? You are not addressing a room filled with shitty, pampered boys in the grand halls of university. We summoned you for a briefing, not a brow-beating. Nonetheless, this is not a place for soft men—you need to harden yourself to this world, or, in one way or another, you will not be part of it very much longer."

"I was not trying to suggest—" interjected Pearson.

"I know, I know," replied Morris. The major eased his sense of hostility and, as much as his cold heart would allow, felt a twinge of guilt for harshly attacking Pearson's character. Pragmatically, he realized continued agitation and insult would serve no purpose. Impatiently, yet with a certain air of calm, he continued, "This war has become a series of shit pageants. We are nearing desperation, and you are more resourceful and able than any we have. Without much powder, you are no use to us here. You believe yourself to be a superior breed, yes? You are a senior officer in the king's army, who is expected to conduct himself as such. That starts with taking an order without discussing or questioning the whys and wherefores."

"What the Major is saying, Captain, is that you *will* face the working end of muskets, but whether they be American or British is your choice," added the colonel, who normally would have reprimanded the major for overly berating a fellow officer in his presence, and, in this case, depriving him of the joy of doing it himself.

Bell was a veteran of the Seven Year's War in America. As a lieutenant, he served beside Major George Washington in the Ohio Valley campaign. His heroics enabled Washington to withdraw the bulk of the colonial forces from Fort Necessity as it was being overrun by the French. Against overwhelming number, Bell rallied what was left of the British outfit, and halted the French from advancing as Washington scurried back to Pennsylvania and safety, where he was later hailed as a champion. Typically, Bell would relish any opportunity to kill Frenchmen, yet this time, his equal disdain for the colonists dampened his satisfaction. Bell witnessed over two dozen men fall before he finally agreed to surrender the fort, a far too expensive price in British blood to save any number of Americans. When he discovered Washington undertook the expedition as a chance to beat his competitors and survey the valley for commercial purposes, Bell was overcome with undying odium. The rebellion was a personal opportunity to hunt the scoundrel, George Washington, and run his blade from his neck to his balls.

It was unusual for the colonel to have bothered to waste a single breath on his reasoning. Likely he would have instantly thrown the seditious, and rather irritating, captain in irons. These circumstances were bleak, and latitude was an unfortunate consequence. For now, Major Morris's scolding would have to do.

Pearson meekly replied, "Of course, sir. I will forever serve our king dutifully."

"Now that wasn't so hard, was it? Ten of Morris's grenadiers will escort you, and Wyandot Panther will be your guide. He's our best tracker, and, after recent events, it is better he is not here," said Colonel Bell.

"The Mohawk? The scout who—" Pearson began desperately.

"He is the one," Bell cut him off to reply. "He knows these woods, and he can follow the stars and the sun better than any scout I have ever known. He's a hideous fucker, but you have no chance to reach the island without him." Bell shifted his attention toward Morris. "Major…"

The major tapped on the map at the southern position. "You know the Continentals are positioning artillery to the south." He continued gravely, "The far redoubt didn't hold."

"Light cannons, yes, Major. They've been scurrying about all afternoon," replied Pearson. "They must have circled around Mount Hope and toward Defiance—"

"Or they are not part of the northern force," interrupted Major Morris. "I think elements have peeled from Albany to join Gates. As of nightfall, I believe they have at least six cannons in position. I would guess fifty to a hundred feet apart. They are either trying to divide our forces between north and south, or are positioning the guns to support an infantry charge. Daybreak tomorrow, I'm going to seize those guns before the colonials can assemble there in force. As far as you're concerned, I'll engage the Americans, which will cover you and your party to break from the lower demi-lune, toward the longboats and downriver…and New York. You'll be out of harm's way soon enough."

"The lower demi-lune of the northernmost rampart?" asked Pearson.

"Yeah, the northern rampart."

Pearson furrowed his brows in a bit of confusion, "I beg your pardons, sirs, maybe this is a puerile question, but—"

"A what?" interrupted Bell, exasperated.

"I'm sorry," replied Pearson.

"This is a *what* question?" clarified the colonel.

Pearson paused to the let moment fester. The colonel felt a level of threat, as it was clear, in the intellectual realm, the captain was by far his superior. Pearson knew this and perhaps chose his words with such intent. "A *puerile* question…um…a, uh, silly question," he clarified.

Bell's disdain for the captain appeared to grow yet more. "So why not just say that?"

Though it would have been simple to fire back one of the many snide remarks that came to mind, the captain, of course, was restrained. He was content to have succeeded in subtly belittling the colonel, in his quarters and in the presence of another British Officer. Pearson continued with a contrived, simplistic tone, "Of course, Colonel Bell, my apologies. I don't know…poor choice of words. Am I mistaken, or does the lower chamber only have a western entryway? We'll have to run across the field of fire to reach the river."

Major Morris coldly replied, "You are not mistaken. You will, indeed."

The captain's urge was to probe this thought for further clarification and explanation. His initial conclusion suggested the plan was more dangerous than it need be. Yet, he would soon come to learn, both Major Morris and Colonel Bell were loathed to field even the most trivial of questions, and even valid discussion was unwelcome, and in this case, pointless. Perhaps a decision he would regret, Pearson trusted his assumption the two veteran officers had considered all avenues in making their decision.

"To be clear, I can offer no assurances regarding your safety," continued the major. "You will be exposed to cannon and muskets. Surely, they will use grapeshot to fill the air with a swarm of lead. I'll do all I can to draw their fire, but I can't imagine everyone one who breaks with you will make it to the longboats. The fact remains, I would be surprised if half do. I have little regard for the soldiering of the Americans, but our decision is a product of desperation, not calculation." As he continued to instruct Pearson, the dire reality of his plan had become more apparent to Morris. He paused and remained silent for a moment or two before he proceeded. "The priority is to survive, to be one who makes it into the longboat. Be fast. Do all you can to ensure our dispatch reaches the general. Do not slow to help the fallen, do not worry to leave any behind, and do not look to engage the Rebels. It is critical the *message* arrives, not you or your party. And if your goal becomes at any point unreachable, make no mistake, you will be held accountable should the Rebels find out the contents of which you carry. Am I, in any way, unclear on this?"

Pearson slowly and despondently nodded his head. "I don't think you could be any clearer. I assure you, the Americans will not get a hold of the dispatch; it will be destroyed should it come to that."

"Good," replied Morris. "My column of grenadiers will continue to engage the enemy after you have set sail, yet stay toward the west regardless. Pass Mount Independence, continue southward no less than ten miles, no more than fifteen, then cross—"

The colonel picked up the narrative from there, speaking over Major Morris. "Keep going east twenty, twenty-five miles into the Green Mountains. Colonial militia is patrolling the lakes and near banks of the river—the west is mostly Tory." Bell's eyes remained fixed on the map, and he made no effort to look up at Captain Pearson. Colonel Bell did not see the purchase of commissions as a right of honor for English nobility. He lacked a certain respect for Pearson and his type, who he believed joined the war only to enhance their legacy through an assuredly easy British victory. The colonel's finger followed his instructions on the map as if he was talking to himself more than anyone else. "Circle back, work your way southwest, back toward the Hudson. At that point, you can simply follow the river southward, and I would reckon at that point it would be wise to dispose of Panther. If you don't get lost, it should take no more than ten days or a fortnight. Make haste, and do not look for problems where you don't see them. I love dead Americans as much as any man, but it is crucial for you, or anyone in your party, to relay our needs to New York. If for any reason, I get news that my report did not reach the fucking Viscount Howe, I expect it will be included with word of your demise."

"I cannot say for sure how many lives I have to throw at the Americans tomorrow, Captain Pearson," added Morris. "I would be surprised if it is less than a few. You need to make sure they were not spent uselessly. I know you are not familiar with the firsthand carnage of warfare. I am not saying this as an affront but as a point of fact. Young men, boys, I can't say for sure how many fathers will become childless, and children will become fatherless—mine may be amongst them. Men will lie on the field in a pool of their own piss, shit, and blood, dismembered, bowels spilled about them; the fortunate among them will pass quickly. The others…we can do nothing for them. Some will cling to their lives for days. At night, when the air is cool and silent, wolves will find them to feast upon their flesh, whether they be dead or alive. Gentlemen allow for the wounded to be collected when the contest is over, yet I cannot be so sure the Americans will follow such conduct. You are soft, and I am not standing before you to pass judgment on this but to state it as to clarify reality. I know, as well as you and the colonel know, you are not entirely fit for this task, yet you must make yourself fit for it. You must find whatever conviction you have, and if you can find none, carry on as though you do. We are spending the years of young men for no other purpose than to buy you a chance to reach the longboats."

"I understand, Major. With deference, I do not need further clarification on the gravity of the task. I assure you, I will give the matter the effort it deserves," declared Pearson.

"I wouldn't sell yourself short, Captain Pearson," said Morris, adding, "You are a man who sees the value of logic. Trust Panther's guidance and appease his savagery, do not burden the party to carry the wounded, and feel free pilfer from the Loyalists if need be. Do what you believe needs to be done, and move forward without dwelling on matters. Take every precaution you must, and act per no code.

"Your party will be mostly lads. Boys whose balls have yet to drop. They do not know better than to be scared, yet they will trust in your intellect and standing. Present a calm image, show no fear, even when you are afraid, no hesitation even when you are unsure, and they will be fine. Soldiers are like dogs, in that they feel the fears and concerns of their masters. When the master is calm, so too is the dog. When they sense you have nothing to be afraid of, they will follow in kind."

Bell interjected with the intent of countering Morris's grim depiction of the situation. "Yes, Major, of course, but soldiers are instruments of war. They are tools, a carpenter's nails. Some will bend or fall to the ground, and because he has so many nails in his sack, he will take no mind to straighten the crooked one or pick up those which have fallen. These are not your mates, Captain; they are expendable for the purpose. Do not befriend them, and do not get to know them. You cannot hesitate when you order them to their deaths."

In a halfhearted, almost comically insincere attempt at reassurance, Morris concluded, "I trust becoming friendly will not be a problem."

"You're going to have to find quarter with Tories, I'm sure. I'd rather you do not rape any of them," Colonel Bell added sarcastically, referencing a recent, disturbing incident involving Wyandot Panther. "The documents you carry detail our ominous state. I'll say this again: under no circumstances are you to be killed or captured with them in your possession. As of now, we are shielded only by the Americans' ignorance."

"Understood," replied Pearson, who had gone from uneasy to impatient, in part to Morris's and Bell's repetitive series of instruction. "The general will read your dispatch, or no man will read it."

"Yes very good, Captain Pearson. Though it goes without saying, I am going to make clear to you, control of this garrison is crucial," said the colonel, in his distinctively strict and straightforward manner.

"General Howe's office is of the assumption it is securely controlled by the Empire. Should he continue to neglect our position, we will not be able to hold Ticonderoga, and the war will most certainly turn against us."

* * *

Five days south of Fort Ticonderoga and one day north of New York Island.

Cole, a beautiful, muscular, midnight-black yearling stood beside the road, strapped to a rickety old cart. His coat was as soft as cotton, as smooth as silk, and as shiny as glass. Happily, he gnawed barley and hay from the feedbag strapped to his snout. He was the product of a grand stallion and a beautiful, sprightly mare, and without a trace of the blood of a workhorse. A prince who belonged at the head of the majestic carriage of royalty, he stood as a serf, within a web of leather straps and harnesses, beside a muddy road.

Post Road ran along the eastern bank of the Hudson. It cut through the thick layer of trees and over the hills of the valley. The path was heavily traveled by the wagon's riders, though unfamiliar to Cole. Still, he pressed forward, almost proud to haul the men who sat behind him. The sky was darkened by the threatening clouds, and a brisk wind whispered through the autumn leaves. Several yards away, beyond a tall maple and large, jagged rocks, where the water lazily washed the shore, stood the two traveling mates. Their shadows swayed on the surface of the cool river water. The Hudson was uneasy and gray with the reflection of the threatening clouds. Both men were just close enough to the edge as to hardly dampen their toes. Though they were companions, they clearly shared no social standing. One was tall, broad-shouldered, and plainly dressed, with heavy leather boots and a crude, wool cock'd cap. At his side stood a more refined figure, with vaguely elegant attire from his exquisitely crafted boots to his fine, beaver skin, tri-cornered hat. The pair gazed at the glittering, gray-blue water and held their cocks as two streams of urine trickled into the Hudson.

Cool taps of faint drops of rain fell on the backs of their necks. As they relieved themselves, the eyes of the more refined character could not help but wander in the other's direction, specifically toward his manhood. He tilted his head and stretched his neck ever so slightly, as to find an angle to size-up his pissing colleague. After a second, or maybe two, he worriedly looked away and was unable to make any assessments on the matter. He tried to give this no further thought, yet curiosity would not allow it. With this, he simply looked forward and fixed his eyes ahead, over the river and on the red, bronze, and marigold leaves on the western side of the Hudson River. He looked up to the sky. "Hope you don't mind getting wet." A distant thundering rumble prodded them to move things along. The weary travelers shook the final stubborn drops of urine from their vagina miners, adjusted their breeches, and set back to continue their way southward.

* * *

Captain Isaac Pearson stood with a cadre of Morris's soldiers within the lower level of the western demi-lune of Fort Ticonderoga. He held his musket formally, several inches from his right hip. His deep-red uniform was pristine, every button and badge placed perfectly, his boots shined to a gleam, officer's sword polished and hat placed straight on his head, pointing as directly forward as it should. He was jittery and fought himself to find the appearance of calm. A hint of rum remained on his breath, a reminder of his desperate attempt to find a restful hour or so throughout the night. Seemingly, every few minutes, he reached for his right hip in confirmation his most highly valued Duval pistol was being brought along with him. Of course, he would never leave it anywhere but close, yet his continued grasps had at this point become a nervous habit. From above, the thundering roars of heavy gun blasts rumbled throughout the open chamber in which he stood.

The rampart rested several yards ahead of the western barrier. It was of triangular shape, built of heavy stone, and stood just over twenty feet in height. The king's guns were positioned at battlements on its hardened surface. Below, in the open chamber, it was dark and dank. Pebbles and dust rained on Pearson and the others. With each artillery burst, the captain needlessly brushed himself clean. He casually reviewed each of the troops as he began to walk along their line. In truth, he did not know what constituted a proper soldier, yet continued his so-called inspection only for perception. Each stood at attention as per the respect of the officer before them. Every man held his musket at his side as a dutiful soldier, and most fought desperately not to tremble or reveal their fear. They were mostly young. Some seemed closer to children than men, clumsy and thin. None of their faces were familiar to the captain, who hardly paid much mind to the rank and file within the fortress to begin with.

Pearson knew they looked to him to model fortitude and courage, but he was as unsure and unnerved as they appeared. Only Wyandot Panther, the bloodthirsty Mohawk scout, appeared to be at all at ease, if not enthusiastic, as he crouched and leaned, almost impatiently, against the wall just inside the entranceway. *The Panther*, as he'd become known, savored the opportunity to kill colonials. In practice, he had become quite the expert.

Though he had an air of aristocracy about him, the soldiers in his command had collectively valued the captain's leadership quality. Pearson had an exceptional, if not uncanny, mathematical mind. He was an excellent artillery officer who hardly wasted a round. He was not an infantryman, nor a cavalryman, and had never witnessed the carnage of warfare directly. Nor had he witnessed the results of his deadly efficiency. The expectation of bloodshed was further turning his already-knotted stomach. In this instance, he was as far from his element as the Panther was from hoity-toity English affairs. Ignorance to this realm would shift his leadership to not rely on calculation, but impulses and hunches.

He walked along the column of men, each of whom stood straight at attention as he bellowed, "Do not overthink our task here, Gentlemen! We are not needed to help win this skirmish, we are needed to survive it. Take only one shot—do not reload, and do not stop or slow yourself for proper aim. We are not firing to hit them, but to keep their heads down. I know you are all eager to kill Americans, to prove your value in combat, and you will be given opportunities to do so…but not today. Today is not the day to pursue that glory. Our charge is far more important to our king than turning this Continental Regiment into a pile of corpses."

Pearson realized he was rambling nervously, overplaying his act, and refocused to be more direct. "The rebels will not risk their guns by advancing or pursuing. Major Morris is going to charge to capture the cannons, and more significantly, draw their fire." He calmly paced down the line of men. These clarifications were, of course, unnecessary. Yet, he was running through the scenario for himself as much as his troops, and in reflecting on Morris's advice, he hoped the trivial directions would suggest he was in control and prepared, thus easing their tensions. "Make extreme haste, and I cannot stress this strongly enough: Do not wait for either me or anyone. Get to the nearest boat, secure the lines, and be ready to push-off immediately."

One soldier within the line began to fix his bayonet, and another followed his lead and prepared to fix his. "No. Keep your bayonets in the scabbards!" barked the captain. "Did you hear me order to fix bayonets? Jesus...Can we please, *please* practice some common sense, Gentlemen? We are racing toward the longboats, then throwing ourselves into them. I am not going to scurry past American cannons to be greeted by one or your goddamn bayonets in my stomach as I land on it."

Pearson closed his eyes and tried desperately to wish away his anxieties. His stomach was alive with fluttering energy, and his penis had withdrawn nearly entirely into his body. His mouth was dry and felt as though it was filled with cotton, making it difficult to continue his verbal badgering. The captain could hardly breathe, swallow, or rest his hands, which were quivering vigorously. The faith he had in his comrades had quickly ceded to his pragmatic concerns about their competence. The typically low opinion he had of his fellow man was fostering a nearly paralyzing doubt. At this moment, Captain Pearson had convinced himself today would be the last day of his life.

Light rain progressed steadily into a constant shower. The sky had grown gray as thick, billowy clouds drifted from west to east and the ground had become soaked with puddles and mud. Pearson's experience had taught him to fire heavy guns low when targeting an onrushing enemy. Cannonballs skip and bounce about the ground wildly, tearing through the ranks of men and splintering limbs. The soft, muddied soil presumed the Americans would be foolish to attempt this tactic, an apparent sign fortune just may have been on their side.

The field was flat, other than a few stones that peeked through the grassy surface here and there. The downpour steadily washed the ground, and the subtle, constant drone of the rain was lost to all ears. Blasts of cannon fire shattered the otherwise sinister calm. The tree line began seventy yards or so south of the fortress, and the rebel guns were lined from south to west between the trees and the stronghold's southern barrier. A line of Redcoats, the rest of Major Morris's grenadiers, formed a single column between the fortress and the American guns. They sat in the muck and wet grass and leaned with their backs against the southern redoubt, which extended about twenty yards before the fortification's inner barriers. The obstacle was made of heavy, interlocking logs and thick hay bales. It zig-zagged as it stretched to west. The Grenadiers' muskets pointed skyward, with bayonets fixed, an unmistakable mark of Morris's command. Traditional protocol in His King's Army would be to fix bayonets only when close confrontation had become inevitable, yet this was not the practice under Morris's charge. The major preferred the enemy to be fully aware of what awaited him, should they charge his ranks. Their uniforms were soaked and heavy from the continued pelts of ceaseless raindrops. The line was almost directly in the center of artillery exchanges. The bastion behind them and the American light cannon lines before them traded volleys of cannon fire overhead. Fired projectiles flew so close over, some nearly knocked their hats to the ground.

The stench of death was washed with the burnt scent of gunpowder as clouds wafted through their ranks. Sporadic cannonballs crashed into the wooden redoubt, blasting the beams into splinters. Four of the eighty-four men had been struck by American cannon blasts. Each lost his life, in one horrific manner or another. Each was dismembered or impaled gruesomely; their bodies remained in the mud. Traditionally, warring parties allowed their opponent the civility to carry back the wounded or killed at the day's end. Yet, this was an existential war for the Americans, a war they sought to win by any means. Good graces and the proper conduct of gentlemanly combat served no purpose toward that end.

The second lieutenant, the most senior ranking of the forward platoon, was struck in his lower ribs. His spleen was ruptured, and his right lung was pierced by a bone splinter. Slow, internal bleeding cost him his life after he clung to it for several hours. Another, less unfortunate, private's skull was blown nearly off by a direct hit on the back of his head through one of the gaps in the wood rails. His body was thrown forward two or three yards, where it still lay, in the mud, face down. Its head was mostly splattered about as if it had been poured from his body, and what remained of his skull was gnarled and shredded. As the torrent poured on the corpse, a wash of light-red bodily fluids streamed outward as blood and rainwater washed from his shattered skull. His remains were hardly noticed for now because Morris's forward grenadiers had all been calloused to the bloodshed and carnage of war. The narrow line of red figures stretched from east to west. The Third Queen's Royal Grenadiers remained ready and vigilant, each man anxiously awaiting the command to charge, a command they had been expecting for just over three days now. The intensified fire of the heavy guns behind them suggested the command would have to come at any moment.

Atop the fortification's outer work, behind the southern redoubt, Major Andre Morris and two mounted cavalry officers sat on their steeds some fifteen yards or so behind the heavy guns. His nerves were mostly still, yet he lacked a bit of his usual confidence. The rain poured in front of his face, streaming from his riding helmet, and his mount, Ajax, was becoming increasingly restless. The heavy cast iron cannons were built to fire twelve-pound balls into the heavy, oak hulls of frigates and cruisers on the high seas. Today, they launched grapeshot toward the American artillery positions. Four men stood two on either side of the farthest gun within the bastion's star-shaped arm. The barrel blasted an incredible roar, and the entire gun and carriage were jolted back violently. A plume of gray-white smoke was thrown forward from the muzzle and then blown back.

"Reload!" shouted the artillery officer who stood just behind the big gun. The first soldier left of the gun's muzzle, the *worm*, as he was known, held a long wooden rod with a heavy wire ring mechanism at the end. He ran toward the open end of the gun, which was still coughing thick smoke, and poked the rod into the barrel, shifting it inward and outward frantically. The worm cleared the barrel of debris, then ran to his position alongside the cannon and rested the rod at his side. From the other side, another soldier jammed a wet sponge attached to a wooden pole down the muzzle in the same fashion as the worm. He was making sure to extinguish the embers within the chamber. As he ran back to his standing position, the soldier behind the worm raced to place a powder charge, wrapped in heavy paper, into the muzzle. The forward soldier rammed the powder shot down the barrel, and the worm lifted a grapeshot case, a dozen or so heavy iron balls wrapped in canvas, into the gun immediately afterward. Finally, the fourth soldier jammed the ramrod into the barrel, forcing the projectiles toward the breech.

"Make ready!" barked the artillery officer from behind. The far soldier from the left position poked a small hole atop the breech, piercing the powder charge's paper shell, and stuck a short hemp fuse into the pinhole. The officer paused for less than a moment, and yelled, "Fire!" as loudly as he could. The soldier in the far-right position cupped the tip of a long match and blew on it profusely, then immediately lit the fuse. After a second or two the massive cast iron hornblower erupted with a thundering explosion, spitting a flash of fire and a plume of heavy white cloud from its muzzle. The entire gun leaped backward, and the five cannoneers were instantly lost in the swirling smoke.

Sitting tall on Ajax's back, the major held a long, brass spyglass to his eye and scanned the Americans' gun positions carefully. The lens was nearly covered in rainwater and was quickly of no use. Frustrated, Morris collapsed the spyglass by pushing it into his palm and grumbled his irritation. He was not at all sure what the rebels had been up to, if the guns had been repositioned in the night, defended by more than supporting units, or if the heavy guns of Fort Ticonderoga were inflicting any damage. Major Morris was virtually blind to what he was about to order his platoon to advance into.

As of dawn, the Americans had six light cannons lined nearly a hundred yards from the southwest corner of Ticonderoga. Morris's best estimation at the time, was each cannon was supported by a dozen or so light infantry and three to four militiamen, yet as of now, there was no way for him to make a truly accurate updated assessment through the rain and hedgerows. Morris was unusually trepid and unsure. For several seconds, he peered into a void, and without any notions, let the rain pitter onto him. The veteran soldier no longer allowed skepticism to guide his course. "Fuck it," he muttered to himself. Morris looked over his shoulder toward two particularly young soldiers; their backs were to the fortress wall and each was wearing a large drum barrel below his gut. He pointed in their direction and snarled, "Now!"

They raised their sticks, held them horizontally at eye level, tip to tip, then began thrashing the drums rapidly to emit the *call to battle* order. Seconds later, down at the near center point of the redoubt, one of the red-clad soldiers within the line alerted the company by hoisting a banner tall. A rain-soaked Union Jack within a field of cardinal red was raised. The colors flapped limply in the faint wind, but were too burdened by the weight of the soaking rain to appear with inspiration. Morris waved his flanking cavalry officers, and they hurried down the bastion ramp toward the column of Redcoats.

The major's stallion sprinted forward, throwing mud into the air with each stride. He moved swiftly through the swirling smoke, and the drums beat loudly behind him. Near the center of the column, he pulled back the reins, and Ajax fell back to his hind legs, lifting and kicking his front two angrily. The two mounted lieutenants followed several yards behind. He faced the Rebel force, his two cavalry officers standing tall on either side, and the column of infantrymen stretched some thirty-plus yards to his left and another thirty to his right.

At this distance, Morris could clearly see a column of American Blue Jackets stretching thirty-plus yards ahead of his line of grenadiers. He remained steadfast and calm while he waited for the rebel unit to expose itself when it rose to fire on his troops. He quickly surmised the Americans were nearly twice in number, much more than he anticipated.

"Present!" bellowed the major, and the forward rank of soldiers, in near unison, got to their feet to face the enemy. Each man held his musket four or five inches from his chest vertically, and steadily awaited the next command. He peered from his left to right as he swiftly inspected each man and each musket. From their position, the Americans launched a round of bullets toward the British column. A single soul was struck and brought to the ground. Every one of the others stood fast in their positions without hardly a flinch among them. The line held strong, and the volley was altogether ineffective.

"Make ready!" ordered Morris, and each of them brought their muskets to their shoulders, into firing position. The major looked forward, both hands grasping the reins eyes fixed on the enemy before him. He waited four or five seconds, nearly an eternity for the tense British column. At any moment, the Americans would again rise to fire after reloading their muskets. Morris had engaged the colonials in combat before. He had seen them determined by a fear that drove them into a panic of irrational actions. This particular band of Rebels appeared a bit more reserved, yet still inferior and inexperienced.

The Americans had a tendency to kneel as they reloaded. This did nothing to make them less vulnerable, yet it did quite a bit to prolong the time it took to reload. The disciplined grenadiers were typically able to fire every fifteen seconds; the Americans took nearly twice as long.

"Fire!" he shouted with all his might the instant the Colonial Band rose to fire another volley. Flashes of fire burst throughout the line, and a collective crackle echoed along the column, which was immediately engulfed in a sea of white smoke. Major Morris's warhorse thrust about until he jerked at the reins tightly to reel him in. The storm of iron balls shredded through the colonial line and tore down nearly a quarter of the American force. The air was filled with specks of blood and flesh. Those who were not hit were overcome by the carnage—splattered blood and bowels of their less fortunate comrades. Like birds flailing with broken wings desperate to fly, the Americans floundered about in terror. The uncommon few of them were so composed as to effectively ready their muskets to fire on the British once more, yet the line was broken.

Without the slightest hesitation, the column of grenadiers systematically began reloading. Ahead, the rebels struggled into wild disintegration, desperately unable to galvanize into an effective force, and were desperately unable to fire any manner of a threatening volley. Few managed harmless, scattered pops up and down the line, but the Redcoats, in unison, completed each step, preparing their weapons to fire on the Americans once again. The major pulled his saber from its scabbard, held it by his side, and repeated his command to make ready. Each man brought his weapon to the ready position, some a bit quicker and more steadily than others, though still as a methodical fighting unit.

Captain Pearson watched the action at the sally port inside the rampart's lower chamber some yards behind Morris's position. His heart was thumping wildly, and his mouth felt as if it had been filled with cotton. The shower had given way to a downpour. The gray stone walls of the fortress had darkened, and the flat battleground had become soft and soaked.

"Disperse!" he barked as he gestured his arm forward and sprinted out toward Major Morris and the grenadiers. Pearson stopped just outside the chamber and waved each man on as they burst out of the entryway. Like drops of water trickling from a spigot in a strong breeze, each man escaped through the chamber's western entryway and sprinted as fast as his legs could manage across the battleground, east, toward the Hudson. Wyandot was in the lead, and the ten Redcoats followed, their packs rattling and clanging, their boots sloshing in the mud and splashing in the puddles. Each man clung to his musket as he raced toward the water some two hundred yards ahead. The company flew through cannon fire toward the longboats and sailed past the colonists' right flank. Captain Pearson was the last in the line and led them from behind, forcing them to continue forward.

Just before him, three of his contingent halted and aimed their muskets southward, toward the rebels. The closest soldier was nearly two yards ahead when he was thrown backward as an apple-sized ball was fired into his torso just above his left hip and just below his ribs. The round pierced his body, blowing a small hole in his stomach. Instantaneously, thick red spray exploded from his hind ribs and through his tattered coat. Seemingly at the exact second, the ball was violently thrust into the shoulder of another soldier, who was directly behind. The trooper's shoulder blade snapped and splintered as the projectile blasted against the base of the demi-lune, firing rock debris in all directions. In a flash, what seemed at once, the cannonball blasted through two men and crashed against the hardened wall.

Pearson's face was dotted with the blood of the fallen men. He felt a rush of horror nearly overtake his senses. He felt as though he roared his command, "Do not stay behind each other!" In reality, he was so overwhelmed by the carnage, he managed only a feckless whisper. One soldier lay motionless, the other writhing on the ground, shrieking in pain. His bone punctured his skin on his back shoulder, causing a horrific compound fracture, and when he instinctively thrust his hand out to clutch at the wound, he sliced the palm with his splintered collarbone. The captain raced along but took a moment to kneel before the agonizing soldier. Fragmented bits of brick were fired against his neck and shoulder as the continued gunfire landed against the fortress wall. He immediately assessed the severity of his injury, then continued his hastened pace toward the lake, leaving the wounded man behind.

Major Morris lifted his saber forward and roared, "Fire!" Another combined thud and cloud of smoke ensued, as the column launched a volley of lead balls toward the rebels. "Charge!" he commanded. He whipped the reins and ferociously kicked his horse, urging him to advance. The major fiercely raced toward his enemies, bouncing atop his steed with his sword held low at his side. His mounted counterparts charged alongside him, swords emblazoned, ready to plunge into the American lines. Trailing the three horsemen, a line of Redcoats rushed along, hurtling the redoubt and charging forward with bayonets leading their way.

A few dozen yards behind Morris's charge, Pearson and his company raced toward the waterline. The first few men had reached the water, and one threw himself into the nearest longboat as the others scurried to cut the ropes that secured it to shore. Several rebel soldiers defending the easternmost cannon spotted them as Pearson and the others scurried toward the lake.

"They are trying to flank us!" shouted one of the Americans. "Come on!" he commanded, hurrying toward them while waving the others to follow. Half a dozen colonial troops irrationally darted toward Pearson's company at the longboats. The American cannoneers turn the wheeled three-pound gun rightward, into the direction of the longboats fixed at the shore.

Pearson was some fifty paces from the colonial charge. Ahead of him was the waterline, and just to his right was the easternmost cannon. From his position, the captain noticed the Blue Jackets who had rushed from their emplacement and shouted at his troopers before him, "Ahead! The rebel guns—make ready!" Pearson and four nearby grenadiers raised their muskets toward the onrushing Americans. "Fire!" he charged, and he and the others blasted a volley toward the American cannon's position.

One of the Rebels was knocked back and rolled along the ground, but the rest continued forward without hesitation. "Hurry!" barked Captain Pearson, and he sprinted toward the others near the longboat. The American cannon roared with a burst of fire and smoke. The breasthook and stem post of the nearest boat shattered into twigs and kindling, the mast blown apart near its base. It clanged about and fell into the water with a massive splash. Instantly, Panther and the two soldiers who had nearly reached the boat turned back, in the direction of the Americans as they stormed toward them.

Three more grenadiers had reached the nearest longboat. They tossed their muskets into the battered vessel and frantically helped cut at the heavy ropes binding it ashore. Two of the trailing Redcoats saw they were about to be overrun by the American charge. One tapped the other and raised his weapon to firing position, and his comrade followed his lead. With the rain streaming down their faces, they trembled, barely able to hold their weapons steady. The breech of the nearest rifleman flashed, and his musket popped as the ball was fired into the surging Continental soldiers. Without hesitation, he turned and sprinted toward the longboat a dozen yards ahead of him. His shot landed on its mark and shattered the leg of the charging trooper. His shin snapped in half just below the knee, and he collapsed nearly straight down, driving the upper bone into the rain-soaked turf. He fell forward, thrusting the bone from the mud, and without making a sound, grabbed and pulled on his breeches as if he were on fire.

The second Redcoat's breech fizzled, hissed, and failed to fire, doused by the heavy rain. For a moment, he stood in bewilderment, unable to process exactly what was happening. He lowered his weapon from his shoulder and inspected it anxiously. Amid the confusion, two of the Americans lunged at him with their bayonets and ran him through. He was stabbed in the stomach and upper chest as he was thrown back to the muddied ground. The young trooper flailed about and screamed as the Americans furiously thrust their blades into him repeatedly. Blood spewed and splattered about as he thrashed and desperately tried to cover himself with his arms. Unmercifully and moved by frenzy, the two Americans brutally jabbed at his arms, slicing his skin and shredding his muscles.

Pearson ordered the three soldiers within earshot of him to halt in their tracks. He was now some thirty yards from the fallen soldier and still in the line of cannon fire. "Reload!" he commanded. The troops earnestly poured powder down the barrels of their muskets, shoved a lead ball into the muzzle, then forcefully jammed the ramrod down the shaft. The captain withdrew his father's officer's carbine pistol and raised it toward the Americans as he barked, "Fire!" Their guns cracked and burst with flames and smoke. Two of the Americans were thrown back, while the other three flinched and cowered. A duo suddenly pulled back toward the eastern cannon position, and the third dropped to his knees, frozen in panic.

Sergeant McAllister unsecured the damaged longboat, and one by one, his comrades leaped into the wooden hull. The front of the boat was broken apart from the gun's blast. The cannonball had smashed through the upper bow and torn through the frame just about mid-portside. The disfigured remains of the lone soldier who had first reached the longboat was pinned against the port bulkhead. A large hunk of his right torso was blown apart, and his bowels and innards were strewn about the inside of the hull.

Wyandot Panther lurched slowly from the longboat, which was now wading a few feet from the shore. The rain hammered against his broad shoulders, and the droplets rolled off his deerskin breeches. It was as though the smell of paralyzing fear had awakened him from a slumber. His long black hair fell flat behind his neck; his eyes darkened with rage as he plodded his way toward retreating Rebels. Slowly, he pulled his razor-sharp dagger from its leather scabbard and tread toward the bemused American soldier who was still lost in a state of terror. The frantic Continental trooper clutched at the wet grass and whimpered uncontrollably as he was engulfed by Panther's shadow. If he was not a boy, he was not much older than one. To Panther, this meant nothing. The native scout did not see the death of Americans as a necessity but as a consecration.

The easternmost American cannon fired a shot toward the boat. The gun belched a deep, booming blast, and a flash of fire and veil of white smoke burst forth. Almost immediately, the upper rib of the starboard frame exploded, hurling a blur of wooden fragments into the air. The ball zipped through the vessels and shattered the knee of the grenadier sitting on the center thwart bench, ripping through the port-side rib. The wooden frame was blistered outward, and the slug splashed twenty yards or so into the lake water. The soldier's calf had been thrown almost horizontal, and his knee was twisted and covered with thick brown-red blood. Instantly and agonizingly, he bit down and grit his teeth with all his might, turning his head, doing all he could manage to avoid seeing a glimpse of the horrific injury.

As the battered longboat continued to drift farther from shore, Wyandot Panther loomed over the feverish Continental soldier. He lowered himself, and with cold deliberation drove his knee into the young man's back. Panther snatched the poor soul's forehead with his right hand and firmly pulled back, while gripping his dagger with the other. Pearson had been approaching quickly. He threw his hand forward, and from several yards away, bellowed, "No! Wyandot, leave him—get to the boat!"

Entranced in a state of barbaric savagery, Panther grimly turned toward Pearson, then proceeded with his bloodlust as if he never heard the order. The young soldier lashed around weakly and desperately gulped for air, unable to muster a sound. Ever so slowly, Panther forcefully dragged the blade along his forehead from ear to ear, slicing his skin as he pulled back the man's long brown hair. The distraught victim gargled most repulsively as the malevolent native wrenched the top of his head from his skull as if he was pulling skin from a grape.

"Leave him, goddammit!" demanded Captain Pearson as he reached Wyandot Panther and grabbed his wrist forcefully. Pearson stood over Panther, his furious stare piercing the shower of rain, and for a moment, his eyes remained fixed on Panther's. With eyes locked, Pearson clutched Wyandot's forearm firmly, not daring to let go. The American soldier remained pinned to the ground as Panther's knee firmly pressed into his spine. The lad weakly jerked about, but was losing strength as his wound continued to bleed profusely. The captain had heard tales about the Mohawk's ritualistic brutality but was unprepared to witness it with his own eyes. With his eyes still locked on Wyandot's, he forcefully, yet with a calmness he did not feel, commanded, "I need you to get in the boat right now. He's going to die. We need to be in the boat." The two men remained still through the test of wills. Wyandot looked down at the struggling colonial soldier, grinned with amusement, and rose to his feet. He was content with the degree of horror he had inflicted and yielded to Pearson's demand. The captain released his wrist from his grip and repeated solemnly, "Get in the boat."

Wyandot and Pearson were the last to jump into the damaged longboat. The two men ran to the shoreline, then quickly waded through the water, knee-deep, until they reached the vessel that was a few yards off the shore. The two of them tossed themselves into the craft. "Push off, and move quickly," ordered Pearson, and two of the contingent grabbed the two oars from the rowlocks and pushed along the bed of the shallow edge of the waterline.

On the bank of Champlain, the artillerymen of the eastern field cannon position turned the carriage toward Pearson as he, and those in the boat drifted slowly southward. A gunnery soldier removed the ramrod from the barrel as he completed the final step toward reloading. The cannon was staring directly at Pearson's company when the cannoneer brought the long match toward the fuse. In desperation, Pearson slowly drew his carbine pistol at his hip. He was nearly drained of energy and emotion, but rested the gun on the top of the boat's bulkhead, pointed his unloaded officer's pistol at the gun emplacement, and pulled the trigger needlessly. The American cannon was nearing firing another blast. Pearson hunkered down, leaning limply against the starboard frame, his arm extended, with the pistol dangling just above the surging lake water.

In a flash, Major Morris charged the unsuspecting Continental artillery crew. He slashed the Americans with his cavalry sword, splattering cascades of blood wildly. Redcoat infantrymen then swarmed the Rebels and tore them apart with their bayonets like a pack of hungry wolves shredding wounded prey. The major turned his stallion and looked out toward the longboat as his soldiers finished off what was left of the colonials. Pearson meagerly lifted his arm, indicating his appreciation and confirmation that he was alive. Morris gazed emotionlessly for a moment and nodded ever so slightly.

Morris then turned toward the ravaged field behind him. A few of his company completed the massacre by forcing their blades into the still-breathing lungs of the last of the American elements. Smoke swirled about, and the rain tapped on the rim of his riding helmet persistently. Ajax gasped heavily as his dark, narrow eyes surveyed the carnage. Intermittent pops crackled through the air as the skirmish faded to its conclusion. The bodies of the many fallen soldiers lay scattered around the field. Each of their stories was complete, each with the same ending. Dismembered bodies, limbs, and ground flesh spoiled the naturally idyllic countryside. Swirls of smoke drifted lazily within the wind to meet the darkened sky. The American cannons had been silenced, for now. Rebel resistance was fiercer than Major Morris supposed, and the cost in blood was more than he would have wagered. Pockets of supporting militia bands scurried southward into the woodlands. It was a certainty they would return in the company of others. Ticonderoga would not be held by a single victory. Convinced Pearson had made it as safe as he could ensure, Morris pulled back to regroup. The American guns he fought desperately to take would yet remain unmanned.

The devastation was as apparent inside the open hull of Pearson's longboat as it was on the field of battle. The wretched, lifeless body of the nameless trooper leaned against the port bulkhead, its head facing forward, tilted almost completely horizontal. Its eyes fixed wide open, its jaw nearly dropped to the chest. Innards spilled out on its lap, and what was once a proud English soldier was now an unrecognizable ghoul.

The captain was on the cliff of composure and shaken by the horrific carcasses. He had never seen the face of death so intimately. He had been a young man, but a minute earlier. A fellow with family, dreams, and regrets. Now, he was nothing more than a steaming heap of ground-up flesh. Recalling Morris's direction, Pearson moved to cleanse himself of feeling. "Strip him of his rations, balls, and powder, then throw him into the water," he barked.

After a moment of hesitation, Sergeant McAllister pillaged through his fallen comrade's packs. He removed all the items he believed to be of some use: his powder horn, a handful of musket balls, cans, rations, and a small flask of rum. Private Holdsworth, the youngest and greenest of the company, sat directly across, gagging and recoiling in disgust until he turned to vomit into the water.

"Fucking pathetic," mumbled Private Manson, who seemed quite relaxed as he sat next to the fallen warrior. Pearson immediately responded, "Do you need a direct order to prompt you into helping your comrade, Soldier?"

Manson did little to hide a grim smirk from his face and casually shifted to help the sergeant lift the lifeless body. Though his effort was more of a token, he and McAllister struggled for a second or two, before they were able to hoist the soldier's remains above the bulkhead. In so doing, Manson felt the bulge of a pocket watch within the fallen soldier's blood-sodden breeches. In an instant, he put forth all his energy needed to lift the nameless soul and shove him overboard. Manson was not sure what the item was, but his instincts compelled him to swipe it for himself before another from the company moved to assist, and before the body was cast into the lake. It was not a particularly ornate piece of jewelry, yet its age and patina suggested it had been passed along from one to another, for some time. Ever so sneakily, his eyes surveyed his company, and he swiped the old pocket timepiece and held it in his clenched fist and out of the sight of wandering eyes. Clumsily, he and the sergeant managed to heave the grisly remains into the water, yet only after further polluting their uniforms and the hull of the boat with blood. It hit the water with a softened splash, head peering toward the sky, and bobbed in the windblown waves.

Inside the boat, Private Hendricks groaned in anguish as he pushed his hands against his badly injured knee. Blood streamed through his fingers as he clutched at his injured limb. His legs were nearly soaked in brown-red, and the blood had amassed into a puddle on the bottom boards of the hull. Behind him, Private Holdsworth, who had collected himself to a degree, drew a linen cloth from one of his packs and leaned in to wrap the wound and comfort his anguished mate. Captain Pearson was positioned in the first thwart, trying to catch his breath and gain a semblance of composure. After a moment, he turned to face what was left of his company and observed the agonizing private and his compassionate brother-in-arms. He waved off the caring young private and grimly shook his head with disapproval.

"I'm sorry, Soldier," he said to him. Without the courage or dignity to look at Holdsworth as he spoke, he continued, "Your benevolence is admirable, yet do not let it overcome good reason. He will do nothing but slow our pace until he either bleeds himself out or becomes infected. Though I wish otherwise, there is nothing we can do for him. His best chance, his only chance, is to swim to the shore, now, before we are too far from it. Throw him over." The company of men were exhausted and almost completely unnerved. They looked amongst each other, and each was perplexed and unsure of what they had heard. None of them made an immediate effort to follow Pearson's order.

Pearson gravely, calmly, and clearly repeated his command, "Private, throw him into the water."

Corporal Browning silently gestured his head in the direction of Hendricks, who continued to groan in anguish. "Respectfully, sir, I don't know about this," muttered the corporal.

"What do you not know, Corporal?" demanded McAllister. "You do not know the chain of command, you do not know the King's English? The captain was not clear in what he ordered?" Browning refused to respond other than with a hushed look of dismay. With McAllister, the two moved toward their injured comrade, and each gripped his hands around a patch of his waistcoat. It was a struggle to lift him, and Hendricks growled a shrill, ear-piercing cry and meekly flailed at the two men as if to move them away. In so doing, his hand left the wound, and a torrent of blood gushed out of the gash within his flesh, which began splattering and spraying wildly. Browning and McAllister were awash with a gush of thick, warm, salty red fluid. Hendricks's floundering caused the two men to collapse onto him, and to crush his badly injured knee against the hull. He roared with agony, and the two soldiers reflexively threw themselves from him. The endeavor was comically pathetic.

"He will not be able to make it back. He can hardly move at all! He will surely drown!" Private Holdsworth insisted anxiously, from the near stern of the longboat.

"And what do we do?" barked Pearson from near the bow. "Drag him along and allow him to slow our pace, to make our charge yet more difficult to complete until he falls? I can promise you, he will indeed die along our path. If you cannot properly prioritize your senses of compassion and logic, I will demand you to join him. You know I am in command, and you should know that, at this moment, we are not afforded the luxury of deliberation or discussion." Pearson hesitated for a few seconds, and with closed eyes, accepted the realization this moment would forever change who he was. Under his breath, he grumbled, "Popular decisions are often the wrong ones. This is the reason men of my stripe lead and men of yours follow."

"Do you want us to strip him of his rations too?" Manson added sarcastically. The sniveling soldier was offering nothing constructive, and despite his effort to the contrary, happened to make a productive suggestion.

Pearson saw the fabric of his company becoming quickly torn to shreds. He resented Manson's sarcasm, yet decided to use it as a chance to appear reserved and to de-escalate hostilities. Though he knew otherwise, the captain acted as though Manson's interjection was sincere. "Good thought, yes. Remove all the weight from him, take his packs, his musket balls, anything that might weigh him down."

Browning and McAllister patted him down and unclipped assorted packs and belts. Hendricks was dazed, oblivious to what was going on or about to happen. The sergeant inadvertently locked eyes with him, then quickly turned away as though he was ashamed of what he was going to do.

"You do this slow," Wyandot Panther said impatiently, and jumped to his feet, grasping the injured soldier from behind. Hendricks writhed around in pain, unsure of what was happening, lost in his anguish. The three men attempted to heave Hendricks overboard, but he was too heavy and too frantic for them to force him over the bulkhead and into the water. His blood was strewn about as they struggled to lift his body into the water. With each attempt, his legs and shredded knee banged against the heavy oak hull, adding yet more agony to his final moments of life.

"Bloody hell, come on already!" Manson pleaded impatiently, yet offering no sign he was willing to assist. Frustration and impatience overtook Pearson's sense of sorrow as he shuffled himself toward Panther and the others to assist as they struggled to heave Hendricks over the bow. The boat swayed wildly and threatened to topple over with furious commotion until finally, the four managed to toss him into the lake.

Hendricks released a most horrid scream and thrashed in the water mindlessly. He was quickly enveloped by a misty red pool as his wound drained into the lake. Through his fury, he managed to grab the side of the boat, nearly tilting it over. The loss of blood was draining the life energy from him. Still upright, Pearson threw his arms out to his sides as he nearly lost his balance, almost falling into the lake. Panther forcefully grabbed one of the long heavy oars from the soldier holding it and poked and jabbed at Hendricks, shoving him away from the boat. Hendricks screamed and grabbed helplessly at the oar, then clutched into the air until he was fatigued and had lost too much blood. His vigor seemed to have seeped from his body. Mercifully, he was now free of pain. His eyes remained fully open as his head rolled backward as though he was watching the rain fall from the heavens. His frame was still until it slowly sank beneath the surface and into the watery darkness.

Twelve men broke from the fortress bastion. Pearson, Wyandot Panther, and five of the grenadiers made it to the longboat alive. The craft was splintered and punctured with cannon blasts. Watery blood and pink bodily innards layered the hull's surface. The air was overcome with silence as each man remained alone with his thoughts. The water was gray and rough, the trees along the shoreline sagging from the heavy rain as though they had lowered their heads in mourning. The once tranquil landscape was scarred with war's desolation. The fallen British soldier's body drifted into the distance, the rain began to let up, and only the methodical rowing broke the silence.

Wyandot Panther, who was immune to such sorrows, leaned close to the captain. With his lips to Pearson's ear, through his long, thick, wet black hair that nearly covered his face, Panther whispered most menacingly, "If you are truly in charge, you would not need to tell us you are in charge." Without uttering another word and devoid of expression, Panther leaned back, his eyes locked with Pearson's until the captain turned away.

Captain Pearson leaned over the port bow and gazed in front of him as the slowing raindrops gently tapped the surface of the water. His heart raced and he gasped long, deep breaths, desperately trying to find some equanimity in the situation he now found himself in. He looked at his hands, which were jittering nearly uncontrollably, the right nearly covered with blood. For a moment, he remained still, then reached to cup a handful of water and washed away Private Hendricks's blood.

"The only thing necessary for the triumph of evil is for good men to do nothing."—Edmund Burke

Two

September 1777.

The wooden carriage creaked and bounced behind the sturdy black yearling that pulled it along. Two riders sat atop the bench with crooked backs, as though the weight of fatigue was slowly pulling them down. Clumps of soil caked the wheel, further taxing Cole as he proudly pulled it along the damp dirt road. The wagon was packed without much care, and the many bumps, rocks, and dips caused the loose, clay jars to clang against each other.

"And here we are," sighed Dedrick as he turned to his companion. The party had traveled some distance from the north to reach New York Island. The pleasant weather initially promised to make the jaunt less unbearable than usual. However, unexpected rain made sure otherwise. Had nature cooperated, it may have only slightly mitigated the typical expectations of boredom, fatigue, and general petulance. Still, the trek from Tarry Town to Manhattan was not without its intolerable moments. "You all right…tired?" asked Dedrick. "You look tired."

His tone dry, Lars simply answered, "No."

"You want to take a nap? I'll take the reins from here and you can have a little nap."

"I'm fine, sir," said Lars.

"Suit yourself friend, no nap. What about a hug, you want a hug?" asked Dedrick.

"Thank you, sir, no," replied Lars with his distinctive deadpan demeanor.

"Let me give you a hug," said Dedrick. Though he was obviously playing, Lars was fully unaware of the sarcasm. "I was more asking for you to give me a hug." Without a hint of expression, Lars lowered his shoulders with a sigh, then slowly stretched his limbs, as if to invite Dedrick to offer him an embrace. "There you are, Big Guy," snapped Dedrick, who then leaned in while tossing his arms around Lars's broad frame. "Doesn't this feel good?" he asked as he patted his back.

Lars was obviously uncomfortable, yet the selfless gesture, from his perspective, framed their relationship perfectly. If the typically emotionless chauffeur had any semblance of humanity about him, it only manifested itself with the ever-so-faint droplets of affection he demonstrated toward Dedrick. Somehow, his manager's unrelenting well-disguised sarcastic torments connected with Lars's undeveloped nature. In turn, Dedrick's unusual humor, which was more to amuse himself than others, entertained Lars on a level he was unable to understand.

"Indeed, sir," replied Lars as he pulled the reins to slow the advance.

Lars maintained his characteristic scowl and focused straight ahead, eyes fixed on the path in front of them. Dedrick sat back, relaxed as one could be, and peered between the many brick and stone buildings toward the horizon. The city hummed with the hustling and scampering of the many residents and the passing winds that flowed between the structures and tall masts of the harbored ships. Their noses had been introduced, yet again, to the stench of ripened trash and manure, which had festered in the warmth of the sun. Every time Dedrick and Lars entered the city, they were reminded of the foul stench. Predictable, yet, each and every time, they were surprised anew at how rancid it was. They had traveled for nearly two full days to reach the City of New York. They had followed the same path along the Hudson that they had followed countless times before, seen the same landscapes, rested at the same tavern, and passed through the same towns. From Tarry Town to the city was not a particularly long journey, and in places, it was quite picturesque with its natural river valley beauty. Though, beauty tends to fade into regularity as its presence becomes routine.

In the bed of the wagon behind the two men was an assortment of jars, sacks, and a stack of pelts laid one on the other. The items bounced about as the carriage rolled forward. They continued along the puddle-cratered road until they were engulfed by a maze of brick and stone buildings. The wagon moved slowly as it passed many others doing the same. Dedrick patted Lars on the knee playfully, hopped from the wagon, and instructed, "If you bring this to the wharf around the back, I'll head inside. Don't unload all of this by yourself. If the *help* dawdles around like fucking…I don't know, blindfolded monkeys in a magic show, let me know. Do not do all the work. I shouldn't be long. I'm in no rush, but we can set back as to not waste this lovely day. Maybe I'll buy lunch. Sounds good, right?"

Lars held the reins and brought the horse to a near stop. "Very good."

"You're amiable, Lars, maybe too much so. It's why people like you, but also why they feel they can take advantage of you. Suppose, it is both a curse and a blessing," advised Dedrick.

"Indeed," replied Lars, who was wholly unsure what Dedrick meant, or what the word amiable meant. "They were speaking of the, the…relations with, the man I cannot remember. The older gentleman who has relations."

Curious, Dedrick prompted, "Older gentleman?"

"Yes, the older gentleman. From Pennsylvania."

"William Penn?" asked Dedrick.

"No, no, not William Penn. The man with the hat and spectacles —the man who speaks."

Simply for his personal enjoyment, Dedrick refused to free Lars from his frustration. "The man who speaks…" he said in feigned contemplation. "Oh! Hamlet. He's not from Pennsylvania."

"No. No, sir, not Hamlet. He's American, from Philadelphia. Ah, what is his name? 'By failing to prepare we are unprepared,' or 'we should be prepared,' he said. Invented the chair you can rock back in. He's from Philadelphia."

"Hamlet is not from Philadelphia, Lars," replied Dedrick with a dry, unflinching tone.

"No," murmured Lars as his frustration grew. "I know. I know he is not, sir. I'm not thinking of Hamlet—Frank…Frank, maybe?"

"Francis Bacon?"

"Who?" uttered Lars. "No, no. Frank someone…"

"I don't know," continued Dedrick. "Well, whomever he is, just make sure you don't do all the work yourself."

Lars removed his lid and rubbed his fingers through his long, dark hair as unusual vexation moved him. "Indeed, sir," he said as he struggled to shake off the unrelenting pangs of a frustration he could not quite understand.

Dedrick hurried along a wooden walkway that led to a rather unstable-looking staircase. It climbed along the outer wall to the second floor of a brownish brick building, where it met an equally rickety-looking terrace that overlooked Cherry Street. He hustled to the top, then leaned on a splintery wooden rail and gazed into the city about him. Gray clouds blanketed the sun, and Dedrick let the subtle rays warm his face. He peered over the tall stone and brick buildings and through the shrouds, jibs, and rope webs from the tall ships docked in the ports along Water Street. Gulls glided aimlessly overhead, and distant bells rang nautical hymns as a tall merchant ship, the *Feloz*, drifted languidly in the harbor as she waited to come to port. Dedrick remained fixated on the vessel, temporarily lost in a state of relaxation. A steady breeze blew from the harbor, and he took a few deep breaths, filling his lungs with its cool air. Dedrick was lean, tall, and rather handsome with his deep blue eyes. His hair was a light brown and lazily tied back at the nape of his neck, as per usual. Most often, a few strands would escape and fall forward on his face and blow about with a breeze. As such, he developed a habit of continually brushing them back behind his right ear, a rather alluring gesture that did nothing to displease the ladyfolk. Although usually dressed in finer attire, on this day he wore functional blue cotton breeches and a plain shirt, half tucked with a few smudges of dirt here and there. Dedrick rarely made much of an effort to trim himself in a manner fitting his social standing, yet his slightly disheveled appearance did more to further his charismatic appeal than to hinder it. After a moment, he recalled his promise of haste and collected himself to continue.

The endless fertile lands of the New World were lying in wait like a fledgling sweet-smelling virgin whore imploring to be fucked. The Old World settlers who managed to voyage here were so aroused, with rock-hard pricks, they poked one another in the back as they pressed forward to stick it between her legs. In Europe, the farmers tilled and the craftsmen constructed and very few could see beyond tomorrow. The Old World was content in the ways of the Old World. Not here. Notwithstanding scattered islands of traditional values, in America, men were driven by the Godly work ethic that prompted them to accumulate ever more wealth. For the more he has, the more He smiles upon him. Here, in the New World, many plainly did not understand the word *enough*.

As the British wasted no interest in the valley's natural splendor, the Americans had evolved to have no interest in any endeavor that offered no potential for pecuniary gain. In Europe, intellectual activities such as art, literature, and music were the reasons for life, but in America, they were merely accepted, until they became distractions from life. In America, the colonials were intoxicated by greed. Nature did her best to sort the winners from the losers, and as such, all would suffer from either indigestion or starvation. Yet abundance afforded plenty of crumbs to fall from the table of the gluttonous elite, to appease the rats as they scurried about their feet. The Revolution was merely a metaphor of the precocious colonials who lived freer, longer, and more luxuriously than their English cousins. The better things are for the Americans, the better they expect them to be. Under the flags of liberty or loyalty, the cause was the same. All Americans were fighting only for their perceived self-interest. Softened by such abundances, the colonists had no immunity to even the slightest inconvenience. Lord Townshend knew this when he cunningly drove the children from their father. And nowhere in all the colonies was this more evident than in New York City.

New Amsterdam, as it was, was settled by Dutch traders and Belgian Huguenots after they were taken by the beauty Nature's God bestowed upon the valley. Hendrick Hudson was unable to offer the Netherlands the passageway to the East, as he had promised, yet the magnificence of the green lands and crystal-blue waterways captivated Dutch settlers all the same. In short order, the deep harbor and network of waterways soon reaped untold fortunes for West India Company. New Amsterdam was and always had been unlike her neighbors. Maryland was settled as a haven for Catholics, Massachusetts as a province to be unpolluted by Catholics. In

Manhattan, intolerance to one's faith served only to threaten prosperity. It was not for seventeen years that the first church was built on the island as the pursuit of the gilder became the prevalent religion. The smell of such affluence was not lost under the nose of the British Empire, who imbued the region by planting her flag over the capital city and renaming it after the Duke of York and Albany. Inhabitants had no concern about the colors which flew overhead, nor did they give any thought if the Director-General or Viscount of Cornbury slept in the capital garrison. New York's merchants, mechanics, and fishmongers had always remained singularly loyal to their bounding fortunes.

Manhattan Island was the capital province, the heart of Colonial America. It was alive today, mostly, as always, yet in an unusually somber mood. An uncertain ambiance slowed the normally frantic pulse. Dedrick was aware of the practical considerations surrounding his current setting, yet still felt as unsure as those who dwelled on the island. Units of red-clad soldiers were in stark contrast to New York's typical riffraff. The streets were drab and dull, and the troopers' crisp, cardinal jackets were as bright as fireflies against an evening sky. The city folk were clearly not accustomed to the presence of His Majesty's Army and, as a whole moved about with nervous deliberation. Discarded cabbage leaves and refuse floated atop the pools of rainwater that flooded the various entrenched fortifications. Gun batteries were positioned between shops, houses, and parlors. The massive masts and yardarms of royal gunboats cast their shadows as a large net that ensnared the city.

Dedrick entered the doorway on the second floor of the import house and sauntered into a cluttered open room. It was an industrial-looking interior with exposed brick walls, ropes, and pulleys dangling from the ceiling, tools scattered here and there. Several sweat-gleaming laborers carried various bags and crates to and fro, and stacks of cloth lay within the corner alongside barrels and lockers that were piled about. The air was rotten with the stench of dried perspiration and sawdust. Frequent clanging and thumping penetrated his ears. Although encumbered by the heavy items they carried, two of the hard-working hands made a point to bow and wave graciously when they recognized Dedrick, who, of course, returned a crooked smile and bow of the head.

Tall windows along the side walls allowed the midday sun's rays to pierce the dungeon-like darkness, casting a very bright light. Ahead of Dedrick was a long wooden desk, behind which stood a short, stocky fellow who waved him forward with one hand and held a large slice of melon, which dripped down his arm, with the other. He wore round glasses that fell low on his nose, a white neck cravat, which was moist with sweat, and a light gray coat, where a small red ribbon was pinned just above the breast. With a mouthful of melon, he blurted, "Mmmmph, there he is. Come, come. It's good to see you, my friend. Especially since I know when I see you, I see money not far behind." As pink drops of melon flowed from his lips, he continued, "I'm not sure we're ready for you just yet. You're here much sooner than I expected."

"Huh…is that so?" said Dedrick.

"It is so," Nate wiped his mouth with his sleeve, then reached over and, although sticky and wet, extended his hand to shake Dedrick's. Dedrick looked about, and his eyes surveyed the counter until he noticed a few loose scraps of sawdust-covered linens or cloth of some kind. He reached for one, flipped it clean of dust, draped it over his palm, and grabbed Nate's hand in return. "You're a piece of fuck, you know what?" quipped Nate.

Dedrick could not help but chuckle, "I'm sorry, did you call me a piece of fuck?"

"Yeah, it's the most insulting thing I could think of at the moment," confessed Nate.

"*Schonen Tag,* Nate. As always it's good to see you, too."

"Shoe tag, what is that," asked Nate.

Dedrick chuckled. "It is 'good day' in German."

"And…am I expected to simply know this? You presumed that, even though I have never once uttered a single German word, or mentioned I know anything about the language, I would understand what that meant?"

Dedrick playfully shook his head. "I think you become more ill-tempered with each visit. You used to be carefree and loved life—

danced and pranced around, sang songs, and had all kinds of hair on your head."

"Danced and pranced? I don't think I've danced nor pranced a moment in all my life. Yet, since you insist on knowing what happened to me, I will tell you. Marriage is what happened to me," quipped Nate.

"Please," replied Dedrick. "Stop this. You love Rosemary, and you know damn well she and your boys are the best things in your life."

"Ugh," groaned Nathan. "For the love of God, why would you bring this shit up? You're trying to get under my skin, right? Trying to put me in a shit mood, I guess? Because I was in a pretty pleasant mood a few minutes ago. Wasn't dancing and prancing, but was in a fairly pleasant mood."

"By mentioning your wife and children?"

"You know I don't like thinking about those things, let alone talking about them. It's bad enough I have to live with her and listen to her, smell her hot breath as she breathes all over me in the morning. I'm expected to think about her now? Can't I even be alone in my thoughts? She has to be part of my day, all day? Can't I enjoy the time away from her? Where does it end? You know what it is?" he continued. "My wife will have a thought or a feeling and will become annoyed if you don't somehow simply feel or think it along with her. Say…I don't know, I clean the table after we eat, she will say, 'Why the hell did you put the dishes away? I wanted to have a second helping.' As though I am supposed to simply *know* she wants to shove more food down her fucking face!"

"You're an irresistible romantic, Nate. Don't listen to anyone who tells you otherwise."

"Don't give me any of that, please. You really don't know what you are talking about. She's just, she's the worst, she really is. I suppose, in company, she has her moments, but at home, with me, she can only be described as…uh…what's the word? Detestable."

Dedrick knew Nate was being flippant, yet was annoyed to hear it just the same. "Rose is not in the least bit awful, and you married her. I would say it was one of the best decisions you've made in your entire life."

"I was young and stupid," replied Nate. "Believe me, she is awful. This is a woman who yells at me for, everything, really. Yells at me for sleeping, yells at me for walking, yells when I ask how her day was, yells at me for making her yell at me, yells at me for coughing."

Dedrick couldn't hide his amusement. "She yells at you for coughing?"

"For coughing," he confirmed.

"This is what I'm telling you my friend. Yells at me for coughing or may even yell at me for not coughing. Its what she does, she yells," confirmed Nate.

"Well, I bet you give her more than enough reason to do so. Perhaps—and I am only speculating—perhaps it's you? Besides, is it ever perfect? If we enter a marriage under the assumption it's easy, there'd be no reason to take a vow before God to uphold it."

"You've got to be kidding," said Nathan. "This comes from a man who attracts women like bees to honey. That is so unbelievably easy for you to say. You have more than a fair amount of choices, but most of us do not. Especially me—look at me. Look at this face and this fucking belly, just look. You see this mess? And…I'll be fair about this, you haven't seen my wife in some time now. Believe me when I say, she is not at all doing well holding off time, and age… and gravity. Perfect. If our marriage improved to merely horrible, I'd be happy. Please, don't feed me shit and say it's porridge, my friend. If you are not happy, I will plainly say I resent the shit out of you."

Dedrick slowly shook his head as if to feebly give up and give in. In the interest of winding down the conversation, he concluded, "I give up Nate. If it makes you feel any better, I'll tell you I'm somewhere just north of unhappy."

Nathan took one last chomp from the melon rind, whipped the juice from his lips with his forearm, and continued. "This is your fault—shouldn't have brought it up. In any event, I'll tell you what *would* make me happy, and that is making money so I can pay my debts. Let's get going here. What did you bring me today?"

Dedrick took a second to transition to a humorless discussion. "Fifty, exactly," he replied.

"Hmm, not bad. And I thought you looked so rundown because you just came from Kitty Fisher's. Who would have thought it's from hard work? I'm sorry to say I can only give fifty per," said Nathan in a suddenly somber and serious tone.

"Fifty schillings? Fifty schillings are hardly worth the trip," said Dedrick.

"When you pay your help as much as you insist on paying them it isn't," replied Nathan.

Dedrick shook his head and smiled wryly. He'd heard Nathan's assertions many times and knew exactly where this discussion was going. "I should have known that was coming. Their children are just as hungry as ours, Nate," he said in passing.

"And they won't be able to feed those mouths if you're bankrupt," sniped Nathan. "Fifty schillings is really the best I can do. I'm not looking squeeze you, especially you, or take advantage. The price of salt and grain…and, just about everything, has reached the sky because of this fucking war. The demand of these sorts has been as tight as the hole in my bum. People are spending the little they have on food, not beaver skin hats, not here and not in Britain. Yet another reason to despise those horse shit Rebels."

Dedrick was dejected, yet not entirely surprised. Nate had never quibbled over prices nor shown any intent to get the better of Dedrick throughout the history of their relationship. "The Rebels?" he asked. "It's not the king who sent Redcoats, the ones who are consuming all of the salt and grain to drive up the prices? It's not because of him?"

"They are not here for kicks. Had there been no upheaval, there'd be no Redcoats burning all the wood and eating all the meat. He was right to send them here. Everything about this uprising is wrong," said Nathan. "It's unnatural."

Dedrick replied in a clearly decisive tone. "I knew it, knew it would come around to this soon enough. Go ahead, enlighten me with your diatribe."

"I will only because you insist. It's lunacy. Lord North will be gone in time, and I am not saying George is not…many things, but he is still our king," said Nathan. Nate was one who relished the opportunities to opine his hardened convictions to anyone who was willing to listen, and many who were not. He made decisions with his gut as opposed to his mind, and as such, details, polite manners, and respectful disagreements were often lost in his exchanges.

"He is *a* king, but he is not *our* king. He's a king who sits on a throne that is an ocean away. He will never see us as proper subjects, and Parliament will never see us as countrymen. They know nothing about our interests, our needs or wants, that or they simply don't care. Either way, it makes no sense to be governed by a distant government," said Dedrick. "*That* is unnatural."

Nathan quipped back, "I had no idea I was doing business with Thomas Paine. Wow, this is incredible. Am I trying your soul, Mr. Paine?" Then he shouted to nobody in particular, "Hey, everyone, it's Thomas Fucking Paine!"

The few laborers in the quarter hardly slowed their pace and merely glanced toward Nathan with a bit of confusion, then continued with their chores. Nathan's horse hand, who had been gathering satchels and ropes at the far end of the room, looked toward Nathan and Dedrick, pausing for a moment with a slightly bewildered look about his muck-covered face. He was Nathan's ideal laborer: hard-working and dim-witted. After a moment of pondering, he asked Nate, "Is that really his middle name?"

Dedrick could not help but snicker, and Nathan threw his head back and his eyes toward the ceiling in a mild fit of frustrated impatience. After a second or maybe two, he scanned the cluttered counter in front of him, snatched a fresh slice of melon, and fired it at his stableman as he grunted, "God help me, I'm surrounded by dalcops." The rind landed well short and splattered, then slid, leaving a wake of sticky juice on the splintery wooden floor. The work hand scurried to refocus on his tasks.

"You were saying, *Rosemary* is the problem in your relationship...?" he said, a brow arched as he darted insinuating glances at the melon. "Nate, I know what you are saying, and I mostly agree with you. Nevertheless, when you force these acts without consent or consideration, it's tyranny. The reaction may be extreme, perhaps. However, the justification is not entirely unreasonable. These men, the *patriots*, will, in the end, be hanged for this, but as of today, I admire their conviction. If nothing else, it will force London to wake to the reality we are not meek and obedient, willing to accept whatever it wants to inflict upon us at its whims," said Dedrick.

"It may be tyranny; I suppose it would be difficult to truly argue otherwise. But, I prefer a tyrannical government to be on the other side of the earth than to be here," replied Nathan. "We should be careful to fight for something we don't know, we don't want. We're so spoiled, in so many ways, and we've come to take this for granted. We are far better off than the Englishmen. We live longer, enjoy bountiful harvests. You think those Lobsters out there want to be here, half a world away from their homes and their families? What choices do they have when their king summons them to war? The choices you and I will never be forced to make. We are prosperous and safe. *Reasonable*…what is reasonable? Is it reasonable for us to continue to reap the benefits of the empire, but share none of the burdens? I say we have been lucky to get away with the king's neglect for so long."

"And I do not entirely disagree. The measures are an overreach, but does that justify treason? The compact of government and governed is the only rule of law. It is what makes us a civil society, it protects order. From time to time, particular parties will not see their best interests served. It is not possible for *all* to have their interests advanced *all* the time—we accept this give-and-take for the greater good. This is how it works, it's that simple, really. We've seen our interests protected for as long as you and I have been alive—well, at least as long as I can remember. I am at least somewhat uplifted to know our city, and our colony, recognizes the clemency and paternal goodness in offering to restore order and protection."

"Hmm, I see what you are saying. I'm not in favor of this rebellion, to be clear. I am simply saying, it is not entirely without merit." grunted Dedrick, who was surprised by the profound nature of Nate's diatribe. "We do well, this is true. We do well enough to complain about shortages as we hurl fresh fruit at hired help. However, this is beyond a difference of opinion or the advancement of one's interests over another. We are at a crossroads; we can continue to be subservient dogs and continue to be treated as such, or we can make our voices heard. The Boston radicals are unreasonable, and a declaration of independence is treason, I grant you, but London rejected *all* attempts at redress, you know this. These problems have been festering for years now, and Rebellion was inevitable. If anything, you should be content it is not being passed to your boys to fight it."

Nathan pressed his spectacles with his fingers, then reached for a small pouch filled with tobacco that rested among the clutter on the counter. He fumbled around the various rags and tools until he found an oddly, fine-carved wooden pipe. The item seemed very peculiar and out of place, surrounded by such rustic and utilitarian tools and such. Not to mention the man who would be smoking from it. He pressed a pinch of leaves and, without lighting it, continued, as it dangled from the corner of his mouth, which was still covered in melon juice. "It's entirely undignified, unprecedented, and I admire nothing about them. Hancock is a smuggler, that's all he is; a pirate who is upset because the king is actually enforcing the smuggling laws his father should have enforced years ago. Sam Adams is crazy, all the rest are Bomkins—Floyd, Lee—there is not a rational or respectable one among them. Oh, yes, and your champion, Thomas Paine, is an uneducated drunkard looking to lecture us on what *he* thinks we need after he's been in this world for only a glimpse. Your family has prospered, as well as mine. Our trade over the sea is safe; France, Spain, any nation, would not dare meddle with the King's Navy. You don't think we are obliged to, at the very least, contribute a fair share?" he asked, and then puffed as he struggled to ignite the pipe.

"Negroes, Irishmen, Indians, Catholics, who knows, maybe even the fucking French, will all run wild in these streets if not for the protection and order His Majesty provides. Would you not say, being subject to some…questionable acts, is a very cheap price to pay?" he continued. "Look, I'm not happy with a great many things coming from London, but rebellion? Declaring independency? We are basically telling our fathers they can suck our collective cocks. It's madness. It is unseemly and it is offensive."

Dedrick rubbed his thumb and finger about his mouth, brushing his scruffy chin. "So *you're* offended?"

"Correct, I am offended, me, the bald fucking fat guy, with the nagging fucking wife. The man who currently has the shit that has tumbled out of his ass smeared inside his flabby, sweaty thighs because he shat himself when lifting a heavy barrel. The guy wearing the sweaty, stinky clothing standing in front of you—that guy is offended."

Once again, Dedrick rubbed his finger and thumb about his scruffy chin and squinted his eyes ever so slightly to process all the information Nate had just given him. With a crooked smile, he added, "In so many ways, that might be the 'Nate-est' thing I've heard you say."

"How so?" asked Nathan.

"Self-deprecation aside, your perception of self-importance enables you to find offense in actions not directed at you."

"I…maybe, maybe I don't really know what you are saying— sounds insulting, though. Whichever…we can debate the merits, but a violent rebellion is futile, and I am not going to be on the wrong side when *this* King George looks for his justice. I have a family, as do we all. My biggest concern is their safety and well-being. The Crown provides that, and I don't think the band of radicals would, or could, do the same."

"I know, I know," replied Dedrick, through a somber tone. In his heart, Dedrick mostly agreed with Nathan, yet, from time to time, he enjoyed the verbal sparring. The long, mind-numbing trip from Tarry Town with Lars, and only with Lars, had left him starved for intellectual stimulation. In this case, stoking Nate's agitation made it that much more fun.

Just when it seemed the discussion had run its course, Nate found a sudden burst of frustration and worked himself into his typically animated state. "We're British subjects, an extension of the Empire here in America. Can we do something properly? Can we conduct ourselves in some way with the dignity befitting our prideful English heritage? Can we represent ourselves in a decent way at all? Or, do we always have to live up to the portrayal of the dumb, fucking, backward Americans?"

Prompted by his lively rant, droplets of saliva flowed down Nathan's chin. He slurped it up and whipped them away with his hand, then wiped his hand clean, against his already-stained cotton breeches.

"What would you have us do, then?" asked Dedrick.

"Nothing," sniped Nathan. "I propose we do nothing, we serve the status quo. The Tories are going to take both houses. This will pass, as it always does. Revolution…? Fine. What happens next? What happens if they win? What do we do with so-called Independence? An American king would be no different than any other."

"How about American democracy?" asked Dedrick.

Nathan grinned with amusement, as he lit the pipe until light swirls of smoke rose around him. "You want mob rule? You have far too much faith in your countrymen, my friend. Most are not nearly as honorable and selfless as you. We will all look to protect only what serves us best—I know I would. Better still, we would be governed by the likes of Sam and John Adams? Men vote for the people they can relate to, and the superior ones are hardly the ones who win elections. At best, we'd have to trust the will of the people, the mindless lot of them; the common farmers who have no minds for law or government. It takes a majority to win an election, and a majority of men are whimsical, ignorant, easily swayed stains of shit. You wish they would determine our fates?"

Nathan remained hardheaded, undeterred to consider a point of view contrary to his. It had become that he was not seeking to listen, but to lecture. Dedrick was not seeking hostile confrontation and was not resolute in any particular perspective on the subject. To him, he was debating as much as searching for an answer.

"So, we are the dumb fucking Americans?"

By this point, he simply wanted to wind down the conversation. Nathan had been very outspoken on the topic; he was steadfast, and the conversation was about to go in a circle. He sniggered and shook his head, realizing he had led himself into his own trap. "Socrates, I would say has some credibility on this issue, no? He said tyranny is probably established out of no other regime than democracy. Now, fuck off."

"Socrates said to 'fuck off?' I missed that in my reading," Dedrick said sarcastically. "Perhaps you are right, I'm only thinking with my mouth. In any event, can you pay me my pittance so I can go overpay my help and be on my way?"

* * *

North.

Wandering within a vast wilderness of the northeast, somewhere near the border of New York and Massachusetts, Captain Isaac Pearson, five British Grenadiers, and a Mohawk tracker, finally allowed themselves a long-awaited respite. The cue to get off their feet was the fading glimpse of daylight chased away by the night's sky. It had been only three days since the company broke from Ticonderoga, yet they were already weary and discouraged. The seven had been hiking fourteen or more hours a day. Trudging along endlessly, yet appearing to advance nowhere. Each step became heavier and seemed to bring them no farther from where they had left and no closer to where they needed to be. The trees, the sky, the ground, the sun, and the stars were all the same, no matter how long and hard they marched. They felt as if they managed only to reach where they already were.

When they weren't sleeping on dirt or shitting in the bush, they would twist an ankle on a rock or feel the sting of low branches and small trees as they were whipped in their faces as they passed. Everyone was mostly quiet; in part, because they hardly knew one another, yet mostly because they were simply too tired to waste a semblance of the energy required to converse. Pearson, most of all, wondered if he lacked the mental and physical stamina to complete the long slog to New York Island. Making matters worse, he spent strength he could hardly spare working to appear composed and in control.

Captain Pearson had little concern about the outcome of the war. In fact, in some regards, he leaned toward sympathizing with the Rebels' cause. He was, however, haunted by the image of the young soldier he believed he ordered to his death, and overcome by the obligation to complete the mission, as to not waste the sacrifice in lives that had already been paid, assisting him to do so. As much as his sense of guilt and duty propelled him forward, it also weighed him down.

When the band reached a small grassy patch within the smothering forest, Pearson decided they had gone far enough for one day. "I suppose this will do," he said as he slowly came to a halt.

The party murmured a collective sigh, and each man began to remove the various belts and pouches that had been weighing him down. One by one, each relieved his aching feet and took to the ground. Though he was tired as any, Sergeant McAllister devotedly began to gather twigs and fallen branches to start a fire. He wandered the tree line and groaned each time he knelt to grab a stick. Wyandot Panther watched him disapprovingly for a few moments until he was sure of the sergeant's intentions. "Why you do that, why picking up the sticks?" he asked.

"I beg your pardon?" replied McAllister.

"Why you pick up the sticks?" he repeated, louder and more deliberately.

"Well, Wyandot," replied McAllister in a blatantly patronizing tone, "I'm glad you asked. You see, I am sure you believe fire to be some spirit or Indian god who warms the souls of the red-skinned men. And you most likely believe you need a sacrifice or ritual to the fire god for him to visit, but that is not true, Wyandot. At least, not for us. The white man can control fire, can start a fire whenever we want. And now I want to start a fire, and this is fairly difficult to do if I do not have something to burn."

Panther was unmoved by the sarcasm. "You have fire, you have Americans see fire."

McAllister paused for a moment, then glanced toward Captain Pearson, who was preparing to settle in, several yards away. Pearson was just beginning the ritualistic procedure that afforded him as much comfort as could be expected. There had not been a single occasion that he stopped where the captain had not followed the precedent begun with the first break. He removed a diligently folded canvas sack from his pack, flapped it, three to four times, then gently let it glide toward the ground. Individually, in some order, he removed utensils, a beaker, teapot, whatever he may have needed at the particular time. He arranged each item in a systematic fashion on the canvas. While doing so this time, he noticed the exchange between the sergeant and Wyandot.

Pearson thought about Panther's assertion for a few seconds. The captain had not had tea this late in the day, and the party had never set a fire after the sun had gone down. Pearson tried to convince himself otherwise, but knew Panther was right. The priority was to remain unnoticed and deliver Bell's communiqué. A fire, while warming, was not necessary. He remained silent for several seconds, waiting until he and McAllister locked eyes. Then, without uttering a word, he subtly shook his head in silent disapproval. Pearson was careful not to risk harming the perception of McAllister's superiority, especially over Wyandot Panther.

McAllister stopped his activity, then acted as though he was considering Panther's suggestion. "I suppose you may have a point," he begrudgingly acknowledged. "Seems to me, living your life in the wilderness like an animal makes you realize such things. Very good, Panther, the fire god will not be visiting you tonight." He then abruptly released the sticks, which fell to the ground at his feet, before he strolled toward the captain and away from Panther.

"Ughhhh…fuck," groaned Private Manson as he slowly lowered himself to sit. Unlike Pearson, Manson did nothing more than lethargically throw his body to the ground. It appeared he was unconcerned whether he was sitting on grass, dirt, or anything other. His breeches were somehow inappropriately soiled with all manners of muck and mud, and yet, at times, he'd taken to sitting on his jacket, thus spreading the dried filth through his entire uniform. The once brilliant white trim about his tri-cornered hat had, in short order, become soiled, gray, and stained with filth. He often lazily flipped it to the ground and could not escape the plague of grime that had spread from the bottom of his boots.

He arched his back and stretched his body to the left, then to the right. "Fucking hell, how much longer?" he blurted to whomever might be listening and willing to answer.

The young Private James Holdsworth was in earshot and either did not understand it to be a rhetorical question or was eager to seem helpful. "Not really sure. It's been almost four days, about twenty-five miles a day. I would estimate about another week or ten days…maybe a fortnight?"

"Really?" Manson responded, sarcasm thick in his tone. "A week, huh? This come out of your tiny little asshole, or you actually know what you are talking about?"

The private just shook his head, as he was stunned by the extent of what an unbelievable prick Manson was. Though he desperately wanted to stay off his feet, he did not want to rest anywhere near him. At this point, the typically considerate Holdsworth could not conclude how to remove himself and sit farther without seeming obvious, awkward, and rude. Whereas most would not have extended Manson the courtesy of manners and simply walked away, Holdsworth sat where he stopped, which was only several feet from Manson. Not by chance, the others all sat some distance away. Manson removed his heavy, madder red jacket, tossed it to the ground, and cricked his neck from side to side. His rickety bones and soft belly confirmed the poor condition in which the private kept himself. Manson's body was aged well beyond his thirty-two years.

Because he knew he had Holdsworth reeled into a discussion, and had no reservations about taking advantage of his good nature, Manson continued to offer unsolicited updates on the status of his discomfort and overall well-being. "I have shit dripping from my asshole, and my thighs are so sweaty it's making a swamp underneath my balls. My feet are blistering, my legs are sore, I'm fucking starving, and we still have, who knows how many days left to go. This is no way to live I tell you."

Holdsworth was tempted to remind the self-centered prick they were all in such condition, yet gave in to the notion that it wasn't worth the time, nor the breath. Without looking in his direction, he simply groaned, "Mmm," acknowledging him, though with blatant disinterest intended to discourage Manson from continuing.

Manson was too involved in his own discomfort to detect Holdsworth non-verbal suggestion to shut the fuck up. "This is some fucking life," he said to Holdsworth as he continued to free himself of utilities and belts. "Not what I had in mind. I've made it this far, and I ain't planning on going anytime soon. I'll give you some advice, kid, you seem like a good little shit."

The young soldier was entirely disinterested, yet resigned to live with his mistake and to offer civility to a man who appeared entirely uncivil. "You're too kind," he murmured insincerely.

"I'm working on that. No, I'll tell you, if you want to live through this fucking mess, do nothing to stand out. Blend in like a leaf on these trees. Security through obscurity. Better to be a living piece of shit than a dead hero, right?"

Private Holdsworth shook his head in disbelief. "I suppose that is one way to see things."

"Damn right it is," blurted Manson. "Hey, I'm going to excuse myself for a minute. I'll be back. Keep an eye on my things. I don't think I trust any of these fucks. Anything goes missing, at least I know I can blame you. I'll only be a few minutes, or…might take a while. Going to try and make it quick, but don't get me wrong, I usually go all kinds of hours, worn down many a bitch, I have. Sometimes I start to think it is strange how long I go. It is a gift, really. Make sure nobody goes through my shit."

Holdsworth had a chagrined look on his face, not at all concerned enough to reply, and yet he knew Manson was going to persist regardless. "Ugh. Where are you going?"

"I need to *unwind*, my boy…lighten my load, as they say."

Manson forcefully tossed his pack at Private Holdsworth. It landed rather bluntly against the side of his head and knocked off his hat, which prompted Manson to bark out a repugnant laugh.

"Good reflexes, son. Glad you're on our side," he said through cackling, loud laughter. "Fucking slow shit…stay outta my way if we run into some Rebels. No, but I shouldn't be more than a few minutes. You can relax. Won't be too long—I know you will miss me."

It seemed to Private Holdsworth, Manson was trying to goad him into asking what he was going to do. Still, not only did Holdsworth not care, he did not want to deal with the inevitable sarcastic response he was sure to receive if asked, or guessed. It was not an easy task to irritate Holdsworth to the point of outward hostility. "Fine, just go shit. I don't need to know how long it will take or what it looks like when you are done," he said in a dismissive tone.

"No. No, I don't have to shit. I am going in the woods to clean my cock. Take a shit? No, not shit. My balls are talking to me, all sorts of sore," said Manson as he grabbed his crotch. "I keep getting hard when my prick rubs up on my pants. Been a few days, and I have to blow this out."

"You are going to masturbate is what you are telling me?" Holdsworth asked.

Seeming almost proud, Manson declared, "That I am. I'm going to masturbate, son, pull my rod, stroke that thing until my big twelve-pounder blows its load."

Private Holdsworth was meek and non-confrontational by nature, yet the levels of disdain and disgust he so immediately fostered for Manson altered his characteristic temperament. "You're not serious? You must be some depraved pervert if that is on your mind. How can you possibly have any desire to do that, now, here?"

Manson grinned with delight over the response he conjured, and he could hardly get the words out quickly enough. "Funny you should ask," he said, as glibly as he possibly could. "I've been walking behind you for three days now. Can't take my eyes from that young ass of yours, thinking about how I'd like to poke it with my cock. Stick it right in your dilberry maker." Manson, again, erupted into his typically obnoxious and excessively loud laughter. He reveled in the look of contempt on Holdsworth's face. Simple, low-brow, juvenile humor was more than enough to amuse Private Manson. Given his general demeanor and level of depth, chances are, he genuinely did find his own joke to be especially clever. "There's never a time for nothing."

Holdsworth groaned at the repugnance. He was not as disgusted by Manson's affirmation as he was at being in the company of such a sleazy cretin. He suspected early on his colleague was a bit sordid of character, yet had no idea it was to this extent. The exchange was enough for Holdsworth to make a vow with himself, never to make the mistake of engaging with Private Manson again.

"Is nature, my boy, natural," continued Manson. "You don't know this? Your body will keep making your jam, so from time to time, you have to open the valve. Let some flow out. So, it seems to me I'm going to leave some of *me* here in this wretched shit-country."

"Well, I have never heard that," replied Holdsworth dismissively.

"Eh, you're still young, still have yet to hear about many things. Doesn't matter if you've heard about it or not, it's true. Stick with me, son, and you'll learn a lot." ...

"Please," he said as he waved him away, "go...take care of...what you need to take care of. From what you describe, it seems you need to do this sooner rather than later."

"You want to come and watch?" asked Manson, then predictably burst into his piercing laughter yet again. He gave Holdsworth a symbolic tip of the cap and scuttled his way through hedges and over some large stones for a distance. In a final act of irritation, he whistled a tune with a shrill, grating shriek.

Captain Pearson hoped the few final glimmers of dusk's glow would offer him the opportunity to read the works he carried along. Even if the light only allowed him two or three pages, the few minutes spent in Elizabethan Europe, and far away from the North American sticks, surrounded by simpletons and masturbating commoners, would be most welcome. He was yet partially in denial over the issue regarding the fire, which for him, meant he could not have his daily Grey Earl tea. The elegance of Shakespearean language would, for now, have to do.

Within the soft leather pouch he held close at all times, were several documents, including Bell's dispatch for General Howe's office. His copy of *King Lear* rested snugly within pages of mostly unimportant military records regarding stores, disciplinary actions, and the like. He allowed himself to relax, as much as possible, and carefully, almost methodically, turned every single page, until he reached the one where he thought he had left off. To him, not a single page deserved the dishonor of being lumped together with another as they were flipped. Rather, each and every one was worthy of the time and effort to be turned, on its own. Thus, one by one, he slowly glided his finger down the edge of each sheet, almost persuading it to gently fall over on its own. When it struggled to do so, he would blow gently, as if to nudge it along. In so doing, a small, red ant scurried over the pages, and Pearson reflexively swatted it away and crumbled sheets within the pamphlet. He groaned in frustration and began to curse himself. "God—"

McAllister had come to rest a few yards from the captain and observed him curiously. "May I ask you a question, sir?"

The interruption perturbed Pearson a bit, yet McAllister was the least disgraceful of his current company, so the captain offered somewhat of a heightened level of tolerance in his case.

"You can, if it is a brief one," he replied.

"Forgive me if this seems blunt. I am only curious—the tea. You seem to drink your tea whenever there is a chance. Can you enjoy your tea in this, um, situation? Would you not prefer to keep the tea for better times, to only drink the fine tea you carry when you can truly enjoy it? I am only saying, for me, I would not want such a pleasure to be associated with this experience."

Pearson was more taken with the question than he anticipated, as he found the premise to be an interesting one.

"Would I prefer," he corrected. "I have no choice but to be here, in this country, in this woodland. Yet, I do have a choice on how I deal with it. Though we are a thousand miles from where we want to be, we will never be away from home if we make it where our heart is."

McAllister was impressed with the captain's assertion. Though it was likely Pearson simply uttered whichever words reached his tongue and without much thought. "You are from Wales?" asked the captain.

"That is an uplifting point of view. Yes, sir, from Newport, Ringland. It is on the Usk—"

"I know where it is," interrupted Pearson. "I've been there. It's… quaint. You are far from Wales, Ringland, and, as it stands, there is not a single thing you can do to change this. In my estimation, you would be better served to accept that and bring as much of Ringland with you as possible. Of course, this is a matter of opinion."

The sergeant moaned and nodded his head as he gave the notion consideration. Sensing he'd established some trace of a bond with the normally uptight captain, McAllister was comfortable enough to be measuredly candid and abruptly shifted the conversation, "You don't believe in our cause, sir?"

Pearson's first inclination was surprise, yet, after a moment, he understood the perception he wasted little sense of urgency on the wide-ranging outcome of the conflict. He may have developed a reputation within the ranks, and for a moment questioned the outward appearance of his efforts. Though he suspected McAllister was keener than the others and, as it was, worthy of a proper response, he cautioned, "I would be careful, Soldier. One could mistake your suggestion to imply treason, or at the very least, disloyalty."

Flustered, McAllister quickly sought to clarify. "Apologies, sir. It was not my intent to question your loyalty. I am sorry for my—"

Pearson was moved by the kindness in the young man's eyes and was not looking to upset him, thus he let him off the hook quickly. "It is fine, Sergeant. Though I would caution you to choose your words more wisely. That said, if they win it will be a revolution and if we win it will be sedition. Right and wrong are simply matters of perspective. The cause hardly matters. We fight for our brothers, we fight for the Country, for our history and for our English heritage. Personally, I am not altogether concerned with the grand scheme. When all of this is considered history, whatever the results may be, I am pleased to think I will not be asked why I did not fight, but why I did. These things are beyond you and me. No, I do not necessarily doubt our cause, Sergeant, but maybe our resolve. We do not seek the same ends. The colonials want to win this war, and we want to survive it. If we fail, it matters little, at least to me. The Americans, the British, French, Spaniards, we are all the same. We are all germs that have spread from our world to infect this one. We have greedily ruined our lands, exhausted the fields to virtual waste, and then struggled by war for the claim of new lands, to do the same. Would require little sacrifice to simply stop the behaviors causing such problems. We are too blinded by what stands directly in front of us to see what should be so plainly clear. Thus, we search for ways to continue, if not to perpetuate our self-destructive behavior. Few can see the world beyond their sphere of direct consequence. The American merchants want to be freed from our yoke to trade with the world on their terms. His Majesty, who sits upon the throne by the fortune of bloodlines, has nothing to lose but his virtuous legacy. Lawmakers with the whims of their constituents, our officers with their prestige of rank and accomplishment, the kingsmen with the next volley, and their wives and mothers with their safe return. Each of these bodies collides with the others and provide the energy for it all to proceed. Most suppose this is all by the grace of God, and this foolish thinking gives birth to foolish endeavors, the offspring of foolish minds. For my part, I am bound by honor to fight for the cause. I'm not bound to sanction it."

McAllister was rather sharp, though in this instance, did not entirely grasp Pearson's long-winded postulation. "I should know the answer was complicated. Nothing is as simple as it seems, even this war."

"Should have *known*," corrected Pearson.

The sergeant was slightly embarrassed, as he feared the captain looked down on him as with the others. Without realizing as much, he was validating the captain's claim by looking for immediate clarity on what was the most immediate concern. "If the Rebels take Ticonderoga, what will happen to us?"

Pearson smirked wryly as he looked up at him. "When sorrows come, they come not as single spies, but in battalions."

Roughly fifty yards away, Private Manson nested himself, like a rat within piles of trash, in a piece of low ground, thirty to forty yards from the rest of the company. He washed saliva through his mouth by swishing it back and forth between his crooked, yellowed teeth. Then he spat on his palms so he could reduce friction and more easily stroke the shaft of his dick. With his tongue clamped between his teeth, a cascade of dribble raced down his grizzled and scruffy chin. The filthy, sweat- and shit-stained breeches he'd been wearing for several days now were at his ankles. He seemed possessed as he pulled and jerked with vigor. Though the air was no more than forty-five degrees, his brow was dampened with a gleam of perspiration. The spit had washed some of the muck from his right hand, and he forcefully slid it up and down his penis, from the testicles to the tip. He paused every so often to rest his aching wrist and catch a breath. It was a struggle between relieving the pain in his sore wrist and dealing with the frustration of delaying his climax. Through it all and despite his best efforts, he could not divert the thoughts of his surroundings and current predicaments. He recalled various sexual exploits and adventures, yet this offered little. It was not until his degenerate mind conjured the picture of Martha Winsted, his landlord's rather mature mother, that he became confident in his eventual success. Mrs. Winsted was a sixty-odd-year-old widow. She was mostly gray-haired, arched in posture and wrinkled in skin. Manson was aroused at the thought of being aroused by her. Her kindly soft-spoken words, which whistled through the remnants of what teeth she had left, spoke of naughtiness and lust. He imagined her, hunched and assisted by her old, twisted walking stick, approaching him to wrap her prune-dried lips around his cock.

He was focused singularly on orgasm and entirely disinterested in enjoying the process to get him there. The blatantly inappropriate nature of the visual seemed to move him toward ejaculation. Occasionally he groaned and grunted, stopped for a few seconds of rest or to lick his hand, or fire more spit into his palm. In his fantasy scenario, she forced herself on him, in lieu of the rent, which, in reality, he hardly paid when due. Finally, he was almost there—the dam needed only another tap to finally burst.

"Yeah, you old fucking bitch, that's what I am saying. Fuck you, fucking slay-bottom hag," he moaned. Strands of his dull-black, straggly, lice-infested hair fell over his face. Gasps of breath blew his hair back when it became too distracting. An electric energy was building inside of his scrotum; it was imminent. To give himself the final nudge he needed, he nestled his free, filthy palm under his testicles and, ever so slightly, lifted them. His fingers were as gentle as if balancing a feather. The orgasmic sensation was building to a climax. It was as if he had been holding his breath for as long as he could tolerate and could no longer resist but to let the air burst from his lungs. The semen began to rush through his shaft as he finally reached culmination.

It was that moment that Private Manson was instantly engulfed by a massive dark shadow from an equally massive brown bear that towered behind him. It appeared as if the slowly encroaching night had suddenly fallen around him. Manson's eyes peered almost straight upward toward the mountainous beast. Like a dragon spitting fire, she thrust her jowls forward and snarled a long, deafening roar that swept through the trees like a sonic wave. Her teeth shone vividly as polished, white daggers.

Manson was immediately overcome with terrible panic until his fight-or-flight reflex urged him to run as quickly as possible. In an instant, he turned and burst ahead, darting away from the furious grizzly. His breeches shackled his ankles, and without taking a step, he suddenly collapsed forward, onto the ground. He floundered aimlessly until he could get back to his feet to run, then fell again, just as instantly.

Pearson and the others heard the thunderous roar from their positions. At once, the entire party snapped their heads toward its direction, and those who were sitting leaped to their feet.

Only Sergeant McAllister could muster a word. "What the fuck?"

For a moment, all remained still with fear and uncertainty.

"Take your weapons!" cried Pearson, and each of the men grabbed his musket and raced in the direction of the monstrous snarl. Captain Pearson was behind and trembling uncontrollably as he struggled to unpack his Duval pistol. Musket balls fell to the ground like the heavy pellets of hail from the sky, and gray powder clouded the air until it settled as dust on the fallen autumnal leaves. Frantically, he charged his gun and rammed the ball into the breech, then surged toward the others. With his first step, his right foot landed on a musket ball and was thrown behind him. He threw his elbow forward to brace himself as he hit the ground with a thud. A large gasp escaped him as the wind sailed from his lungs.

Wyandot Panther slowly, and with no urgency, rose to his feet. It was as if he was more annoyed to have been disturbed than he was distressed. He strode four or five steps, then stood over Pearson with an insipid look on his face. On the ground, the captain was dazed, and his awareness took a few moments to reprocess his current predicament. Wyandot bent low and, with his brawny right arm, snatched Pearson's red coat behind the neck and heaved him slowly to his feet. Panther's arms resembled the trunks of an old sequoia, and the task of lifting all of Pearson's one hundred seventy pounds was nearly effortless.

Each of them began to file into the woods some thirty to forty yards away from the brown bear. In turn, they shared the same wide-eyed expression as they came to see the angry, massive grizzly before them. Between them and her was the cowering private. Manson was on the ground with his bare ass staring at the sky and his trousers at his knees. She reached her arm aside and whipped it across Manson's back. Her long, black, jagged claws carved three deep slices into his backside and lower nether region. Thick splatters of dark-red blood and scraps of pink and white flesh were launched several yards in the direction of her swipe. His cry was so shrill it would have pierced the ears of the bewildered Redcoats had they not been so overcome with distress.

"Shoot! Fire—fire!" barked McAllister. "Don't wait for the commands, kill it!"

Blasts of musket fire popped, and the soldiers were engulfed by clouds of thick gray-black smoke.

Pearson and Wyandot scurried toward their position, and the captain unloaded a shot from his pistol. "Reload—keep firing!"

Two of the shots landed, yet neither did more than further enrage her. She snarled in anger and moved toward the Redcoats, who were frantically reloading their weapons. Without regard, she crawled over the bloodied and torn private as she advanced. Her first step landed at his lower right ribs halfway from his spine. His rib cage could not bear the weight of her nine hundred pounds as it was displaced through her paw. She stumbled forward and snapped his rib cage as though it was made of dry twigs. The splintered bone tore through his skin and pierced his right lung. Bowels and innards were forced into his throat as if being squeezed through a tube. Thick chunks of blood were spat from his mouth as he bellowed a gruesome gargle.

Pearson raised his pistol and did his best to aim it toward the wrathful brown grizzly. His hand was quivering, his cheek was throbbing and swollen, and his vision was still partially blurred. A fiery blast threw his hand back with the recoil as he squeezed the trigger. The shot struck her just below the left eye and cracked her skull. She snarled and was thrown backward, off her hind legs. Without hesitation, Pearson horridly scuffled through his belt pouch, took another ball, dropped it down the barrel, rammed a powder charge after, and reloaded.

From their positions, Privates St. Claire and Holdsworth, Corporal Browning, and Sergeant McAllister launched musket fire at her as she snarled angrily. The shots hit their mark, yet were little bother as they pelted her heavy coat. Enduring unimaginable agony, Manson meekly writhed about the ground. His body fluids and bowels were plastered into the dirt at his side. The meaty entrails outside of his body were strung with the veins, organs, and stringy flesh to the parts inside of his body. As he shifted about more of his insides were pulled through the large open gash at his ribs. Manson had become a bladder of skin that was oozing pink, red, and yellow sludge. The filthy white trousers that had been wrapped at his shins had become cardinal red as they soaked up all the blood that continued to gush from the slices across his ass. He wheezed as he struggled, gasping for air, inhaling and spitting blackened blood as he toiled to breathe.

Wyandot Panther gradually appeared from the veil of swirling gray smoke. He was a brooding and dark figure, and he approached ponderously and without haste. With his head low and his carved stone Iroquoian hatchet held at his right side, he advanced. The heavy stone blade swung like a pendulum with each stride, and a long, sinew strand, which was tied from the base of the blade, swirled in the breeze as if it was his personal banner. The blade was old and antiquated, though in his hands not the least bit ineffective. The Mohawk had long since developed superior blades of iron and copper, yet the Panther had no mind for progress. He was loyal to the heirloom inherited from his father, who inherited it from his father before him. His blade was no tool, it was a rudimentary weapon, crafted specifically and wholly to kill. It was without the ornate carvings, paintings, or embellishments of its kind. The sharpened edge had pierced the hides of countless beasts and even more men. The weapon of the hunter of hunters.

In a seamless motion, he flipped the weapon into the air, caught it with the blade high, reared his arm behind his right shoulder, and launched it toward the behemoth. The hatchet twirled, blade over handle, through the air, and flew as a blur past Browning, no more than three or four inches from his ear. With a loud thump, the edge pierced the bear's coat and drove itself into her thick layer of fat, just below her shoulder. Her groan nearly shook the remaining leaves from the trees, and she flailed back and forth wildly until the hatchet fell to the ground. The wound was not at all fatal, and hardly painful, yet this was an unfamiliar sensation; one she had never felt in her life.

Her eyeball had come to rub against the broken bones of its socket, and her primal instinct for survival told her not to continue the struggle. For a moment, she stood motionless, seeming unsure and maybe even afraid.

In that instant silence was a thick paste that blanketed the air and prevented all from moving. McAllister, Browning, St. Claire, Holdsworth, and Pearson were as equally unsure as they were still. Only Panther, who continued about his deliberate stride, showed a sign of life amongst the statues of men. He was maybe fifteen yards from her and, without hesitation or the slightest trace of fear, approached. She fell to all four and twisted her massive skull to her right. From the shrubbery, a fifty-pound, brown cub scurried, like a field mouse running through a barn, and scampered back into the woods, away from Panther and the others. Seeing him flee toward safety, she followed in kind, making sure to push her cub forward as she rumbled along. The protective mother and her offspring crushed twigs and snapped branches as they trampled their way south and away from Panther and the others.

Panther and the cadre of British soldiers collectively sighed as they dropped their shoulders in relief. The captain's heart was still thumping wildly in his chest, and a flood of adrenaline was still surging through his veins. Still, he closed his eyes and willed himself to appear calm. He felt he had to say something. Even if it be meaningless, it was important for him to break the silence and demonstrate fortitude. As he began to utter some feeble attempt at assurance, the first few syllables that fell from his mouth were slurred and mumbled to the point of inaudibility. "It left, Gentlemen, well done," was all he could muster. Slowly, his sense of dread and panic yielded to the pain throbbing from the immense bruise on his swollen chin.

Lying on the ground, Private Manson groaned weakly and disturbingly. His lungs struggled to capture air through the thick wall of bloodied innards from his stomach, which had been forced into his trachea and now clogged his breathing passage. His splintered ribs had punctured his lung, sliced his liver, and torn through his skin. Small and large intestines, glazed with bodily fluid and blood, were worms strewn about the forest floor surrounding him. He was more a chewed piece of raw meat than he was a man. Manson was still living, hardly, though enough to see his viscera that had been spread about the woodland ground.

The state of the ill-fated private had been temporarily lost amongst the sense of terror shared by the party. When his wits found him, Holdsworth was so overcome with disgust, he immediately vomited profusely. He threw his hands on his knees and coughed and gagged. His lungs gasped a massive breath as if reloading, and he hurled another round of the acidic digested rations he had eaten for breakfast. Mostly the spew landed on his chest and legs. His heavy red coat and cotton trousers sucked in the chunky yellow-green bile like a dry sponge. As he struggled to gain composure, streams of warm, dark yellow-brown juice flowed from the corner of his mouth. Instinctually, he choked it back, and swallowed, once again, the rations he had eaten hours earlier.

The captain nearly did the same, yet managed to maintain his composure. He was at a loss, and when McAllister looked upon him as if requesting guidance, Pearson had none to offer. The captain was torn between his commitment to protecting His Excellency's men who served under his command and the practical nature of the current reality. Perhaps in haste or indecision, he already felt responsible for the death of a young man. The vision of Private Hendricks splashing about the red water of Lake Champlain had not stopped tormenting him. Manson was now effectively nothing more than a punctured, leaky bag of mush. Yet his heart was still beating, and as despicable of a louse he may have been, he was a soldier in His Majesty's Army. The blank expression on Pearson's face noted the bewildered nature of his thoughts. His company stood idly as they peered in his direction. Through the haze of his still-foggy vision, he felt their eyes upon him.

"Captain?" asked McAllister in a shaken voice.

Pearson closed and opened his eyes several times, slowly pressing his lids downward with force. Thrusting his eyelids closed continually would have presumably washed the blur from his vision. More so, the captain was procrastinating, delaying a decision he did not want to make. Strangely, he turned toward Panther and could not help but to lock eyes with him. Wyandot remained kneeling after he retrieved his ax and offered a blank stare.

Unlike the others, Panther was not in the least bit unnerved. He casually rubbed the blood and thick strands of brown hair from the stone blade with his deerskin tunic and hardly acknowledged Manson's terrible moans that came from only a few feet away. All the while, his eyes remained fixed on the captain. His savage nature and cold heart had never been more apparent to Pearson than at that moment. Panther's deep black hair lazily flapped in the autumn breeze, and his darkened eyes peered straight through Pearson's wide-eyed gaze. While still cleaning his weapon and without uttering a word, Wyandot turned his eyes toward Manson's direction, then back to Pearson. Not a single thought or a second of conscience reflected when Pearson subtly nodded his head.

A thinly veiled grin was drawn upon Panther's face as he slowly rose to his feet. He threw his European leather pouch from his back and placed his ax into it, then thrust the pack across his back again. He reached both arms behind him, to remove his bone dagger from its sheath at the small of his back. With the blade held forward, he lowered his shoulders and moved with a menacing posture. Panther proceeded like his namesake, slowly and cautiously, as if he was looking to remain unseen in the tall grass of the plains. The thick strands of his black hair covered his face. The dry leaves crackled below his feet with each purposeful step.

McAllister caught the captain's eye when he suddenly turned toward him, yet Pearson refused to fully look in his direction. The sergeant knew what Wyandot Panther was intent to do and felt the urge to react, yet did not, remaining still and silent.

The shattered, tiny shards of glass, broken from the pocket watch, twinkled like stars within lumps of mangled, red and pink flesh. Panther was blinded for nearly a second, then, with his left hand, grasped Manson's long, stringy hair, and with some might, pulled it back. He had muscles of stone, and each one in his arm flexed firmly. Manson gurgled and groaned until his eyes widened unnaturally with terror. Pearson turned away and refused to allow himself any thoughts on the matter. As though he was sawing the branches off a fallen tree, Panther sliced Manson's throat and cut away the stubborn skin that held his head to his body. An indescribable swilled groan pierced Pearson's ears, whose willful ignorance could no longer shield him from the horror.

Large spurts of warm blood showered Panther's face, and the taste of salt drove him to slice through Manson's body with more ferocity. The body twitched violently until, after ten or fifteen seconds, Panther managed to finally pare the skin and lift the head from the shoulders. As Panther yanked the skull from the neck, air was swallowed into the body cavity. Manson's vertebral column was attached to the skull and ground and slurped as the bony edges ensnared soft flesh. Panther thumped his heavy foot on the spinal cord and yanked his hand forcefully, separating it from the chain of backbones. With Manson's head completely removed from his body, Panther held it with the same care he would an infant. He turned it upright and looked it straight in its eyes, then tossed it several yards into the brush. The decapitated head crashed against the ground and rolled along several feet, leaving splatters of blood in its path.

Though it felt like an eternity, all remained speechless and still for less than a minute. Only the faint sound of the gentle wind whisking through the trees broke the silence until finally, Panther turned to group and grunted with no trace of emotion, "We take his rations?"

* * *

South.

"Hmm," Dedrick moaned through a yawn. The heavy bearskin blanket was remarkably soft and comfortable, yet inconceivably warm. He cast it aside, and a brisk wave of cool air crashed against his balmy skin. Gently, he then moved the silky-skinned, arm from the quiescent woman whose bed he shared. She had fair skin, occasional spots of light freckles, a toned arm, though not enough to suggest she was not petite and feminine. Her hand appeared soft and delicate, tiny fingers with shiny green polish over her nails. From time to time, she mumbled, ever so softly and adorably. With the greatest of ease, he slowly and carefully pinched her wrist with his thumb and fingers and shifted her arm just enough for it to be out of his way.

She grumbled and mumbled, then tossed about for a moment or two, yet remained asleep and snuggled under the heavy brown cover. He squinted his face with the anticipation of waking her, though he was lucky, as she happened to be a fairly deep sleeper.

The room was nearly covered in shadow. Only the dying embers in the hearth and lone candle clinging to its last flickers of life helped the weak, very early morning beams of the sun as they struggled to find their way over the horizon and through the thick glass window. He sat up, placed his bare feet on the cold, old, wooden floor and took a moment to arch his back and stretch the last glimmers of sleep from within his bones. His hair was more unkempt than usual, nearly untied from behind the back of his neck. A few annoying strands fell in front of his face and were cast back with a swift blow from his lips. Still carefully, he peeked over his shoulder to ensure his movement had not woken her. For a few seconds, maybe more, he remained silent and still. Her breaths were deep and heavy, and he was convinced it was safe to continue.

As he rose to his feet, he did all he could to lighten his step, yet the hickory planks beneath him offered what seemed to be earth-shattering creaks within the still silence. He peered through the nearest window mindlessly, still partially asleep. The dawn's light cast a warm glow on the glassy surface of the Hudson River. Through the western facing window, Dedrick's dark blue eyes were caught by the inherent beauty of the valley and the kindly resting river water. From the west bank, some miles away, three tiny crafts polluted the serenity as they struggled to cross the waterway. The vessels were cluttered with Blue Jackets, and the sculls and wake sliced the calm water as they moved eastward. For a moment or so, Dedrick fixed his gaze on them, until she tossed about in her sleep and removed him from his relaxed trance.

Dedrick's nude body glistened from traces of sweat. The unreasonably warm bearskin was not the only culprit to cause this perspiration. Rather, certain strenuous nocturnal activities were more to blame. A bowl and pitcher rested on a beautifully crafted basin, nearly fifteen feet from the bed, near the corner of the room. The toilette was equally ornate, and the entire arrangement seemed strangely at home within the heavy, dull-gray brick walls.

It seemed as if Dedrick found himself within the chamber of an upper-crust Parisian debutante who had been recently adopted from serfdom. The room was designed with opulence, though without reason. It was a hodge-podge of the expensive and common strewn together without style or cohesion. Nautical images presented within silkworm tapestries did nothing to complement the oriental ceramics that rested on the continental-style mahogany table. The pastel colors within the French needlework pillows clashed with the dark red rug strewn under an aged wooden table, which, in turn, clashed with the bronze-yellow chandelier, so carelessly hung, just off the center of the ceiling. Strings of beads and cheap gemstones hung from the chipped and knotted, old oak beams at the foot of the bed. The contrast of the faux elegance did more to accentuate the unfinished nature of the carpentry than to create the feel of luxury. Much in the way a thick, brown wig atop the head of an aged man serves only to add years to his face. Still, the haphazard and garish interior stylings had a credulous sense behind them, and in a way, helped to make the room feel charming and unassuming.

Where the Palisades Cliffs gazed across the river, lay The Hacklemesh Weaver Inn. The Inn, as it had commonly come to be known, was a three-floor, simple, gray brick building that rested atop a high point on the western banks of the Hudson, a day's stroll from northern Manhattan. To the south and to the west sat the tranquil hills of the Valley, and at certain times of the year, faint swirls of smoke could be seen rising from the many buildings on the northern end of the island. The weathered, drab stone, Quaker-style structure offered not the slightest suggestion of what transpired within its walls. Originally, The Inn was built to provide a place of refuge for religious dissenters when such diversity became unacceptable. For decades, the walls had shielded those without like-mind or faith from the peril of intolerant hordes. Subsequent years had seen the same walls to be the shields of far different dangers. The many chapters of the Inn's story, yet concludes with far different happenings.

Still sure to remain silent, Dedrick held the pitcher low as he poured. The water blurred the intricate and decorative floral pattern within the wash bowl. He was yet to fully wake and clumsily clanged the pitcher against the bowl as he brought it to rest on the basin. Instantly he turned back toward the bed, expecting the noise to have woken her. She grumbled inaudibly, then rolled from her side, yet remained quite at rest. He closed his eyes with mild relief. In truth, he partially hoped to wake her.

He cupped his hands and splashed the lukewarm water onto his face. After he repeated this, then patted himself with the soft cotton linen resting beside the basin, he looked about the room for his clothes, or at the very least, something to cover himself to some extent. He was virtually at home and knew Turkish towels were usually folded neatly within the drawer chest at the other side of the room. After a quick survey, he curiously saw no sign of his clothing. Once again, he trod lightly, but quickly to the other end of the room for a towel. His hunch was she was going to wake at any moment and see him completely unclothed. The sun was gaining in strength and size, casting its light through the eastern windows and washing the shadows from his naked body. Dedrick hardly lacked for confidence, yet on a certain occasion, he was more than a bit bashful. In particular, he was very insecure about the size of dick, and being flaccid at the moment made him even more uneasy. Over the years, he'd loathed the need to recognize the fruitlessness of his denial on the subject. For as long as he remembered, uncountable, opportune glances had mostly confirmed his suspicion. At night, or by a candle's light, his diffidence was softened to enough of an extent to allow him to freely use it without much concern. Nonetheless, it was an area of his character he preferred to reveal only when absolutely necessary.

Sally woke to the image of Dedrick's bare ass staring back at her as he was hunched over, searching for a towel within the drawer. Looking to swiftly take advantage of the opportunity, she slyly looked about the bed for whatever may be within arm's reach. She snatched one of his wool stockings, balled it up, and flung it toward him. Startled as it landed against his back, Dedrick sprang up straight, immediately crashing his head into the cabinet above the drawer.

"The fuck…?" he uttered.

Through a delighted giggle, Sally asked, "Aw, are you all right, darling?"

Dedrick merely gave her a look of displeasure and draped the heavy cotton cloth around his waist. He was restrained, though he felt an insulting remark fostering about his tongue. His frustration did not allow him to only partially assuage his scolding. "This is funny? Hitting my head makes you laugh? You're a fucking child if you think that's funny."

"Oh, please," she said. "We are all entitled to our petty amusements, my love. I do think it is funny. I think it's funny because you are more embarrassed than hurt. I would say that I am sorry, but my apology would be insincere. Now, are you going to continue to pout, dear? You want me to make it better, do you?"

Gently, she bit down on her lower lip and gradually, seductively drew the bearskin aside, revealing her perky, round breasts. She was wearing nothing aside from an unpolished, silver necklet, with a pearl-embedded clasp. The soft beams of light gleamed through the heavy glass windows. Traces of perspiration caused her fair skin to shine as though she were a porcelain statuette resting in the late-day sun. She moaned with pleasure as she fondled her left breast with her right hand, then, with her finger, gently rubbed around the tip of her taut, rosy pink nipple. Her breasts were firm and fair, though not altogether large. Even though Sally had been told of this capricious shortcoming to the hyper-superficial on occasion, she was unlike Dedrick in this regard. She chose to celebrate the so-called imperfection as a unique part of who she was. She found no shame in her attributes and would be the first to joke about the subject in a playful, self-deprecating way. Consistent with her nature, she felt that anyone who saw her breast size as a flaw was someone whose opinion meant nothing to her.

Sally was certainly blessed with many of the natural, womanly qualities most men would find hard to resist. She had a way of pleasing all senses. Because she suffered severe colic as an infant, her voice had just enough huskiness to be alluring. A tiny brown birthmark dotted just above her chin drew the eyes toward her mouth and her thin, blushing lips, which perfectly encircled her flawlessly white teeth. Her auburn-brown locks fell just to her shoulders, and her eyes were as large and as blue as a Caribbean Ocean. No matter where and no matter when, she always had the smell of fresh spring flowers. Even now, after a rather long night of physically exerting deeds, followed by an even longer night's sleep, she smelled only of jasmine on the vine. For his part, Dedrick could not understand how the entire world of heterosexual men did not succumb to her spell. Of course, his only reference was Lars, his insipid valet, so he was not entirely sure it was not. Regardless, as far as Dedrick was concerned, Sally was the brightest flower in the garden.

The existence of The Inn was not discussed freely with those who did not visit it, and not at all by those who did. Most had learned to accept it was simply an immaterial, stone and brick building, and those who entered and left, though familiar, were merely nameless faces of no consequence. Only the foolish dared to openly challenge commonly accepted perception, despite the obvious evidence to the contrary. Within its halls, New York's most important and influential enjoyed the rather expensive comfort of discretion to revel in whatever debauchery their depraved minds could conjure. One did not seek to visit The Inn; The Inn sought those to visit. All inquiries in this manner were met with an irreversible lifetime ban, at the very least. Only a very select few were invited to enjoy the many pleasures The Inn had to offer, and once removed, guests would never be welcomed back. Mostly, though infrequently, services were simply exchanged for money. From time to time, special favors were required in lieu of precious metals or currency. Thus, the more one was able to offer in regards to influence, in one form or another, the more welcome he would be. Failure to uphold the standards of these expectations would be met with varying outcomes. Typically, the veil of discretion would be removed, though, at times, a breach of contract had resulted in more severe penalties.

Patrons, as they were, guests of The Inn, were always treated and addressed in a way meant to show appreciation for their standing and worth. For as long as good fortune chose to smile on them, servants of The Inn would ensure all guests' total satisfaction. Fresh rose petals were drizzled into large, warm, Roman-style baths every day, all year. A vineyard on the grounds grew the most delicate grapes in the northeast, and pure opium was imported regularly. The food was always fresh, and the beer always cold and stout. Offerings were limited only to the guests' imagination and levels of restraint. Women or men of all types: curvy, thin, short, tall, old, young, demure, or innocent were to be enjoyed by request. Guests were free to delight in whatever behaviors they find most satisfying.

All worries and woes from the most common of nuisances to the trouble of war, remained outside the walls. Once inside, few rules applied, the first being that discussion of ill manner, anxiety, fear or concerns of any kind, were never allowed. In The Inn, such considerations did not exist. All guests were neither better nor worse than all others. Social standing, wealth, title, political influence, and all the like were not a part of the inside world. There were no rivalries, grudges, or outward ill will from any guest, toward any guest. Inside The Inn there was no such thing as Loyalists or Separatists, no Puritans, Anglicans, Jews, or Catholics—there were no consequential differences of minds or opinions from the outside world. As a gesture or commonality, guests were never addressed by surname and were required to surrender all footwear aside from stockings. Any sole that had trampled the rude soils of the outside were not allowed to spread a speck of its dust inside. For Dedrick, and by fortunate association, Lars, The Inn had become such a routine stop it may have been more accurate to describe them as residents, rather than as guests.

Since his introduction, Sally had been Dedrick's preferred pleasure. At times, he had ventured to taste the other many delights from The Inn's menu. And they were truly delightful, yet they were not Sally, and he was disappointed each time. It took very little time for him to learn he would find no better. He'd become infatuated with her awkward humor, natural charm, and raspy voice. Among her many qualities, was her creative talent, and with this, she was above reproach. Irrationally perhaps, Dedrick had made the decision, while as a guest, never to engage in certain behaviors. This was to say, Sally would never bear his child. Given this self-imposed restriction, Dedrick always deferred to her good judgment, and as of this occasion, had never been disappointed.

When he gave the matter some thought, as he tended to do, he would not know what he found particularly appealing about her. Outside, Dedrick was accustomed to being the alpha dog, the one who barked the orders to keep all the others in line. With her, he was uncharacteristically unsure and longed to be nurtured. Sally had a unique manner about her. Surely, the perception of her childlike simplicity along with the confidence to be the authoritative figure in their relationship was what inspired his affection. It may have been any number of things, yet regardless the reason, she kept him coming back. On this morning, though, he had exhausted all his sexual urges, and her seduction did nothing to arouse him.

"I'm fine, thank you," he said as he rubbed the top of his head with his right hand.

"You're right about that, my darling, you are very fine," she purred, and with the bearskin resting on her naked body, crawled along the bed toward him.

Dedrick was as flaccid as a dead fish and not particularly swift at effectively expressing polite disinterest in such a situation. Now, he was hoping to communicate his apathy without saying as much verbally. He scurried toward the large carob wicker trunk she had aside from the head of her bedstead, where the magnum of wine they poured from the previous evening rested. The large bottle and empty crystal glasses caught his eye, not that he necessarily wanted another glass, but rather, this was a chance to shift the direction of the exchange.

He was not sure which glass was hers and which his. His hope was to drink from hers and for her to want to drink from his. Affectedly, he assumed whichever he chose was hers and she knew hers was his. The bottle was surprisingly light and offered little more than a few drops. Still, he tilted the magnum until it was vertical and facetiously held it over the crystal wineglass for several seconds. Carefully, he picked hers up at the stem and gestured for her to retrieve it. With a disappointed look about her, she slowly crawled back toward him and accepted the glass.

"I can't believe you want to drink right now," she said.

"Shhhh," he replied as he reached for his glass atop the chest. He fixed his eyes on hers, lifted his glass, and they clanged them together gently.

"And to what are we drinking, my love?" she asked, her tone mildly sarcastic.

He paused for no more than a moment and replied, "Can we just drink? It always needs to be for something or to something? It would be so trite to drink 'to us,' and I think I can do better. Health is always important, as is happiness, and—wow, your breath is really bad."

Immediately she threw her free hand over her mouth and blurted, "What? My breath? I'm sorry, did you say I have bad breath?"

"I did," he said. "I'm sorry, but I have to be honest. Maybe we can drink to the shit coming from your mouth. Damn, my lady—and I'm only saying what I would expect you to do for me—but goddamn! Smells like a fish, or a school of them, died in there. The hell did you eat? Respectfully, please, maybe look away or wrap something around your chin. Better still, don't breathe at all." He held his arm out as if keeping her to a distance. She had a confused and resigned look about her.

Still holding her hand up to her mouth, she asked, "You need to stop. Is it really that bad?"

He felt a degree of guilt, seeing as he was fostering an indignant manner about her. His proclamation was mostly, though not all, in jest. His inkling suggested he wanted a measure of revenge for causing him to bang his head against a rather hard, wooden cabinet. Mostly, this was one of his typically clumsy attempts to gently belittle her into a position of insecurity, so he did not yield to her mild, though apparent despondency.

"No, it's not *that bad*, it's *worse* than that bad. I can't even exaggerate if I tried."

Without the slightest hesitation, she leaned into him, speckled his white towel with droplets as she spilled flat wine, leaned to within three or four inches of his face, opened her mouth as wide as she could, and blew bursts of air directly at him. She continued blasting him with her breath until he dropped his glass to crash upon the floor and fell back into her pillow.

"Ah! Shit, please, no. Stop! Mercy!" he cried.

Her glass shattered when she carelessly tossed it to the floor. She crawled atop him, tickled him by poking and prodding him about the ribs, and shoved her face beside his, firing more billows of her allegedly warm shit-smelling breath upon him. Dedrick was laughing, though he was not necessarily amused. "All right, all right, you win—stop," he pleaded through a gasp.

Still, Sally continued to wrestle with him until he tried to lift himself upright to remove himself from her. In so doing, a quick honk escaped from his ass. He froze for a second or more and hoped it went unnoticed. The flatulence was too loud to be ignored, and Dedrick's face became warm and flushed with embarrassment. Desperately, he tried to think of something clever to say, to save face, while his brain seemed frozen in shock.

"And what was that, my dear…?" she said as a cunning smirk grew upon her soft lips.

"All right, all right. It's your fault—it's fine, it happens," he awkwardly replied, then grabbed both her wrists to restrain her from continuing. Undeterred, Sally tugged and pushed her hands toward his stomach to tickle him some more. The two playfully poked and shoved one another until both of their heads crashed together. Their mutual laughter instantly morphed into a painfully frustrated groan.

"Fucking shit," said Dedrick. He was partially relieved, as he instantly moved on from his embarrassment. He thrust his palm against his forehead. "That's twice now. I'm starting to think you either want my brain to be permanently damaged, or you have some sort of pain fetish."

Rubbing her head, she replied with a patronizing tone, "Oh, please. I suppose that was my fault too because it is clear *nothing* is ever my love's fault. How can we make it all better, sweetie? What can Sally do to make everything all right?"

Still sitting on the bed, rubbing his head yet again, Dedrick's eyes were taken by a scattered pile of haphazard trinkets resting on a tabletop near the far corner of the room. The utilitarian construction and aged wood helped the table to fit as perfectly out of place as everything else in the room. Curiosity drove him to walk toward the table for closer inspection. Resting on top were a number of unrelated items; a small portrait of a young, nameless noblewoman in a gilded frame, a finely crafted yet overwhelmingly tacky, colorful gemstone silver brooch, delicate ceramics, assorted jewelry, a lavish jewelry box, a pair of silk and satin slippers, and most unusual of all, a velvet bag of marbles. The small velvet pouch, loosely tied closed by cotton yarn, held a bundle of marbles. He tugged the pouch open, peeked inside, and with the minimal light being cast, was taken by the vibrant colors of the tiny crystal spheres.

"This was here last night?" he asked as he gestured toward it. "What is all of this?"

"What is all of what, darling?"

"This…shit, what is all of this? These are gratuities, aren't they? Please tell me otherwise because that would be pathetic."

"If by gratuities you mean gifts, then yes, they are. They are gifts, well-meaning gifts. You're impressed by them?"

Dedrick barely shook his head with timid antipathy. "Gifts. I don't think I'd use the word *impressed*, curious, though. These have been given to you by your many admirers?"

"You are too sweet, my dear," she replied with a proud grin.

"I'm wondering why you leave them displayed as such. Are these some trophies you wish the world to see?"

"Oh, darling, you need to stop," she said. "I'm starting to hear a hint of jealousy in your voice. Suppose that should be flattering and I should thank you. More, it is a bit surprising and really quite unappealing."

Dedrick gently shook his head with mild amusement. "You really are in love with yourself, aren't you?"

Sally seemed very naïve, yet had honed an inimitable skill which empowered her to detect intentions beyond the spoken words of men. She could hardly contain her smile as she realized Dedrick was desperate to hide his resentment.　Though she could have easily appeased him with honest reality and assured him the various gifts were, in fact, meaningless, she chose to let his insecurity dangle on its fragile rope. "I am one of a kind, my darling. The girls who need showers of praise are as common as wishful thoughts. Now, if I was as shallow, I suppose your continued visits would be enough to support my sense of worth. No, these are simply gifts; they are attempts to win my favor. Each has a story all its own, all with the same stale and sad chapters. It is all very silly, but you are all very silly. You think you can win my charms with material offerings, that I will be so overcome or impressed with your generosity, or your means, I will somehow become smitten, if I was not already. It is very peculiar for you men, I should say, to know the world inside these walls is fantasy, yet refuse to believe it. And, what I find most interesting is each of you see the pile of gifts on the table, which you noticed I make no effort to conceal, yet still think yours will in some way be outstanding, that your lure will catch my affection when all the others have not. The professed domineering gender, especially the guests here, boast of practical mind and self-reliance, and each and every one of you believes yourselves to be an individual, unlike all the others. Which, I would say, makes you exactly the same as all the others. Claiming to be distinct has become a predictable and uninspiring cliché, and I can never figure out why you all insist on relying on it. Desperation clouds good reason, I suppose. But, I indulge, and go along with the charade, pretend every bounteousness gifted to me has won my heart, or made me soaking wet with desire. Sometimes, I suspect some of you know I'm being insincere and don't even seem to mind. It is pitiful, really."

Sally carried on as though she had given this speech a thousand times. She seemed more interested in admiring the shine of her recently painted nails than concentrating fully on what she was saying. "This is all very predictable. The more you boast of your confidence, the more expensive the gift you will give me. Very, very pitiful, yet still, in a way, fascinating."

Dedrick sneered and drolly replied, "I'm impressed. I suppose you think you're pretty clever? You think you solved the riddle and have a handle on the simple of the genders—maybe you have, as you seem to be doing more than well for yourself. So, it looks as though I must humble myself to ask if I may have one of your…many gifts, one of the pathetic attempts at winning you over, the lures to snare your affection. You wanted to know how you can make it better? *That* is how you can make it better."

She snickered gently. "You want something, dear?"

"If I may, yes. I like this sack of marbles. For the life of me, I can't imagine who would give you this, or why. For whatever the circumstance, it certainly is not a cliché, I'll give him that much. In any event, I'm sure you value my patronage and assume you have no use for them," replied Dedrick as he tossed the velvet sack of glass balls up into the air repeatedly. Without paying it much mind, one of the many books stacked on the shelf before him caught his eye. "Oh, and that, that book too."

Dedrick walked closer to the dark, rosewood bookshelf and lifted a leather-bound copy of Jonathan Twist's *Gulliver's Travels*. He brought it close, blew off some of the dust, and examined it for a moment. "This one."

"Those are marbles, jacks and fivestones, sweetie. Why would you want such a thing? I can't see you finding amusement in such simplicity."

"I would like to tell you, *sweetie*, but remember, my business is just that, my business. It all remains outside of these walls."

"No need to be sensitive, dear. It was merely a question," said Sally. "I don't care for the marbles, perhaps you can have those, but not the book. The book was not a frivolous gift, and I would like to read it…someday. It sounds interesting to me, Gullible Travel, it is?"

Through a gentle laugh, Dedrick corrected her. "No, not *gullible*, Gulliver—*Gulliver's Travels*. Are you really going to read it, or are you just looking to give me a hard time?"

Sally was surprised by her reaction, her inclination to take offense to his tone and implication she was in some manner, unread. Yet, she was aroused by Dedrick's confident candor. Without trying, he now appeared much more assertive than he usually was with her. Normally men who shared her company placated and flattered her to no end, which, to her, had long since become tiresome. She tossed the bearskin aside to reveal her fully naked body. Through a seductive grin, she slowly moistened her lower lip by stroking it with her tongue, looked him directly in the eyes, dropped her bare feet to the floor, and slowly sauntered toward him. Her long, silky smooth legs cast her tiny feet, one over the other as if she were walking on a tightrope. She moved slowly, her approach to build anticipation. Without breaking the spellbinding stare of her crystal-blue eyes, she rubbed her right hand through the lips of her vagina and continued her two fingers upward along her flat stomach, creating a faint trail of gleaming moisture. When her hand reached her mouth, she rested her fingers at the base of her lower lip and thrust them gently between her soft and moistened lips.

When she reached him, Sally leaned against Dedrick and, from behind, tenderly draped both of her petite arms around his hips. Together, they gazed through the thick, old heavy glass window as it overlooked the sleepy hills and rising sun. Her chin rested on his right shoulder and very leisurely, she let her hand slide gradually down his firm abdomen through the heavy cotton towel he had wrapped around his hips, until it reached his not-so-firm crotch. With a delicate touch, she wrapped her fingers around his penis. Softly, she pecked tiny kisses along his neck as her breath blew into his ear.

Softly, she whispered, "Speaking of hard times…you can have your book and bag of balls, darling, and you can shine your dick between my tits, for five pence."

A slight twinge of arousal shot through his body; still, her seduction was met with cold resistance. Dedrick slowly spun his head toward hers. "That is tempting, but, at this moment, I'm dried out. For now, I'm only interested in enjoying the continued pleasure of conversation, the marbles, and the book. Regardless, I already paid for the other."

"I don't think so, love," she said. "Your time has come, so to speak."

Dedrick chuckled again. "Really? And how did we reach that conclusion? When did 'my time' end?"

"Now," replied Sally.

"Now? *Now* is not a time. What did I pay for when I paid last night?"

"You paid for the evening…sweetheart. Look." She removed her hand from his crotch to push her finger against the glass, then continued in a manner as though she was speaking to a child. "You see that *tiny* glimpse of the sun as he peeks his head just above the trees along the horizon? See him—there he is, see just over there—look at him and say 'guten morgen.' You paid for last night, love, and it is now this morning."

Dedrick shook his head, and though he found her gestures entertaining, he was still a bit taken back. "Aside from telling me to talk to the sun as it rises, I'm not sure if you are being serious right now."

"A girl has to make a living," she replied, with a most satisfied look upon her face.

"Yes, fuck, I suppose she does." Dedrick flippantly surveyed the bookshelf. "Hmm, I don't see *The Wealth of Nations* on the shelf—clearly, you've read *that*."

"What is that?" she asked.

"An Inquiry into…The Wealth of Nations, um, Adam Smith."

"Oh, yeah, of course, Adam Smith," she replied with a hint of sarcasm.

"Adam Smith. His views on the exchange of goods and money, profit motive. You're aware of his treatise?"

"Of course, who isn't?" she replied with the same sarcastic tone.

"You know, even when you mean to be shitty, you are quite charming, you know that?"

She gazed into nowhere as if she was contemplating his suggestion. The name was familiar, though clearly quite common. "Exchange of money. He's been here?"

Dedrick sighed with amusement. "Has he been here?" he asked himself. "That is a…yeah, that's an interesting question. Is this appropriate to discuss? Hmmm…maybe, I mean sure, he could have been here. I don't know. Not even sure I should answer that, really."

"I fucked him?" she asked with blunt, heartfelt curiosity.

Again, Dedrick was mild, though outwardly entertained with himself. He stroked his grizzled chin with his fingers, partially out of habit, but mostly as a reflex to hide his smile. He allowed himself a few seconds of glee, enjoying the entertainment of the thought. In many ways, Sally was the shrewdest and most cunning of anyone he knew. She was also sweetly ingenuous, and after spending many nights over the course of many months with him, Sally still had trouble distinguishing his sarcasm from his sincerity.

"It's possible. I don't know. You might have fucked him. I can't say, really, right? If forced to guess, I'm going with no, you have not fucked Adam Smith. Yet…who knows, it still is possible you fucked Adam Smith. I don't know, though. I heard he is very much into crazy things, fetish type, um, things, like with pee-pee and whatnot. Piss and shit, well, not shit. Piss…and shit, meaning stuff, not literally shit. Surely you would have remembered this." It was apparent he enjoyed repeating the absurdity of the discussion's basis.

By now, Sally recognized his mockery, and by this point was on the border of amused and annoyed. "That's lovely—what is your point, my dear?"

With a straight face instantly drawn, Dedrick responded, "All right, all right, Adam Smith, he said, in simple terms, individuals are driven by money, by profit. Money is the reason we do whatever it is that we do; it is the reason we try and care and work hard. Our ambition and all our efforts correlate with the money we earn. Those who put forth no effort make no money, and those who do, do. It is all about making ourselves money. He called this the Vile Maxim. The butcher does not care that you or those you provide for are hungry, he's not interested if you eat or collapse from starvation; the butcher only cares that you buy his meat. He does not seek to feed you; he seeks your money. That is what motivates him."

"Well, this Adam Smith sounds like a very cynical man, and I'm glad I don't know him."

"That's true, it is a very cynical perspective. That is one way to look at it," replied Dedrick. He lifted her chin with his fingers, then stroked his hand gently across her cheek, brushing her hair behind her ear. "Another would be that he has described what you do perfectly."

She welcomed his soft affection and leaned her head toward his hand and placed hers atop his as if she wanted to make sure he did not remove it from the side of her face. "My hunch is that was an insult, but I'm still not entirely sure what you are trying to say. Is it because I take your money, because you must pay to stick your cock into my ass, is that it, dear? I don't know you on the outside, how you live, or by what means you are able to pay me, and none of it matters. I don't really care. I care only about the time we spend together. And you know, Sweetie, we don't always follow the house rules."

Dedrick sensed the tone of the exchange shifting from light-hearted teasing, to preliminary exchanges of amorous overtures. Through the dawn's light and the quivering tenor of her voice, he sensed the genesis of romantic feelings. His emotional state had been altered with the realization she held such sentiments of him. Without trying, she was breaking through the wall of apathy he had built with the bricks of her objectification. He was moved from what he believed to be a child-like infatuation to a truer sense of affection. She had demonstrated her humanity and fragility via the perception of hurt feelings. It was as though she gave permission for him to allow his emotions for her to overcome his guarded senses. He was struck by a cannon, dazed by his infatuation. Dedrick never fully grasped the reality that he saw her as anything other than the beautiful being who sucked his cock and made him laugh. Now, it was as though his feelings had been given free rein to blossom.

He struggled to formulate a coherent response to express the conflicting feelings within him. "I'm not judging, at all. It's nothing, never mind. I'm sorry. I shouldn't have brought it up. It doesn't even make sense anyway. Let's just forget it."

"No, no," she cried. "You started this, and you can't simply share a thought about me, one which you apparently believe to be profound in some nature, then simply move on because you believe me to be too simple to understand, or you don't have the inkling to waste your time explaining. Nope, I am not letting you off the hook with 'forget it,' my love. And I couldn't 'forget it' now even if I tried."

"You really don't see what I'm getting at?" he asked.

Her tone seemed to shift, yet Dedrick was unsure if she was becoming perturbed or being playful. "I think I do see what you are getting at. I might have an idea, though it seems obvious and pointless—you are saying I only do what I do, to you, because you pay me, to do what I do. Is that right?

"This man, *Adam Smith*," she continued with emphasis as she locked her stunning blue eyes with his while drawing her face closer. "He came up with all of this on his own—yes, he seems to be very impressive indeed. I hope I did fuck him. Him, I would fuck for free. But you..." she added as she rested her finger gently up against his lips as though she was ensuring he remained silent. Her voice drifted into a seductive whisper. "No, you have to pay, my love, and you have to pay a lot. And I know you will. I know you will pay me, and pay me again and again. I know you are going to leave this chamber and as soon as that heavy, old door slams behind you, you will be anxious with anticipation for the next time you can rest your eyes upon my fully unclothed body, until you slip your hard cock into my warm, slippery pussy. You will pay fortunes driving you into despair for me to be yours, and only yours, for these few hours. You will, darling, because you know the sun shines from my cunt, and that I taste sweeter than any fruit to have touched your lips. You will pay because every hour I am with you, is an hour I am not with any other."

She sauntered back toward the bed, slowly and with the purpose to entrap his stare. Slyly, she turned her head aside and glanced back, ensuring his eyes were fixed on her. Convinced he was looking, she bent back forward, and with no urgency, took the bearskin and tossed it over her shoulders, where it rested to cover her body. Without breaking eye contact, she turned and lowered herself onto the bed, sat up straight, crossed her legs, then leaned forward, toward him.

"My poor, delicate flower is hurt?" she asked with an inauthentic pout. "This is surprising, I really must say. Well, don't be, dear. I happen to *very* much enjoy the time we spend together. That is, I *usually* enjoy our time together. This conversation is anything but enjoyable, but I don't charge you for conversation. You are...hmmm, how can I put this, love? I don't want to say you are my favorite because that implies you are somehow part of all the rest. No, you are very special to me. I always thought you knew as much. Evidently, my suspicion was wrong...again. I tend to feel others share my feelings. That seems rather silly and self-absorbed, so forgive me, dear, please. Since we are here, I suppose I should have been more open about it. There is something about you, and at times, my mind keeps me up all hours, racing to figure you out. You are not here, you are not in my bed, but you manage to keep me up until the sun fills my room."

Dedrick felt a warmth inside of him and truly wanted to believe her flattery, yet was begrudgingly skeptical. He continued as though he was prodding her just enough to accept her assertion as truth. "I keep you up at night? Why do I feel this is something you say to other men?"

"I really am surprised. I thought this was something we both felt. I cannot believe you have never picked up on this. I am better at hiding my feelings than I thought. No, I have never said this to any other man, sweetie. My heart flutters when I know you are here. There is something to you. Maybe it's the way everyone is when you are around. I don't know, but you have a way about you, an effortless way to connect with everyone, to make each person you greet feel special, whomever it may be. Madame Jeanette, with the stable help who tend to your horses, the other girls, with me. And that connection, no matter how insignificant it may be to you, changes who we are when in your presence. In this way, you must see the world differently than all others, you must see only the best versions of those around you. At times, I feel…if I were someone else, I don't know if I would like me very much. Never when I am with you. I like who I am when I am with you, maybe that is it. I don't know. Could be so many things: Your square jaw, the way you walk, that you sleep with a pillow over your face, or that I've never, ever seen you laugh. Maybe it is because you refuse to give up and continue one awful joke after another, even when I seem not the slightest bit amused. Maybe it is all those things, or maybe none of them. I don't know what it is exactly, and I think I don't care to know. After all, not knowing what draws me to you, is exactly what draws me to you. Mystery is always far more interesting than what is common. Sweetie, there is something to you, there is no mystery to that.

"During those sleepless nights, those many sleepless nights, these two fingers…they slip into me as you, your fucking face. I hear your voice, and I slide them deeper into me, moan your name, and my pussy warms with sweat. Days go by when I cannot wait to go to my bed and be with you in fantasy." Sally brushed her front-bottom sensually, then straightened herself up for a moment, paused, and fanned herself with her hand.

"Whew," she sighed.

By now, Dedrick was, to say the very least, moved. Dryly, he could only say, "Wow, that was…wow." He could barely hide his jitters, and she could hardly withhold the faint grin and look of satisfaction on her face. Reflexively, though negligibly, she nodded her head as she approved of her performance.

Flustered with sexual excitement, he continued, "I don't know how to react to that. I really didn't know this, for sure. I had inklings, but you are a tough one to read. When I'm not here, I miss you too, a lot. Don't know that it keeps me up at night, though I can't sleep regardless, but I do hate leaving here and trying to find reasons to make the trip—well, I shouldn't—yeah, I feel something for you. I know I'm supposed to forget all of this, forget about you, and when I walk out of the door, my life starts again. I'm back to *the world* where you do not exist. Doesn't matter, you continue to live in my mind, and…well, you know, every time I smell bread, I get a flutter in my stomach and my dick gets hard. That has to mean something."

Sally scrunched her expression into one of utter confusion. "Bread? That's…interesting. Who knew you had such feelings for wheat products?"

He could not help but giggle at her attempt at humor. "This place smells of fresh bread. Right? You don't think? Well, every time I walk through the door I'm overcome by the scent of bread. I associate you with the smell of bread." Dedrick turned away from her, chagrined and humbled to have removed himself from the pretense of indifference he had always maintained with her. He strolled toward the other end of the room and gazed out of the eastern window. A light mist blanketed the calm river, and the dew on the autumnal leaves glistened with the light of daybreak. In a sense, he regretted his declaration, yet, in another, he wished to continue. He felt more naked now than he had before he wrapped himself with the soft towel.

"I'm sure you're thinking it's all about what we do, it's all sexual. Of course, clearly that is certainly part of it, but…you know, you're pretty fucking cute and charming and really hard not to fall for," he uttered through a grumble. "I would love to know you outside of here—nevertheless, what can we do? We share more of ourselves than we certainly should as it is. We can't expect more, right?" he asked with rhetorical intentions, perhaps, conceding to the notion their relationship was to be confined to the current setting and definition and nothing beyond. Yet, he turned to her and hoped she would in some way have a response suggesting otherwise.

Sally's delicate lips quivered like petals in a gentle breeze. She tilted her head and paralyzed him with her sparkling, blue apatite eyes as they grew with sorrow. "Oh, sweetie, sweetie, sweetie, you should tell me everything you want to tell me. My heart raced hearing that your heart raced." She crawled along the bed toward him, reached for his hand, and then tugged, helping herself to sit straight. The sun's light from the eastern window had grown stronger and radiated from behind. Her soft, sandy red-brown hair was cast in its warm glow. Down her long neck, it sparkled on the links of her necklet and wrapped her slender and delicate shoulders.

Still clinging to his hand, she rested her other atop his and clenched both tightly. "You are too sweet, my love. Other than a bad name, I don't think I would have much to offer you. All the same, we know it cannot be. This is our world, darling, this is ours, and whenever you are here and for as long as you are here, this is our world and only our world. My eyes, my lips, my breasts, and my cunt are all yours, only yours."

"I suppose." He sighed.

"I don't want to be sad," she continued. "Besides, you know we shouldn't be speaking of sorrow or sadness, and it seems as though we are getting dangerously close to doing so. We have us, we have today, and many more sleepless nights filled with anticipation. Whenever you are a guest, I will always be here for you. I am your Hero and you are my Leander."

A smile began to crack Dedrick's face as he warmed with her optimism. "Yeah…You're right. That is a good way to put it. But, did you say I'm your hero? That's a little strange, and you just may have killed what we had going," he said in his typically sardonic tone. "Flattering yes, but that's not really what I'm looking to do here."

"No, no, silly, not a hero, Hero, and *I* am Hero."

He lowered his brows as he tried to contemplate exactly what she was saying. "You lost me."

"Hero and Leander."

"These names are supposed to mean something to me?" he asked.

Sally twittered and could not resist. "Oh, so I should make fun of you for being unread, should I?"

Dedrick could not help but smile at her discomfited attempt at mockery. "Fair enough. Can you please tell me who these blokes are?"

"I should make you beg," she said in teasingly flirtatious way. "Hero and Leander were two Latin lovers, Ancient Greek folklore. Hero and Leander could only be together at night, so every night, she lit a torch for him to see. And every night, Leander, strengthened by his passion, would swim across the river guided by the light of her torch to reach his love, his reason for being—Hero, his Hero. They did not spend their time together saddened by the thoughts of the time they would not be together. It's romance—it is a tragic, beautiful riddle. The more in love we are, the more we need of our lover and, in this way, our need is really never met. Hero and Leander had the unbreakable bond of love, and it had to be enough because it was all they had."

"Leander and Hero?" he asked.

"Yes, Leander and Hero, two lovers…well, that is until the night the wind blew out the torch and he lost his way and drowned. But, before that, it was so very beautiful and romantic."

Dedrick was snapped out of the weak trance she had managed to put him in. "Ah, you're a jester now? You tell jokes? Is that what you do?"

Her face was lit with satisfaction as she sneered with childlike glee. "Oh, love, we have our entire world together. Let's delight in that. We have it all, and it is only you and it is only me." She fell back onto the bed and tugged his hand forward. He allowed himself to gently collapse onto her, with only the Turkish towel that was now falling from his hips, between them. She closed her eyes and pulled her head back as he gently kissed the milky-white skin on her delicate neck with tender pecks. Softly she groaned, and at the back of his head, brushed her fingers through his hair.

"I can get rid of this fucking thing," he grunted and lifted his waist and tossed the towel to the floor. Sally began to lower herself toward his crotch until he held her shoulder. "No, no, I don't want to do that. If this is our entire world, I want to share as much of it with you as I can."

A coy smile grew upon her face. She knew precisely what he intended, but she was going to make him say it. "What do you want to share with me, dear? What do you want?"

"I want to fuck you," he replied.

Almost sinisterly, she smiled. "Mmm, yes," she groaned. "I have wanted you inside of me for so long—yes, let's fuck." As he continued to softly kiss her around the neck, he purposely nipped her skin with his teeth, stinging her ever so slightly. The pricks of pain within the sea of delight nearly brought her to orgasm. She opened her legs and clamped them around his hips. Dedrick thrust and adjusted, positioning himself to penetrate her swampy-warm, wet vagina. Her delicate hands rested on the back of his broad, sturdy shoulders. "Wait, my darling, wait just a moment."

Confused and frustrated Dedrick paused, lifting himself above her by straightening his arms against the feather bed. "What happened?" he asked.

"You said you wanted the book…and those marbles, yes?"

Even more perplexed, he went along with an unusual line of thought, determined to conclude this as swiftly as he could. "The book? Yes, I was interested in the book and the bag of marbles."

"I wasn't sure if you really were, sweetie, I am sorry." Then she lifted her head toward his, placed her lips against his, and slithered her tongue into his mouth. With her hand firmly behind the back of his skull, she pulled him tight and continued to swirl her tongue against his inner cheek. After some time, she pulled back and quietly spoke into his ear. "I said ten pence, right? That is fine, for the book and the marbles?"

By this point, he had nearly forgotten about both of the items, and completely forgotten the details of the brief discussion regarding them. "Yeah, yeah, ten pence is fine," he said hurriedly.

The same sinister smile stretched her lips, and after her head fell back to the pillow, she drew him close, thrust her lips to his, clenched the shaft of his cock, and slid it through the soggy, tepid slit between her legs.

* * *

At Crown Point, where the cold water of the East River lazily washed the stones that lay at the shore, rested a lonely timeworn stone and brick building. The northern and southern chimneys were cracked and barren of bricks, and the wood frames were splintered, coated with chipped and faded paint. Each of the four lower and four upper windows on the broadsides were as sullen and sunken as the eyes of a dying old man. The lone doorway was narrow, with a slight arch at the sill suggesting a most unwelcoming frown. At the southern end a decaying, brown willow threatened to collapse onto the structure at any moment. The northeastern corner was littered with the thick vines of the weeds that had crawled along the stone to greet the deep green moss that had nearly covered the roof. Wildflowers had mostly overtaken the stone footpath leading to the doorway, and at night, the flickering lanterns within the windows cast the ghoulish gaze of a late October jack-o'-lantern. Inside, the old, musty air was filled without joy.

Mr. Douglas Gordon was a hardworking man, a man who was unashamed to express the adoration he felt for his wife, son, and twin daughters. Mr. Douglas Gordon was as devout as any Blessed Puritan in the New World and honest and charitable as any man, anywhere. He was soft-spoken, often agreeable, even when he didn't agree, and particularly mild in manner. Mr. Douglas Gordon was stricken with a condition that restricted all his efforts at restraint. Despite all the cruel realities about him and despite the souls that relied on his nourishment, he could not stop disappointing. His sickness made it truly impossible for Mr. Douglas Gordon to practically express the love he had for his family or to manifest his philanthropic wants. He was a man with a solid heart and a weak will.

The hardened, musty scrap from an old sail was quickly thrust from atop his face. A metallic grommet nearly cut his left ear as the cloth was ripped away. A flash of blinding sunlight reflected from one of the carefully placed mirrors at the ceiling to burn his eyes, which had been exposed to only darkness for days. He grunted and ground his distress through the heavy, damp linen, which had been tightly tied between his jaws and behind his neck. Resting on a wooden plank for so many hours caused his back to gnaw when he shifted his weight. Still, he thrust his head about, grumbling and teary all the while.

His abrasive, makeshift blanket had been removed only from his face and still rested just above his shoulders, covering his body. Though he could not see them below his cover, Mr. Douglas Gordon was latched down by two heavy, leather straps at the chest. When the intense glare was finally acceded by his watery eyes, he was overcome by the distinctive cardinal red from the waistcoat of a king's soldier who peered down at him. Mr. Gordon lay, perhaps several inches from the floor, on a crude bed of rigid, splintered pine. The infantryman grinned with a certain juvenile delight as he examined Mr. Douglas Gordon, who continued to thrash about. A few large beads of sweat met at the trooper's chin and fell as a large droplet into Mr. Douglas Gordon's right eye. After a moment, the bristly Redcoat turned his head aside, straightened his back, and threw the old sail back over Mr. Douglas Gordon's face to once again cast his eyes into familiar darkness.

As the rifleman drifted from the bound soul, his steps were replaced by those of another. Each thud was uneven as if created by one with a slow and unusual pace, or limp. With each stride, the clang of crashing wood echoed within the empty chamber, and dry floorboards screeched beneath his feet. Mr. Douglas Gordon was still with fear, wrapped within his own hot breath, which could not escape his thick linen cocoon. Gradually, and almost carefully, the cover was once again removed. As the musty, gray cloth was lowered from his eyes, the horrible image of Doctor Cornelius Van Leeuwen became clear.

Van Leeuwen's twisted, barbed fingers continued to diligently fold the old sail cloth about Mr. Gordon's neck. One of his long, sharp, fingers scraped against Mr. Douglas Gordon's gentle skin close to his cheek, nearly drawing blood. "Good morning, sir," chimed Van Leeuwen. "Hope you are well rested. I believe that was not nearly as uncomfortable as you had expected, yes?" The clear sky opened the sun to shine brightly into the large window within the eastern facing wall. The wind from the water crept through the cracks and creaked as though the old house was alive with a trace of breath. Inside, the room was devoid of furniture or design. Large, knotted oak beams ran along the unusually high ceiling, and at night, glimpses of candlelight from the second floor peeked through the many cracks and gaps. The walls were bare stone, and the floor was blanketed with dust. An old lantern hung lifelessly in one corner, though it had not been lit for some years, and any such light would find it difficult to penetrate the layer of dust and grime in which it was ensconced. Patches of abandoned, gray spiderwebs dangled about the ceiling and corners. The room was barren aside from Mr. Gordon's rudimentary bed, a few partially opened crates, a scrap or two of rank old clothes, pellets of rodent shit, and a dented tin bucket partially filled with a peculiar, dense, blackish/red fluid.

Mr. Gordon mumbled, groaned, and gagged from the strap within his mouth. "This is a bit of a shame, my dear friend," grumbled the doctor. The poor fellow continued to choke on the rag, yet the doctor refused to budge and assist. Mr. Gordon's eyes asked for mercy, but the frigid Doctor Van Leeuwen was unmoved. "No man can serve two masters," continued Van Leeuwen. "For either he will hate the one and love the other; or else he will hold to the one, and despise the other. You cannot serve God and mammon."

Still constrained by straps and muzzled by a canvas band, Mr. Douglas Gordon could do no more than writhe about and groan inaudibly.

Van Leeuwen was a ghoulish, decaying figure. His skin was drained of color; eyes were narrow jades, and his nose was long and sharp. It was familiar for him to have leaned on his well-fashioned walking stick, yet his spine was bent like a threatened cobra. Long white hair fell from his head to his slender shoulders as a cascade of streaming spiderwebs. He wore black from head to toe, as he often did. On his head rested a dark, clerical type hat, his chest bore a heavy, midnight cloak, and his feet were cast in finely crafted, black, polished, leather low-heeled shoes with gleaming silver buckles. Within the stench of dismay cast by his shadow was the faint suggestion of aristocracy.

"I am pleased to share a bit of welcome news, Mr. Gordon. Your debt is paid in full, which is to say as far as my concern, you are free to go about your day," said Van Leeuwen to the still-groveling Mr. Douglas Gordon. "Forgive me, if I may. At the risk of being presumptuous, I feel compelled to advise you to consider your decisions more wisely. Debts are slavery, which is why I tend to live without them. Our word is what distinguishes our worth amongst one another. In the end, you've come to doing what needed to be done, and I suppose you've earned a morsel of honor. Perhaps you can avoid such…circumstances such as you presently find yourself if you rely on prudence over urges. Particularly unwise is to wager money you do not have, and even more imprudent is to do so with persons whom you do not know. Nonetheless, I will not keep you to be the subject of my pontificating and moralizing. You have fulfilled your obligation here, and in so doing, regained a measure of deference."

Van Leeuwen fully removed the cover from Mr. Douglas Gordon by swiftly tossing it to the floor. In an instant, Mr. Douglas Gordon pinned his chin against his chest to see his lower body and filled the room with a deafening squeal as he cried through the fabric gagging his mouth. Violently, he thrust himself about and cast tears as though they were fired through a spigot. With dread and sorrow drawn upon his face, his innocent, big brown eyes turned toward the doctor. For a moment, he was still, stricken by disbelief, and his eyes shone like glass as they welled with moisture. He peered at the doctor with the look of complete desperation.

"It appears we are all through here, my good sir," said Van Leeuwen. "I have a good feeling you and I have crossed our only paths. In fact…" The doctor dug through the inner pocket of his wool cloak and removed a handful of coins. With his walking stick still in hand, he fingered through them until he could find the one he was looking for. "I am embarrassed to say, you overpaid me, and I owe you a bit less than a farthing." With his thumb, he casually flipped the silver *New Yorke Token* and, end over end, it tumbled through the air until it landed on Mr. Douglas Gordon's forehead with an abrupt thud. The desperate soul clasped his eyes and grimaced. The coin rolled from his cranium to his shoulder, then clanged onto the hard, wood floor.

Mr. Douglas Gordon's legs had been severed from his body. At his hips were two dried blood-caked, yellowed, soiled cotton bandages that had been carelessly applied. Blunt, blistered, raw stumps, no more than four inches long, flopped purposelessly from his waist. Inside his right thigh, a small stream of blood trickled from the stitches to a small puddle below where his hips rested. His right and his left arms had each been detached at the shoulders. Two mangled, twisted, bloodied stubs protruded from his shoulder blades. He was entirely without clothing, and what was left of Mr. Douglas Gordon lay on a solid slab of old, dry wood, soiled with the stains of his piss, shit, and blood.

Though he gasped uncontrollably, he flailed about helplessly, much as a large turtle that was tipped onto his back would do. He had been put to sleep with all four limbs, and had awakened to being nothing more than a torso and skull. When he was put under, the doctor used heavy, sharp steel to slice each of his limbs with a circular motion as if wrapping them with twine until the flesh was carved away. His bones were hacked with jagged blades to the point of allowing one of the doctor's wretched, money-whore minions to barbarically snap them from his body.

"Be well, sir," said Van Leeuwen before he respectfully bowed his head and strolled from the chamber. As when he entered, his rod and the wooden soles of his magnificent shoes clanked against the dry boards and echoed throughout in a rhythmic pattern. The beat of his strides and the groans from the unfortunate Mr. Gordon created a horrifying symphony. When he reached the doorway, the Royal sentry quickly shoveled a heap of stale, cheap tobacco into his maw and chomped away. With his chin swollen as he gnawed the repulsive weeds, he asked, "What should we do with him now?"

Van Leeuwen made not even the slightest effort to hide his condescension and shook his head in disgust. The gesture was mostly lost on the uncouth soldier. "He has paid his dues; he is free. Show him the door," replied Van Leeuwen.

The Redcoat was unsure, though he assumed the doctor was being glib. "Should I get the Grave Digger?" he asked.

"No," replied Doctor Van Leeuwen. "That is not necessary…yet. Unstrap him, carry him out to the streets somewhere. Better yet, bring him with you on your way north. Leave him in the woodlands."

"The woods?" asked the soldier.

"The woods," repeated Van Leeuwen.

Drips of brown dribble ran from the soldier's lips. "But…well, how will he get back? He can't even crawl."

"I cannot say, Private. Such as it is, bring him to the forest of the northern hills and drop him there. He claims to be resourceful, and he is a mostly honorable man from an honorable family, and I have no reason to doubt him. I trust he will figure something out. And, if he does not, he will be eaten by coyotes before the night ends. The fact remains, he paid his duty, and either way, this is not my concern, and it should not be yours."

"The Evil that men do lives after them; the good is oft interred with their bones."—Marc Antony

Three

September 1777.

The early morning air over the Hudson was bitterly cool as it swathed Captain Prescott and the other thirteen men of Nicholson's New York Regiment. They crossed the waterway on two flat-bottomed ferries, slicing the calm surface as a tailor clips a linen. The faint mists of warm breath followed along the gentle wakes of their passage. Most of the company shivered and pressed their arms into knots as they looked to keep free any semblance of warmth their bodies managed to conjure within. It was no more than unseasonably cool, yet the days before were unseasonably warm. Their deep blue wools seemed dulled by the autumnal haze floating above the water's surface. Prescott stood the tallest amongst his comrades. He was aboard the ferry with seven others, and six further, trailing aboard the second vessel. Two sturdy, yet clearly overburdened warhorses stood motionless near the center of each of the ferry transports. Imposed by heavy packs, utensils, and barrels of powder strapped on their backs, the pathetic animals appeared as though they were nearing collapse.

The band of Continental soldiers refused to be still and wobbled to and fro as they struggled to maintain their balance as the crafts were pushed forward. They were weary, yet alert, uncertain, though eager, and each, in his own way, apprehensive about their plight and their cause. Prescott was neither, he was an island of resolve within a sea of disillusion. With one arm across his chest and the other resting on his scabbarded sword, the captain proudly thrust his chin forward as if to guide their way. He was as still and proud as any majestic figurehead within the Royal Fleet.

The boys of the Dobbs Ferry Company toiled feverishly to paddle the heavy crafts from the western to the eastern bank of the Hudson River. The water was nearly as smooth as glass, a slitter of blue-gray that gently cut through the folds in a blanket of emerald and juniper. "Forward, pick up the pace," ordered Prescott with a grumbled scowl. "Give it all yer might, boys. I know you are stronger than this. You're young, bucking lads, push forward our time is pressed."

Prescott was both a gentleman and a ruthless businessman. He joined the rebellion when London began requiring oversight on all colonial currency. This, above all the Intolerable Acts, most hurt the Prescott family's fortunes and urged the captain to take arms. All the same, Prescott had never been one to let others fight for his interests. At his core, he believed the subject would settle itself in one fashion or another. As a matter of practicality, Captain Prescott saw the Rebels winning this war or the Empire yielding to the colonies demands. To him, the Revolution was as much about honor, as it was about fending off the threats to his continued prosperity.

His current charge was personally directed by Washington's trusted aide-de-camp, Major Benedict Arnold, and it was a matter of some importance. A well-renowned individual had recently landed in America, having sailed from Austria; a man of such importance, General Washington had been said to believe he could singularly shift the tides of the war. Prescott was tasked with safely retrieving him from the snug little hamlet of Hanover, a day's ride north of the city. From there he would escort him back to General Washington's nearly defeated colonial army in New Jersey. Legends of the Prussian officer Freiherr von Steuben and his unique talents had spread like a wildfire amongst the American ranks. His support for the rebellion promised to single-handedly tip the balance toward the Rebel's favor. Von Steuben offered his service, and life, to transform the American Army from a band of ill-mannered, ill-fit planters and brickmakers to an efficient, deadly fighting force. His safe travel was critical, and Prescott had been chosen to ensure he arrived safely.

The captain caught a glimpse of a small British patrol and their garish red fucking coats, a few dozen paces past the water, near the parallel running Post Road. One hundred or so yards short of landing, he peered through his brass spyglass and confirmed. "Aye, you fuckers, you fucking fuckers," he muttered. "Looks as though we are not going to be welcomed ashore by horny whores and happy wenches, boys!" he barked. "The company who awaits us aims to clip the nuts from our sacks and feed them to our sons. Load your weapons because it looks like we're going to send a few more the king's men to their graves!" A wave of energy suddenly engulfed his company, and each man scurried to load his musket and prepare for battle at Dobbs Ferry.

* * *

Far to the northeast.

Captain Pearson's company of beaten, discouraged Lobster Backs was finding it increasingly difficult to continue. Dictated by disinterest, outward frustration, and an overall deficit of morale, each of the six kept to himself. They were each spread ten to twenty yards ahead of the other in an uneven, lazy column as they slogged through the brush and over the jagged stones and harden soil at their feet. Wyandot had lost the sun some as it rose from the eastern horizon and led them miles unnecessarily eastward. Pearson suspected something to be amiss given his skilled acuity in regard to the personal disposition of the party's guide. Panther appeared to be strangely unsure. All the same, Captain Pearson saw no value in confronting his tracker, given the expected result of the potential outcomes in so doing. Quietly, he hoped and presumed Wyandot had not led them too far astray and the rest of his band remained content in their ignorance to the matter. The party pushed aside the low branches and dense brush as they tiredly lurched forward, each step seeming heavier than the one before. The uneven ground was littered with thick roots and stones that would not even allow the troop to mindlessly move along. Every stride was required to be a mindful one. Trudging through the heavily wooded New England terrain felt as though they were walking through a lake of molasses. The trees and shrubs snagged and clawed as they marched. Their stomachs ached with hunger, and their chins were covered with uneven, matted beards. Every shoulder hung low, all legs were numb, and all their feet were heavy and raw. The cumbersome packs had graduated from uncomfortable to painful; their straps chafed and scraped their skin. Only the captain appeared to be no more than mildly fatigued; though his lethargy was masked by his somewhat cleanly shaven skin and well-kept uniform. His swollen chin was tender to the touch, flushed with a purple hue, and his jaw stung every time he opened his mouth. Pearson's spoiled tongue had been accustomed to the textures and tastes of tender meat and fresh vegetables. The consumption of dried rations was a survival necessity, not a meal. By now, chomping the old potatoes, dried beans, and tough, salted meats had become a chore.

None were quite sure where they were, yet all were very sure they were hopelessly behind the initial expectation of where they were supposed to be. Faith in only a ten-day or two-week journey had long since been smothered by grim reality. Above the unfallen leaves and fingers of tree branches, the sky was becoming deep blue, still dark and flecked with tiny stars. The company was lost within a wilderness of all the brilliant colors the recurrent palette had to offer; striking reds from the sourwoods and maples' muted cider sassafras and the evergreens' shades of moss and juniper. All the seasonal beauty of the northeast was wasted on them.

The morning was young, having only offered perhaps a few hours of light, but the captain's fortitude was on the brink of collapse, and he considered ordering a premature break. From the northeast, a distant, quick blast echoed through the trees. Pearson and the others, suddenly infused with energy and vigilance, immediately halted in their tracks. Panther threw his hand toward the sky, warning the troopers to remain still and silent as he slowly and methodically peered through the shrubbery and low branches. Reflexively, each of the grenadiers cowered by suddenly crouching or lowering his back. Ahead, perhaps one hundred feet, perhaps more, the native scout noticed the faint traces of swirling white-gray smoke. Without a moment's hesitation, he unsheathed the long knife he wore at his back, then skulked forward like a predatory wildcat approaching an unsuspecting prey.

"Wyandot...hold, wait," ordered Pearson in a loud whisper. Pearson was not altogether surprised his command went unheeded, yet he was agitated just the same. Whether Wyandot Panther had not heard or had ignored him mattered not. The captain knew the instant he rushed from the bastion of Fort Ticonderoga that he was going to, in no way, manage to control his Mohawk escort. Since the moment Wyandot Panther was hired by Royal officials, only by chance had he done anything to conform to the rules of conduct required of all native aides-de-camp. Tales of his brutality and inhumanity had been valuable propaganda tools in the Americans' effort to recruit enlistments. By now, Panther was nearly uncontrollable; his effective tenacity at finding and killing Americans bought him the leniency to enable such unhesitant barbarism. Pearson's only recourse was to hope Panther controlled himself, or at the least, was too tired to do enough to jeopardize his command. Watching him stray from the company and advance into the woodlands stirred mixed feelings within Pearson. Were he true to his soul, he would admit a good part of his heart was pleased to see the savage man race toward his potential demise.

Panther shifted with a graceful swiftness as he steadily breezed over the large roots and rocks and through the shrubs and low branches. His movement was strangely silent, and he picked up his pace as he continued farther from Pearson and the others. Firmly, he held the bone handle of his jagged blade high, ready to strike and slash. The Panther was now a hunter who was in a primal trance, unaware of anything other than stalking his prey.

An unusually large, gray-brown cottontail exhausted his last gasps of life with a few twitches until finally, he came to lie motionless on the soft ground. His body rested on a gentle bed of tall green grass. The musket ball had been fired cleanly through, leaving the matted blood on his soft coat as its only trace. The excited patters of childish footsteps quickly grew louder as young Benjamin Winthrop eagerly ran to fetch the prize his older brother had shot.

"You got him!" he yelled with near disbelief as he approached the animal.

"I see it. You really don't need to yell about it," replied George, as he and their younger sister, Mary Beth, casually appeared from the shrubbery. The smoke was still steaming from the barrel of his old Dutch Lock musket, and as hard as he tried, he could not help but contain the joyful look of accomplishment on his face with an awkward smirk. In truth, it was quite an impressive shot; such a small target hidden within the tall grass and with such a horribly inaccurate firearm. Though a few years older, he was only marginally more mature than his younger siblings. For George, it had always been a matter of importance for his younger brother to emulate and admire him, just as he had with their oldest brother. With that, he was intent to maintain the perception he was completely confident in his ability as a marksman.

"Ew!" cried Mary Beth.

"What is 'ew'? That's all you have to say is 'ew?' You've eaten rabbit a hundred times," replied Ben.

"So…I don't want to eat him! Why did you have to kill it?" she pleaded.

"Now you don't want to eat a rabbit? Remember that next time Ma prepares rabbit stew. This is how it looks before he is cooked. How can we eat him if he isn't dead? You want to cook him when he is still alive? That would be worse. Or do you want to eat him when he is alive? He will be kicking around inside your belly, and he'll try and crawl out of your mouth or out of your butt. He'll crawl from your butt, and he will be so mad he'll probably bite your nose off because you tried to eat him," advised Ben.

"Ew! Stop! No, he won't," she said. "He won't crawl out of my butt."

"'Cuz he is dead," answered Ben.

"To hell—will you both shut up!" demanded George as he approached. He then asked Ben, "You know how to skin him, right? I can do it if you can't, but tell me because we don't have much left to eat and can't waste him."

"Or her," chided Mary Beth.

Both ignored her. With an odd sense of honor, Ben was proud to be considered for the task. "Yeah, I do, I remember. I can skin him, and get him ready to be cooked." He lowered himself before the small animal and poked him to see if he was truly dead, then continued without hesitation as if he knew what he was doing in regard to preparation.

Hovering over his shoulder, George asked, "You know how to hold the blade, right? Start at the belly…"

"I know, I know how" Ben replied impatiently.

"And you know how to clean his ears before you skin him too?"

"His ears? Yeah…I—yeah, I know how," confirmed Ben.

"Idiot!" exclaimed George. "You don't clean his ears. I knew it! So stupid. Let me do it before you mess this up."

"I won't, I promise," assured Ben. "I really can do this."

As George knelt aside his brother, he shivered from a cold gust, then the two boys rested for a moment beside the lifeless animal silently. The young siblings had strayed a bit far from their home in Eagle Creek. George was mostly certain he'd be able to lead them back, yet was still burdened by a gnawing sense of concern. They were surrounded by knee-high grass, which fluttered like the waves of a calm ocean in the autumn breeze. The profound nature of their collective sense of appreciation was beyond their years. Eating meat was uncommon these days, especially rabbit, and though they were not directly aware, the influence of their oldest brother and father's guidance touched them. His father's large, old beaver skin cocked hat, which George wore, despite being forbidden otherwise, continually fell over his eyes. He was frustrated, yet refused to remove it. Daybreak was quickly encroaching upon the midday sky, and they hurried their pace, to be home before their mother realized they had left.

Little, wide-eyed Mary Beth could not have been much more out of place, as she stood barely a few inches taller than the grass. Her clean, bright white, soft linen frock beamed like a light against the dull, brown autumnal grass, brown leaves, and gray tree limbs. She clutched her cornstalk doll and remained still, curious and filled with remorse as she listened to her brothers' banter.

Suddenly, Wyandot Panther burst from the foliage. His figure was the blur of a darkened shadow. In one swift blow, he knocked the musket from George's hand, flung it several yards into the woods, and snared the queue of bowed hair behind the boy's head. The old hat flew off his head as it was caught in the breeze to land some yards away on the grassy field. Panther thrust George back by the hair and snatched his left arm at the wrist. He held his blade pressed against George's throat with his right hand, and with his left, tightly clutched the boy's forearm. George was virtually paralyzed by his overwhelming sense of panic, and Wyandot held his wrist so tightly it nearly crushed his bones.

Mary Beth shrieked with fear until, feebly, George struggled with a whimper and wheeze and urged her, "Run, Mary Beth, go! Fast, run!" Immediately, the tales his father shared of native brutality, the routine scalping and flaying of Americans filled his panic-stricken young mind. He caught the image of the dead rabbit and could almost feel the cold blade of Wyandot Panther's jagged edge sliced through his skin. He was too afraid to resist and placed his fate at the mercy of hope.

Stricken by dread, Mary Beth dropped her doll and cried with horror as she dashed into the trees and out of sight. Wyandot's eyes followed her for a moment, then consented to accept, for the time being, her escape. The bloodthirsty Mohawk warrior easily could have carved George and Ben with quick slices, impairing them and freeing him to chase. Humanity did not slow Panther. He looked forward to the thrill of a good hunt.

Ben's eyes nearly popped from his skull, and he managed nothing more than to allow his jaw to fall nearly to the ground as he urinated uncontrollably. A gentle geyser of warm piss flowed into the gray-white cotton breeches he had inherited from his older brother. He was compelled to run, but even if he could muster the composure, he would not dare leave his brother to die alone. For a moment, Wyandot Panther peered into Ben's eyes and gazed so deeply it was as if he looked straight past them. He was sure to terrorize Ben, ensuring to keep his gruesome attack a personal one. Strands of dark hair had fallen over his face and were brushed back with every exacerbated pant blown from his lungs.

A grin slowly grew on Wyandot's face as he recalled the countless images of slain natives and all the inhumanity brought to bear. The Panther would see to it Ben would witness the mutilation of his brother, to infest his soul for as long as he was alive. Ben's death would certainly please the Mohawk, but the permanent scars of anguish would be a far sweeter revenge. Panther saved his most gruesome practice of brutality for occasions such as this, when he could slice through the heart of the young. Ben would be showered with George's warm blood, then forced to endure the barbaric native's act of ritualistic vengeance learned from his warrior uncle, Hawk's Shadow.

Onekwenhtara Ronkwe would require bits of George's flesh to be sliced from his body and bones to be broken and wrenched from within his muscles and tissue. Warm, meaty pieces, organs, teeth, and splinters of bone would be driven into his brother's mouth and down his throat. Panther would forever change young Ben, and in a sense, become part of who the boy would be until the day he died. The forced cannibalism would disturbingly alter Ben for all his years. The immediate scars of Wyandot's brutality would come as gashes within his bowels when he inevitably shits the jagged teeth and pointed fragments of George's bones.

Pearson burst from the woods as Panther grappled the child. The remaining members of the party followed seconds behind. Before he figured or uttered a word, the winded captain rested his hands on his knees and gasped. He took several quick pants, and between bursts of air, ordered, "Wyandot, no! What are you doing? This is unacceptable…release him, now."

All of the Grenadiers remained speechless until McAllister barked, "Panther! What the fuck are you doing? He's a boy! The captain told you to let him go. Let him go." McAllister's exacerbated demand did more to motivate Panther into slaughtering the lad than it did to sparing him. He refused the captain and pulled George closer still. Panther forced his blade firmer against George's skin, drawing a thin line of blood. The boy cried, "Please! No…please."

"They are only boys, children," Pearson pleaded desperately. "Please, Wyandot, I implore you to release him. There is no value in murdering this young boy. I'm ordering you to leave him. Do not force me into doing something to stop you."

"You are wrong, I see some value," snarled Panther. "A boy. A boy is a price for the many my eyes have seen murdered by his kind."

Pearson slowly lowered his right hand to the grip of his Duval pistol, as it hung from his hip. "Wyandot, to be clear, you will not harm this child. This is not warfare, this is murder, and I promise you, it will not go without punishment. I am required to stop you by the means of my discretion."

The threat did nothing to deter Panther, who merely smiled wryly and without a trace of compulsion to comply with Captain Pearson's order. He struggled and shifted his body after George flailed about, and he tightened his grip. Panther's veins appeared as webs up and down his powerful arm. The blade was pressed more firmly into the young man's throat and nearly choked off the wind going into his lungs. George gagged and hissed as he pushed to breathe. "There is joy in killing a boy. You know you will feed on his life energy when your soul swallows his. A boy's heart is alive unlike a man's…sweeter to the taste."

"The captain is going to order us to fire on you and we will not hesitate to do so Panther. If he dies so too will you." Sergeant McAllister told him coldly as he raised his musket to his shoulder and in firing position. "I can live with the haunting memory of a dead child if it means I can properly remove you from this earth. Even with all this misery and angst, killing you would warm my soul. Goddamn savage—murder him, cut his throat. Do me that favor. Kill him, and I'll be sure to have been compelled by duty and not by my personal inclination to bespatter your brain about this field." Pearson was taken by the soldier's callous declaration. He had not expected such rage from the impressionable young soldier. All the same, the Captain felt the warmth of satisfaction.

The more Pearson and McAllister challenged him, the more Panther was driven by spite.

He drove his blade farther into the boy's tender throat. George began to gargle and choke on his blood. "You know where we are?" asked Panther.

Pearson and McAllister turned toward one another with the same confused look on their faces. "Do I what?" asked Pearson.

"Where are we?" continued Panther. "Where is it that we stand? You know where we are, how to journey by the stars and the sun? You know where is south, you know where is New York? You know how to trap or hunt, what berries and bugs you can eat and what berries and bugs will kill you? Do any of you know these?"

Pearson glanced toward his colleagues, each of whom remained silent. He hung his head. "No, Wyandot, I don't. I don't know any of those things. None of us know any of those things."

"I know you don't," groaned Panther and he pulled his blade closer, into George's neck. He turned to completely lock his eyes on Ben, who was nearly petrified with horror. Panther carved and sliced from side to side, forcefully driving the knife's jagged edge through George's flesh. His expressionless gaze remained fixed on the younger of the brothers. It was likely Panther reveled in the poor youngster's sense of dread, yet offered no clues of emotion. Blood erupted from the boy's neck and spouted into Panther's face. Panther held still, even as his eyes, nose, and chin were washed with the warm fluid. George thrashed about violently, splattering thick, current about his dull, unbleached linen shirt, worn trousers, and the faded green grass at his feet.

On the bank of the Hudson.

The miasma of powder was still fresh within the air as the last traces of smoke whisked away in the gentle wind. Prescott's company lay scattered along the riverside. Some moaned feebly, others rested still and silent—all are bloodied and beaten. Both the flat wooden ferry boats glided lazily, just off the eastern bank of the river. The hulls were cracked, splintered, and beset with damage. The remains of each young man from the Dobbs Ferry Company drifted along the watery surface like leaves fallen into a pond. It had not been a battle, but a massacre. Prescott and his unit expected to engage the disciplined force of king's men, yet their enemy was far more ruthless, sinister, and ruinous than they, or any, could have imagined.

The brave Continental officer led the charge valiantly, but was shot on his right side about his neck, shoulder, and hip. Before he could fire a volley, he was overcome by a hailstorm of lead shards that tore through him and his men. He was hardly upon the shore when his body failed and was nearly lost in the tall grass, the placid waves of the river washing against his boots. The beaming sun was cast into his eyes, though he could hardly see through the haze of his blurred vision. Slowly, in dribs and drabs, blood was seeping through the torn flesh on the side of his neck, and he could do no more than desperately groan. Prescott had accepted that he had met his end.

The trouncing of heavy steps approached, and he could make out a dark grayish figure, with shiny, glass eyes which shimmered with the sun. It was faceless, cloaked in gray, and it snarled as air was thrust through a thick tube latched about his mouth. It blocked the sun's glare as it hovered over the captain. Prescott's body was cooling rapidly as the warmth of blood escaped him. The captain's body was dying, and his mind was absent of thought. This was not a Royal soldier who happened upon him to practice the custom of benevolence extended a fallen enemy by swiftly ending his life after the battle. An angel, or perhaps a ghost but an agent of the afterlife to carry him to eternity. It snatched Prescott's wrists and tried to heave his body from the water, toward a small pile of bodies, some thirty paces closer to the road.

As it tugged, Captain Prescott's right arm nearly gave as the bone was completely removed from the shoulder. He grunted with agony, and the gray trooper refused to let up, twisting and yanking his flaccid limb. Skin and flesh were stretched, nearly to the point of being torn, yet the gray figure stubbornly pulled with vigor. Prescott was bothered to near madness. He felt only the intense pain, helplessness, and confusion. The figure was a drab blur within the blinding light of the sun as it yanked Prescott's body several feet along the ground, repeatedly crashing his skull against the hard surface in so doing. The captain was too heavy and too mutilated to be moved enough to be heaved onto the mound of fallen men. For a moment, it yielded, became unsure and frustrated. It turned toward the road and the line of mounted Redcoats as though it was seeking instruction.

"Leave him. He can stay where he lies," commanded the crimson-arrayed cavalryman who was positioned amongst a small unit of soldiers on Post Road. After a moment of inspection, it turned back, then scurried back to the heap of lifeless and injured American soldiers piled on the embankment several yards from the water's edge. It snatched one of several tin cans that had rested off the road and hurried back toward Prescott's position. He doused the captain with a cascade of lamp oil. Prescott's face was engulfed with the oleaginous, oily fluid. He groaned with pain as it scorched his eyes and inflamed the open wound at his neck. "You…fucks," he gasped through a wash of oil and saliva. As though it was going to be his last, meager breath, he pushed to speak, "Fuck…your king. He can suck the piss from my cock."

The gray trooper appeared entirely disinterested in Prescott's attempt at honor or insult, gave him a glance, and continued toward his company of gray troopers. From behind, another blurred gray figure replaced the one who had disappeared. Prescott was only able to distinguish broad shapes and general color tones, yet by this point could realize a dark shadow and glimpse of quivering light. Prescott belted such a discordant scream it nearly cost all the life from him. He was swallowed by a blaze of fiery flames that instantly raced about his body. His skin blistered into a gurgling patch of molten muck. His eyes burst like boiled eggs. The proud, blue Continental uniform was scorched, incinerated with his bones and body. Though his lungs slaved to choke in the smoke, they were quickly seared as he inhaled the flames until he was unable to breathe. It was a hellish horror until his fate was finally met with the benevolence of death. Less than one day after being trusted with his consequential task, Captain Prescott's charge ended with his life, incinerated on a knoll, alongside the banks of the Hudson River.

From Post Road, several dozen yards from the waterway along the high ground, five mounted cavalrymen held their posts. Each was cloaked in particularly brilliant red coats and sat tall and confidently in their saddles. They were spaced what seemed to be precisely fifteen yards apart, overlooking the river and the activity of the gray troopers. Lieutenant Harris was flanked by two of his comrades to his left, and two at his right. The look on his face offered no joy, dismay, discontent, or satisfaction. Battlefield victory had become routine. Harris's conquest at Dobbs Ferry was merely one of countless others, and he had come to see no emotional value in the outcomes of combat. His cold eyes surveyed the carnage as though he was taking inventory of his enemy's loss. Along the ground, the gray troopers toiled to gather the remains of the Americans, the living and the dead, into one pile.

"Hold! It seems he is not altogether badly hurt," Harris snarled as one of the gray troopers stood above an injured colonial. "From what I can see here, he has only superficial wounds—his leg? In any event, the others are dead, or certainly soon will be. Regardless, I cannot see better alternatives. Take him…carefully. Bear in mind, we need him alive. Act as though your fates are tied to his."

In the woodlands, north.

Carelessly, Panther tossed George to the ground and watched as his body twitched weakly. Dark red blood was pumped through the gash in his throat and rained on Pearson, who abruptly threw himself to his knees doing all he could to help the dying boy. Awash in blood and driven by distress, Pearson could do no more than desperately cover the wound with his hands by choking George's throat. Holdsworth, Browning, and St. Claire could manage no more than unsteady composure as they observed the display in horrific disbelief.

After a few moments of continued struggle, Pearson came to accept the futility of his efforts: The boy's departure was inevitable. His hands, neck, chin, and uniform were soaked with scarlet. He held himself on his hands and knees above George's lifeless body with his eyes secured to the boy's unwavering dead stare. George's eyes were eerily still, unmoving, as though they were glass balls plastered into his skull. The captain's rumbling heart broke the tense silence, and he was unable to utter a sound.

Browning offered slight condemnation when he docilely uttered, "Captain?"

Pearson turned toward the corporal with a bewildered and desperate look. He was stained with a child's blood, overcome with guilt, grief, and rage and knew it was critical to suppress each feeling and stay within the limits of pragmatic reason. Wyandot Panther towered over Pearson and the remains of the innocent, young boy. As commander, he was moved to act on the behalf of expediency and rationality. Killing Wyandot Panther would have saved Ben's life and satisfied a number of feelings, yet doing so would have served no purpose but ensuring the party's failure. He considered men of his ilk, lineage and standing are obliged to make the difficult decisions. Pearson did so without yielding to the simplicity of emotion. The boy was an unavoidable causality.

Panther's steel was coated in warm blood, and his repulsive look of contentment tore through Pearson's bulwark of conscious resolve. At any moment, the rush of wrath-infused adrenaline was going to thrust the normally measured gentleman to irrationally charge the hardened, burly murderer. There would be no contest of brute force, and Panther could easily toss the softened statesman as though he was blowing the petals from a dandelion. Pearson's hands were unfamiliar with force, while Panther's were as hardened and calloused as the stones at their feet. Understandably, the captain's good senses overruled his rage.

Sergeant McAllister was as measured and composed as one could expect. In terms of practical reality, he was now in charge. Loyal to the chain of command and unwilling to neuter Pearson in the presence of His Majesty's soldiers and the native tracker, he did not outwardly question his superior's indolence. However, he was not willing to allow Pearson's weakness enable the massacre of another child. "Go!" he demanded of Ben. "Run, boy! Are you a fool? Go— go away from here now!" He waved him away furiously.

Ben was trembling, without any self-control, and yet unable to gather himself to rise to his feet and flee. His panicked state caught the discerning eyes of a hungry predator, and Panther slowly began to creep closer. McAllister threw his hand forward and demanded he remains in place. "Don't you dare fucking move! I don't care a-fuck if we roam these woods until we die of starvation. You *will* be shot down, Panther." Wyandot hardly shifted his eyes in McAllister's direction and continued to inch closer to the cowering boy on the ground.

"Let's see him home. Make sure he arrives safely and notify his family. It is the decent thing, we owe them this much," declared Holdsworth.

McAllister lowered his head, "You know we cannot do that, Holdsworth...Save we kill the Indian."

"Son of a bitch," grumbled St. Claire, who leaped before Ben, grabbed his coat behind the collar, and hoisted him to his feet. "Do you want to join the other? Get out of here, boy. Save yourself— run!" Lightly shoving, he urged him to be on his way, but the overwhelmed child did not flee. He remained stricken with fear, too afraid to move.

Panther did no more than grin. "Yes, run, boy…listen to them. Do not shiver in your fear, run fast. I am already bored of this and have no wish for you to die today." Ben's eyes were as wide as the valley's greatest lake, and he could do no more than keep them fixed on his brother's butcher. Coolly, Wyandot opened his hand and allowed his blade to fall to the grass at his feet. "You are either a fool, a weakling, or you wish to join him. Now, run away," he pleaded calmly.

St. Claire clutched young Ben by the wrist and forcefully yanked him forward several yards. "I am not going to tell you again, lad. If you want to live, get away from here. Go—go!"

"A waste of time," uttered Panther. "The soft heart of the American is only brave when in large number. The boy is bred to shit himself. He does not have the mind to save his own life, for that will mean he will have to fight another day." With that, Ben found enough wits about him to scurry as fast as he could over the grassland and into the trees. He panted and huffed mightily as he pushed his muscles beyond their limits. Though by chance, he was heading toward his home, in the northwest, he was charging aimlessly.

The company remained still, eagerly awaiting Pearson's inevitable order to kill Wyandot Panther. The sinister, tangled trees and tall grass stood as witness to the carnage. The quarter moon had yet to seep into the day, as though it was intent to observe from the pale-blue sky. Though it was not even a minute, it could have been a year. Pearson appeared lost within a feverish state of anxiety. Every man's conviction to honor was tested as each sought to fire a musket ball into the slaughterer's skull. Private Holdsworth held his head low and slowly approached the fallen child. He knelt beside his remains and began to whisper the Lord's prayer. The remaining troop stood without intention.

Panther was as curious as he was amused. "Why do you do this? Why do you speak to the dead?"

"I am praying for him, Savage, not speaking to him. All souls require our prayer, and with them, they enter the Kingdom of our Father. For the wages of sin is death, but the free gift of life is Christ Jesus our Lord—yet, I'm not sure any amount of prayer can save you. I would consider hell to kill you for this rather than to pray for your soul."

"You speak of the gods, then?" asked Panther.

"God," corrected Holdsworth. "I am calling on God. There is but one. The trees and the wind are not gods. They are *from* God, not to be bowed before. I, the Lord your God."

"I have seen this. You pray for the souls of the men you kill? Why kill them, or why pray for them?"

"Sinners need our prayers more than anyone," replied Holdsworth. "The Americans reject the Church, they reject the will of the Lord and the king. I am a soldier for His Majesty and Our Father who has put him on his throne. I don't know why the Lord has included you as part of all of this, but I have faith in Him. I pray for the Americans because they need my prayers."

"Your god has made him…your captain? This is not a wise god," grumbled Panther.

"The Lord is beyond our reckoning. He has chosen our captain, and we do not need to understand, we only need to accept it. I am humble as to question the Lord, yet I cannot see now why our captain will spare your life."

"You are such fools. He is a coward, and you do not see this. Some god has made your king a king and this coward your captain. He is a coward, a coward surrounded by warriors. You follow him because a foolish god told you to, but he is nothing without you. Fruit rots without its skin. Why would I want my spirit to live among this god who makes cowards leaders of men if I have to beg him and have others plead to him?" Panther grunted. "You say we are the mindless ones. Fuck your god—fuck him."

Holdsworth's will was on its last thread. He was ready to take the bait and charge Panther, honor be damned. Pearson managed to slowly rise to his feet. He was at a loss for words, actions, and emotions. His underlings did not respect him, he had no control over Wyandot Panther, and his indecision had by now, cost several lives. He knew all if this, and he knew the entire party knew all of this. Though he accepted these truths, his only choice was to press on and ignore reality in favor of perception. "Private Holdsworth, Corporal

Browning, bury the body. And do it quickly so we can be on our way. We still have our orders."

Panther could not help but offer Holdsworth a look of complete gratification. Both the soldiers were astounded. McAllister and St. Claire quickly glanced in their direction, and Panther subtly nodded his head and pressed his lips, surprised, though quite satisfied. He bent his back, swiped the blade from the ground, then cleaned the blood off with his breechcloth. "Your commander gave you an order," declared McAllister. The duty-bound sergeant was not without reservation, yet understood the grand scheme of their charge, and his respect for the tradition of command and loyalty knew no limit. "I know you heard the order," he said as he turned toward Holdsworth and Browning. "We are not leaving this child to be picked apart by the vultures and crows. Put away the stupid fucking look upon your faces and bury the goddamn body!"

"This is fucking unreal," uttered St. Claire just under his breath as he turned toward Pearson. "Captain, what the fuck are we doing here?"

McAllister's eyes quickly became alive with rage. He immediately turned his attention from Holdsworth and Browning, then stormed toward St. Claire. "I'm sorry. Did you just challenge the captain, Private? I cannot believe you are stupid enough to address an officer in the King's Army in such a manner! Surely I was mistaken."

St. Claire was instantly submissive, though confused. "No, Sergeant. I was…I don't know, you don't have a problem with any of this?"

"It does not matter if I have a 'problem with any of this.' What *does* matter is the problem I have with treason," replied McAllister. "Our duty is to follow orders, not to question them. Our thoughts, concerns, and opinions are meaningless. Our job is to do, not to think—that is always how it has been and that is how wars are won. You should know this…If you have a problem with *that*, our code requires me to address it; I will shoot you dead, here, now." He was torn with a sense of denial. McAllister's disapproval was weaved within his declarations of unquestioned duty and blind loyalty to authority.

The tension was unbearable. McAllister had just lost most of the respect he had for Pearson, was as eager as any to have killed Panther, yet was true to the words falling from his mouth. The oars of all rowers must follow the same rhythm, or the craft will drift aimlessly. Should the need to trim the trouble-making soldier ensure this, then so be it. Order was critical, and he was experienced to know chaos would doom them faster than starvation or enemies. St. Claire did not wish to challenge McAllister, yet would have a difficult time following Pearson any further. The standoff remained non-violent, though threatened to escalate with the most insignificant misspoken word.

"Thus far, we have marched into the bowels of the land without impediment," said Pearson from a distance and without emotion in his tone. Each of the men became baffled and still. "Thank you, Sergeant. You are a quality soldier and a noble Englishman," he continued. By this point, the irresolute leader was acting as a thespian from one of his favorite performances. In truth, he felt no command of the party and no confidence in himself. By this point, his only recourse was to act. Pearson knew it was best to move ahead, for if he remained fixed in this battle, he would lose focus on the next. "And…you are not entirely wrong; normally I would consider the formal charge of mutiny, though, these are trying times and… unusual circumstances. Like you, I will question my actions here and mourn the soul of this boy and the tragedy which befell his family, but not today. Today, I seek only to survive so that I may live to reach the general in New York and to complete what has been required of me. I assume you all agree this is the priority. We must trust there will be a time when proper correction and recognition for all who are deserving of either. Perhaps the day will not come when we see such things, yet if we ponder this now and do all we can to separate the right from the wrong, it would have all been meaningless, as we surely will not survive. We need Panther and we need one another, and I will not allow our differences or judgments, as vulgar as they may be, to divide us now. Consider the upheaval wrought by the misguided will of the Americans as the murder of this child…and many others. Such is the result when proper order fails…We are going to refocus all our efforts to the task before us, as we are bound by our responsibility to the king, our country, and our honor to reach New York."

Each of the Redcoats looked about at each of the others, as if awaiting another to say something, to say anything. Yet, all remained silent. For the time being, it appeared Pearson managed to keep the party together, yet the seeds of discontent had been sown. "Let's get moving and not waste such daylight," prodded Pearson. Both Holdsworth and Browning were completely chagrined, yet obediently followed the command given them. Holdsworth snatched one of George's wrists and Browning the other. The two struggled as they heaved the remains of the lad forward along the ground. Private Holdsworth fought to keep his stomach from turning, yet felt he was going to vomit at any moment. As they dragged the lifeless body forward, it painted a brown and red trail of blood along the grass, until George's skull clanked awkwardly against a large root. His head, which was attached by mere strands of flesh, was thrust sidelong under his upper back, hoisting his body several inches from the ground. The stretched skin, which had been holding the head to the body, nearly gave, and George's head was virtually separated entirely from his shoulders.

"Ugh, good God," groaned Holdsworth, who immediately dropped George's hand and retched bile from his effectively empty stomach. Once again, the green young trooper lost himself and vomited uncontrollably, then clenched his arms about his stomach, bent his back, and spewed acidic chunks on the departed. Fluids and digested bits seeped into George's open neck and mixed with his blood and entrails.

Pearson was disgusted and felt himself following in kind. Reflexively, he overreacted by harshly scolding the soft private. "Holdsworth, for Christ's sake. We can't have this. Not a minute ago I made our priorities clear. You are going to have to find some fortitude within you and lose your tender nature because I am not going to let your delicate sensibilities slow our progress. This is not a knitting circle; this is war and all its inhumanity. You are Grenadier in the Army of the British Empire. You need to get a hold of yourself." In a sense, the captain appreciated the innocence which had not entirely been lost with the private. Still, Pearson was compelled by an overreaction to save his own composure, demonstrate hardened leadership, and somehow shift the collective focus from the unfortunate episode involving George.

Panther giggled with delight, while the others grimaced in disgust. McAllister was both annoyed and sympathetic as he rested his hand on Holdsworth's back in a halfhearted attempt at comforting him. "It's fine," he said. "I'll take him."

"I'm sorry," muttered Holdsworth through a spew-glistened pout. "I don't want to be a burden."

"I know you don't Holdsworth," replied the Sergeant. "Please, just...get out of the way."

McAllister and Browning continued to haul George's mutilated remains toward the tree line, where they would search for soft ground. The remainder of the party continued several dozen yards from the scene of the incident. Wyandot Panther lurched forward and snapped the boy's old and worn Dutch musket from the ground. From the corner of his eye, he spotted young Mary Beth and her great big green eyes peering back at him from within the forest of blades of tall grass. Her soft, pristine white gown shuddered with the breeze. Her lids refused to blink, and her heart pounded as though it was going to leap from her chest. Panther turned to his left, then to his right, as if assessing the attention of his comrades, but none seemed to be aware of her, or to be paying him any mind.

Panther peeked to the ground to catch a glimpse of the smiling face on her cornhusk doll. He remained fixed for no more than a few seconds before he glanced about his party once again. His British cohorts were too involved in their own activities or anguish to give him any notice, or more simply, they refused to accept the reality he was still alive. Quickly, he knelt low, snatched the doll up, and hurriedly flipped it toward her. It flew over her head until it landed some yards behind, where she remained cowering. With such a delicate whisper he could hardly hear it himself, Wyandot murmured, "Sweet dreams, girl," as he strolled toward the slain rabbit to fetch what would presumably be his dinner.

The sky offered no suggestion of rain, yet, in the distance, faint rumbles of thunder announced the coming of another autumn storm. The wind picked up, as did the whooshing sighs from the leaves. The two senior men, McAllister and Browning, continued to struggle and plow George's corpse over the unyielding ground. A sense of anxiety began to fester within the pair as both looked about the ground frantically for a spot of giving soil. As the thunder claps grew louder and nearer, Pearson ordered the two to abandon their effort. "We'll have to leave him, woefully and without dignity, yet we have no other recourse. The weather will not allow further delay. We must press on."

"Humbly , Captain, I think we can bury him without much time. Please, sir, it is the least we can do for this soul," pleaded Browning.

Pearson appeared grim, and the notion of another challenge to his authority thrust a surge of angst through his body. He remained speechless, as simply, he was wholly unsure how to respond with the proper balance of resolution and empathy. Fortunately, his trusted aid McAllister seemed to find the right words for the moment. "The best we can do for his soul is to free it from the obligation of forgiveness through our token gestures of decency. There is no such creature as an honorable fiend."

Browning released his grip on the boy's remains, and it appeared McAllister's declaration resonated with the whole of the party. Solemnly, yet hurriedly, the company once again began to head southward. St. Claire moved ahead swifter than necessary, several yards ahead of the others, as though he had no desire to be within the group. Holdsworth kept his head low with shame as he dragged the butt of his musket along the hard forest ground. Pearson was trailing and moved with such deliberation as if he was seeking to be lost, left behind. Wyandot, with the Dutch Lock firmly in hand, pressed ahead without any care. Ahead of his tracks was George's large beaver skin hat. It rested snugly within the green, sage blades and spots of blood. Through it all, the boy's father's hat still shone as if it had never been worn. It was taut and clean, nary a wrinkle nor scrape of dirt, only soiled by a lone blade of grass, which rested on its brim. Panther's heavy foot trampled upon it as he trudged forward. It was pressed into the grass, collapsed and encrusted by the mark of Wyandot's foot within a seal of mud.

* * *

Dedrick Hereen and his dedicated valet, Lars, sat on the wagon's bench and peered straightforward, as if they were each alone. Lars was hardly one to initiate conversation, and Dedrick was simply too tired to converse. The silence was stolen by the muted rumblings of distant thunder. The sky was suddenly dark and the air brisk and ripe with the smell of fallen leaves. Clouds muted the rising sun, which flickered between the nearly leafless trees and into their eyes as the cart was pulled forward. Because Lars demanded too much haste from Cole, the empty wooden wheels jolted horribly against the hardened path. The travelers were eager to get home, to eat and rest as they wished, without company, in their own beds. Now, with the river on their left, they continued once again, along the familiar Post Road.

For a moment, Dedrick considered breaking the stillness, as he was overcome with curiosity regarding a matter that had recently come to his attention. Inappropriately, Sally had shared some thoughts, which is to say, tales with him that had reached her ears regarding Dedrick's burly and mostly quiet chauffeur. Without offering much in specifics, she suggested Lars typically elected not to directly engage with Sally's peers while a guest at The Inn. Rather, Lars instructed his female companions to become involved with one another while, aside from occasional groans, he observed silently and stroked his unusually large penis. Rumors were furthered along with frustration, as his escorts were only teased by glimpses of his gifted endowment. From what Sally had gathered, at least as soft voices suggested, Lars had developed an affinity to having a stream of warm urine wash his bare chest. At times, he had required his companions to drink very specific teas, which he recognized as producing the most desirable piss to flow from their slits. It had also become acceptable for a few stray droplets here and there to find their way into his mouth. It had been several miles and over an hour, and Dedrick had yet to get the matter from out of his head.

"So, Lars, let me ask you," said Dedrick.

"I will, sir," replied Lars with his usual absence of charm.

"You, um, you like our stops, right? Or would you rather we just get to New York and then home again as quickly as possible? That is to say, we don't have to always go…where we go."

"'Tis fine, sir," grumbled Lars as he peered straight ahead with seemingly no interest in advancing his thoughts. "We can stop."

Dedrick's face became a bit animated, and he felt as though he may have actually cultivated the seeds of a productive conversation. "Right? Good, I am glad you do not feel put out. I know you are very particular about sleeping in your own bed, which you are pretty sure to have it facing north-northwest, in your own room, and that you make sure to eat the same breakfast every single morning, at the same time, at the same table…

I can appreciate such things; routines are comfortable. It would be nice to bring them with us on our travels. So, let me ask you this: what is your feeling on piss?"

Lars's character held steady as he grumbled a response, "I'm sorry, sir?"

Dedrick was playfully frustrated, yet amused all the same. "How do feel about piss, uh…urine. Do you…enjoy being around urine, or…no? Generally speaking, do you like piddle? Let's say, for whatever reason, I had a bottle of piss, and I offered it to you. Would you say 'no, thanks,' or maybe, 'that's great, thank you. I love this stuff?' If you had a choice to be near piss or not, what would you choose?"

Strangely, Lars appeared visibly uneasy as it became somewhat clear where Dedrick was going with this line of questioning. "I… relieve myself when I need to, sir. Not before then."

From this, Dedrick learned what he required to know and decided to free Lars from his state of unfamiliar embarrassment. "Right… well that's good Lars. That was, more or less what I was trying to get to. Good…I hear it can cause problems to wait. Good."

Both were, in their own ways, sullen and tired, yet not entirely eager to end the journey. The two were approaching the village of Dobbs Ferry, no more than half a day from their home in Tarry Town. Jeremiah Dobbs had settled the village when he incorporated his ferry service to and from the Palisade Cliffs. Evidently, British war planners recognized the same value as young Jeremiah had a generation prior. The typically restful parish had been fouled with earthworks, bunkers, and redoubts. The boots of His Excellency's throng and the hooves of their beasts had blemished the normally pleasing countryside. Dobbs Ferry was a humble community, though not without charm. Sturdy log and red-brick folk houses overlooked the Muh-he-kun-ne-tuk or *The River That Flows Two Ways*.

From the north, the heavy gallop of warhorses announced the arrival of two striking British soldiers, festooned with magnificent red jackets. A thick, tawny cloud of dust seemed to push them through the smothering brush and trees aside the path with ease. Their tall, Tarleton riding helmets were as dark as the midnight-black stallions they sat upon, and the soft rays of the covered sun beamed off the metallic ornamentation worn about the riders' chests, nearly blinding Dedrick as they neared. A curious suspicion propelled Dedrick to nervously press Lars at the shoulder and order him to bring the carriage still. Cole whinnied as Lars pulled the reins close, and, from behind, the screen of dust almost immediately engulfed the oncoming wagon and riders.

Both cavalrymen were uncommonly composed and sat uncommonly tall; these were not the typical rank and file of the royal officer corps. A gold-covered plaque at their chests depicted cross swords and blackened stone crown below the Roman Numeral IV. Dedrick, who was quite familiar with the empire's fighting forces, aside from the rank insignia, could not recognize many of the symbols and regalia upon their uniforms as any such Royal regiment in America. The lead rider shifted his horse toward Dedrick's direction, and his sturdy and towering frame blocked the cloud-covered sun as he neared.

Within the mingling billows of dust, Lieutenant Harris pulled his beast, Windstorm, aside the front of Dedrick's carriage, less than two or three feet from where Lars sat. The mist of the swarming dry dirt was soon washed away with the breeze to fully reveal the man before them. He was an abnormal sight to lay eyes upon. Harris's left ear was a flap of blistered hide stuck to the side of his skull, his chin, down across the right side of his neck, was peppered with raw, pocked skin and dried blisters. One could be fooled into believing the British soldier was half covered in wet oats or porridge. His mouth appeared stretched where the upper lip met the lower, as if he were snarling like an angry dog showing her teeth. Below his jaw, near the leftmost side of his neck, traces of heavy stitches remained as dry scars leading to a calloused hollow of withered skin revealed a trace of his jawbone left exposed. As he gripped the knob of his old saddle, Dedrick could not help but notice his right hand had only a thumb, two fingers, and two suppurated nubs. The various horrendous wounds and grotesque disfigurement would seem to suggest the trooper had survived the apocalypse.

Harris's narrow, obsidian eyes surveyed the traveling companions and the contents of the mostly empty wagon bed. He remained expressionless, almost as in a transfixed state, and did nothing to reveal a hint of any tell that may have suggested his thoughts or concerns. His voice was ghastly and plain in tone. "You are friends of the king, or are you agitators?"

Predictably, Lars remained silent, calm, and too unaware to have been unsettled. The officer's disfigurement had Dedrick a bit unsettled, however, as his eyes were virgin to the ghastliness of war's remains. His assumption was the soldier endured some manner of horrific battlefield wound, or perhaps, several of them. He tried to coyly work an extended glance, without seeming to do so. "We are not sympathetic to the rebellion," he answered. "We are loyal to the Empire and King George. I am Dedrick Hereen, an associate and personal friend with Governor Tryon. This is my secondary, Lars, and he's loyal to whichever my loyalties may be. We have no business with the Rebels, sir. I don't wish to continue without knowing whom I am speaking."

Harris offered no suggestion that he had heard Dedrick's claim and continued to silently scrutinize both men. He was direct, uncordial, and with his gape unflinchingly secured on Dedrick, he continued, "You are Tories, then?"

"No," replied Dedrick. "Not exactly. I do not look to limit myself within a political label. However, I do not view killing one's countrymen over a political disagreement to be particularly noble, so I am understanding to the party's position on this matter. I'm a merchant; a fur trader, specifically. My enterprise has done well in part due to the protection of His Majesty. Instability and upheaval are not good for business, at least not for mine. In fact, as we speak, I am wasting time better spent on more productive affairs. Now, my apologies for seeming abrupt, if there is nothing further you need from us, Lieutenant, excuse us so we may proceed."

Harris appeared unmoved. "Would you agree it wise to wear the red ribbon of our American friends?"

Dedrick turned to Lars, who was typically stoic throughout the exchange. "Hmmm," he mumbled. "I think he's right. The fucking red ribbon, Lars…The red ribbon. That's is I knew I forgot something."

With a twinge of desperation, Lars replied, "Red…? You never had a ribbon, sir. I have never seen any such ribbon."

Still without revealing a thought, Harris slowly nodded his head, then turned toward his similarly scarred cohort, Lieutenant Murray, and coldly ordered, "Get the Mole Rat." Murray nodded his head in affirmation, kicked his steed below him, and waved the reins angrily. His horse hurried, though not urgently, back, northward along the same path from which they came. The trots faded to share the distance with the rolling thunder. Dedrick sighed with annoyance and became instantly impatient. "Jesus! What are we doing here, Lieutenant? Aren't there any Yankee Minutemen somewhere you can shoot? You want to search my cart, is that it? Would that make you feel good? Go, please, enjoy yourself. Please hurry, though, as I would like to beat the rain. I have a few empty sacks, a couple of barrels of nothing, some fucking salt, some apples—I don't know, what else is back there, Lars? You remembered to stow Paul Revere in one of those crates like I told you to?"

"No, sir, when did you ask this?" replied Lars.

"Lars, it's fine. Listen, Lieutenant, as I stated, I am an acquaintance of the governor, as well as other such influential men around these parts. Typically, I maintain these relationships by not troubling them with petty concerns, thus they know when I do express a problem they should consider the matter with the weight it deserves. With that, I would hate to bother them regarding this…affair."

Harris was too steady and disciplined to react, and yet seemed oblivious as Dedrick became more agitated. Really, Dedrick's tone mattered little to the lieutenant, who was looking to neither escalate tensions nor to be polite. The lieutenant simply gazed into the trees, fixated on the trembling red and gold leaves. From time to time, his eyes would glance in Dedrick's direction, yet he remained mostly uninterested in him and more so in Cole.

"Your claim has the character of an ultimatum, sir," uttered Harris.

Dedrick caught himself amid his diatribe. "How is that?" he asked.

Harris was no longer interested in continuing the discussion. "This is a fine-looking stallion, congratulations."

Momentarily gracious, Dedrick sighed. "Thank you, Lieutenant. That is very decent of you to say." For a glimpse, it appeared tensions had settled to a degree.

From the north, Murray returned with another horse and rider tethered to his mount. His escort sat atop an old brown mare that lazily trotted alongside Murray and his nag. Like the other soldiers, McBrain was clad in a cardinal coat and adorned with the same unfamiliar medallions and insignia. He appeared to be a far older chap than his comrades, with long streaks of stringy white hair that dangled in knots from his riding helmet. His skin appeared cracked, pale, and wrapped tightly around his skull. Folded, dry flaps ran from his chin to his chest, as if they were frail pilasters hardly able to hold his head to his shoulders. McBrain was an infirm-looking figure who appeared to exhaust all his energy as he clung to the saddle's horn. His body bounced with each stride and seemed on the verge of toppling over and onto the road at any moment. Murray moved ahead and guided with a heavy rope tied to McBrain's horse's harness as though it was a leash. The clanks of both animals' trots grew louder as they neared, and as they did, Dedrick's impatience changed to uncertainty and then fear.

Lieutenant McBrain gasped desperately with each breath as his lungs struggled to capture the cool air. His elderly face appeared without eyes. Beneath his bushy, dull, silver brows were scarred cavities sunken within his skull. Stark, thick clefts of skin ran from left to right across his face above his eye sockets. Dedrick could not help but gawp, without regard to manners. McBrain was not only an extraordinarily old-looking trooper, he was one who had no eyes.

"What is this?" asked Dedrick with a shaken tone. His agitation had immediately shifted to concern. "What is going on here, Lieutenant?"

Harris waved Murray toward his direction, then received the leash to easily tug McBrain and his horse closer. Murray pulled himself aside and positioned his warhorse toward the center of the path, looking southward. His weapon was secured sturdily behind him at his left flank. When his mount came still, he reached for his long Dragon musket and rested it on his lap. The firearm represented the highest quality in craftsmanship within all the royal armory.

"Mister Hereen," replied Harris. "Like you, we have matters that need our attention, and just as you claim to desire, we seek to put down the uprising swiftly. The Ministry is funny in that they expect us to take our responsibilities seriously. In so doing, you and others may endure mild inconveniences from time to time. Perhaps you can draft a letter of grievance to Mr. Washington of Virginia, whom I believe is somewhere in New Jersey as we speak, though I am not entirely sure. Until then, you can make this easy for all of us by answering the fucking questions without trying to be funny. Please, continue telling us about your friendship to the governor."

Dedrick was tense, though not intimidated nor completely impatient. "Very well. *Friends* may be a bit generous, mind you. *Friendly* is perhaps more accurate. I am an associate to the governor, that is to say we share common ventures. Point being, Tryon is loyal to the king, and I see you as the good guys in all of this. If you will forgive me, I would prefer to offer no details on my relationship, as they are of no consequence, regardless."

"You speak in a riddle, sir," replied Harris.

Still outwardly frustrated, Dedrick realized mentioning the governor's name had been a miscalculation. only serving to further Harris's suspicion. "I speak in riddle," he repeated. "I suppose I'm being vague. This subject affords me very little liberty, and...for our purposes here, I suppose you have to trust me. I am loyal to the Throne. I abhor this rebellion and reject its cause. I do not see a break from the Empire as anything other than treason and a break from the Church as anything other than profanity. For my part, I am doing well here in America. I can provide for my family to the point of affording luxury…I'm a known friend of the Empire. My name must be among your records. And I have no motivation nor inclination to promote disorder. I have offered quarters, stores, and horses to the king's forces and wish you the best in your endeavor to suppress the uprising. Clearly you can see, I carry no contraband nor any evidence to suggest otherwise."

McBrain kept his head tilted back, remained silent, and appeared to observe the exchange through his tiny nostrils, which flared at the end of his long, crooked, hooked nose. His frame was skeletal, slight and lanky, and his brilliant red coat hung on his narrow shoulders like the flying jib of a clipper tied to port on a windless day. His corn nibble teeth were a drab yellow. They appeared as autumnal sunflowers planted within a bed of ash, contrasted by his pale, gray skin. The struggling muscles in his neck could hardly keep his dome from quivering like a pebble during an earthquake. Each breath was as deliberate and as forceful, as though it was going to be his last.

With his crown pulled back, he sucked the air through his fibrous hairy orifices at his nose like a fish swallowing gulps of water into its gills. All the men's eyes stayed fixed on the ghoulish soldier, waiting for him to utter a sound. He gasped deeply and strained to urge the words from his lungs, "Traveler…you, uh, are a—I say, your breath smells of twat," he said. "Your breath smells of the twat of a heavy young woman, Mister. I can smell twat, and I smell Tuesday on you."

Immediately, Dedrick spun toward Harris. "What the fuck?"

"You…you are loyal to His…?" asked McBrain through a fading breath. The archaic bastard whistled each 'S' through his gums, as though he were a newly hatched spring chick.

Dedrick was confused, frustrated, and outwardly dismissive. The question was clearly a silly one; a question which had only one answer. Only a fool would claim to be a traitor, and an even greater fool would make the claim while surrounded by armed officers in the King's Army. "His Majesty?" he corrected. "Yes, I'm not a traitor. Once again, I am not sympatric with the rebels. I am not sure I can be any clearer on this. I've heard the provincial royal offices have been covered in letters of complaint regarding the conduct of your brethren. Apparently, I have heard correctly."

Once more, charging his feeble old lungs with a deep gasp of wind, McBrain continued, "Your heart...it is racing, my...little lad. What, sir—I say, what, sir...what is the nature of...your, your business today?"

At this point, Dedrick turned his attention toward Harris, who had been idle. Perplexed and increasingly vexed, he asked the lieutenant, "Is it really necessary to continue this inquiry?" After Harris offered no suggestion to the contrary, he continued, "My business today, is that I am heading home, north. That is my business today."

"Ah," groaned McBrain, and then pressed further. "You live north, do you? Do you, uh, do...Where in the north?" He paused and took a moment to catch some wordless breaths, then appeared a bit frustrated at his failing mind. "Apologies, I seem to be, uh, I'm having some troubles here. That is, I am sorry...give me just a..." He paused another time for a moment, then glanced about aimlessly as though he sought some assistance. Harris became uncharacteristically irritated and was hardly able to mask the frustration about his face. McBrain was an old warhorse, one who had figuratively seen his best days long ago. Still, he had a strong heart, and the old man pushed on. "Is that—It is a woodchuck, over in the field there? A squirrel or a wood...or I think maybe woodchuck eating grass or grain, right? Ah, all right, so you...do you have—you understand...I say...you have loyalty to the Monarchy, you say?"

Dedrick was doing his best to remain calm, yet impatience, hunger, and weariness seemed to be getting the better of him. "You had trouble thinking that question through? My answer is the same, I do not support the Continentals. I am not a dissident nor a mutineer. I carry nothing linking me to the Rebels, so yes, I'm loyal to the fucking Monarchy. I plead with you to release us so we may continue on our way. Your persistence to ask me the same questions in different ways cannot be a productive means of seeking whatever you are looking for. By your leave, good sirs, I would like to get the fuck home."

By this point, Harris was no longer amused, but perplexed and concerned. There was no mistaking McBrain's failing state of mind; however, the lieutenant was not aware it had reached this point. Still, he decided to offer his elder comrade the benefit of the doubt.

"Ah, he is a rude one," grumbled McBrain. "Rude, yes…and smells of twat."

"Rude, perhaps," quipped Dedrick. "I offer my regret, Chronos. I did not wish to become hostile toward you. I do, however, tend to act this way when I find myself in ridiculous situations."

Finally, Harris entered the exchange, "I find it confusing for one who attests to be loyal to our king to find such a request to be ridiculous. Certainly, you value our diligence in rooting out his enemies?"

"I'm sorry," sneered Dedrick. "Are you really suggesting this is not ridiculous? This decrepit, wrinkly, blind fuck introduced himself by telling me I smell like Tuesday—"

"And twat," added Lars.

Dedrick shot Lars an exasperated look, then continued, "And twat. You trust his opinion on this, his judgment of me? If this is the diligence required to uncover Rebel sympathizers, I should expect the Rebels to win this war before the sunsets."

Without losing his calm disposition, Harris looked toward McBrain, who was exhausted and seemed to quickly lose the fortitude to remain upright on the back of his steed. "I see…I see, no…reason not to let them pass." The old man once again lifted his head and sucked the air in through his stringy nose hairs. "Aye, yes, they…they are no trouble to us at all, Lieutenant Harris. He's a foul little muck-spout, but not our enemy."

"Thank Christ," sighed Dedrick.

Harris gestured Murray forward, and the two cavalrymen trotted aside Cole and toward the front of Dedrick's cart. Windstorm whinnied as if greeting Cole, who silently glanced, then swatted his tail about. Harris and Murray essentially pinned Dedrick and Lars toward the side of the path, just a few yards from the tree line. Lieutenant Murray tugged McBrain closer by drawing on his leash. The old soldier mumbled under his breath and nearly fell from his saddle. Through the commotion, Harris gestured Murray to urge Cole a bit farther off the path by thrusting his head toward the direction. "Press him over more, onto the grass."

"What's going on?" asked Dedrick. "He said we are not your enemy—did you hear him? Tell him, Grootpapa. You said I'm a fucker, but we can be on our way. Why are you not allowing us to pass?"

Harris calmed Dedrick. "I know what he said, Mr. Hereen. You are free to go, sir. Because you are in fact, an enemy of the rebellion, we are considering your well-being. I can strike you down without effort, yet I am not, thus you are free to believe me. Wait for our contingent to pass before you proceed."

Dedrick no longer challenged his confinement and oddly, immediately trusted Lieutenant Harris. His interest grew as he heard stomping hoofs and creaks of wooden wheels against the hard, rocky road ahead of him. The rumbling was escorted by the thunderous booms overhead as it slowly approached, the clocking strides measured and the crawling wooden carriage wheels sounded as if they were rope-bound pulleys struggling to lift the weight of an elephant. As the procession neared, Murray could not help but inch himself farther from the center of the roadway. At one point, his warhorse bumped against Cole, until the lieutenant managed to pull him ever so slightly away. Still, he made sure to keep himself as far from the pathway as he could manage.

From within the shadows of the maple and evergreens appeared a cavalcade of mounted soldiers, ahead of a horse-drawn wagon with an open bed. The brown, dry leaves along the clearing parted to the left and to the right of the pathway. A thin line of brave foliage remained in the middle as the party moved forward pulling through it. Narrow, twisted branches stretched desperately toward the center of the road as each fought for the sunlight. The peaks of the great pines stood atop the bed of emerald, where it met the pale blue and gray foreboding sky. Two lead riders wore dazzling red jackets over and crisp white vests and equally crisp white breeches. Their tall headdresses were adorned with glistening pewter ornamentation, and each and every one of the many medallions and buttons shone like mirrors. Both the mounts were magnificent, muscular brutes, untarnished with the typical scrapes and cuts found on breeds of British warhorses. These were not the common men of the king's command.

Behind, a rickety old wagon was pulled by two, grayish Percheron horses who plodded along ungracefully. The cart was flat, with low sideboards, rusted hardware, and short, spoked wheels. Two men, a driver, and an armed escort sat on the bench atop the carriage. They appeared as stone statues within the ruins of a classical city, fully clad in dull gray. Neither displayed a semblance for any of the king's regiments, no rank insignia, nor sign of military affiliation. The pair wore only plain gray. Heavy cotton, dark-gray hoods draped from their backs, over their skulls to nearly cover their faces. Thick, tall glass cylinders covered their eyes and made them appear to be owls or some other nocturnal bird of prey. Long, brownish hoses hung from their mouths, where they appeared to be held by a series of buckles and straps. A hard leather muzzle was clasped at the nose and mouth. From this, the breathing funnel was clamped. It snaked down, toward their side, where it dangled near the toe board and swayed as they rode. Their breaths were flushed into the apparatus in heavy gasps like a winter's wind. Not a scrap of skin was exposed; leather gloves were met at the wrists by tightly wound bands, their ankles, each dressed with bindings, the same. Under the heavyweight cloaks that hung from their shoulders, their bodies appeared to be wrapped as the preserved remains of the Pharaohs of the ancient world.

As they passed, the driver purposefully turned his neck toward Dedrick, who could not help but scrutinize the passing convoy with dreadful curiosity. It was a nightmarish sight, one which would surely haunt him for some time. Within the dark cloak appeared a devil of sorts, a man whom he would have believed born of the undead. Beneath each of his heavy glass eyelets was a white globe within a sea of baneful darkness. The Phantom Trooper cast an air of dread as the stench of sour meat stung the nose. A shiver of terror ran from Dedrick's neck along his spine, until he turned away.

Behind the ghoulish soldiers sat a sole, badly wounded Continental infantryman. He rested atop a mound of straw, which was nestled toward the front of the wagon. Forlornly, his body leaned against the grayed sideboard and bounded, carelessly, as the wheels clashed against the path. His right wrist was hastily bandaged with loose strips of blood-soaked linen, and his heavy cobalt coat was tattered at the right shoulder. The wound was obvious, even partially concealed by the heavy cotton of his jacket. The wealth of the grapeshot pellets landed on the right side of his skull. A full half of his face was a lump of sagging meat, pocked with gashes and holes. Below his cheek, his flesh was ripped apart to expose his jaw and teeth. One slug had blasted into his temporal plate, nearly lodging itself into his brain. The most apparent damage was caused by the ball that blasted above his cheek, just below the right eye. His zygomatic bone was fractured, and his eyeball sank into the cavity of his skull. The lead pill bore all the way through, into his mouth, from where he swallowed it as his body crashed to the ground. By this point, the colonial soldier was numb to the pain and apathetic to the specter of the continued torture he presumed was to wait for him.

Trailing the cart was another. Like the flatbed before it, the enclosed carriage had a rider of the Phantom Regiment at the reins, though no other. The bed was completely covered with heavy, gray wood planks. Only a small, barred window at the back within the gate offered any clue as to what could be inside. The two horses tugged it along, and it creaked and clanged as if the contents within were rather heavy. Dedrick shifted his head about his shoulders as he was trying to peer through the wooden boards, a needless reflex driven by intense curiosity. He could not help but imagine what horror could have been loaded into this wagon. His assumption was the cargo was a troop of soldiers, Redcoat or Yankee, yet so gruesomely injured the image of such would have haunted any passerby.

Harris held his right arm firm as the convoy passed. He warned Lars and Dedrick, "Stay back. Wait until the line is nearly out of sight." For a few moments, the riders and wagons rumbled along the path, southward. The growing claps of thunder accounted their arrival, and the dim fog cast by the impending storm followed them along the sky. The Hudson's surface had darkened and stirred with anger. The gentle hills were blanketed by the storm clouds' shadows, and a cool, penetrating chill filled the air. Now, the fallen brown leaves on the path wafted in the wind as though they were looking to flee from whatever happened to be inside the enclosed wagon. The shadowy convoy of wagons and gray soldiers rolled slowly past Dedrick's probing eyes. He could not help but lean back on the bench, away from its direction, as the last of the wagons rolled some distance southward.

"You would be unwise to speak of this, Mister Hereen. Matters nothing to me regardless," said Harris, who then bowed his head respectfully. "Let's go," he ordered as he and Murray kicked their mounts, yanked the reins, and slowly galloped southward.

"We are setting out, hold on," said Murray. To which, McBrain clutched the saddle horn and prepared. Murray held the connecting line lightly, as if trying to ease Lieutenant McBrain's horse to proceed gently. He followed, and the three trailed the others, southbound along Post Road.

Without expression, Dedrick turned to Lars. "That was… something. I suppose we can go," he said. "Are you alright?"

"Indeed," replied Lars, who offered no indication of concern nor wonderment as to what had transpired. He merely whipped the reins and grunted, "Yah!"

As expected, Lars gave the episode not a single thought. His excesses in goodness and naïveté were made up by his deficit in wit. In some sense, Lars was blessed to understand the world in overly simplistic terms. He was serenely ignorant of his personal shortcomings, unburdened by bigotries, envy, spite, and humility and free from worldly concerns. There had yet to be a night in which Lars struggled through restlessly. The sight of disfigured men and ravaged bodies would do nothing to change this. Conversely, Dedrick could not help but give the incident most of his attention. The unfamiliarity was troubling from many avenues. Hitherto, he believed to be kept abreast of all the events and actions of the Royal forces in America. Perhaps his web of friendly connections was not spread as far as he understood. He tried to place the unit markings, contemplate the contents of the covered wagon, the Empire's procedures on hauling the wounded or deceased, and most pressing, the account of the ghost-like soldiers.

For a moment, his weariness and homesickness yielded to his uncertainty and fear. Lars once again tugged at the reins, and Cole began to pull forward. The bench bounded on its springs and the cart lurched along. After a second or maybe two, Lars yanked back on the reins suddenly, prompting Cole to halt. "Whoa!"

Dedrick had a confused look on his face when he asked, "What happened? Why did you stop?"

Lars poked his chin forward, toward the right side of the path before them, as if he was gesturing for Dedrick to follow with his eyes. "You see?" he asked.

Just off the road, at the base of a beautifully golden-leafed honey locust, sat a fleece, tawny and white chipmunk. Tiny black eyes were hardly above the tip of the grass. His mouth was furiously nibbling, and his back was straight as an arrow, as though he was excited to watch the traveling companions pass. After a few seconds, driven by disinterest or fear, he dashed back from the pathway into a bushy patch and out of sight.

* * *

North.

More than a few beads managed to escape the clouds, though the rain mostly held through the starless night. A thin layer of gray mist blanketed the damp ground, and the air was still and silent. It was late morning, and the company was once again on the march. Their chins had all become covered with uneven beards, their clothes were rank and matted with muck, their feet were swollen, and their resolve was setting to escape them. Still, the captain managed to hold the party together only enough to continue and press forward.

Pearson hiked several yards behind Panther and several yards ahead of the pack. McAllister shadowed him, just to his left. As was typical, the only sound to reach their ears was the constant trampling of their strides, the clanging of their packs, and a rare moan of some sort of displeasure. The Ben and George incident was not more than a day past, and the specter of the boy's lifeless body kept his ghost very much alive in their minds. Each man had his own feelings on the matter and yet, those feelings remained undiscussed. For his part, McAllister elected to suppress his instincts and remain devoted to the respectable traditions he held close to his heart. The diligent trooper would not allow his festering hesitation to influence his determination to loyalty. Perhaps with the assistance of denial, the sergeant willed himself only to see the upstanding qualities in the company's superior leader.

No longer interested in the droning silence, McAllister offered a conversation. "Sir, to be candid, I have to say, I was a bit concerned when I was selected for this expedition. Forgive me. While I was assured I would be in good hands, I knew little more than your name. Well, I could not help but ask of you to the men in your unit, and I am glad I had. From what I gather, you have been selected to lead this charge because you are an incredibly gifted artillery officer, that is, as per the troops under your command."

"I should only forgive your candor, Sergeant. I would expect a responsible soldier to prepare and educate himself prior to any undertaking. Your assessment, if honest, is flattering, Sergeant," replied Pearson. He grimaced and threw his open hand toward his tender, swollen, off-colored chin. It was becoming increasingly difficult to chew and speak through his broken jaw. "Though, unfortunately, not altogether accurate. I was chosen because I was expendable. My contribution, if you will, was wasted at Ticonderoga because we were desperately short on powder and more so on balls. As it is, the mighty guns of Fort Ticonderoga are nothing more than a pretense of power. Guns without powder and balls are as useless as those who command them."

"I see," sighed McAllister. "That still does not make you any less talented. Nobody doesn't get the reputation among the men he serves without having quality. We talk—we know who is a fraud and who is not. I've heard about the Battle of Brooklyn. They say each shot you fired from sea killed ten Yankees and four more horses. The Hessians are not easy to impress, and well, if they have respect for you, so too do you have mine. You say expendable, but I think Bell would not risk this task to a soldier he did not trust, a soldier he did not feel would succeed."

Pearson grinned coldly. Though his aura of arrogance and condescension was unmistakable, he was not a man who relished flattery. In fact, Pearson mostly saw verbal praise as meaningless. No question this was a manifestation of his hardened upbringing, where compliments were as rare as precious gems. "Nobody *gets* the reputation," he corrected.

McAllister responded with a silent, confused look.

"You said 'nobody doesn't get,' which is a double negative."

"I'm sorry, sir?" asked the confused young trooper. "Double negative?"

Pearson paused and considered how to reply, "Yes, nobody doesn't is akin to everybody does…*Nobody* doesn't meaning, no one does not…Think of this as math. Adding two negatives equals a positive, thus phrasing two negatives, such as 'nobody' and 'doesn't' equates to a positive outcome. You see?"

"Umm," grumbled McAllister. "Sure, sir, yes, yes, I see what you mean. *Nobody gets.* An embarrassing mistake, sir."

"Mistakes are learning tools, Sergeant. Nonetheless, it seems the tales of my exploits are exaggerated." For a glimpse, Pearson became fixed in proud recollection until he found himself. "We timed our fire with the waves to aid the trajectory. When we listed portside our guns were raised. It's not important. We were effective and we won the battle, this is true. Regardless, if the fables of my actions were accurate it would do us no good where we are, wandering aimlessly in this forest."

"You are being modest, sir," assured McAllister.

"And you are being unreasonably kind, Soldier."

"Well, I do not consider myself to be of simple mind, and I believe you are qualified to lead us to a successful operation. Nature chooses who will lead and who will follow. You were born to command, to be in charge. A leader is a leader, whether he be on a ship or in the middle of the woods."

"I didn't mean to insult your understanding, Sergeant. In fact, you are quick in mind," replied Pearson. "I am merely suggesting… Nothing. I don't know what I was trying to suggest. I appreciate your, um, faith."

Panther paused for a moment, surveyed the land around him, and then looked up at the sky, trying to gauge the sun through the clouds and consider his bearings. He shifted his attention back toward the others and growled out, "Come…this way." He began to trek toward his left.

The sergeant looked at Pearson and softly and carefully asked, "We need him, don't we, sir?"

Peering straight ahead, the captain replied, "Yes. Yes, we do."

"Not killing him had to have been a difficult decision to make, sir. I am sorry you had to make it."

Still with his gaze fixed ahead, Pearson replied, "That should go without saying, Sergeant. I mean that literally. It was more difficult than I believe, even you would understand. It was also a decision I want to consider as infrequently as possible, and we are not going to discuss this further. We'll leave it with leaders being born."

"Indeed, Captain" confirmed McAllister.

The two men walked nearly side by side, sharing an awkward silence for another dozen or so yards. "Hold, Wyandot!" commanded Pearson. "I think we need to get off our feet. We will stop here for a few minutes." Panther turned his back and predictably offered no inclination he had heard Pearson, nor that he cared if he had, until he began to slowly plod his way back, toward the rest of the contingent. The party emerged from the woods to a treeless dew-glistened meadow of some size. It rested on the base of rolling foothills and revealed a glimpse of the early day's sun not directly to their right. The low mist was chased away by the dulled rays, and the cool air was finally beginning to warm. The clear water of a shallow creek twisted through the field a few dozen yards to the west. This was a welcome sight to the men carrying increasingly light canteens. It was not a particularly opportune time for rest, yet given the day's break, the prospect of a fire and long-awaited tea was a strong possibility. By chance, perhaps, it was an ideal spot, and it seemed to be met by the shifting winds of good fortune. Almost as if the sky was rewarding his decision, the clouds were yielding to the light of the sun. For the first time, in some time, Pearson felt optimistic.

Buoyed by this swiftly uncovered good faith, the captain's swollen jaw seemed less painful and his mood seemed almost cheerful. "Now," he said to Sergeant McAllister, "let me offer you something to distinguish yourself from the likes of rabble of most men. The image we choose to portray to the world is a window into our character. Just as the poisonous snake is scaled in yellow colors, he is telling the world who he is. Yes, of course, we 'get to know' one another, yet this is tedious and wasteful, and in spite of the prejudice within us, dictating our will to feel a certain way based on the appearance one presents. If we know perceptions become reality given the innate superficial tendencies of human nature, why rely on the rare inclination otherwise? We need to appear not as how we feel we are at the time, but how we wish to be. As an example, here: our firearms. Your musket is no different than any others, it is made of the same wood and is branded by the same proof marks. What separates yours from all the others is how you present it. Like everything about you, the musket is an extension of your person. What type of man would let his weapon rest on the ground to be soiled with dirt or mud? Though it may fire just the same, it gives us a clue as to who he is."

"Hmm. I see what you are saying, sir," replied McAllister. The sergeant was not an aristocratic or judgmental young man. He was, like his father and like his father's father, a craftsman, a hard-working carpenter. Like them, he gave little thought to society's social hierarchy, the coming and going of politicians, the fancy nobility, or the success or failure of others. He was honorable, honest, dedicated to his country, and content to be content. The McAllister clan had done well given to the acceptance that men such as Isaac Pearson sat on a cathedra, and men such as the sergeant sat on stools. Perhaps superficial perceptions mattered in Pearson's world, but they had no place in Sergeant McAllister's. Still, in accordance with his good manners and general respect for his captain, McAllister indulged him. "Yet, let me ask you, if you will: How can we say in this instance the man's gun was not covered in mud through the course of a battle? Perhaps the mud shows him to be an active participant on the field and not a lazy oaf?"

Pearson was impressed not so much in McAllister's assertion, which was a bit simplistic, but in his interest in exploring the discussion from varying perspectives. He struck the captain as being intellectually curious and interesting. "Clearly the mud or mess may have been caused by countless reasons. You may very well be right, on this occasion, our instinctual predisposition may mislead us. And this will be the case from time to time, yet, if we explore this in mathematical terms, it will occur far less often than not. In other words, most of the time, the soldier will have a filthy weapon because he is an indolent, lout…or a lazy oaf. This is natural, and yet we find it necessary to force our behavior against our better instincts. I would ask, when you see a snarling dog showing his teeth as foam gushes from his jaws, do you take the time to empathize with his perspective, to understand this dog beyond a superficial level? It is far more practical to rely on prejudice than not." He removed his scabbard from his sheath, and yet again, ran through the various steps of his routine before taking rest. "I plan to never use this in all of my life," he continued. "Yet, for as long as it is in my possession and while I can control its state, the blade of my bayonet will remain untarnished and as sharp as a razor."

Throughout the conversation, Pearson surveyed the crew in an attempt to gauge their perceived opinion on his decision to break so early in the day. St. Claire stood tall, cracked his back by twisting his body left and right, while Holdsworth and Browning lazily fell to their feet, surprised, though not upset to take such an early respite. A glimmer of certainty grew upon McAllister's face as he was reassured by Pearson's relaxed nature. Even after the explanation, Pearson's ways made little sense to McAllister. The impressionable young soldier was more mature than his boyish expression would have one believe, yet he was not fully relating to Pearson's assertion. Fitting as such, as Pearson, who acknowledged acting from perception, had treated him more as a schoolboy than a capable sergeant in the Twenty-First Queen's Royal Artillery. McAllister learned early in his life to open his mind and emulate the habits of those he deemed successful. The others only saw in Pearson a coward born into privilege, a minnow swimming within a pool of sharks. McAllister saw a superior mind they did not understand. The sergeant continued, in a half-hearted manner, "Well, sir, I am bound by honor to tell you, I can't speak for the sharpness of the edge, but can for sure, say it is a bit dirty."

Clearly, McAllister was hoping to further tear down the boundary of soldier and commander, or even become friendly with the captain. Pearson chuckled patronizingly and had a difficult time maintaining his uncaring demeanor. In fairness, he recognized it was he who began the discourse and blurred the appropriate line between them. "Were you not the one who claimed to have a problem with treason?" he quipped.

"Very good, sir," replied McAllister. "I am going toward the water. If you will, I will wash the blade and take your canteen to fill, sir?"

Captain Pearson knew the river water would not properly polish his blade, yet recognized the young soldier, for reason's unknown, emulated his commander and sought to be helpful. He dug through his fine, soft leather pouch and retrieved a small cotton handkerchief. It was a white and red headscarf, embroidered with simplistic floral designs. The item had a bit of emotional value to it, as it was a small gift given to him by one of his students. Pearson saw it fitting to pass it along to McAllister who, in this sense, was a student as well.

"It'll be one less thing for you to worry about, Captain," explained McAllister.

"One fewer. Thank you, Sergeant McAllister, you are a young man with potential. I appreciate our exchanges—now, if you will forgive me," replied Pearson. "It may be some time before I have another opportunity at tea. I do not wish to appear rude, yet, drinking tea and reading Shakespeare are pleasures I tend to enjoy alone, and undisturbed."

"Say no more," uttered McAllister. With that, the sergeant carefully accepted the folded neckerchief and held the base of the blade with his right hand, rested the steel in the palm of his left, and lowered it onto the cloth with as much care as he believed Pearson would see fit. It was silly perhaps, yet McAllister wanted to believe Pearson was sincere and this was a not a trivial matter, but one of importance. The blade and the task had a special meaning to him now that he was invested in its care. As he strolled westward, toward the flowing waterway, between the intermittent smudges, McAllister caught his blandished expression looking back at him against the steel bayonet. After an awkward moment, he realized Pearson had neglected to pass him his canteen. He paused and gave this a bit of consideration, then concluded to continue without disturbing Pearson. For now, Pearson's canteen would remain dry.

From the northern tree line, some fifty paces ahead of them, a crackle echoed throughout the field. In an instant, Private St. Claire's neck erupted with blood and flesh as a lead ball blasted its way through his throat. A bolt was fired into his neck just below his jaw and another at his right hip. The force of the blows threw him from his feet, four or five yards back to the ground. The exit wound at the base of his neck was torn through. Pulpy, wet, pink nubs of meat were tangled within his long, light brown hair. The trooper's breeches were tattered instantaneously, and his hip became covered in a dark red blotch. With each gulp for air, showers of blood pumped out the back of his head. In less than a blink, he found himself thrashing about in a sewer of blood. His arms helplessly clasped his neck, until after only a few moments, he became still other than faint dying twitches.

McAllister turned and raced toward the brush about thirty feet behind the company. He leaped over the creek, landed clumsily, and collapsed headlong, tripping over his own feet. Reflexively, he threw his arms frontward, all the while gripping Pearson's bayonet. The near razor-sharp blade tore through his abdomen as he crashed to the ground. It had run through his stomach, nearly severing his spine, and pressed his heavy red coat upward. McAllister's body jerked about wildly, and he screamed in agony.

A screen of powder smoke whirled in the distance. What seemed to be nearly twenty armed figures emerged from the cloud and advanced toward Pearson's company. They halted, and in an organized column, raised their weapons to their shoulders to make ready for another barrage of fire. Wyandot Panther was stirred into a primal trance. He hunkered low, removed his old warrior's dagger from its leather scabbard, and darted back to the direction in which the band marched. With a quick stroke, he flung his blade into the soil, where it landed like a spike. Without a trace of panic, he pulled his pack from his back and retrieved his old Mohawk hatchet, tossed his pack aside, snatched his dagger from the ground, and lurched his way into the woods. Like a shadow in the rising sun, he disappeared without a sound or a trace, swallowed by the dense forest.

With empty canteens in hand, Browning and Holdsworth were casually heading toward the stream. Both jumped within their boots, startled by the sudden clap of gunfire. The corporal tossed his head from side to side, noticing his musket resting on the grass some thirty yards from where he stood. Realizing they were outgunned, in an untenable position, he threw himself to the ground. In his panicked state, he caught a glimpse of Pearson, who had tossed aside his teapot and utensils and staggered for his musket. The reality of impending doom had set into Browning's subconscious mind just as his conscious mind told him Captain Pearson and his charge were unworthy of the risk to his life. In an instant, he sprang to his feet, let his tin canteen fall to the ground, and tore into the woodlands beyond the creek. With his back facing his comrades, he sprinted with all his might into the trees and away from harm. Holdsworth held his head low as he shouted, "Wait! What you doing? You can't!" Then, after a moment of confusion, he followed in kind. The wide-eyed young private knew he was deserting his unit, yet by this point, bravery and conviction succumbed to Pearson's ineffective leadership.

From his position, Pearson remained small as he furiously crawled toward St. Claire, whose mouth was spewing blood by the bucket. The fallen soldier whimpered with the faint trace of life within his lungs. A volley of musket fire buzzed overhead. Taps and ticks clattered as the balls splintered branches and whipped through the leaves. With air thrust heavily and rapidly in and out of his lungs, Pearson kept to the ground. St. Claire's face resembled a melon, fallen from a wagon. The whites of his eyes were as gleaming as polished pearls as they peered straight through Captain Pearson. For a moment, Pearson felt himself rising to his feet and thrusting his arms above his head, yet the urge to surrender was lost the moment his eyes caught his elegant, leather pouch as it rested a few yards from his reach.

With lightning speed, he snatched the leather pouch from the ground and threw it over his back. He then grabbed St. Claire's shoulder strap and heaved it with all his might, trying to drag the soldier to the tree line. The immense and nearly insurmountable struggle to drag one hundred sixty pounds of St. Claire while remaining low to the ground was well beyond Pearson's stamina. The private gasped and despairingly flailed his hands, smacking Pearson in the face repeatedly. The captain lifted himself to his feet, arched his back as low as he could bear, and yanked him forward with all his might. The more Pearson tugged, the more intense the flow of blood gushed from behind St. Claire's neck. The soldier's body left a thick trail of blood atop the grass, and he was heaved along. The militiamen charged closer, stood tall, once again took aim, and blasted another round in Pearson's direction. A volley of musket balls hummed over them, one hurling the captain's hat from his head but somehow missing his skull. Captain Pearson collapsed to the ground, landing on his backside. He became frantic and unfocused, looked about wildly, and was unable to make a decision. The sound of the militia commander barking his order to reload and make ready prompted Pearson to take action. Intuitively, he released St. Claire from his grip, jumped to his heels, and soared toward the woods with every bit of energy he had in him. His legs felt as though they were as heavy as iron, yet he forced them forward with increasingly more effort. Heavy gasps nearly choked his breath, and his pack rattled and bounced against his back. After nearly seventy yards or more, he leaped into the heavy brush and landed forcefully on the solid ground. Landing directly on his left shoulder, his arm was stung by the rock-solid terrain. All his fingers were numb, and his arm felt limp, almost lifeless. His body was quivering like a feather in the wind, and his lungs were pumping air furiously. The militiamen seemed to be growing as they neared. His eyes remained fixed on their approach, yet he felt he had exhausted all the energy within him. His charge was the priority. Pearson refused to listen to his muscles and the voice of reasoning, which urged him to surrender himself and turned again to charge into the woodlands.

Low branches and brushwood whipped against his face as he dashed through the forest. His chest became heavier with each gulp; he did not look back and had no idea where he was heading, yet dared not slow his breakneck pace. After more than a hundred yards, he tumbled over a large fallen tree and burrowed himself underneath while lying on his front side. The captain's legs had nearly given out, he was on the verge of collapse, and despite all his will, his body would not allow him to continue. With his chest thumping wildly, he was breathing so briskly his lungs felt as though they would burst from his body. Through his panicked state, Pearson hurriedly and desperately shoved some leaves and dirt over himself, and the movement caused a shock to race through his right shoulder. Spending all the might left in him, he slowed his breath.

A dozen paces perhaps fewer before the tree line, the militia band slowed to a halt when they reached St. Claire and the British packs and weapons that were piled about on the grass. Fortuitously, they seemed to have little interest in pursuing the captain. Content to have disrupted the band, and to have killed at least one Lobster, the militia unit methodically harvested the remains of Pearson's company. One by one, they lowered themselves to pick at the abandoned packs and weapons that lay scattered. They were a rag-tag bunch. Gruff and dressed not in uniform. A few were old men, perhaps beyond fifty years in age, others were boys. As they carved up the spoils of their conquest, they relished in the victory. The group was a pack of jackals tearing at the carcass of a lion. The unmistakable look of satisfaction was collected upon their faces. None had understood nor particularly cared about the consequence of their victory, but killing any number of Bloodbacks was satisfaction all the same. They tittered like foolish young boys and carried themselves without the dignity of honorable European warriors. One playfully jabbed Pearson's un-bayonetted musket into the chest of another, who feigned death and fell to the grass, with a juvenile look upon his face. Whoever this band of misfits were, they were not of the Continental Army. They were not under the command of General Washington.

Sergeant McAllister was facedown, moaning weakly, surrounded by a puddle of his own blood. The blade had carved him up rather viciously, and he had by now nearly bled out. His spine was nearly in two, and his small intestine was sliced; releasing acid brown liquid within his bowels. A few of the colonials stood over him and observed the horror and disgust with only disinterest. They wore ragged attire, gray and brown coats, dirty, floppy hats, and heavy leather boots. These men were not disciplined soldiers, nor did they abide any code of military honor; they were farmers, smiths, and carpenters. The carnage of war was unable to govern their cruelty. Though their cause has been born recently, these were not fledgling warriors. They had been told, by leaflets and broadsides, pamphlets and papers, by their neighbors and by those who claimed to know better: the Redcoats were butchers and the Patriots heroes. The English began by slaughtering their kind in the streets of Boston, and since then, they had graduated to freely raping, pillaging, and taking as they willed. They had no regard for the Americans, and never would. These men had been told the king merrily watched it all with a shit-chomping grin drawn about his fucking face. They had been told, time and again, the Empire had no use but to exploit the Continentals in the manner the Continentals exploited the Negroes. Their simple minds had been marinated with the Patriotic propaganda of Rebellion, and as a dry sponge tossed into a puddle of water, they soaked all of it in.

"What do we do with him?" asked a boy amongst them, his pubescent voice cracking with uneasiness. The deep green and dark blue banner of the Green Mountain Boys fluttered lazily in the gentle breeze, held sturdily against his shoulders.

"We will put him down," replied his father, the infamous militiaman Ethan Allen, who was standing by his side. "We cannot help him; we can only end his pain and extend him the Lord's mercy —if he deserves it, I cannot say." He lifted his old, flintlock musket toward his shoulder and placed the muzzle directly on the back of McAllister's cranium. Quite noticeably his hands shook, and he squeezed his eyes closed forcefully. The cast iron barrel rested against the sergeant's skull for what must have been ten to fifteen seconds. Through his agony and desperation, McAllister feebly pleaded for his life. He was hardly able to muster a sound and was enveloped within his blood and sense of doom. "Sirs," he cried through splats of blood. "Please, sirs, please…"

The name Ethan Allen was a chilled wind that had swept through the northern woodlands as an apparition of doom. He and his craggy troop had done more to prolong the war and infuriate war planners in London than the might of all of Washington's men. Commander Howe had uncharacteristically defied traditional conduct when he issued a standing order for his generals to bring him Ethan's head and only his head. The cold-hearted militiaman appeared unmoved, yet was unable to pull back the trigger. The field was silent under the sagging banner, and the young boy's face was grim with anticipation. Joseph wanted to turn away, yet knew it to be cowardly. The others had no such consideration and looked away, backed down to their knees, covered their ears, and trembled with the expectation of the horrendous blast.

With a thundering bang, the blast blew McAllister's skull to pieces, spraying brain matter and blood to speckle the grassy field.

Ethan threw his musket to the ground and wildly slapped at his face, desperately trying to remove the splatters of blood that landed on him. He coughed and spat furiously after he tasted the salty tang of the few drops that found their way into his mouth. He looked about for a moment until he fixed the location of his son. Firmly, Ethan clutched Joseph's wrist and tugged him forward to stand over the ghastly remains of what had been Sergeant McAllister. Both Ethan and his son lowered themselves to one knee. The young boy gulped, as his father declared with a steady voice, "When…a long train of abuses and…usurpations, pursuing invariably the same Object evinces a design to do, to reduce them under absolute Despotism, it is their right, it is their duty, to throw off such Government, and to provide new Guards for their future security—"

"Even by means of bloodshed," Joseph broke in to say. Still kneeling above McAllister's body, Ethan lowered his musket and held his hand out toward Joseph. He waved his fingers, gesturing him closer. "I would say, that is all the respect this one requires. Please, our colors."

Ethen rose to his feet, and Joseph Allen passed the banner of the Green Mountain Boys to his father, then stood back, with hands clenched and his head held low. Nonchalantly, Ethan flicked a few patches of dirt and a blade or two of grass from the base of the thin, cast iron pole. Firmly, he clenched both hands around the shaft, lifted it above his head, and thrust it with all his force into McAllister's spine. He twisted and churned the staff of their flag, driving it down through the soldier's body.

The militia band had earned a reputation as an unmerciful force who relished the chance to slaughter the New Yorkers who were brazen enough to settle within the Green Mountains. Ethan Allen and his vigilantes had long ago lost track of the number of wandering New York colonials who drifted a bit too far north and had the misfortune to encroach upon their territory. The regional rivalry had manifested itself within the rebellion as New Netherlanders remained mostly loyal to the Crown, while the Northerners fought for independence. The Green Mountain militia were carelessly unhesitant to dispatch any New York colonial given the chances he was loyal. At the very least, Ethan Allen offered no remorse for the slain who were foolish enough to have been born in fucking New York, regardless of their allegiances.

The smell of burnt powder filled the still air, and a bevy of white-breasted nuthatches dashed from the trees. With the deep green flag sagging atop the crooked post impaled through McAllister's body, Ethan turned to his band of citizen soldiers and announced, "Our colors fly with pride. For as long as they continue to send them, we will continue to make piles of their dead bodies! The dumb-fuck Brits. They will run out of red dye before we give up or give in!" His comrades threw their guns toward the sky and cheered vociferously with animated approval. "And look at this one," he continued as he glanced down toward the fallen McAllister. "The poor bitch was unlucky enough to be alive when the Lord decided to make George the Third his king. Had he been born under another regime, at a different time or in a different country he would not be lying here in a pool of his blood. Fate dealt him a cruel hand. Well., now he can settle that grievance with the Good Lord in person."

"Hear, hear!" cried one of the militiamen.

"The day is still quite young, Gentlemen, let's collect our prizes and continue to find more." The men of the Green Mountain Boys scurried like worker ants; some collected the muskets, while others picked through the various pouches and sacks. Pearson's opulent and delicate silver teapot lay on the ground within the grass. It was pristine, if not for the few small blotches of blood cast upon it. The silver was polished and the lid was still firmly in place. Its glare caught the attention of one of the Americans, who moved toward it, knelt, and held it for a moment. He took a few seconds to take in the tea kettle's beauty; he had never held an item of such fine quality. The luxuriant cauldron had perhaps more worth than this man's entire estate, for what it was. His rudimentary mind was unable to fully comprehend its value, yet he knew enough to understand it had value. Quickly he peered to his left and to his right, worried the others would notice what he had. Most hurriedly, he turned to place it inside a large pouch he wore at his side. The bulge was plainly noticeable, yet he carried on all the same, contending to deal with inquiries when and if presented.

"Suicide is Confession."—Daniel Webster

Four

October 1777.

Hereensburg Manor, by contemporary standards, was relatively humble and sleepy, yet considerably warm and welcoming. It lay along the western bank of Mill River, which ran from the Hudson on the east and cut through the valley to Connecticut. Hereensburg was comprised of several buildings; barns, sheds, a slave house, a guest house, and a scattering of huts and cottages. The impressively large wharf, mill house, and manor house suggested the manor had been constructed with substantial care and at a great expense. The gristmill stretched across the river with a sturdy wooden dam. During uneventful days and virtually all nights, slow rushing water could be heard as it streamed through the many pillars and fell to the lower river. To the east, some fifty yards' proximity of the river, rested the manor house. Built of sturdy construction in the Dutch style, the manor house was constructed with white fieldstone, a gabled roof, and large shuttered windows. North of the manor house lay several hundred acres of green, rolling pastures, a few lone maples, rows of carefully placed orchard trees, a split rail fence, short stone walls, and lush woodlands for as far one could see.

Within the eastern shadow of the tall manor house sat a considerable, well-kept garden. Watching over the sprouting vegetables was an inelegant, crookedly placed scarecrow. Emily toiled on her knees, poking at the soil, and although she was not required to do such manual labor, she enjoyed it much the same. To her, gardening was one of many time-passing hobbies, and just about any reason to be in the fresh air and sunshine would do. Emily was to horticulture what she was to virtually every avenue of her life. She had become quite the gardener; in the summer, she grew fruits and berries, then squash, potatoes, and mums in the fall, and in the spring, hardy vegetables, turnips, and carrots. Today, she was picking one of her favorites, sweet potatoes, which she tossed into a wicker basket beside her. Caesar, the affable old Shepherd, sat at her side loyally and lovingly. His damp, pink tongue dangled from his jowls as he panted endlessly. Emily sat upright, placed her hands on the back of her hips, and straightened her back to stretch, then sighed as she allowed herself an infrequent respite. She tilted her head back, closed her eyes, and let the warm late-afternoon sun warm her face.

From within the nearside of the house, she heard the scampering of excited footsteps. The corner of her eyes noticed two pint-sized figures sprint from within the large house before her. The pattering of little feet thumped along the wooden porch, and a tiny voice cried out with jubilation. "Daddy!" shouted Eliza as she and her older sister, Sarah, raced along the stone pathway. The two charged toward the northern gateway, with frocks flapping about them like flags in a brisk breeze. Caesar dashed forward with the two girls, kicking a spray of dry dirt into the air behind. Emily's heart trembled, and from her knees, she turned and followed their path forward with her gaze.

Her soft, auburn hair shone in the western sun's light as she raised her hand above her brow to hide her eyes from the glare. Large, sapphire eyes nearly teared with joy. Her beaming white smile could be seen from a mile. When her grin stretched more still, she covered her mouth with her hand as if to hold all the joy from escaping. She was nearly overwhelmed with excitement. Quickly, she tossed her gloves to the ground, patted the smudges of soil from her frock, then pulled her hair back, straight behind her neck.

Dedrick's figure was bathed in the warm glow of the sun. Behind, Lars whipped the reins, and Cole lurched forward, hauling the nearly empty wagon that rumbled toward the stables. Shadows from the limbs above him crawled along the green pasture to greet his arrival. His face was alive with delight, and he knelt to the level of his onrushing daughters. Before he could find his balance, Caesar lunged into him, with his tail whipping about wildly. He cried and groaned as though he was about to burst with joy. The old dog could not contain his excitement, and simply touching his master was not enough to exhume his delight, it was though he wanted to burrow himself into Dedrick's chest.

"All right, all right, I know, it's good to see you too," he said as he scratched and rubbed the lovable mongrel's furry coat. Caesar pounced about with a mad fury and leaped forward to lick Dedrick's face. He crashed his paw into Dedrick's groin, thrusting his entire eighty pounds into his crotch. "Dammit!" cried Dedrick, who then shoved the animal away from him. "Fuck, Caesar—bad!" The scolding did little to temper the mutt's jubilation, though he tilted his head and lifted his ears in confusion.

With his testicles throbbing, Liza threw herself into his arms, nearly knocking him back to the ground. "You're home!" she cried. Then her little arms wrapped around his neck to squeeze the life from him.

"I'm home," he said. His enthusiasm was temporarily dismayed by his sudden discomfort. Lars observed the exchange and could not help but giggle at the sight of the canine thrusting his paws into Dedrick's sensitive area. Casually, he flipped the reins and proceeded toward the stable.

"Did you bring us anything?" asked Eliza.

"Lizzy! Are you kidding? That is rude," scolded Sarah, who sauntered near. "You don't ask people for presents. And…we haven't seen him in days, you don't think you should be happy to see him? You don't think you should at least say, hello? Welcome home, Daddy." Little Liza's elation turned to sorrow as she ruefully lowered her wide eyes.

"I'm sorry, Daddy," she pleaded with a solemn look in her big, young eyes.

"Go!" he snarled and shooed poor Caesar away. "You're an asshole. Now, get—go away." In his typical fashion, Dedrick could not resist leaving her on the hook. "Don't worry, Princess, it's fine. It is a little rude, your sister is right, but its fine. You ruined the moment, and probably my day, but its fine."

"Dad!" cried Sarah. "Stop being mean. She's going to cry—it's all right, Lizzy, he doesn't mean it. You didn't ruin his day, but that *was* rude. You shouldn't ask for presents. You should be happy to see him, even if he did not bring us any."

"Sarah, please, I'll take care of this," he said and pulled her close to wrap both in a huge bear hug. "You've asked me about presents more than a few times. And that is horrible advice. If you're going to lecture her, think it through a little more. 'Be happy,' as though she has a choice in such things? Regardless, she does not need two mothers—one is more than plenty. In any event, I did happen to pick up a few things, as I usually do."

"Really?" asked Sarah in a suddenly excited tone. "So you brought us something?"

Both of their sweet, young faces lit up with anticipation. He pulled his old, canvas pack from his back and fumbled through the contents. After a few seconds, he finally found the items he was looking for within. "Ah, now you're not so upset with her. Now you are all sunshine and roses. See…see what you did? You're a shrewd one, Sarah, very shrewd."

"I don't understand," cried Sarah. "What did I do? I didn't even do anything."

Dedrick subtly nodded his head and continued through a crooked smile, "I think you understand. You're a clever girl, Sarah. Embrace that, don't be coy about it. Being clever is a gift. One cannot be taught to be clever, she cannot practice being clever. You are clever, or you are not…and you are. The 'Be happy' thing notwithstanding. Clever people are the leaders, the ones who rise above the rest. Remember that and take no shame in being wise."

Confused, yet feel strangely gratified, Sarah was both curious and basking in the compliment. Her emergent young mind urged him to continue, "No, I really don't know what you mean. What did I do?"

Dedrick rubbed her head playfully. "You took advantage of your sister's naïvety by amplifying the situation regarding the presents I may or may not have brought. You used her as a tool to pry into the gift situation. You scolded her as a means of inquiring about presents. A little sinister, but sinister and clever are not far off."

Sarah remained silent as she considered the matter. She was a bit thrown as her father perfectly summarized her intent. It was not that she was willfully attempting to deceive her father, but was as curious about her actions and his perception of them. It may very well be her developing mind is clever as to attempt such a ruse, yet not quite advanced as to fully understand empathy.

"Anyhow, I don't want to belabor this. I missed the two of you… Let's see, my princess. This is for you," he said as he opened his palm, revealing a small velvet sack filled with glass and stone marbles and jacks. "It's…Jacks and…something. Fivestones, Jacks and Fivestones?" She clenched the pouch from his hand in a flash, and her smile extended to reach both ears. With curious excitement, she untied the pouch and poured the contents of the balls into her hand, spilling some onto the grass.

Though she was trying to appear patient, Sarah was just as excited. Nonetheless, she could not let an opportunity to scold her young sister go to waste. "Eliza! You need to be careful. He just gave them to you. Are you going to lose them already? Pick them up! Sheesh, they are dirty already. God…I'm sorry, Daddy. She is being so—"

"Seven?" asked Dedrick. "She is being a seven-year-old? What did I just say? Sarah, I know you love your sister, I know you care, and I know you are trying to be helpful, but she does not understand it that way. She only thinks you enjoy nagging her with no purpose other than to nag her. She spilled the marbles on the grass. Do you think she truly needs to be reprimanded for that? You need to be patient and let her be a child without correcting or underscoring every mistake she makes. Poor kid is going to feel like a beaten dog, afraid to make a move. Or…your constant nagging will have become routine to where she no longer hears it or cares about what you have to say."

Lizzy felt oddly warmed by her father's protection. She was far too immature to process such emotions, yet, on some level, felt vindicated to see the pack leader take her side and satisfied to see her rival brought down. Dedrick's warnings warranted merit, as they became the reality in the relationship he had with his elder daughter. Sarah had heard similar proclamations time and again. Occasionally, she withheld her overly badgering ways, yet always returned to form within a short time. "I know, Daddy, I wasn't trying to pick on her, but you just gave those to her, and…she's going to need. I know, I know. You're right. But…I don't think she will really share them with me, anyway. It's fine, though. Those, um, are the marbles for both us, right, or…?" Her young mind was not yet fully able to grasp the nuances of diplomacy.

Dedrick's face lit up with a slight grin when he recognized his daughter's clumsy ways. "I know I'm right, it should go without saying. I'm right all the time…mostly. There's been, what, three times when I wasn't right? I hate repeating myself. Have we ever told you the name we had picked for you, had you turned out to be a boy, instead of the beautiful baby girl you are?"

"No," she said. "I don't think so."

Dedrick shook his head in confirmation. "Hmmm, wasn't sure I hadn't. In any event, it was *Paralipsis*. What do you think, would you like that? Paralipsis Hereen. It's Greek. Your mother wasn't fully married to it at first, but she came around."

"Para…para-sis—What? No, ugh—no, not one bit. That was my name? What kind of name is that? It's not a pretty name at all, Daddy. I'm sorry, nobody should name a baby…that."

Dedrick was amused with himself, chuckled, and replied, "Well, I suppose, then, it is a good thing you weren't born with a little pee-pee between your legs."

From behind, Emily finally reached the others. Caesar was wandering beside her clumsily, still unsure of what he had done to upset his master. She walked progressively slower as she approached Dedrick and their daughters. It was as if she longed to extend her blissful anticipation of being in his arms. Her fantastic blue eyes were locked onto his, and she took no care to hide her obvious glee. Emily was Dedrick's nearly perfect mate. She laughed often and fell victim with each of Dedrick's sarcastic mind-games. She was graced with uncommon beauty and a respectable nature forbidding it to influence her character. Inappropriately often, the male laborers on the manor conjured petty excuses to be in her company; needless questions or quests for approval and confirmation on trivial, inconsequential matters were the norms. Of course, she was too polite to be bothered and too sweet to recognize their intentions. Despite being told time and again to count her blessings of material wealth, charm, and a marriage to an admired, handsome, and well-connected husband, she had always been grounded in humility.

Dedrick caught her stare and nodded, then rose tall to match her eyes. He brushed his hair from his face, as he often did, and a smile cut through his grizzled, unshaven chin. She stopped just ahead of him, tilted her head ever so slightly, and simply peered back, as if with admiration. Coyly and playfully, she tilted her head and extended her arm as if to shake his hand, formally. He sighed with mild amusement, yet was not taken to play along and extend his hand.

He felt unexplainably uncomfortable and shifted his attention quickly. "No, the marbles are not for you, of course not…but share them," he said as he turned and poked his head near Lizzy's. "This is for you," he continued, and once again riffled through his pack. His tongue was thrust between his teeth, and he could hardly wait to see the look on Sarah's face. "Ah…here it is," he said as he presented her with his gift.

She had a bit of a puzzled look drawn upon her face as she was not quite sure how to react. "A book?" she said with a twinge of disappointment. "This is really…nice. It looks…nice. *Gulliver's Travels.* You read it? What is it about?"

Her apparent letdown seemed lost on Dedrick as he continued with enthusiasm, "I have read it, and it is quite good. It's exciting and funny…I don't think you will want to stop reading once you start. Especially you, because you'll understand everything within the story. Lemuel Gulliver is shipwrecked and needs to travel the seven kingdoms of the world. And, well, you tell me. I don't want to say too much. Sometimes expectations can ruin the experience."

Sarah's look of disappointment shifted to mild interest as she began to flip through the pages. Her mood was perked by the sense of pride her father bestowed upon her. She valued his opinion and sought his approval more than her mother's.

Emily shook her head and teasingly asked, "Are there any presents for me?"

Taken off his guard, Dedrick instantly realized he simply did not consider bringing his wife home a gift. He takes trips to the city often and on virtually every occasion he comes home with a souvenir. Awkwardly, he did his best to think on his feet, "Yes, of course, you think I wouldn't? Your present is my presence."

"Oh, wow," said Emily through a blatantly mocking tone. "That was...not good. 'Your present in my presence?' Did you really say that? That gave me goosebumps it was so bad. I'm a little embarrassed to have even heard it. Please, make sure to never use that one again."

"Mom!" cried Eliza. "You're not supposed to ask someone to give you a present."

Emily squinted her eyes in thought and paused for a moment, then turned toward Sarah, then back to Eliza. "I think you might be right, that was inconsiderate and gauche. Thank you, Lizzy," she said as she rubbed the top of her young daughter's head approvingly. "You are a well-mannered little girl." Sarah offered a frustrated glance toward Dedrick, who deliberately made effort to not notice.

"So...you will give me my present later, in private?" she whispered to Dedrick.

Dedrick simply replied with an empty grin and suddenly remembered. "Wait...You know what I bought? I almost forgot... Rock candy. You two enjoy sucking on sugary rocks, right? Silly, of course you do. Who doesn't like chewing on diamonds and cracking their teeth?" Again, he searched through his pouch and became a bit frustrated when he could not find the pack of candy. After a minute, he hummed in contemplation as he stroked his chin with his fingers. He picked through the smaller pack he carried along his back, only to realize it was not within that one either. "Shit," he mumbled under his breath. "I might have left Lars with the wrong bag—dammit."

"Did you look through them first?" asked Emily.

He paused and offered her a blank expression. "Did I look through the bags? Hmm, that's a good question. I did. I looked through the bags, realized this was actually the wrong one, and decided it would be better to leave the one I want and take the one I don't."

Emily was struck by a wave of disappointment. She lowered her head and gave herself a moment of pause. She hadn't seen the man she loved for several days and was overcome with joy to finally fix her eyes upon him. Within a few minutes, he had managed a biting response as though he shared none of her enthusiasm. "Nice, Dedrick. Thank you for that."

"Please, you need to stop being so sensitive," he griped, then grabbed Lizzy and heaved her body into the air. She giggled with delight as glass marbles trickled from their pouch and back onto the grass. He spun her around a few times, nearly lost his step as he turned himself among marbles, then gently rested her on the ground. His foot rolled along one of the small crystal balls, and he nearly lost his balance. "Damn," he said as a twinge was fired through his hip. His daughters were delighted to near laughter. "You like that? Better pick those up before one of your mothers' yell at you, or someone, probably me, winds up falling on his face." Sarah glanced over and was instinctively inclined to reprimand her sister, yet decided otherwise and diligently flipped through the pages of her new book. After a bit of thought, she appreciated the gift and was excited to both read it and talk about it with her father.

"I didn't hear 'thank you,' young ladies," said Emily.

Both girls rolled their eyes and mumbled a collective, "Thank you, Daddy."

Together, the family strolled leisurely along the walkway toward the manor house. "You were gone longer than we thought you would be. It took you almost four days. Was everything all right?" asked Emily. "We thought, and were hoping you would return yesterday. We spent the afternoon making fruit pies, and I tried to make beet pancakes. Girls were excited and wanted to have them ready for you. I don't know how well they kept overnight. All night they asked about when you'd be back. Wasn't easy to keep these two mouths from eating them. I think Lizzy nearly—"

"Christ, Em, sorry," interrupted Dedrick. "I get it. You're lecturing me as though I was happy to be away. Do you think I enjoy trudging back and forth to Manhattan? We were hung up. The rain, stopped by a British patrol, Lars wanted to rest last night instead of continuing through. It's a long haul—shit, I'm sorry. I'm sorry I ruined your pies and pancakes. You're right, I suppose I could have strolled on past the armed troopers to hurry back. 'Sorry, mates, I see you are considering shooting me right now, but, my wife is annoyed and would like me home as soon as possible. You know how it is, right?'"

"No, no, I wasn't attacking you, Dedrick. Are we a bit testy today? Sorry I brought it up. Obviously, I did not know any of this. We thought you would be home Tuesday, or yesterday. I'm sorry I missed my husband."

Dedrick rubbed his hands against his chin, frustrated with himself. "You're right, I apologize, it really has been a long trek. I'm tired, hungry, and as it is, grouchy. Lizzy is dumping marbles all over the place, Caesar nearly pushed my balls up into my stomach. I just need to eat and get some sleep." He wrapped his arm over his wife's shoulder and gently tugged her near. Without consideration, she forgave him and was happy to bask in the family's warmth.

"Your balls, what balls, Daddy?" asked Eliza. "You have balls too?"

Sarah giggled outwardly, and Emily was relieved to hear his contrition and tried to hide her amusement with a gentle slap on Dedrick's shoulder. "He means, Caesar jumped on him with his *paws*...on his tummy and hurt him. He is happy to see Daddy, just like you are, and you know he gets crazy and jumps and bumps into people. But he is fine, and Caesar is sorry."

The confused little girl was yet satisfied with the explanation and simply grumbled, "oh" insincerely. "Bad dog."

"No. No, no. Why lie to them?" Dedrick shrugged. "Not paws, *balls*. Mommy is just...I don't know what Mommy is doing. Boys have two balls on either side of their pee-pees—well, no. One on either side of his pee-pee, I should say. Nonetheless because Caesar is a moron, he jumped on me and crushed one of them, *with his paw*. The thing about our balls is, they are quite sensitive. And hair grows on them, and they get sweaty and...it's bad, they are bad. Yucky. I'm telling you this because if a man ever tries to assault you, you need to kick him or punch him there, in his balls. They are yucky, but I promise, he'll leave you alone."

Eliza wore a blank expression on her face and meekly grumbled, "Ew."

Emily shook her head, playfully, though a bit irritated all the same. She threw her hands open in dismay and rebuked, "Dedrick, wouldn't you say that...isn't, um, appropriate?"

"What is not appropriate? The truth?" replied Dedrick as he rubbed the top of poor, confused Eliza's head playfully. "Come on, let's go. I want to try some of those pies you girls made," he continued as he pointed toward Caesar, whose tail was still thrashing about wildly. "You stay away—get!"

Dedrick hoisted Eliza on his shoulders with a groan, rested his arm around Sarah, and the family merrily strolled back along the stone pathway toward the manor house, which waited to greet them. They passed Emily's garden and reached the front stoop, where the wooden planks below creaked beneath their strides. Inside, the vestibule was outfitted with as high-quality antique furniture as any in the area. Tabletops and shelves throughout held pewter and brass candlesticks, crystal decanters, fine china, and earthenware. Portraits, landscapes, maps, and clocks hung on the walls. Handcrafted designs were carved into the ceiling trimmings. The images mostly reflected the picturesque river valley; images of beavers were a central theme. Silk curtains muted the fading sunlight from the many thick glass windows, and a beautiful Etruscan statue of a wolf mother suckling Romulus and Remus rested atop the mantle at the central fireplace. The décor was old, yet timeless and untouched, and though the quarters were filled with the air of opulence, it retained a certain unpretentious welcoming feel.

To the right was the upper kitchen, where several utensils and cooking tools were suspended under shelves. Ceramics, jars, and small boxes abounded on the various shelves, cupboards, and cabinets. Dedrick noticed Vesta, the reliable slave hand, crushing grains in a clay bowl in a most mechanical manner. He poked his head beyond the stairway toward her direction, then lowered Lizzy to the floor. "The older I get the heavier you become. This has been true since the day you crawled from Mommy's belly. Good to see you, Vesta."

"And you, Mister. Come now, Sweet Eliza," called Vesta, and little Lizzy scampered into her arms.

"Look!" said Eliza as she proudly presented her bag of Fivestones and Jacks.

"Ah, little thing, those are as beautiful as a young lady's eyes. Such a lucky little girl to have such a caring father." Vesta patted her on the head and showed her into the other room. "Welcome back, Mister Dedrick."

"Thank you, Vesta," replied Dedrick with an insincere smile. "It is good to be home."

*   *   *

North.

Isaac Pearson staggered through New York's northern wilderness. He was the last of the twelve men Colonel Bell dispatched to be alive or accounted for. He'd been wandering, mostly aimlessly, for nearly a week. He had not eaten a speck of nourishment for two days, and before that had not eaten more than a few scraps of dried meat and a handful of stale beans. He was jittery and weak, filthy and soiled to the point where his own stench repulsed him. The once-brilliant and proud red coat he wore on his back had become soiled and dampened to a cheap wine. The forest had been and continued to be smothering, unyielding, and frustrating in its refusal to come to an end. The trees seemed to be collapsing in on him, strangling his faculties, and choking from him the will to continue.

This day was nearing its end, and the setting sun was ushering in another long autumnal evening. Within the past many days, he had managed no better than a few restless hours of sleep. There was no cover from the frigid air, nor comfort from the rigid ground. The crackle of crickets droned away, gnats nipped at him relentlessly, bugs of all type crept within his filthy uniform. When his limp shoulder or throbbing jaw did not deny his rest, fear served the purpose with effectiveness. Pearson dreaded the darkness most of all. He shared the shadows with nothing that did not intend him harm; natives, wild animals, American militia.

With daylight, he did his best to follow the sun, yet had done so with little success and had continued to wander the woodlands like a ship without a rudder. When he reached a patch of grassless soil at a small knoll, he allowed himself to rest. He was surrounded by an army of trunks and limbs, thin and thick, straight and twisted, all competing for the sky as they reached upward. The woods were silent and still, the only sound being Pearson's heart as it heavily thumped within his chest. His arm hung low, and his shoulder continued to pound him with pain. He took a long, deep breath and leaned against a tree as he clutched for his canteen. It was not that he was necessarily thirsty; he had been lucky to have found sources of water. For some time, he followed the same shallow stream. About a day ago, maybe two, he drifted from it, hoping to track a direct route from the woodlands. The absence of apparent progress was drowning the motivation to continue.

Pearson propped himself against a sturdy honey locust and pulled his tin canteen to his lips. A few drops dribbled down his chin, and he sighed with relief as he felt the lukewarm water run down his throat. The shooting pain in his shoulder caused a groan as he struggled to reach for his Duval pistol, simply for the purpose of fixing his eyes on it. Bereft of thought, he peered into the barrel, making sure it was properly loaded and ready to fire. Somehow, it was as pristine as the moment it was presented to him. He gently rubbed the carved notches aside the barrel with his thumb, and once again lost himself in the speculation on what or whom they could have represented. Still, he was unsure if he would carve one himself, given the need.

He looked around, to the right and to the left, and felt smothered by what seemed to be never-ending seasonally colored trees and limbs. For a second he suspected McAllister had somehow been trailing him. Pearson was resolved to conclude the sergeant had been liberated from the angst of their struggles as a prisoner of war. He would be cared for as needed, fed and stowed on His Majesty's ship to be sent back to Ringland. The weight of hopelessness hung on him like a saturated old, cotton coat. The glow of the cast iron barrel caught his eye, and he recognized how quickly and easily he could escape all of this. His calculated mind concluded the reality offered little chance for his quest to end in any way other than with his death. Was it wise to prolong his anguish before he was greeted by the inevitable? Did prudence call for him to accept the likelihood and release his desperate grip on weakly founded hope? There'd be no more pain, no hunger, no need to push on, and no guilt or despair. He would be free of the torment from the ghosts of Hendricks, Manson, and the slain colonial boy. The ghastly images of their demise would no longer be scorched into his memory. Why was he set to press on to live as they no longer could? What force would protect him when he was more deserving of death?

His recourse was to give the matter no further thought. Grimly, he pulled the pistol's hammer back into firing position, raised the weapon to his face, and wrapped his lips around the end of the barrel. Though his arm trembled wildly, there was no more pain in his shoulder. Heavy drops leaked from his eyes, and he could not help but pout as he had not done since he was a child. Resolved to do this, Pearson managed to mute his reservations to pull the trigger.

The impression of Elizabeth, his young wife, spoke to him like a spirit from the beyond. In the cold wilderness, he felt the warmth of her body next to his. "I'm sorry," he cried with a broken voice and shower of tears. He regretted veiling his appreciation for her tolerance of his idiosyncrasies and impatience, her agreeable ways, her warmth and caring, and her selfless character, which at times had been the foundation of their relationship. He could hear her voice clearly pleading him not to buy his commission, to stay home, safe with her. Perhaps he had come to take her for granted or had grown jaded, and perhaps her amiable manner had both attracted and repelled him.

"No, I'm not," he said as though he was speaking to her. He lowered the gun from his mouth, then lowered his lids to keep his eyes closed for a few seconds. Reflexively, he peeked over his shoulder, as if making sure nobody witnessed his moment of weakness. With a click of the thumb, he removed the hammer from its position and with extreme care, rested the pistol back in its holster. We are not a single being with a fixed soul. Pearson always believed, today we serve our future persons and, in turn are served by our past selves. The fools are burdened by the neglect of their past selves and the superior man thrives as his past-self served him well. Now, at his lowest point, lost, hungry, filthy, weak, hurting and desperate, Pearson refused to let the current incarnation of himself destroy who he will be.

He was filled with remorse and humility, ashamed to have displayed to himself such moral weakness. With a few refreshing breaths, he rested his eyes and thought to regain his fortitude.

With a twinge of drive returned, Pearson swigged a few more gulps of the warmish water, and in so doing, noted a rather odd, gangly tree, with an unusually split trunk, a few yards above the roots, several dozen yards ahead of him. He narrowed his eyes a bit, paused, then approached it slowly. Pearson threw his head back, halted in his tracks, and in a fit of utter rage, fired the canteen against the knotted and twisted trunk.

"Ballocks!" he cried. "Fucking cunt! Fuck! Fuck you, Jesus. Fuck you!" He paced in an irregular circle pointlessly for nearly a minute. Captain Pearson had seen the very same tree and the very same patch nearly a day earlier. He had walked for nearly a full day on end, only to arrive exactly where he had left.

* * *

Northwest of Central Manhattan Island.

Madame Jeanette held Doctor Van Leeuwen's hand gently and moved forward as though she was tugging him along. She was a sultry woman, and though it was not by intent, every move she made was a seductive one. She glided with a certain grace, as though she could not help but be alluring. Her long, silky dark hair was tied at the back and rested on a fine, soft lace neckerchief. The elegantly adorned gown and apron she wore were impressive, yet could do nothing to hide her curvaceous figure. The heels of her exquisitely fashioned silk shoes clanged against the stone pathway and echoed throughout The Inn's wide-open cellar. "Here we are, handsome," she said as the pair reached an enclosed doorway. Her mysterious dark eyes peered into the doctor's. With a gentle tug, she pulled the wooden door open, then graciously and respectfully waved Van Leeuwen ahead. As he passed, he removed his black hat and lowered his head in a gentlemanly effort, and she returned a blown kiss in his direction.

The chamber was nearly engulfed by darkness, windowless and filled with a damp, chilled air. The walls were coated with heavy white paint, and sturdy beams ran along the length of the ceiling. Along the wall directly in front of the doctor, four long, sturdy oak panels ran from the center point, to fan out along the right edge of the wall, and four more from the center to the left edge. The pattern of the beams' construction resembled a massive spider, crawling along the bricks. A ten-foot, narrow harvest table ran across the room near the far end. Two dull pewter candlesticks at either end flickered in the shadows. Behind sat The Council; three figures, the center of whom appeared to be no more than four feet if standing. He was cast in virtual darkness, and his face was covered in blotted white powder, yet, his youthful expression was clear just the same. Some would generously describe him as a young man, but more truthfully, he was a child. The lad was lost under the top rail of the large oak chair in which he sat. Atop his head was an overly large powdered wig that rested clumsily and crookedly just above his eyes. The finely tailored waistcoat dangling from his shoulders could have comfortably fit two of his bodies within and still buttoned with ease. He sat in the stead of his father, the Director. Flanked on his left and his right were seated increasingly impatient, elder members of the triad. Like the Nameless Boy, they wore bow-tied, white powdered wigs, though their faces remained unpowdered and clean. They fit perfectly into their midnight-black, finely tailored coats. Either could have been old enough to be the boy's father, and both were most content they were not.

The Nameless Boy's eyes were fixed on a massive, crudely bound book. It may have weighed more than he. It lay carelessly on a sea of parchments and pamphlets upon the table before him. His itty finger followed along the lines of text as he toiled by silently moving his lips, most clearly unable to understand what he was attempting to read. He held his finger in the air, demanding the doctor wait, silently. After a few seconds, he struggled to slam both ends closed dramatically, disregarding where he had left off and turned his attention to his visitor.

"Good morning, Cornelius," he uttered through a cracking, pubescent voice. "We hope your stay with us last evening was enjoyably. Yes? Enjoyably? Please, come forward, if you will, please."

It was late afternoon, though the doctor had no wish to correct him. Van Leeuwen approached silently, as his shoeless feet landed delicately on the rigid surface of the floor to leave no trace. As he approached, the dark silhouettes of two imposing figures appeared, standing straight at attention behind the Council and Nameless Boy. Mostly, they remained under the cover of shadow. Though they were very much alive, they appeared as stone statues positioned sturdily, with both hands held clutched over the handle of a sword that reached the ground. Only their broad profiles could be seen, still, more than enough to intimidate Van Leeuwen into an uncharacteristically submissive state. "It was *enjoyable* indeed, thank you," he said. "I am a bit confused why I was summoned here. If I am not mistaken, I have no outstanding balance. You know I never run into debt. Is there a problem?"

"No, nothing like that. Not a mistake, you are in an *extra-carious* uh, place, Cornelius. The Inn needs you to provide a uniquely service, only you can provide. You should lavish this. Is it good...yes? The will be given a nice credit, and we always take care of our clients. This is good for you. This is prosperous...prosperously, prosper—right? You will do it anyway, Cornelius, you will do this. The Inn is asking you for this, and The Inn does not ask, it demands. Remember, one cannot drink a fish."

The doctor's confusion was overcome by irritation. His head collapsed into his chest, where it hung in a mildly frustrated fit. Services were typically not the preferred method of payments, as they were much more often than not, beyond their monetary value. There could be no conciliation, nor compromise. At times, The Inn requested a payment in service, and the so-referred requests were non-negotiable demands. For his part, the talented doctor had gotten by without such a request for some time. Though he was dismayed, he was not entirely surprised.

Van Leeuwen did not wish to continue the exposition beyond where necessary and bluntly asked, "What am I needed to do, good sir?"

"Good, Cornelius. That is the spirit we fragrance here—yes, good. To the north, a day, two days' ride a day—either a day or maybe two, they said two days—your care is needed. A very significantly, a significantly important individual person has taken ill. She needs the care only you are able to offer, and this must happen before the snowfall. Her time is unique, thus it is important to hurry with your haste."

Van Leeuwen furled his brows with confusion. "Exactly where, and exactly who, and what is her problem?"

The Nameless Boy shifted his gaze toward his left then his right, as though he was looking for help answering Van Leeuwen's inquiry. "Uh, yes…who—Cornelius is asking who," he uttered with an unsure tone. The elder councilman sitting at his left snatched the quill pen from its ink bottle and impatiently scribbled onto of the scraps of parchment about the table. As he finished, he slid it along the surface to the Nameless Boy. The lad was near illiterate, and the dim light and sloppy penmanship certainly did nothing to help him understand. He proceeded to read it out loud, haltingly, "The cown kill…will make… inform"—both of the Councilmen on either side of the table shared the same look of exasperation—"will make infinite—infinite?" Without a further effort to read the note, he chose to extemporize what he believed to be a proper response. "The particularly details are not fully known in total. When I learn them, they will be learned to you. For now, Cornelius, just know you will be called on, summarized, soon, and when you are, be ready to travel. You are greatness in men, Cornelius, greatness. Oh, I was told to remind you, Cornelius: Do only what The Inn demands, your ice is thin. We would hate to see another reprimand on you. Now, please leave right away. Please now, please leave us and enjoy the rest of your visit."

* * *

Upriver, between one to two days of Manhattan.

The moon looked down on the manor, the reflected light danced along the surface of Mill River, the crickets sang to one another, and stars gleamed in the blackened sky. Inside the house, the curtains swayed softly in the cool night's breeze and pushed through the windows to flutter the soft glow of the candles. Dedrick was nearly asleep, snugly tucked away under a soft cotton cover. Emily sat near the eastern window within their bedroom chamber, lost in a world empty of thought. Her feelings dulled the magnificence of her green-blue eyes as they peered in no direction, and her smooth auburn hair was cast against the fair skin on her gentle neck. For some time, she'd been cloaked in willful ignorance, afraid to confirm her suspicion, until she finally pulled back the top of her gown about her neck. Slowly, she pinched her blouse at the collar and tugged downward, revealing a patch of reddish-yellow blisters and lumps. The dull moonlight could not hide her terror. Immediately she let go of her frock, as she could bear to look no more than a second. Her eyes welled up, yet she did her best to hold back the whimpers of sadness and distress. She felt the need for comfort, and though she understood Dedrick finally looked to be at rest, she sought to find it from him.

She twisted her head from side to side as to unfurrow the locks and pointed her stare directly at him. Leisurely, she pulled loose the lace atop her long white gown and let it slip from her body and onto the cold planks at her feet. She was nearly flawless; her teeth were as white as newly fallen snow, where not blighted by infection, her skin was as supple as a newborn's, and she moved with the grace of a winged angel gliding in a gentle breeze. The scarlet nips on her firm and perfectly formed breasts were as hard as pebbles. Between her shapely hips, her blushing vagina smiled gleefully. Her long legs lurched forward until she reached the base of the bed. From there, as a jaguar in the tall grass, she approached Dedrick on her knees and hands. Her chin rested on his shoulder, and she folded her nude body into his, as though they were one. Slyly, she slipped her hand under the light cotton cover and inched it down his side toward his crotch.

"Mmm, no," he groaned as he reached for her hand. "I'm sorry. I'm not really…I'm tired. Save it."

Frustrated and disappointed, she fell back into the bed and peered directly at the ceiling. "Save it. Of course. I've been saving it. I haven't seen you in almost a week. You hardly talked to me all night; you ate, played with the girls, and went right to bed. I swear you were happier to see Caesar than you were to see your wife. What is going on with you?"

"Ugh," he mumbled in irritation. "So, you're not going to let me sleep, is what you are saying? What do you mean, what's going on? Nothing is going on. I'm tired, I suppose that is what is going on. I'm tired. I apologize for being sleepy. Moving forward, I will do my best not to be."

"Cute," she replied. "Maybe I'm wrong that I want to have sex with the man I love, the same man who has not seen me in days." Emily's insecurity had manifested into outward agitation. Her sense had always been Dedrick's acceptance of her was unconditional, that he was the one to make her feel good about herself despite her misgivings. Rather, his distance and indifference had only been adding to her self-doubt.

"And you think nagging me into it is a good idea?" he sniped. "Would you rather I say 'fuck, all right, let's do this and get it over with'? I'm sorry," he continued. "I am really tired and have to get up early again tomorrow—or today, rather—so, please. If you love me, let me get some sleep."

"Get up early...for what?" she asked. "What is happening tomorrow?"

As Dedrick's frustration grew, so too did his compunction to become tetchy. "I swear to Christ you have selective memory. I told you I was going to visit Pieter when I returned, and as you pointed out to me in my sleep, I have returned."

She shook her head as though she could not believe the words she was hearing. "Please tell me you are not serious right now, Dedrick. That means you will be gone for another, what...two days? I suppose I should say I am sorry, it looks like I've taken for granted the twelve hours you've spent with your family. Go, go visit your friend. I'll be here waiting, as I always do." As she continued, her eyes welled with tears, and her voice was overcome with despair. After a few seconds, she was unable to continue with her spiteful façade. "I'm really hurt right now. I'm hurt you don't love me and don't want to be around me anymore. I'm hurt that you don't care about how sad I am. I don't know what I do to make you hate me so much. I don't have much time, and you—"

Prompted by guilt and the desire to simply conclude the discussion, Dedrick sat up, rolled over, and held himself over her. While looking down into her watery eyes, he said, "Em, stop, please. You don't think this is a bit dramatic? You know I love you, you know I would throw myself off a cliff for you. You are the mother of our daughters, my wife, my partner, the most important person in my life. I *hate* when you get like this. You're being negative and assuming only the worst. You are acting like we are at the end of the road, that the cruelest possibility is the most likely possibility. I'm not giving in to that—you are doing all you can to see the prophecy of doom is fulfilled. The more you let thoughts dance through your head, the more likely they are to become truth. Even if you believe otherwise, you must think only positive thoughts. First, you think, then you believe. Really, you need to stop talking like this, because you are convincing yourself it to be true."

His attempt at reassurance did little to sway her mood. "I see, Dedrick. I'm annoying to you. You hate my grief—that is fantastic to hear. On top of the world of concerns I face, I have to make sure now, not to upset you in the manner in which I deal with them. It sounds as though you are telling me to leave you alone, is that what you want?"

Dedrick felt a burst of crossness fired upon him. He threw himself back into his pillow and turned his back on her. "Jesus, Emily, that's what you heard? It is not at all what I said. I'm not discussing this further. If you want to wallow in self-pity, I will leave you to do so. Just do it quietly." Emily did not reply other than to weep and sniffle. Dedrick rolled to his side and pulled the covers tight, then threw his pillow over his head. Quiet and still, the couple lay within inches of one another, in the same bed, yet in their hearts and in their minds, they were miles apart.

*　*　*

The Trials—Evolution XII

Carso Wick, North Ronaldsay of the Orkney Islands of Scotland.

Soft glimmers from the rising sun meekly fought to penetrate the wall of dull, dark clouds above the faded, brownish grass. The gray water of the North Sea hummed gently as it lazily washed the rigid, rocky coastline. As was typical, the air was heavy and dank. Citadel North, the once proud northern fortification, rested just beside the waterline. The old bricks and stones of the heavy granite walls and inner towers appeared as a gray-scaled reptile that had crawled from the sea to sleep upon the shore.

The pinnacle sat tall above the keep, its arrowslits peering beyond the jagged pattern of thick, dense stone walls. Two inner baileys and a small chapel rested within the pale, dying grass of the inner ward. The bulwarks were desperately trying to uphold their once impressive integrity, yet seemed to be succumbing to age at last. What remained of the northeastern curtain wall faded into the sea, and the countering walls rested among a bed of rubble. The many cracks and fractures were the remembrances of the fortification's long-battered being, yet the foreboding shadows of the stronghold refused to die.

Carso Wick was eerily still, other than the sheep who lazily fed upon the seaweed carried ashore and a pair of crows overhead, who danced in flight as they soared from north to south. The sea winds' heavy air were the soft voices of the many souls who had seen their lives fall on this island. The remains of countless men rested within the soil surrounding Citadel North. Englanders and enemies alike shared their story's ending.

At a grassy foothill where the northern and western walls ended, a doorway opened to a long and narrow path that had been dug within. Chiurgeon Alard was escorted by a king's infantryman as he approaches the pass's entryway. The soldier carried a softly glowing lantern in one hand and a makeshift leash, which was tied to the neck of a small lamb, in the other. The animal slowly trailed behind, prompted by occasional tugs forward. Neither of the men exchanged words, yet moved slowly ahead as if the other was not there.

Alard had deep, dark eyes and thick, ash-colored hair, which he had tied into a tail behind his neck. The links of a thin chain hung low from his neck, and the iron keys suspended from it clanged together with each stride until he reached the solid oak door. He held high a rustic, tin lantern and fumbled through the keys until he found the one he needed. The lock screeched as he joggled the key, removed it, then struggled to force the heavy door as it scraped along the rocks and weeds along the ground. Alard's old body was only able to pry the door partially open, yet the clearly younger and more fit rifleman appeared unaware and offered no immediate assistance. After a moment of toil, he managed to force the old gate enough to allow their passage. Both men slinked through the doorway and began down a long, darkened chamber. The passageway was confining, with jagged old stone walls and patches of spiderwebs. The glow of their lanterns surrounded them, and the clinks and clanks of the lamb's hoofs echoed about the hardened walls.

The subterranean passageway continued some distance, perhaps a hundred paces or more, before it bent toward the right and continued another fifty-plus feet. The rock walls were crude and ill-fit, as if constructed by unskilled masons, and the air was dank and festered with the smell of mildew. Ahead, another heavy oak door awaited. As they neared, Alard dug through his coat for a cotton handkerchief, then held it within his hand. With the same hand, he slid open the rusted wrought iron bar that clamped the door closed from the outside. The chirurgeon waved the soldier back a few steps, who docilely complied and yielded three feet or so, allowing Alard to fully open the door.

The story of the northern fortress, which had been constructed as Storm's End, had many chapters. It had been the shield between the Empire and invading barbarous, Norwegian hordes, French and Spanish landings, and had served as a stronghold for Royal Forces against frequent Scottish rebellions in opposition to the rule of the Throne. As threats to the Empire died, Storm's End became Citadel North; the home of unspeakable terror and torture. Criminals, debtors, traitors, religious zealots, and any number of perceived or actual enemies of Britain, had been imprisoned within the fortification's darkened cells and subjected to unimaginable methods of torment and pain. The dungeon's walls had witnessed routine dismemberment, burning, and most commonly, slow, gradual excruciating persecution of countless souls. Echoes of the agonizing screams had become so familiar, their cries and shrieks had hardly been more than an annoyance to those within earshot. Maggots weaved within the mutilated, lifeless bodies that offered the insufferable stench of death to those who would soon join them. Typically, most were forced to bear witness to the torture of others to preview their own end.

Alard clutched his handkerchief over his nose and mouth, and the Redcoat grimaced when the foul stench quickly reached his nostrils.

As he stood in the doorway, he lifted his lantern, and the darkness gave way to reveal an open chamber. Old webs were tangled along the rough, stone walls, and the ceiling was low and confining. The open space was buried several feet under the surface and allowed not even the slightest ray of light to penetrate the blackened darkness. Several men lay atop the hard dirt and pebbles on the cold ground. Each man was fully naked, with his body coiled in such a fashion as to protect whatever semblance of warmth and comfort he could manage. The lanterns' glow only partially illuminated the rectangular hollow and as each man awakened, he turned and squinted as his eyes struggled to adjust to even the faintest trace of light.

The chamber was mostly empty. A few clay jugs, splintered shards of wood, torn strips of rags, and ropes and broken chain links lay scattered here and there. Noticeably, the corroded remains of *barrels*, as they were commonly called, rested in small piles in one of the far corners of the chamber. Over many years, criminals, heretics, and the disloyal had been bound at the wrists, with hands behind their backs, and placed into a tub of water. His head remained atop the barrel, wedged within two wooden half-discs that were tightened around the neck and covered the top of the barrel. With the sufferer secured on his knees within the barrel, it was filled with water. For days on end, he remained on his knees, trapped within an enclosed barrel of tepid water. To onlookers, it would appear he was only a head resting atop a fully sealed cask. The victim was fed spoiled meats and sour milk and remained bathed in a pool of his excrement. Slowly, the skin would prune and weaken, finally peeling from the body, and in so doing, the putrid, contaminated water caused massive infections. Death was welcome, yet always stubbornly slow.

Alard had an instructional quality of speech. He delivered his words deliberately, yet with commanding certainty. He wasted few and offered not a semblance of eloquence. Standing at the doorway, he announced, "You've reached a new evolution and are one step closer—we will begin as soon as you finish breakfast."

He waved the mostly obedient soldier forward, who pulled the lamb into the chamber. The animal bleated nervously as his handler tossed the leash. In an instant, the trooper stepped aside, and Alard forced the door closed and slammed the locking bar down. The crash echoed back through the long, enclosed passageway. Alard gave a quick glance to his escort, then proceeded back the direction they had come. The lamb's cries from within the enclosed chamber were muted, though no less dire and gruesome.

"I only regret that I have but one life to lose for my country."—
Nathan Hale

Five

October 1777.

The tranquil water of Eagle Creek was the canvas for the painting of
the natural beauty on which it rested. The pastoral greens, reds, and
golds had nearly turned to solemn browns and grays. Only scattered
traces of grass managed to peek beyond the layer of carob-colored
leaves that had fallen and come to rest. Above, the sky was covered
by foreboding clouds, and the air was chilled and heavy, yet still. A
band of some twenty men, one bound by chains, lurched onward
until they broke from the trees to meet the creek's southernmost
shore, where they came to rest. They were little more than a stone's
throw from Eagle Creek Village, which overlooked the water. The
Green Mountain Boys were not yet finished with their hunt, though
the prey they had managed to trap prematurely called their present
expedition to an end. Though the militiamen were victorious, they
were somber and stricken with a sense of defeat. The respite was
appreciated and perhaps needed all the same, for more than a simple
reason they were more than eager to continue their tracks.

Wyandot Panther's wrists were clasped within heavy irons and
bound by thin, hemp rope to a nearly one-hundred-pound, knotted,
solid pinewood post across the back of his shoulders. The massive
beam had been chopped from the trunk of a centuries-old evergreen
a day prior. The raw stubs from its branches gnawed on his shoulders
and dug into his flesh with each stride forward, and the sticky sap
that bled from the bark stained his neck. He was without a strip of
clothing, and the many scrapes, cuts, and abrasions on his muscular
frame were as unrelenting as they were common. His bare feet were
linked by cast iron shackles at the ankles, which chafed and slit

through the skin and flesh to scrape against his bone. For more than a day, he had been offered no relief from the massive trunk against his back, the sun against his skin, and the jagged shards of stone along his path.

A small number of the colonial militia excused themselves, heading toward the creek, where they would do their part to fill it with piss. Most, however, took rest around Panther on the soft grass, while they stuffed their mouths with provisions and swallowed the crisp, cool water that had recently filled their canteens. By now, they had grown disinterested in him, mostly. The thrill of his capture had nearly waned, though not entirely. Panther stood, without food or drink. He bore this weight like a mule trudging a plow through the field, some forty miles, was given little water and no food; lashed routinely, his strength was still maintained to continue for forty more. His eyes slowly scanned his American captors as he appraised each and every man's worth. The Panther was overcome with regret to have been taken by such a sorry gang of shit stains. The entire lot of them were frail and cowardly, and not one, nor all, could beat the malevolent grin from his face. It was a regrettable way for the hunter to meet his end. All the same, he had been long prepared to walk among the spirits of his kind.

The Puritan community at Eagle Creek was made up of a tiny cluster of crudely constructed, white-shingled cabins and small log homes. It was snuggled within the forest of maples and pines along the foothills encompassing the tarn. All the residents made sure to rise with the sun, feared the grace of God, and knew the names of all the others. This was how it had always been. The village did not take kindly to passersby and seldom welcomed change. Oddly enough, one such passerby introduced the community to the most radical change in colonial history. Oliver Wolcott's persuasive tongue easily swayed their simple minds to embrace Bostonian radicalism and to take up arms for the cause of the Rebellion. It took as little time as it did cunning to convince the residents of the sleepy village the tyrannical and coercive nature of London was the genesis of many ills, and only by violent upheaval would they be truly free. Freedom, as it was to be, to pursue the continued mundane interests they had been freely able to pursue just the same. The inhabitants were largely isolated from the world of colonial politics and the comings and goings within the Empire, and for their part, consumed Wolcott's propaganda as a famished glutton would feast on freshly butchered meat. More than half of the menfolk heeded his call to join the revolt.

Wisps of smoke leaked from the gray, stone chimneys and struggled to reach the air. A rickety, crooked, wooden gate zigged and zagged along the western edge of the water, following a narrow footpath. It led from the village to the outpost where Ethan Allen and his company took their rest. The settlement was made up of two log buildings, modest in size, though sturdily constructed, and a nearly dilapidated lean-to, which was nearly lost within a hive of weeds and vines. Within it were scattered a number of metal hand tools, tin cans, and empty buckets. By far the most striking structure within the outpost was a great, black, cast iron lamp oil tank. The massive vat could hold perhaps five hundred gallons and sat upon four pillars of heavy brick beneath a blanket of moss, some three yards from the ground, just off the footpath. Ethan rested his palm against the outer shell that had soaked in the sun and warmed to the touch. He let his fingers softly glide along the crude iron surface, until he was interrupted by Ira Allen, who declared, "I believe that to be them. I think they are coming." Ethan's young cousin was the first to notice the arrival of three riders approaching along the footpath.

Ethan sighed, then confirmed, "I cannot imagine they be any other." As the horsemen neared, he strode closer toward the pathway, near the direction of their pace to greet them. James Winthrop and his son, James, along with their militiaman comrade, Seth Warner, pulled their steeds to a halt just before Ethan. He remained still, with a very dire look about him, until he whistled and waved his own son forward. Joseph was sitting with his back against one of the large tank's sturdy posts, paring the rotten parts from an apple. Mostly, he was giving no attention to the events and persons about him. His packs and weapons were scattered about him carelessly. Upon hearing his father's call, though, he quickly tossed the fruit aside and scampered to his feet. Instantly, he snatched his musket from the ground and clumsily hurried toward his old man, near the Winthrops. After taking three or four strides, he realized he had the wrong weapon in his hands. Hastily he turned back, flung his Brown Bess to the ground without concern, and grabbed the other that was nestled within his mess of items. He relayed it to his father, who took it, then held his son's shoulder as if to ensure he would not stray. Ethan strode forward, still clinging to his son's deerskin smock, and presented the old musket to James Senior, then asked in a subdued tone, "A good day to you, sirs. I regret we do not meet under more uh, pleasant contexts. Do you recognize this weapon? Does it belong to you?"

Both James and the younger turned toward one another with the same look of confusion and dismay. The elder did not need to scrutinize it for long. With his mount ambling about impatiently, James leaned forward in the saddle and accepted the familiar Dutch Lock musket. "Aye, sir, I do recognize it because this is my gun. This was my father's gun. How did you come to get it, Mister Allen?" Ethan paused for a moment, then removed the nappy, old raccoon hat from his head to hold it at his chest. He felt a lump of sorrow well within his throat, and at the moment, wished desperately to be in any location but this one.

"Well, good sirs," replied Ethan, yet more somberly, "I am afraid the circumstances to that regard are quite grim. My heart is heavy to bear such news. It was taken from your boy after he was slain by... that fucking Indian over there. Yesterday, about this time, we caught up to him. He managed to take half a dozen of our troop before we corralled him. He brought us to your boy, some twenty miles to the southeast, and we confirmed what he told us. You have our profound sympathies. I cannot envisage the weight you must feel, and I pray it gives you some solace to know that all your brothers here, including my son and I, feel it with you. You paid more than any man should be asked to pay in the fight for our cause, sir."

In an instant, James's head had fallen into his chest, pushing his fantail hat to the ground as he was overcome with a wave of distress. His young boys and Mary Beth had not come home by the morning. The small band of men mustered to scour the wilderness had yet to return, yet the faint glimmers of hope had died with the cold breeze. Acceptance of their fate was now inescapable. The grief was choking him to no end. "No. No, sir, you are mistaken—please, no." He began to sob. His son could muster no words, though he nearly fell from his saddle. "It cannot be, there has been a mistake, sir. How? No. My son has not been killed. This cannot be—I don't...this cannot be. Please, stop this, sir, please." Desperately, he further inspected the Dutch Lock, imploring it to be another. The familiar scratches and markings confirmed otherwise and ushered a wave of dreadful sorrow. This was unquestionably his weapon.

"By God's grace, there is no mistake, sir," replied Ethan. "He's been missing for some days now, yes? His body was at rest within a bed of grass. We buried him properly. The British employ these savages for their services. This is the one who took your son from you. He confessed as such. I wish it not to be so."

Tears streamed down James's cheeks, and he reached to clutch his oldest son's hand, as though perhaps, together, they may be able to deal with the pain. With his face awash in tears, James's sadness instantaneously turned to rage. "Who? Which boy did he kill? Which of my sons did this animal take from me?"

Ethan threw his hand against his mouth as though he was contemplating a question he did not expect. He stalled for a moment by placing his raccoon hat back atop his head. His eyes shifted toward Joseph, as though he was imparting the inquiry to him. Ever so subtly, Joseph clenched his lips and shrugged his shoulders. Still speechless and uncertain, Ethan astutely glanced over his companions, desperately hoping one would be able to assist. None were forthcoming with any such resolution. "I cannot say," Ethan finally replied. "We were not aware you had another. He did not kill more than one, there is that. I don't think..." He paused and once again glanced toward his son, who nodded his head to confirm. As both distraught men before him sobbed, he continued, "Yes, we are sure he did not kill more than one, my friend. But, we are sure he did kill one, but not *more* than one. That is to say, as far as we can tell, he only killed one. He has confessed to killing one. I did not think to ask if he killed any others, but it is likely he only killed one of your children, sir."

From his position, Panther giggled with sinister delight. "I will leave this world with laughter in my heart, and for this, I thank you. Ask yourself, Father, which do you prefer it to be? Which of your sons do you prefer to have lived? You will not say with your mouth, but in your mind, you have already spoken. There is no shame in sharing your thought."

In an instant, Ethan whipped his head toward Panther, then burst toward his direction. He waved his hand toward another of his young cousins, Remember Baker. Remember was a step from Panther and promptly and forcefully thrust the butt of his musket into Panther's stomach, just below the rib. Panther grunted, with drabs of saliva dribbling through his lips, though he remained composed and mostly unmoved. He was expecting a harsher reprimand. His malevolent eyes shifted toward Remember's, and without making a peep, his cock stiffened, as though he was aroused with the thoughts of all the misery and misfortune begotten by his hands. Without offering any hint to care, Panther fired a stream of deep yellow piss from his nearly erect penis. The warm urine doused Remember's cotton trousers until he leaped back and threw his arms up in disgust. Remember held his arms apart and was thoroughly repulsed as Panther's piss set through his cotton pantaloons and canvas hunting shirt. The look now drawn upon Wyandot's face could not be described, though it represented the unbelievable sense of satisfaction felt within. Several of the militiamen could not help but snicker. Remember gathered himself and once again, with all the might he could muster, rammed the stock of his long musket into Panther's gut with such force it managed to knock his raccoon hat forward, over his eyes. Yet again, Panther anticipated a more severe reprisal.

In an instant, Ethan's somber demeanor turned into outward hostility. "Fucking—what the fuck is going on?" He charged toward Panther and shoved his face directly into his. "I am sorry, it could be I failed to make myself clear. You are swine we are considering to slaughter. Everyone around you wishes nothing but to see you die a prolonged, insufferable death. It could be your primitive mind does not understand, but you are now at our mercy."

Panther did not blink, nor budge. "Mercy? This how the white man tells jokes? You have extended me no mercy, no matter, and I'd want none of your *mercy* if you had. You are all sad creatures. I did not pity the deaths of my kind, I avenged them. What do you do?

You weep for the boy, you pray to your stupid, fucking god for his spirit? No good has He done you, and you will pray to Him more still. I am at rest, and I would welcome death to dance with the souls of those you have taken away, had this meant I would no longer be able to kill more of your kind." He spoke more loudly and turned his attention toward the Winthrop men. "You want to know which of your rat sons I slaughtered, do you? I will tell you, it was the one who did not shit himself and cower like a frightened bunny. That one lived, and did nothing but watch me slice apart his brother. He lived and will forever be tormented by the memory of your other son's death; in his memory, he did nothing but whimper and watch. He is the one I did not slay."

"Gentlemen," Ethan said to James and the younger, "this is not my place to say, nonetheless I feel you deserve to suffer no further part in this. Your hearts need to mourn, to be free of continued anguish and the presence of this monster. Yet, this Redskin fuck is rightfully yours. You must choose his fate, and you must do as you wish. We will honor it, whichever it may be. Though, if by your grace you should trust my judgment, I will say to you, we do have a suitable...how shall I say, conclusion in mind. You can be assured the remainder of his life will be nothing but unimaginable misery. I suspect you would not like to see him die a quick death?"

"We are God-fearing people, Mister Allen, and we have never lived to seek the suffering of those who have wronged us, no matter how heinous they may be. It is our morality which makes us who we are. It would make this Indian more of a murderer for me to allow him to take this from us. His torture will do nothing to bring...my boy back to me. The Lord would have us pray for him, to turn another cheek. Yet, if I am true to my heart at this moment, I believe none of that and only wish for him to suffer as though he was already in hell," replied James. "It seems...my faith is yet another causality of this war. I will not insist you cause this man to endure pain before his death, though I will not insist you do not. In time, I am sure in some way, I will deal with our Lord's judgment. Until then, I will defer to your prudence."

Ethan nodded his head and coldly glanced in Panther's direction. He was more than satisfied with James's assertion. "You have my word, sir, our measures will be appropriate."

James slowly lowered his eyelids as though he was hoping to lose himself in blindness. "Bring him here, first, bring him to me," he demanded.

His son looked upon him with bewilderment and disapproval. "Dad, no!" he cried. For his part, he did not want to be anywhere near the savage who stole the life from one of his younger brothers. "Leave him here, why speak to him?"

"It's fine, James. Bring him over, please," he repeated. Ethan shrugged his head toward Panther's direction, prompting Ira and Remember to push Wyandot forward. The immense beam over his shoulders nearly tipped him to the ground until Remember heaved him upright. Both men stumbled and struggled to stay on their feet. Panther's seemingly endless strength appeared to finally be waning. When they neared James's position, Panther raised his eyes toward him to offer his contemptuous expression.

James Winthrop Senior peered directly into Wyandot Panther's sinister stare. "You are going to die today, Indian, whether you are at peace with it or not. And, you are too much of an animal to realize, I am, in fact extending you mercy, because, despite your nature, I am of a moral and kind heart. I am sparing you to witness what will become of you and your kind. The Lord has already seen to it, we have his blessings. The god you mock has chosen us to be the victor. Now and forevermore, there will be nothing you can do to stop us from slaughtering every last one of you. I'm sparing you to see what will happen after we win this war and butcher the Indian at will. When we run our bayonets through the bellies of those with child and rape those without. The old, gray longhairs who dance like fools for your false gods will hang from trees. We are going to carve all your little red children into bits so we can feed them to our dogs. Then, we will create holidays to celebrate the various massacres and get drunk as we joke about your sad demise. You can do nothing to stop any of it—nothing to stop us from laughing, and dancing and pissing on all your graves before we build our cities atop them. This is all by the grace of our Lord.

"Do you know the story of Pontiac, the wise and compassionate chief? Pontiac was desperate to protect his pathetic clan of savages from an especially bitter winter. We approached, not in sheep's clothing, but as the wolves, to offer him the blankets we could spare. Because he was so easily fooled, he accepted them and thanked us for the gracious generosity. He thanked us after we infected them with our deadly diseases. All manner of pox and plague-riddled your kind, and we laughed to ourselves, as we could not believe how stupid you all were. We felt guilty only because it was too easy. Pontiac is only one chapter in the story we tell our children, the story of slaughtered pigs who were such silly, stupid creatures you ate our bullets by the bushel. The tales will be told for generations beyond us, of the white men who have become fat and rich beyond our dreams at the expense of red men. That is, until we grow tired of such stories and you will matter not at all. I'm extending you mercy by ending your life before you see all of this."

Panther was unmoved. "The world may remember what we say, but never forget what we do. Your boy is dead by my hands."

"Get him out of my sight," demanded James. Two of the nearest militiamen immediately grabbed Panther and thrust him back. With that, James pulled his mare aside, clicked her ribs, then trotted back toward the village of Eagle Creek. He knew it was imprudent to be disloyal to his disposition and confront Panther, particularly in the company of his oldest son. Among his emotions, a strong sense of regret grew within. He wished he had kept his feelings private and had not let the man who murdered his son know his pain. James the younger could not help but set his eyes on his brother's murderer. He'd never heard such words fall from his father's mouth, and felt the reality settle over him, which was that Panther had not only slain flesh but the soul of his family. After no more than a few seconds, he'd seen enough and followed his father on horseback. Both men had seen their fill of death, and neither man had any desire to see what was in store for the Panther.

The claps of the Winthrops' horses followed back along the trail. The Green Mountain Boys remained silent and mostly still until the riders were at a distance. With his eyes fixed on the Winthrops, Ethan bellowed, "You know what to do?"

"We do," replied Ira, one of the oldest members of Green Mountain Boys militiamen. Panther was dragged back toward the massive, black, cast iron lamp oil tank. He struggled if only to give them a hard time, until they reached the base of the nearest brick footing. Ethan Allen strolled a few feet behind, with his son, Joseph, trailing. The commander made a few pointed gestures, and the remaining members of the company each grabbed his musket and encircled Panther. He was surrounded by the working ends of a dozen loaded American muskets. Remember drew a small dagger from his side and sliced away the binds about Panther's shoulders as he and Ira held onto the huge beam. Both men leaped back as it crashed to the ground with a deep thud, nearly crushing their feet. Wyandot did his best not to show relief, but could not help but to crick his neck from side to side, stretch his fingers, and clench his fists.

To the west, a patch of marigold pumpkins lay along a patchy field of brown grass, and each of its members observed without expression. Behind, was a pane of gray mist where the heavens had fallen to meet the damp, tawny sward. The barren trees clawed at the sky with their twisted, knotted fingers as though they were desperate to climb into the clouds. The breath of death had filled the air.

"Don't get too comfortable, Indian," uttered Ethan. "You see, we are going to kill you now, Squanto. We are going to kill you because you murdered a boy. I think even you accept that. But we are going to make you suffer because you are a Cherry Negro. Take a look around, for this is the last time you will see the trees, and the grass, and the sky. The breaths you take now are to be the last gasps of air to enter your lungs, and my voice will be the last one you hear, you fucking Indian."

Panther was speechless, and for the first time, perhaps in all his years, he was frightened. His inkling was to plead for a quick end, yet he refused to surrender his honor. The once-unmovable grin had morphed into a look of terror. His skin was pale, and he was hardly able to keep his feet, requiring both Ira and Remember to drag him along. They yanked him forward, near the head of the colossal tank, scouring the blades of grass with the heavy links from his ankle chain. At the front of the large, iron container was a brass, elbow-shaped valve, and above it, a sturdy cast iron lid. The hinged lid was some three feet in diameter and closed by a narrow iron wheel. Routinely, *scrubs*, as they were, were required to enter the tank and clean the residue buildup from the old whale oil. Mostly, though not always, scrubs were young men who physically grew out of the occupation. The hinged lid was how the scrubs entered and exited the otherwise sealed tank.

Ira exerted all his strength to turn the wheel and open the lid, yet required Ethan to step in and assist. "For the Good Lord's sake, are you a man, yes?" When the two were finally able to pry the heavy iron cap open, the tank seemed to exhale a faint breeze of smelly, oil-infused air. The lid opened as though the massive tank was famished and ready to ingest a large meal. Inside, it was as black as the darkest night, the air was overcome with the horrid stench of lamp oil, and the inner walls were slick to the touch of the oily residue. Wyandot considered charging the band of men, choosing death by musket ball over anticipation and suffocation, yet his urge suggested he would merely gag a bit before simply falling into a terminal sleep. Perhaps suffocation was not as horrific a fate as he expected. Without being coaxed, he approached the open breach without resistance. To which Ethan remarked, "You are a wahoo who takes to instruction quickly. I can see why the Lobsters hired you. Help him in, Ira."

Ira and Remember gripped Panther's bruised and bare feet and hoisted forward, toward the opening. Wyandot clanged his head against the solid, cast iron base, causing some of the militiamen to chuckle with childlike pleasure. A buzz rang through his skull, and for a second or two he was lost in a daze. His hard, dry skin scraped along the metallic edges until he finally managed to secure his way to the inside of the tank. Ira swung the immense latch closed. A spearing clang rang throughout and tore through Panther's ears as he was immersed in total darkness. He could see not an inch from his face. His nude body slinked against the slick iron surface until he settled in as best he could. The fit was so tight, Panther's arms were pinned to his chest. With every gasp, his lungs were pressed to breathe the hot, stinking air. Remember sprang back some distance from the tank after Ira had forced the heavy latch closed. Shrill, metallic squeals rang as he managed to turn the wheel, fully confining Panther within his iron tomb.

The company was silent and still. "I hate to say this," said Ethan. "Well, maybe I don't really hate to say, but fuck it, I'm saying it. That was too easy and not much fun. Disappointing, really, as he seemed to be a feisty bitch, and I thought he would put up a fight. So be it. Hopefully the next one will."

The troops dispersed, each heading in no particular direction. Their eyes were fixed toward the ground as though they were searching for something or somethings. One by one, they snatched fallen branches or large sticks and by the bundle, carried them toward the lamp oil tank. Each tossed his gathering under, then continued to collect more. Two of the troopers hoisted Panther's massive pine yoke and tossed it under the tank. Remember pillaged through the lean-to, lifting the cans and shaking them as though he was assessing their contents. After he found one, which seemed to be at least mostly full, he brought it toward the others, near the base of the large iron chamber. He unplugged the lid and immediately doused the timber with the lamp oil from within the container.

"Very good, very good," proclaimed Ethan. A few more stragglers quickly tossed odd sticks and twigs onto the pile beneath the iron tank. "Joseph!" he called. "Where is he…?"

Despite being told otherwise, the young man had drifted from his father's side. "I'm coming," replied his son with his typical tetchiness. He was near his belongings and carried with him a number of items, which he nearly dropped from his clutches as he appeared overburdened and careless. Ethan rolled his eyes and mumbled his impatience. As Joseph neared the tank's post, he knelt to one knee and allowed his collection of utensils to fall. After a few seconds of fumbling through them, he dangled a long, linen strand, while holding it above his eyes as the gathering breeze pushed it westward. He peered back toward his father, who observed from his position silently. Joseph removed a dry strip of char-cloth from a cylindrical tin; a black patch of cotton about four inches by four inches in size. With the char-cloth wrapped around a small flint stone, he struck it with a thin, steel striker. He whipped his arm several times, smashing the striker against the flint stone.

"Go easy," advised Ethan. "Striking it forcefully is not as effective as striking it smartly." Joseph shook his head, eagerly acknowledging his father, then continued, but at a more deliberate pace. After several more strikes, the cloth was finally alive with the faint trace of fire. A satisfied grin grew on his face. Joseph was careful, yet hurried and put the burning cloth to a knotted strip of pine that quickly took to the flame. He blew gentle breaths, coaxing the struggling glow into a fire. Once again he peered back toward his father, who remained still and attentive. "Anything to say, Dad?" he asked.

Ethan looked at his company. Each face that looked back at him was covered in filth, yet their sympathetic looks were clear. Most were leaning against their muskets or standing in some manner of relaxed posture, and all remained speechless until Remember volunteered a eulogy. "I do," he said. "I would like to say something, Ethan. If you do not mind, that is."

Ethan appeared to be a bit taken aback, as he mostly assumed nobody would elect to say a thing. "Please do…"

After another hushed moment or two, Remember uttered, "Fuck off."

Ethan rolled his eyes and grumbled under his breath, "Beautifully stated." Then he turned toward his son. "All right, let's get on with this, Joseph. Be careful." Young Joseph nodded once more, and with ease and deliberation, approached the bundle of oil-soaked kindling below the sturdy, iron tank. It was as though one of the branches was stretching itself to meet Joseph as he neared. He connected the small torch he had in hand with an oil-glazed branch toward the corner of the nearest brick support. In an instant, the flash of flame slithered through the pile of kindling and burst into a bright, blazing pyre.

The logs and sticks crackled within the blaze, and almost immediately, each man was bathed in the fire's warmth. The flames flickered and danced. "Get more wood," ordered Ethan. Ira and a few others again trod back near the trees, to poke around for whatever timber they could find. The others simply peered into the waves of flame. The glowing embers floated toward the sky, and the bale of large sticks blackened and twisted as though they were struggling in agony.

Thin lines of dark smoke from the unseasoned wood smothered the tank and slipped away to join the clouds above. Among the flame's crackles began muted, deep thumping. Joseph's boyish brown eyes were thrust toward his father, who returned his look with a remorseful stare. The thuds grew louder, more frequent and more frantic as the fire continued to grow in size and fury. Each rumble had a hard time escaping the thick, iron casting, yet the anguished pangs filled the cold, autumn air.

From a hundred paces along the footpath, overlooking the creek, James slowed his mount and turned against the direction of their pace. Against the backdrop of drab, brown foliage and the pale gray sky, he could see the still figures surrounding the black, iron tank. The winds had died almost in an instant, and The Green Mountain Boys' limp and lifeless banner sagged to perfectly represent the collective sentiment of the militia unit. From a distance, glimmers from the glowing flame spoke to their hearts. The Winthrops had been contented to live within the shroud of ignorance to the specifics regarding Panther's fate. The glowing blaze against the sullen field announced his demise in very clear terms. James's mournful gray eyes locked with those of his oldest son. Neither made a sound, yet both knew exactly what was happening within the oil tank. James's forgiving soul was taken by the bitter senses of revenge and hatred. Their home would sleep one fewer soul, their table would serve one fewer mouth, and they would be forever changed. New concerns now festered within the father's mind. He could not help but wonder which of his boys was lost, and if his other children would find their way home, to question his judgments, his leniency as a parent, which he believed enabled his children to often question, if not disregard, his instruction. He wondered how to tell his wife she had lost a child. The tired mare beneath him groaned and strode about, and he pets her neck affectionately as though he had a newfound appreciation. James Winthrop aged nearly a decade in one day and was as ashamed as he was saddened. The events of this mid-fall afternoon would never be discussed by any of the family. At daybreak, they will find George's remains. He will be put to rest yet the memories of this day will live to torment the souls of his loved ones.

After what seemed to be an eternity of silence, James finally announced to his son, "Come, let's go home." Side by side, the father and son trotted away from Ethan Allen and all the callous men within his militia. Safely from earshot, Ethan pierced his son with a menacing glance, "You did not think it to be helpful to let me know he had more than one fucking son?"

* * *

Elsewhere.

The forest had awoken. After the long hours of autumnal darkness, the shadows were chased from the western sky. One by one, the stars faded into the pale blue heavens, though the striking quarter moon refused to retreat with the night and remained proud as it peered over the woodlands. Fallen leaves rolled along the ground, swept along by the eastern breeze. Captain Pearson had been wandering with the windblown leaves for the better part of the evening. He was without food and water, yet his invigorated sense of determination pushed him forward. Desperate for sustenance, he chewed on blades of grass and swallowed worms and beetles. On occasion, he was fortunate enough to find a muddy patch to stick his mouth against the ground and suck a gulp or two of muddied water. His right arm had been slung lifelessly for such a time that his fingers were numb and hardly able to move. The pants at his waist had become so loose he was forced to tie them with a makeshift belt fashioned from a scrap of cloth, his muscles had wilted, and he could feel his body considering surrender.

As he trudged along, he held his side just below the ribs with his good arm. His stomach was fiercely cramped with a sharp, unyielding pain, making it even more difficult to continue. He had come to the point that he was endlessly hunched over and floundered aimlessly without lifting his head. His vision was quickly blurring, and it was a certainty his frame was going to give in at any moment. He thrust his left hand against his knee, felt a pulsing wave within him as if his body was preparing to vomit, then began to lose his equilibrium. All the color had drained from his skin, and his eyes wandered in all directions. He swayed like an old drunk after a long night, from his right to his left, forward and back. His body urged him to hit the ground. No longer conscious, his arms fell lifelessly, and he collapsed forward. Before he reached the soil, his body was immediately snatched from behind by one of the two men who had been following him closely.

Pearson's unknown escorts were as silent as a gentle breeze. Each of the figures were clad in a heavy animal skin cloak and hood that cast his entire face in shadow. Within the arms of his captor, Pearson's body remained limp, with arms dangled at his sides, eyes rolled back into his skull, skin as gray as a stormy sky, and a slight beck of saliva struggled to stream from his lips through his stubbly chin. Captain Pearson was insentient, and as his muscles gave, his bowels released a stream of watery shit into his breeches.

*　*　*

Some miles to the west.

North Ridge Path cut from Concord through Lexington and all the way to Boston. It was routinely pounded by the boots of Continental Soldiers and the hooves of their many horses. Off North Ridge branched a far less traveled corridor that followed the Charles River for a distance westward. The path would be found on no official map, yet the Nipmuck Passage was most active as it carried smugglers' contraband, spy dispatches, and harlots from the whorehouses of Massachusetts Colony to American army camps. Most familiar with the route was Otetiani, the lovely, young Mohawk who routinely visited Colonel Israel Putnam to slurp the semen from his sagging, old cock.

The burnt-orange blanket of descended leaves made it difficult for one to see where the trees met the ground and to further conceal the mysterious pathway. A small open wagon, drawn by a single horse, rolled from the west, slicing through the layer of foliage. The cart was short, though built with heavy, tall sideboards and sturdy wheels. A young trooper of the Third Connecticut Regiment held the reins, and next to him sat an even younger trooper of the same regiment.

Their blue jackets looked as though they had never been worn, and their tri-cornered hats were as stiff as if they had just been pressed. The white bands about their lids and the white linen of their breeches were wholly unspoiled. Both of their youthful expressions appeared no older than the uniforms on their backs. The driver seemed somewhat attentive, yet his partner not as much, as he casually leaned with one foot on the footrest and the other tucked on the bench with his arm bent over his knee. From his teeth dangled a long hay straw. From time to time, he nipped a piece from it, then spat it toward the back of the cart. Within the wagon's bed were two large, enclosed wooden barrels, a dozen or so flintlock muskets of varying type, and a small number of inconsequential-looking crates. The charger looked as if she had been worked beyond exhaustion. She could hardly manage more than to haul such a relatively undemanding load. Her coat was matted and worn, and her muscles sagged. All the harnesses about her swung loosely, as though she had been strapped to the wagon with little care. Her collar was a soiled, tattered, and torn Union Jack flag of the Empire. It rested on her shoulders toward her spine, underneath the back strap.

Within the droning clanks and strides, the pair continued in conversation. "I think I'm confused," said Dixon as he gently furrowed the reins. "I'm not sure I am following completely. I get it, I think, but I don't know. Explain it different."

"For all fucks, all right," replied Ryan impatiently. "If you die in this war, you would be a martyr, or someone who dies for his cause, yes?."

"Yes, I get that; I'm not really sure what you are asking though" confirmed Dixon.

"Alright," continued Ryan. "I'm simply asking, are you willing to die for this cause?"

Dixon creased his brows with confusion. "Certainly. Wouldn't all of who are fighting for it be willing to die? Wouldn't you?" he asked.

"Me?" snapped Ryan, "God, no. I wouldn't die for this, for freedom or for any cause for that matter. I'm going out of my way to survive this shit. Can't enjoy freedom if your dead."

"You know, Jesus was a martyr," replied Dixon.

"Well, he's Jesus, right?" said Ryan. "I'm not looking to be Jesus, I'll let Jesus be Jesus and me be me. Fuck that, I wouldn't be willing to die for any cause. I wouldn't give my own life to save myself."

A silly grin grew on Dixon's youthful expression, "What? That doesn't even make any sense. You wouldn't give your life to save your life?"

"Exactly," replied Ryan with satisfaction as he tapped Dixon on the knee.

"I'm not sure how that would work, exactly, but to be safe I would say no. Jesus is in the Goddam Bible, he deserves it. He died for our sins? I don't even know what that means. That's why I'm not Jesus, because I would need much more of an explanation before I signed on to agree to that. 'So, they can keep sinning after I do this…Is everyone going to reimburse me in heaven for this somehow?' I'm fine being forgotten, I don't need to be read about in a thousand years from now. Just let me…" Before another syllable could escape his tongue, the jagged edge of a stone arrowhead tore through the back of the soldier's throat, thrust between his jaws. The long shaft of the arrow pierced the back of his neck and grazed past the spine to jut out of his mouth as though he had swallowed half of the projectile. Ryan's eyes widened as he desperately and hysterically threw his arms about. Blood-curdling groans were forced from his mouth as dark current shades streamed down his neck, and as he thrashed about, the feathered end of the shaft struck Dixon forcefully in his right eye. Ryan continued to flail about wildly until he leaped from the bench toward the ground.

Dixon was thrown back, in shock and pain. Instantly the blur of another arrow whizzed through the air and flew directly into his ribs below his right arm. The stone head wedged its way into his rib cage and fractured two of his bones. He shrieked with agony, and the tired mare pulling the cart neighed and kicked her front hooves into the air in a fit of rage. The missile punctured his lung. He was still alive, yet lifeless, and he tumbled from his position to crash against the cold, hardened pathway. The young soldier whimpered meekly until all life was drained from within him. Dixon's death was mercifully swift. His comrade was not so fortunate.

With blood dripping from the sharpened stone point of the arrow, Ryan stomped about frantically. The gush of blood continued to flow from his mouth, and his state of panicked despair grew more panicked by the instant. From within the heavy thicket of trees painted with the brushstrokes of autumn emerged the shadows of two figures. Beams of the sun were pressed against their backs to create oddly angelic silhouettes. Both were cloaked in crudely patched animal skin hoods. A long, arched bow was extended from one's hand and a quill of arrows from the other. They remained unmoved as they watched Ryan batter about for a few more seconds until he collapsed to his knees. The arrow's blood-sodden shaft extended nearly a foot from his jaw and the fletching another foot from the back of his neck. His heart raced and the grinding gurgling continued with each pant of breath for which he fought. Ryan's hands were trembling like leaves in a storm as he looked to wrap them around the projectile and somehow, reflexively remove it from his mouth.

From their position, the assassins slowly skulked toward him. Their figures blocked the battered American soldier from the sun. Without concern or thought, they remained still in observation. After some time, perhaps ten to fifteen seconds, the archer withdrew a fresh arrow from his quill, rested the arrow on the base of the hand at the grip, and yanked the string with all his might. The bow's limb rasped as it was gradually bent as though it was going to snap. The jagged stone arrowhead was pointed at the center of Ryan's forehead, directly between both of his shaggy dark brown brows. The head-point was no more than a foot from his temple when the grip was released, firing the arrow through his skull. The arrow drove cleanly though Ryan's cranium and pinned it into the earth pathway as a broadside was nailed to a wall. The arrow that had pierced his neck was driven forward and tumbled toward his chest to finally come to rest on the layer of leaves on the ground. Ryan was killed in an instant; his remains were nothing more than a limp sack of meat and bones.

The archer lowered himself near Ryan's fallen body, rested the bow by its side on the ground, and removed his hood. He was entirely bald, with blisters and twisted protuberances covering him nearly to the top of his head. His left eye was covered in a stringy

224

linen wrap, which was bound to the base of his skull, and his right was nestled between the dry, scarred, and calloused skin. The demonic figure's nose was collapsed inward and would seem to lack any trace of cartilage. His entire jaw consisted of no flesh or bone and would appear to be wholly inorganic. Two thin, long narrow metallic shafts ran from the nape of his neck above his back shoulders to his jawline. The shanks supported a crudely, unevenly carved artificial wooden jaw. At the mouth, a net of misshapen, heavy brass and copper wires filtered the air entering his lungs.

The enigmatic creature examined Ryan closer to ensure he was no longer alive, and when convinced as such, strode toward Dixon to do the same. Private Dixon lay on the leafy grass a few yards away with his face planted into the ground and the fletching end of the arrow protruding from his ribs.

"They're done?" asked his companion, to which the assassin slowly nodded his head. The other removed his heavy, dark brown hood to reveal the pale skin and faded blue eyes belonging to Ensign Shaw of the Fourth Order of Aquitaine Light Horse Guards. "Do we want the horse, Lieutenant?" he asked.

Still crouched just above Dixon's remains, Lieutenant Stone struggled to turn his head, as though to offer a negative response. When he rolled Dixon's body over, he saw the young soldier would forevermore wear the mask of dread. Under Stone's dark brown cloak, a scabbarded, long, steel dagger was strapped to his hip. He slid the blade from its leather sheath and brought the edge to Dixon's temple, along the length of his brows. The steel glimmered in the daylight and shone the distorted contours along his disfigured face. With his hands bound in heavy, dark leather gloves, Stone clasped a handful of Dixon's thick brown hair as though he was pulling back the reins of a wild stallion. He thrust his knee into Dixon's chest and, with great force, yanked the hair back with his left hand. Stone's right hand slid the razor-sharp edge to and fro as though he was sawing the trunk of a fallen tree. He sliced away the skin as streams of thick, warm blood spurted from the widening gash. Without the slightest agitation, he wrenched the peels of skin and flesh back from Dixon's skull to the rhythm of a grotesque slurping. The blade frequently scraped against the hardened skull as though it was being sharpened against a stone. Finally, the last stubborn strip of skin was torn from the base of the parietal bone.

Dixon lay as a large, lifeless lump, with the surface of his head torn off, the lids of his eyes locked fully open, and jaw nearly to his chest. His bloodied mangled scalp dangled from Stone's grip. He looked about for a moment, then forcefully flung it into the hedgerows a few yards from the path. It landed partially tangled in the low brush. The gleaming pink scrap of flesh would become an inviting meal for the crows, who would surely pick it away before the night came to pass.

Shaw stood ahead of the wagon and gently rubbed the long neck of the lovable, old overburdened mare. She shifted about as though she enjoyed the affection, then tossed her head from side to side. Her matted, unwashed mane fluttered about, and she turned toward Shaw with a demonstrative look about her eyes. "I know, I know," he said in a comforting tone. Shaw's face was youthful, yet oddly aged, with dry skin and sunken eyes. His hair was as thick as when he was a boy, but as gray as the memory of his father's. He was perhaps forty years old and could convince some he was twenty or seventy. The dejected trooper peered beyond the tired workhorse and noticed Stone, who held his crimson-swathed blade low to his side as he stormed toward Ryan's remains. His comrade's image was an immediate reminder of the final task, which was perhaps the most unpleasant of them all. He sighed with a large gulp of air and rested his eyelids for three or four seconds until he was fully able to conjure the fortitude to continue. Despite his efforts otherwise, he could not help but notice the kindness in the horse's eyes. Once again, he glanced over to Stone, who had his knee forced into Ryan's chest, about his neck. Falteringly, Shaw slowly unsheathed the fiercely sharp dagger he wore at his side. With his hand firmly clamped at the shoulder of the weary animal, he rammed his blade into her neck, then twisted and churned with all the force he could manage. Infused with a burst of energy, she kicked wildly and thrust about. Shaw's feet were thrown from beneath him as the old mare vaulted forward and threw the rickety old cart nearly a foot into the air. With an abrupt thud, Shaw's back landed against the earth to knock the wind from his lungs. She tramped about, spewing heavy squelches of deep-red blood as her wild heart pumped it through the pit where his blade remained. The scream of her horrific cry carried through the woods.

Stone had yet to make a full slice along Ryan's brow when the clanging and high-pitched whinny caused him to toss aside his blade to grab his bow and a fresh arrow. Shaw threw his arms over his face and was nearly lost within the frantic dance of the horse's heavy hoofs. With a blur, Stone's arrow whooshed over Shaw's eyes to drive its way into her neck. The entire shaft was nearly lost within her, with only a few inches standing from her coat. With a flash, he fired another, which landed no more than a finger's length from the first. It, too, was driven almost entirely through the dense muscles about her neck. She gave two or three wild kicks until she folded over to crash against the roadway, wrenching the wagon to its side with a loud racket. The front wheel axle nearly split in two, the side boards snapped from the base, and leather ropes were strewn about as the tentacles of an octopus. Most of the contents were spilled onto the pathway, and one of the two barrels burst open to let loose a fuming cloud of gray powder that engulfed the cart and departed workhorse.

Shaw remained on his back, with his pulse raging, and he was slowly blanketed by a thin layer of ashy gunpowder. He coughed and winced, then rubbed some of the dust from his eyes. Stone took his time strolling toward the wreckage near Shaw's position. When he neared, his large frame blocked Shaw from the sun, prompting the Ensign to groaned through winded breath. "I was not eager to kill the beast. I should have acted with more resolve or had you do it. Perhaps half-measures are more dangerous than no measure." Stone offered nothing more than indifference and slung his bow over his shoulder, offering no assistance. Confirming his cohort was alive and at the very worst, virtually unhurt, he simply moved on. From the pile of muskets strewn along the pathway, he gathered the two that appeared to have incurred the least damage. With his free hand, he heaved the unbroken barrel over his shoulder and trudged back toward the tree line. Shaw took another moment to do his best to quickly pat off all the powder he could manage, to gather himself, then slowly ascended to his feet to dust himself more briskly. He followed the lieutenant after snatching the nearest of the wooden crates that had rolled several feet from the fallen wagon. It took much of his strength to heave it upon his shoulder, and the pinch in his spine caused him to moan with pain. After a few strides toward the trees, he turned back to see his silhouette marked on the ground by the gunpowder that had settled around where he fell. Subtly and without drawing Shaw's attention, he glided back toward his powder-drawn image and swept his feet about the powder to ensure it covered over.

* * *

Captain Pearson stirred to life by rolling from his side. His injured shoulder burned with an incredible tingle, having been pressed by the weight of his body. As his vision cleared, the blinding glow before him refocused into the beams of sunlight that sliced through the large gap within the rugged stone above. He found himself resting on a bed of dry dirt, loose stones, and pebbles within the womb of brown and gray jagged rocks, coarse within a forest stalagmite pillars. He moved to sit upright and grunted as he realized his ankle was imprisoned within the iron clasp and chain in which it was bound. The links are no more than a yard in length and ended at a sturdy, cast iron pin that had been driven into the stone surface. The iron links rattled along the rocks as Pearson posed himself into an acceptable position. With his senses finally realized, the beleaguered captive felt an odd pulsing energy and heat within him. The air was cool to see the mist of his breath, yet he remained unusually warm.

He was emaciated, nearly unrecognizable, and almost lost within his filthy, matted, and torn uniform. A long, uneven, nappy beard nearly buried his sullen and beaten expression. Still, he grimaced whenever he moved his arm suddenly and could hardly open his mouth without the pain from his jaw cutting into him. Searching about from where he sat offered no trace of clues as to where he was. With his good arm, he desperately and pathetically tugged at the heavy chain, yet accomplished nothing more than to exasperate his senses of hopelessness and frustration. From a distance, the diminished echo of footsteps began to grow louder. The clattering suggested more than a single man was approaching. A faint, flickering glimmer was cast against the sides of the narrow and irregular cave-like passageway. It grew as it neared, as did the clapping sounds of boots against the dry, stone surface. Pearson writhed about in near panic, then once again wrenched the chain with all his might. His reflex compelled him to grab at his hip and snatch his pistol, yet it was not to be found. Violent and frantic jerks did nothing to free him, and he began to kick his leg wildly. The rough edge of the shackles around his ankle began to scrape into his flesh, yet he continued thrashing about. A pear-sized stone lay several feet yet within the range of his grasp. Desperately, he stretched his throbbing arm as much as it could be stretched. The jolt of pain raced through his body as if he had been struck by a crashing bolt of lightning. He clenched his fingers closed, then open, as though he was struggling for the last fractions of an inch to reach the stone, which sat a hair from his touch. A thunderous groan escaped his lungs as he grazed the rock with his fingers, nudging it ever so softly. He could not extend himself to wrap his hand around it, and the small boulder remained motionless and just far enough to be free of his grasp. The inert rock appeared to be taunting the desperate captain.

He released the stress from his body, eased his muscles, and sighed, resigned to accept whatever fate had to offer. Pearson closed his eyes and waited with unusually calm anticipation. After a moment, the heavy stomps came to a sudden halt. Pearson opened his eyes to see what had approached. Two men, covered-over with distressed, deerskin cloaks looked down on him. Both seemed faceless as their hoods cast them into darkness. One held an old lantern with an unsteady flame in one hand and Pearson's superbly crafted leather pouch in the other. To his left, his companion held nothing other than the animal skin cloak behind the other's shoulder, which he clung to.

"Please, listen, listen," pleaded Pearson. "The Empire serves your interests—the British are killing your enemies, the Americans. The Americans are the enemy. *We* are not your enemy. I am not American, please. I am a British soldier, and we are on your side. We commission your kind. We, um, we pay your people to work with us against the ones who kill you. Wyandot Panther, he is one. The Quebec Act protects you from the colonists. Our king does not permit the Americans to expand into your territories, your lands."

"You are not only a fool but a cowardly fool," replied the nearest figure. He spoke the King's English well, and his accent immediately suggested he was neither a native nor a colonial. "You would plead with the natives as though they value your reason, as though they care what the king is wanting to do? The Quebec Act? I cannot believe you are a soldier in our army. You should be ashamed to drape yourself with crimson and claim to fight for the Empire. We are not Indians, fool. Had we been or had we been intent to kill you, you would leave this world stripped of any self-respect."

He tossed Pearson's pouch to the ground near his side, causing a few articles of parchment to flutter in the air. The looming figure removed the hood from his head to reveal his face in the few beams of daylight that found their way into the cave. Colonel Bowman's face was gruff, and his chin was covered with thick stubble. A few strands of gray were mixed within the dark brown. The lantern's soft light captured his face as though it was in a painting. The scars and abrasions remained, though he looked to have aged not one day since he fought the French over a decade ago. "You managed to stray entirely in the wrong direction and are nowhere near Manhattan Island, Captain. It seems your quest has ended without feat but with failure, and General Howe will do nothing to save Ticonderoga."

Despite Bowman's declaration, Pearson was relieved, though bewildered. After a moment of silent contemplation, he rummaged through his pouch to hastily inventory which of its contents remained, and from what he could immediately gather, nothing of note was missing. "What are you concerned to be missing? The dispatch you failed to deliver?" asked Bowman.

"I don't understand," replied Pearson. "You are British? What am I doing here? Why am I chained like a prisoner?"

"We are your countrymen," replied Bowman. "We could have left you to be eaten by the coyotes, though that is not generally our way. Good fortune seems to suggest you offer value to our mission, at least this is what I am going to assume. Nonetheless, I would not expect you to be aware of such things and wanted to keep you around, to see if you belong. Now, we require you to submit to *our* questions."

With that, Wilkinson threw his hood back to his shoulders to reveal his eyeless face. Below his brows was a toothed, blistered scar that ran from ear to ear. His sockets were littered with lumps and abrasions, as it seemed the body could not fully heal whatever wounds may have been caused. Bowman continued, "As of now, I have no wish to harm you. That is to say, I cannot promise you will not be harmed. How we move forward hinges on your behavior, Captain. Valor be damned, you are a soldier who will be treated honorably. However, I can certainly promise, one way or another, you will not be leaving us. All your travels *will* end with you here. I expect you to speak truthful and straight. Do not look to tell us what you think we believe to be right, only speak what *you* believe to be true. Be assured, my companion will surely know if you are being anything other than forthright."

Bowman guided Wilkinson forward by gently tugging at his arm. The lieutenant was eased forward by the colonel, and with a gravely sinister voice, he demanded, "Finish telling us who you are."

Pearson's nerves had him shivering, and with an uneasy tone, he answered, "My name is Isaac Pearson. I am a captain in the Twenty-First Queen's Royal Artillery."

"How did the captain find himself here?" hissed Wilkinson.

"I was dispatched by my commander, Colonel Oliver Bell, to lead a party of infantrymen and one Mohawk scout from my position as a battery commander at Fort Ticonderoga. We were overrun by a patrolling band of American militia some days, perhaps a week, past. I cannot say who survived. Since then, I have been lost, hopelessly trying to find my way from the woodlands to satisfy my charge and deliver the communiqué. I am humbled, though being truthful to say I was unfit for such a task. With all my conviction, I offered all my strength to the charge. As it was, it was given to me out of desperation, and plainly, we can see it resulted as probability suggested, good sirs."

"Captain," sneered Bowman. He surmised his accent, choice of words, and demeanor to suggest Pearson was either nobility or tended to hob-nob with nobility. "Those details are not important. How did you get here, to America, to fight this war? Bearing in mind

E. THOMAS JOSEPH

your misadventures and the elegance of nobility in your tongue, I assume you are not a career soldier."

Pearson was not sure what his captor was suggesting or where he was going with his questions. "Well, sir, because you insist on truth and candor, I will tell you, I do not see how the question is germane."

"How can you make such a declaration when you don't know where my line of inquiries is heading?" groused Bowman. "Seems I may not have been as clear as I had thought—I require answers, not conversation."

Pearson rested back and yielded to Bowman's authority. "Are you curious about my loyalty to the Empire, or to the cause for which we fight? My decision to join in the suppression of the rebellion was made with the understanding of the dangers. I was called by my sense of honor and devotion to the King and Country. I'm here as any loyal Englishman. I believe in the cause all the same. Stability cannot be taken for granted. I have little faith in my fellow man, and this affords me a bit of latitude in regards to tyranny, I suppose. For my part, I will gladly sacrifice liberty if it means my countrymen are required to do the same. As it is, I cannot be idle when I see chaos reign at the behest of American rabble."

Bowman's interest in Pearson had just been piqued. Though he was not fully convinced honor or loyalty compelled the captain to enter the war, he admired his efforts and perceived intellect. "Commendable. Reasonable. Through chance or incompetence, or... some other means, you put yourself at a crossroad where either direction promised a profound consequence. You believe in fate?"

With a confounded look, Pearson replied, "Fate? Fate is an obtuse concept. It is meaningless and offers nothing to believe. I believe we are carried by our decisions, that our actions stimulate reactions. Where we are and who we become are products of our will. If you choose to call this fate, I will not quibble. If you are interested to know, I do not believe in a pre-determined destiny beyond our control. I do not believe a mystical entity has determined our...*fates*." Pearson struggled to sit upright and to find a semblance of comfort. "I am imprisoned in this...bloody cave, as the result of my actions and my decisions. I suppose I will concede as much as to acknowledge, I put my fate in your hands."

Bowman was impassive, seemingly unmoved. His soul had long surrendered all sense of joy and sadness to the weight of the Kahontsi Ehnita. He was not driven by pride, nor a personal dislike for Captain Pearson. He was compelled by an evangelical spirit to serve the Moon's Eye. "Fate did not see you born into nobility? Fate has not chosen you to be a citizen and not a colonial? Fate does not decide which troopers will hear the bullets fly and which will be struck by them? What is your judgment, Lieutenant?"

The eyeless companion responded with a ghostly tone, "His mind is as sharp as a blade. He believes in his intellect and trusts it more than instinct or superstition. It is a mathematical mind and requires to act on reason. He believes his words, yet his heart has more to say. He is as immovable as the stones around us. We cannot remove him from the world in which he lives."

Bowman lowered his head in defeat, rubbed his brows, and declared, "That was not what I was hoping to hear. You are sure of this?"

"I am quite sure, Colonel," responded Wilkinson. "He is scared, but truthful. His mind is reasoned and cannot be moved by implausible suggestions."

"Captain Pearson, do you believe there will be a day when the sun will set in the east and rise in the west?"

"No," uttered Pearson. "Of course not. It would be an impossibility."

"Do you believe there will be a day when we can stay the grip of death?"

"No, I do not. Death is inevitable. We can treat illness and injury, yet will never learn to escape death," said Pearson.

Colonel Bowman subtly nodded his head as if to confirm his lieutenant's conclusions. With a buoyant voice, he continued, "I am Colonel Emrick Bowman of the Fourth Order of the Aquitaine Light Horse Guards. We had been summoned to America to rescue Braddock after he was trapped in the Highlands by a throng of Huguenots. We sank three of Louis's tallest ships before they could land in Quebec. With two scores of the king's men, we seized Carillon from the Frogs and pried each of his hearts from his chests, then piled the corpses like a cord of wood before a long winter. We won the war for the Empire, then swept it free of malcontent colonists and troublesome Indians. I cannot fully remember the extent of our triumphs, nor can I fully recall the extent of the carnage which has been wrought by our hands." Bowman paused for a moment as if to consolidate his thoughts.

"Today and forevermore, we serve the Moon Relic, the *Kahontsi Ehnita*, the Giver of Life. You're feeling its warm energy. It has chosen me, and, in time, it will choose another. As long as we are alive, we will see it never touch the fingers of any corrupt and ill-fit monarch, especially the one whose fat fucking ass presently sits on the throne in London."

Pearson was entirely confused, anxious, and lost for proper manners. "I'm sorry, what is this?" he uttered. "I would like to be on my way, sir. I have no interest in taking anything from you, the Giver of Life. I wish you well."

Bowman seemed oblivious to Pearson's plea. "During our war with the French, the king's aide tasked us to consider a curious circumstance. A small number of native captives were oddly disfigured and impaired. They did not appear inflicted with any wound or condition our surgeons had ever seen. They appeared as living ghouls, with leather skin and white eyes. With persistence, we managed to pry the stories from them. They spoke of a Chieftain who had lived many lifetimes and a medicine to extend life, beyond the realm of natural death. The blind man at my side stated it to be true, insofar as they believed. Word traveled over the ocean to the right persons in London; those who need only to utter a command and have another risk his life to follow a whim. We were then ordered to track this mysterious medicine and retrieve it for George's father, the Second, and so we did. We've slaughtered our own to ensure its privacy and safe-keeping, and by our misguided oath, we set to deliver it to His Majesty. I call it the Moon Relic, though it has been called many names. As I have air in my lungs, I will see it never turned to one who régimes by fortunate blood. I will not extend the reign of any king unworthy of rule. Our long lives will be spent defending it, keeping it safe, until it chooses another to do the same. I believe, like you, order is essential; a higher order than your hierarchy of royal blood."

"You don't actually believe this? This is nothing but Native superstition," replied a shocked Pearson.

"I would expect you to dismiss this, yet wanted to be sure. I will not waste my breath trying to convince you otherwise."

"So why tell me all of this, Colonel Bowman?"

Bowman once again nudged Wilkinson and asked: "What do you think?"

The lieutenant subtly shook his head and grumbled, "No. He's not with us. He will die before he is broken. He is sincere in his claims and believes it only to be Indian fairytale. His intellect requires him to accept only which he deems probable until proven otherwise. Regardless, he is soft and accustomed to comforts. His heart is thin on conviction. He will escape your clutches before he is reborn."

Bowman paused for a moment, rubbed his fingers against his chin, and coldly replied, "Some see the light and others are blinded by it. I decided you will never leave this cave. I have concluded to have no choice other than to have you killed, and I believe your honor is worthy of an explanation. It is an act of necessity, and I take no joy in it. We are not heathens. You have my word, Captain, your end will be met with mercy and without pain. I cannot allow you to walk from here now, and for that I am sorry. Blame the winds of chance that have swept you in this direction. You have seen me, seen our dwelling, and have felt the warmth of the Moon Relic. These realities are to be guarded, and only your demise can ensure that."

Pearson's face was full of dread as he desperately looked upon Bowman, who seemed mostly indifferent. "I will make sure you are provided with as much comfort as we can offer…in this cave," added Bowman. "If you like, I'll have a meal, venison, sent to you. We will allow you as peaceful of a night's rest as you can manage. You will witness the sunrise for one last time, then you will be put down forever."

Pearson was overcome with a rush of anxiety as he understood Bowman to be an irrational man with an unsound mind. "No, Colonel, please. I won't, I wouldn't dare say a single thing. I do not even know where I am. You see what an awful, unskilled tracker I am. Please, sir. We are both Englishmen, we are brothers-in-arms. I have a young wife, please."

Bowman was moved only to offer Pearson a passing glance and suggest, "There is nothing I can do." He then reached over to collect a few of the documents that had fallen from his reach. The pages included Bell's dispatch. Bowman slid them closer, then fanned through a few until he came across Pearson's copy of *King Lear*. The colonel rested it on Pearson's chest and placed his makeshift lantern against the stone surface beside the captain. "I'll have your final meal sent to you soon. I can imagine you to be quite famished. Then, please, sleep well if that is what you choose."

Bowman and Wilkinson turned their backs to Pearson and began to slowly walk down the same narrow passageway they arrived from. After three or four strides, Bowman turned back to the captain. "I'm sorry. I nearly forgot," he said. He then reached toward the hind part of his right hip to withdraw a pistol from its holster. Bowman rested it within both palms and admired it for a second or so, then knelt and stretched his arms out, as though he was presenting Pearson with the ceremonial sword of knighthood. "I'm not a thief and this belongs to you. It is a magnificent weapon, sir. A proud weapon I trust served you well. You have my word it will be kept with your remains." Pearson understood continued groveling to be meaningless and respectfully nodded as he accepted his Duval pistol, then Bowman once again turned to walk away. Bowman clutched Wilkinson's wrist to lead his direction. In so doing, without turning back toward Pearson, he bellowed, "It is not loaded. I will give you your balls tomorrow morning."

* * *

Manhattan Island.

"If you are still this will be less painful, I assure you," pleaded Doctor Van Leeuwen. "Less painful for you, and less agitating for me." His subject was bound with a tight leather strap within his jaws and incredibly tight straps at his waist, wrists, and ankles. Against the far wall, the heavy wooden plank on which he was lashed was marked with blots of dried blood and yellow stains. The two men shared the room with spiderwebs, dust, broken bottles, buckets, and scattered raw utensils and tools. Van Leeuwen's brows bowed to note the curious look on his face. He held a long, thin metallic shaft with sharpened end almost as though it was a twelve-inch needle. Heavy mirrors positioned near the ceiling encouraged the light to gleam from the steel. The doctor forcefully jabbed the point into the man's palm, which caused no immediate reaction. Still, the unfortunate soul continued to wallow and grumble in his misery.

"You did not feel that?" asked Van Leeuwen as his ghastly voice echoed through the chamber. The bound subject's response was only to offer an already petrified stare toward the doctor. Once again, he thrust the point into his palm. This time, the subject offered a reply with a quick groan and shake of the head.

Van Leeuwen removed the large, beaver skin hat from his head and ran his fingers through his long, grisly, thin white hair and sighed with annoyance. On the bed before him the subject was unclothed but for filthy, tattered linens draped at his groin. He appeared to be middle-aged, thin, and a bit shorter than most neb. Heavy and quick pants were pressed from his lungs, and his heart was pounding so furiously his chest appeared to pulsate. His right arm was unusually large, more muscular than his frame would suggest, and unusually off-colored with a purplish shade at the flesh. It dangled by his side, lifelessly. At his shoulder, it was met with a glut of blisters and abrasions, glazed with soupy pus and caked with dried blood. A trail of sinewy-looking sutures circled the joint. Van Leeuwen ran his finger along the orchid-infused flesh at the subject's forearm, then pressed the inner elbow. He squinted a bit and moved his eyes closer. "You feel nothing, then?" he asked as he peeked toward the subject's face. Once again, his inquiry was returned with a grunt and an immediate head shake.

Van Leeuwen was visibly irritated. He gazed through one of the dust-covered, eastern windows for a moment or two until he noticed the faint traces of an approaching party of wagons and horsemen in the distance. Slowly, he turned his head toward the agonizing subject. "Excuse me. I will return shortly…and with God's good grace, we can figure this out."

The caravan of cavalrymen and horse-drawn wagons rumbled along an overgrown pathway and came to a halt, just at the northeastern corner of The Mandrake. Two Dragoons rode forward and two more followed, between were a pair of uncovered wagons. The first of the carriages was mostly empty, the trailing was occupied with what could be near a dozen gray-clothed troopers of the Phantom Regiment. Each appeared expressionless with a covered face and cloaked hood. The company's arrival seemed escorted by a chilling breeze and threatening clouds. The grassy field began to swell as the surge of an angry sea. The eyes of the cloaked soldiers cast the light of the struggling sun with blinding beams.

The mounted troopers' brilliant madder red coats could be seen for miles on this solemn, gray worn day. Behind, a tired and nearly beaten horse toiled to haul a hefty, rugged utility wagon. The driver was draped in dull gray, with a hood covering his head, thick glass disks over his eyes, and a triangular leather nozzle over his mouth. By his side sat his near mirror, whose sturdy Blunderbuss musket rested on his shoulders. The cargo within the wagon was as valued as their lives. With a clink and a clank, the wheels slowed to a churn, and the darkly clad figure of Doctor Van Leeuwen emerged from the structure's doorway. As would be expected, he was draped in blackness and gloom. His eyes were as shadowy as the night, and his gray skin could hardly be seen against the stormy sky. With a cold glance, he peered toward the approaching wagon with the closest expression of approval as was possible to be worn on his face. Following several steps behind was the one who had come to be known as the Grave Digger.

She was lean, yet strong and tall enough to look most men straight in the eyes. After one long stride, she stopped near the doctor and stood just over his shoulder. Her midnight hair flowed from her shoulders nearly to her hips and fluttered in the wind like the black flag of Satan's army. She was a temptress with pouting red lips and eyes that could melt steel. She wore the breeches and light great coat of a soldier, with a ceremonial longsword at her hip. Unlike most men, Van Leeuwen was indifferent and unmoved by her seductive appeal, yet continued to find himself impressed by her effectiveness to complete any task she endeavored to accomplish. He offered her a quick glance, then moved forward to meet the oncoming carriage until it crawled to a halt.

Several yards ahead of the wagon and several yards from the Mandrake's doorway, Lieutenant Harris pulled Windstorm's reins and commanded him to stop with a firm, "Whoa, boy." He threw his boots over the saddle to dismount and passed the harness to Lieutenant Murray, who remained on his steed, then sauntered toward the doctor and the vixen Grave Digger. His black, beautifully fashioned tri-corner hat cast his demonic eyes in shadow. As he approached he pulled his riding gloves free from his fingers as his sword swayed at his hip and his packs and tin canisters clanged like tolling bells. "We managed to ensnare one for you, Good Doctor. Mind you, 'twas a costly and difficult task." he said with a dire tone. "He *was* alive, though now I can no longer say for sure. It's not easy not to kill the men you are firing upon."

The company of the Phantom Regiment poured from the back of the trailing wagon to file in a line alongside it. Each man stood at attention with his long musket at his right shoulder; butt to the ground, barrel to the sky. They were indistinguishable from one another. Each was draped in a heavy granite-colored cloak over diligently wrapped bandages at the neck, forearms, and ankles. Not a single strip of skin was seen throughout the lot of them. Their collective breaths rumbled through the air as they struggled to force it from the long hoses that dangled from the thick, leather veils strapped over their mouths. Ahead, the two remaining troopers scampered toward the tail of the carriage to unload the prized haul.

The Fourth New York Regiment Corporal Henry Beekman Lynn had fought daringly; he was one of the first to charge from Dobbs' Ferryboat and of the last to succumb to British fire. He managed six volleys and struck down four of the king's Phantoms before he fell. Fate would oblige his heroics to meet a cruel and ill-fit end. With his neck and shoulder shredded by the many pricks of grapeshot, the hero now lay with only a glimpse of life within him, facedown, in a torn and blood-soaked uniform within the bed of a rickety, old wagon.

"If he is dead, he is of no use to me, Lieutenant. I trust you are not altogether heartbroken about the loss of these creatures spent retrieving him. Though they are interesting…Still, you will be required to waste more of your time retrieving another, with his heart still beating," said Van Leeuwen from his position just outside the entryway.

"Such trouble for such a simple task, Lieutenant Harris? You must work hard to keep your reputation," mocked the Grave Digger as she stood a few feet from the doctor.

"I wasn't sure that was you," replied Harris. "I thought the stench of dead fish was coming from the river. Should have known it was your twat."

She chuckled and was undeterred by his attempt at an insult. "Come now, Lieutenant, you can do better than that." With a brazen flare, she puckered her lips and blew Lieutenant Harris a kiss.

Harris smirked coldly. "It seems my lady does not bring out the best in me. If I valued your opinion, I would take the time to enlighten you about the difficulty of such a task. Though, ladyfolk should not be expected to know of such things. Ignorance in these matters is part of what makes them ladylike. It has always been for the best for the women to be as unfamiliar with warfare as the men are of feeding infants the milk from our tits."

The Grave Digger shook her head as though she was confirming his assertions. She found amusement in the exchange and delighted in knowing the harsher his tone, the more she was getting to him. "An example of your quick wit? Or are you being sincere? What a pity for you. Your closed mind certainly deprives you of so much the world has to offer. Given the chance, you would be surprised to learn what this woman is capable of."

"Would I?" asked Harris with a coy look on his face. "Perhaps one day madam will be so kind as to clarify with demonstrations?"

"Easy now, Lieutenant," she quipped. The Grave Digger lifted a coquettish smile on her lips, then stroked a thick strand of her raven-like hair behind her ear. She kept her eyes locked with Harris's as she sauntered toward the wagon as it rolled to a stop.

"Enough, children," scolded Van Leeuwen. "Is he still with us?" he asked as the Grave Digger climbed into the bed of the wagon from behind. Her cagey, dark eyes surveyed the corporal. His body was facedown, contorted, and forced awkwardly into the forward corner of the wagon bed. The bone above his left knee had torn through his skin and breeches, with the splintered edge protruding from his flesh, and his calf was folded unnaturally from his body. She was hesitant to move closer and noticing the frail gasps of breaths forced the expansion of his lungs was sufficient to convince her he had not expired.

"Congratulations, Lieutenant Harris, it appears you did your job," she beckoned. She then hopped from the carriage and continued, "I'll wager he wishes otherwise, but he is alive." Seemingly disinterested in appearing steadfast in the face of such horror, she quickly pulled herself several paces from the badly wounded Continental soldier.

"Excellent," droned Van Leeuwen. This was, perhaps, the most excitement one could reasonably expect from the doctor. "Excellent, indeed. Have them take the cart back and put him in the open pen… carefully. He's made it this far—would be a shame to lose him now. I'll see to his wounds shortly." He then offered both Harris and Grave Digger a quick glance and strolled back to make his way back toward the doorway.

"It should be said, this seems very wasteful, Doctor. I mean not to tell you your business, yet you have been dictating to me my business. We are far too valuable to be spent on such a meaningless task. The Americans are inferior soldiers, yet any man with two hands can fire a musket. I can assure you, in certain terms, this will be the last time we snatch a fucking Yankee for you. You are cunning, no? Figure something out if the need arises for another," griped Harris with a frustrated tongue.

Van Leeuwen was not keen on explaining his intentions, yet sought to remain diplomatic, given the arrangement he had made with influential figures in the Royal Offices and elsewhere. Thus far, his ventures with the British Army had been very prosperous for the doctor. Harris was not an expendable, rank and file Redcoat officer. He required Van Leeuwen's respect, and the doctor knew this. "Nothing is simple in these regards," he replied. "I need to assess all variables and to recreate battlefield conditions as precisely as they can be recreated, to say nothing to conclude workable procedures to handle such dangerous weaponry. I do not need to be reminded of your worth and can assure you, no action you take, insofar as I am concerned, will be meaningless. You are offering a valuable service to your Empire, Lieutenant.

"Brute force may win battles, but science can win wars. Study the country's history. Your army vanquished a French one, ten to a man at the Battle of Agincourt. The Empire had longbows while the French did not. British archers cut the Frenchmen to pieces from a distance beyond the reach of any French arrow. The next war, the French were not so ill-equipped. From my perspective, the Americans gave to us a magnificent gift; opportunity. This rebellion brings with it occasions we would be foolish to let pass by. It is a chance to sharpen our blades and cultivate tenacity in warfare for when we meet more capable opponents on the fields of battle. I do not profess to be a trooper, nor do I understand the intricacies of tactics and operations in war. I do, however, understand quite well the lethality of an infectious virus. Should we harness this to effect, the right virus can kill more of our enemies than all the muskets and cannons in the king's command.

"I am pressed, as I fear the rebellion will not hold much longer and we would have squandered such an opportunity. I am humbled to admit an obstacle I have yet to hurdle. The heat from the blast sterilizes the projectiles, neutralizing their effectiveness to a simple bullet." Van Leeuwen caught himself rambling and sought to end the conversation. "So it goes...I have a few thoughts, and we shall see how the subject you returned to me reacts. Needless to say, you are providing a valuable service to your country."

Harris was content with Van Leeuwen's explanation to the point of discontinuing the discussion. "We are patient, Doctor, yet we will not be so amiable if you cannot hurdle whatever fucking obstacles you need to hurdle in good time. If you are unable, I suppose we will see the value of brute force...so it goes." The disgruntled soldier was not interested in understanding as much as he was at telling the doctor to fuck off. Harris understood such ventures as an insult to his virtues and was not interested in progress. He was compelled by his oath and dedication to his command. "You heard him," he barked. Lieutenants Murray and Dickenson had been still, straddled on their mounts, silent and stoic. Van Leeuwen respectfully bowed his head as he slinked toward the doorway, where he was swallowed within Mandrake's walls.

Murray waved his arm forward and ordered, "Let's go!" He, the wagon, Dickenson, and the trailing Redcoats proceeded once again. Harris wasted no time and turned toward the Grave Digger, who was unable to mask the supercilious look upon her face. She remained on the pathway approaching the Mandrake for a moment and peered back at him. Her hair fluttered like a weather vane announcing an oncoming storm, and the mystery in her eyes chilled Harris's bones. The hardened trooper was not easy to move and was seldom at a loss for words when he needed them. "You are impressed, I won't make you say as such," he said as he paced toward Windstorm.

She strolled a few steps closer toward Harris, then tilted her head. "I will admit, you've come as close to intimidating the doctor as I've seen. And I also will admit infecting the colonial and capturing him alive with these…creatures…is not a feat many men would be able to accomplish. Despite yourself, you have your moments. Still, I am not so easily impressed. I hope the lieutenant does not feel hollow because of it."

"I believe the lieutenant has much to offer, madam," replied Harris.

"He does, does he? I would extend him every opportunity to prove as much. Yet…it may be wise to keep some distance. Such a shame, really," she said with a playful tone. "Danger is always thrilling, but good sense urges me not to let you get any closer than frolicsome conversation. Your thrills are too dangerous."

Harris felt further emboldened by a strengthened sense of confidence. "So, I have struck fear into the Grave Digger's cold heart. It seems as I have come to misunderstand you. You have my promise, with you, I am quite safe."

The Grave Digger groaned with mild amusement. "You? Hardly. Being infected by a deadly virus; this is something I feel no shame to admit I fear."

With a soft gasp of laughter, Harris replied, "Is this what you fear? You believe I may have been sloppy enough as to allow myself exposure to this virus? I can say for certain, I would not be who I am, where I am, if I was not as good at what I do."

The Grave Digger narrowed her eyes and offered the sinister smile of an experienced vixen. "You certainly are something, Lieutenant. I think you would be fun to fuck," she said.

Harris remained collected as he continued, "I think you are right, and I think you are entitled such pleasures. I'd be happy to oblige them. You can consider it a favor, a favor I will call on you to return one day."

The Grave Digger's smile widened to reveal her clean, white teeth. "This is kind, sir. The charity is appreciated, though not necessary. It was just talk, as you are not especially my type."

"And what type is that, madam, brave, stout, and smart?" he asked.

"No, male," she replied.

Murray led the contingent around the old stone building toward the bank of the East River, where a series of five, small, roughly constructed outbuildings rested. They were positioned behind a wobbly looking, wood-post fence and a large field of patchy and worn grass. The stench of foul meat filled the air and stung the party members' noses. Flies buzzed about and crows circled overhead. The clapping hooves and heavy rumble of the wheels pressed against the hardened dirt surface. The nearest pen was approximately four feet in length and the same in height. It was boarded with splintery, dry planks, with no windows, but a solid, hinged gate that clamped shut at a heavy metal lock. It was built with purpose and without style. Long, jagged, twisted iron nails protruded from some corners. The wall boards were uneven and assembled with gaps and mismatched planks.

"That is good," commanded Murray from the back of his warhorse. "Bring him into the first pen, with extreme care." With that, the two Phantom Troopers leaped from the wagon's bench and trotted toward the tail of the bed. They sprang into the back of the cart and slowly approached the badly injured American corporal. Lynn was hardly conscious, yet able to manage a weak groan as the stomps from their steps rumbled against his ear, which was firmly pressed against the floorboards. Each of the soldiers clenched one of Lynn's shoulders and, with great ease, tugged him forward toward the tailgate. They turned his body headlong and urged him forward, scraping him along the crude slats along the wagon bed. As he progressed forward two or three feet his jagged femur bone, which was compounded through his flesh and uniform, caught a gap between the boards. His body was hoisted nearly straight into the air, and the sudden throng of immense pain hit him like a thunderbolt. Lynn growled a horrific yelp, and each trooper suddenly turned their heads back toward Murray.

"Hold," cried one of the Phantom Troopers. His voice was muted within the heavy, leather mask about his face. After a panicked moment, they peered toward Lieutenant Murray, who returned an irritated look. "Either he will be locked inside or the two of you dew-beaters will be." The gray-clad figures turned toward one another, then continued with a bit more concern. The wagon was drawn along the flat, grass pathway behind the northeastern edge of the stone Mandrake. A narrow, jagged wire cage was constructed at the base of the western wall. Within the tall grass swaying in the breeze, the remains of a human carcass that had come to lie flat on its back was nearly concealed. There was not much more beyond a torso and a twisted and badly mutilated face. The eyes had been pecked out by ravens, and the flesh around the neck and shoulders were alive with a sea of gray and white maggots. Glimpses of bone and vertebrae appeared through the decaying and tattered flesh. It had no legs, and but one arm. The stench was unbearable, and the mist of buzzing flies swarmed endlessly.

Lined along the edge of the eastern river was a series of roughly constructed wooden box pens. Each coop was no larger than four feet wide and maybe even less in height. Within three of the five pens slumped a barely animate body of an African slave, and in the remaining two lay the lifeless bodies of others. These unfortunate souls had been the test subjects for Van Leeuwen's saltwater experiment. For days, each of the young men had been given only salty seawater from New York's harbor to drink. One of the servants had reached delirium due to the constricted blood flow to his brain. For days, he howled continuously, then began to crash his head violently against the sturdy oak posts and hardened surface within his pen. After thrashing about so viciously, he managed to collapse his glabella into his skull, deforming the shape of his face. The fate of the other deceased subject was slightly less loathsome, as he merely endured severe cramps, nausea, and ferocious vomiting before he succumbed to organ failure.

Those who were, as of yet, alive suffered varying degrees of dehydration. Their skins had become pale-gray, and their nerves shivered furiously to no end. Van Leeuwen's recent distractions enabled their prolonged existence. The recent rainfall had afforded them mud-mucked drabs of water they had been lucky enough to suck into their mouths by thrusting their tongues between the barbs of metallic wire at the surface in their cage. As it will, the doctor was sure to discover his failure to account for such a variable, then correct it and conduct his research from the start, yet again.

The near pen, opposite the western cages, was, for now, empty, yet would forever more be Corporal Lynn's home. The young Continental soldier would be locked within the small wooden box for the remainder of his life. His wounds would be treated by Van Leeuwen, though certainly not with care or a kind heart, but to stave off infection and further damage that might cost the soldier his life too soon. The doctor needed him alive to further his research. Van Leeuwen would observe and note his condition, occasionally slice a scrap of flesh from his skin or drain a cup of blood from his veins. He'd be fed leftover pigeon bones, foul, maggot-infested meat from an animal or otherwise, and polluted, piss-warm water. Like a caged dog with no hope of freedom, Lynn would rest within his own shit, trapped inside the dark, wooden box. He would never wear fresh clothing nor would he ever be bathed. This would be his life until he was no longer among the living, or no longer of use to Doctor Van Leeuwen.

* * *

A day north of Manhattan Island.

Pieter Borst had a kind heart, large stomach, and quick wit. His thoughtful, narrow eyes were nearly lost within his bushy brown hair, and the warm smile within his thick beard cast the light of a hundred candles. He found enjoyment wherever he could, and would hardly refuse any opportunity to eat, drink, or fuck. Pieter's jovial nature was infectious, and even his normally apathetic good friend glowed in the face of his delight. He'd been one of Dedrick's closest mates as long as either could remember, so long, in fact, neither was able to recall how they came to become such. He may well have been the only soul Dedrick could tolerate for more than a day before the invariable and inevitable personal flaws within became apparent. And he may have been the only one who could indefinitely bear Dedrick's sarcasm and intolerance of humanity. Pieter's nature inclined his good friend to share everything with him, from the most inconsequential and mundane of matters to the most personal and private of them.

Dedrick sat across from Pieter along the long, dark, mahogany bar within the Van Wyck Inn. His shoulders hung low, as did his long, russet-colored, unkempt hair. A tall, plainly ornate pewter stein with a final layer of warm beer within looked back at him. He was intoxicated, but only to the point that he was beyond his usually guarded demeanor. Typically, the key to unlocking the door of his characteristic introversion was found at the bottom of the third or fourth stein. He had shared some of his problems and concerns, yet had more still, though good manners and humility compelled him to worry about dominating their time. Dedrick's visits to his old friend's tavern were as relaxing and enjoyable as they were therapeutic.

The Van Wyck had rested along the eastern side of Post Road for three generations. After he arrived in the New World, Augustus Van Wyck, Pieter's grandfather by adoption, built it as a sturdy, humble one-room cottage. Its size and impressive design had grown in correlation to the Dutch merchant's good fortune. During the last war, it served as an improvised hospital, brothel, and tavern, where Brits and Yankees could expect to find relief from injury, sobriety, or lecherousness. The Van Wycks bequeathed the estate, as it were, to their espoused son, Pieter, on the conditions the faded, drab yellow exterior paint and the family name remain. Inside, the tavern was dark and rather rustic, offering pragmatism to style. Patrons would never sit at a wobbly table nor walk on a dusty floor. Outside, the midday sun warmed the valley along Post Road to cast hardly a shadow. The Inn's few, large windows tempted the regulars with glimpses of the valley's autumnal beauty. Yet, those inside the darkened chamber of the tavern preferred the warmth of an intoxicating beverage. One would not expect Pieter to be as diligent and dedicated to the upkeep of his inheritance given his mostly infantile nature. The Van Wyck was the one area in his life where he found pride.

When he noticed Dedrick's mug to be nearly empty, Pieter offered, "Huh...huh? Good, right? Here, give me that, and I'll top it off."

Dedrick took a long breath as if to buy a second or two of consideration. "No, I can't. Thank you, though."

"So, you don't like it, is what you are saying?" asked Pieter.

"No," replied Dedrick. "No, not at all."

Pieter nodded his head, and with his playful eyes fixed on Dedrick's, he continued, "I knew it. Why not just say that, you fucker?"

"Say what?" snapped Dedrick.

"I knew you didn't care for it. Could tell by the way you were taking time sipping it down like a, uh...I don't know someone who sips slowly. Like a tadpole or...I don't know."

Dedrick's habitual gesture of contemplation had him stroking his fingers along the scruff about his chin. Calmly and coolly, he scrunched his brows, and while looking straight at Pieter, said, "Tadpole...what? Pieter, I have no idea what the hell you are talking about."

"The beer. You said you do not like the beer," replied Pieter. "Here I am, I'm serving you this beer, glass after glass, and we're talking, and I thought, but apparently not, enjoying the conversation. Yet there *you* are straining to swallow the shit the entire time, probably not even listening to what I was even saying, as you were too preoccupied with the filth I was making you drink."

"That's...no." Dedrick shook his head quickly from side to side. "No, that's not...I wasn't saying, *no*, I don't like it. I was saying, *no*, that is not right, that I don't *not* like it. Meaning no, you are wrong to suggest I do not like it. You said, 'you don't like it.' To which I said, 'no,' as to mean your statement is incorrect."

Dryly, Pieter asked, "Then, why not just say you like it? Why the riddle? Why all the 'No, I don't not dislike it this and that' wordplay? Just say you like the shit if you like the shit."

Dedrick lifted his head to look up at the ceiling and struggled to contain his frustration. "I did say I fucking like the shit. This is on you, you fucker. I said…You asked me in a negative manner requiring me to respond negatively. You're the one with the confusion and word fucking play, you bearded prick. You think I would sit here and gulp down one stein after the other if I did not enjoy what I was drinking?" He stopped himself when he realized his agitated exhibition was for his friend's amusement. "You are an ass. I swear to Jesus Christ, you really are," he quipped with a deflated tone, then poked his finger into Pieter's full mug of beer and flipped a few droplets into Pieter's face.

Pieter pressed on with a guilty chuckle. "You're too easy. But, in all honesty, you would tell me, right?"

"Yes, Pieter, I would tell you if I did not like it," snarled Dedrick.

"You would be clear? Maybe, 'I really don't care for this. This does not taste appealing at all? I'm not really enjoying this right now.'"

Dedrick remained as deadpan as possible. "Yes. I may not phrase it as you had, but I would make it clear to you that I did not care for the beverage."

Pieter clenched his lips and stirred his eyes in thought. "Would you tell me if you thought I was overweight?"

"Does that need to be said?" Dedrick sighed, then continued with a muted mumble, "That shit goes without saying…" Quickly, he shifted his tone and said more clearly and loudly, "Alright enough, can you please continue about your…inamorata? I was actually interested before we got lost in this aside."

"Ah, right," said Pieter. "Really, there's not much left to say. It's love. That's it, it's love. I'm in love."

"Love?" asked Dedrick. "That doesn't seem a bit premature? You told me you only spoke to her while they unloaded the firewood. How long have you known her, ten minutes?"

"No, stop with the ten minutes," cried Pieter. "Fifteen, twenty… why does that matter? You knew you liked my beer right away, yes? When you know, you know, and I know. I love her. She is amazing— she's incredible. She's warm and gentle, caring and charitable. Her family is…amazing. She is so adorable in her little frock and bowed hair. Mmm, I just want to eat her up. I want to chew on her and swallow her, then shit her out and eat her again. She has the cutest laugh. Amazing. Everything about her is amazing. Her *nostrils* are amazing. I'm telling you, this woman has amazing nostrils. I love her. I can't even think about her because it's too much—I can't take it. When I'm occupied with thoughts of her, I am so pleased as to cause discomfort. I have to punch myself in the face to bring down the unbearable ecstasy I feel. She is that amazing. I can't even find words. I feel as though I need to *invent* words to describe her.

"I would slice one of my fingers off if it meant I could fuck her— maybe even two fingers. I think she could probably talk me into slicing two of my fingers. If she said she really wanted to suck on my cock, but has this strange fixation with sliced-off fingers and insisted I cut two of them off, I think I'd be busy cutting them off. If that isn't love, I don't know what is."

Dedrick snickered, though with a certain reserve and evenness. He chuckled, not only at the humorous proclamation but at Pieter's pathetic nature. "Wow…that's…something. She's charitable and from a good family? You've had fifteen minutes to talk to her. That would have had to have been the first thing she mentioned, which, it seems to me, means she is an obnoxious cunt. 'Pleased to meet you, sir. I do a lot to help those in need, and my parents are outstanding folk.'"

"Good Lord, you've become negative in your old age, Dedrick," replied Pieter. What happened to you? I don't *know* as a matter of certainty she is charitable, but you can tell. She seems charitable and seems to be from a good family. The manner in which she spoke, her tone and vernacular —oh, I don't know…it tells me she cares for the less fortunate in a, well, very deeply."

Hardly able to maintain a straight face, Dedrick conceded, "Fair enough; you win. I'm not going to argue, but trust your judgment. She has beautiful nostrils and is quite charitable. I'm happy when you are happy, my friend. Cheers.

"So, let me ask you this: if she said you can do anything to her, anything, whatever it is you want, anything, but you also must do the *very* same thing to me, what would you do?"

Pieter furrowed his brows as if pondering the inquiry. "Hmmm. In other words, if I shake your hand, I can shake her hand, and if I fuck you in the ass, I can fuck *her* in the ass?"

"Yes, exactly." Dedrick chuckled. "If you pat me on the head, she will let you pat her on the head. If you have a long talk with me, you can have a long talk with her."

Once again, Pieter gave the matter some thought. "Interesting. That's a good question. That is a good one. Whatever I do to you...I think I would grab your tits. Maybe play with your tits a little bit. Perhaps rub your ass." Dedrick laughed forcefully and could not help but nearly choke on his last warm gulp of beer.   As his uncontrollable chuckles got the better of him, he held a closed fist against his mouth, as if to keep himself from dribbling. "That's good. That is pretty good," he said. Both men allowed themselves to enjoy frivolity until the last gasps of laughter died with long sighs. It was suddenly as if the tavern had quickly become darker, quieter, and more melancholy within.

"All right, forget that," replied Pieter. "It's your turn now, you do this all the time." He gestured the fingers with both hands as though he was waving Dedrick forward. "I have been waiting all night. It's time for you to talk to me—you know what I am talking about."

Dedrick's face came alive, and it was as though Pieter opened a valve from which suppressed thoughts flowed like water. He could not wait to tell Pieter, as much as Pieter could not wait to be told. Dedrick had completed the trip to visit his friend in just more than half a day. He rode his three-year-old mare, Willow, from Tarry Town to the Dutch village of Fishkill, as he was consumed by the fresh memories of Sally. "Yeah, I can't, well, I shouldn't even really discuss too much of this. I suppose I can in general terms," hummed Dedrick. "In any event, as I said before...she's incredible. She is everything I love about a person. It's almost not fair. It's almost as though something is not right because she is too good to be true. Maybe not charitable, but I've never met anyone like her. I'm that smitten."

"Hmm...wow," groaned Pieter.

"I know," confirmed Dedrick before he continued. "She is not real. It's almost strange that by chance, so much has gone in her favor. She is confident, very confident—she has confidence dripping from within. She takes herself just a little bit too seriously, has just a little bit of an over-inflated self-worth. Not enough to be unbearable, but enough to propel her to overachieve and present herself with pride. Enough where she takes it as though everyone cares about what she has to say. She's narcissistic only to the point of being appealing and without being obnoxious. She is fun and funny, yet not to the point of annoying. Innately, she knows where the line is between fun and inappropriate. It's all confidence—to make fun of herself, to celebrate her flaws, to command a room, to venture into unknown social situations, to live her life without personal inhibition or hesitation. She's adorable—she's *fucking* adorable. It's unnatural how adorable she is. It does not even make sense how adorable she is. Whatever she does, whatever she says, is adorable. She can tell you it's raining outside and it would be adorable. She has it. Whatever the fuck *it* is, she has it.

"It must be confidence. Confidence cannot be contrived, or…I don't know, feigned. Confidence manifests itself as charm, and confidence feeds itself exponentially. Charm is the magnet that draws others in as though they are interested in you. Thus, further bolstering your confidence. Last time I saw her, I, well…ugh…I passed…you know, wind alright? So I…well," Dedrick caught himself and paused for a moment. "She's brimming with confidence. I really…shouldn't. I think I'll have to leave it at that."

"You have to be joking with me?" groaned Pieter. "You led me down this path, then stopped right in the middle of it. It's like you put this, this, uh, fresh turkey in front of my face because you know I'm a fat bastard. You let me take one bite and yank it away from my face. That's it? It's done, you can't go on?"

"I know. You're right and I'm sorry. I shouldn't have brought it up. May have had too much of this shitty beer."

"Fine, I won't pry. What about home? You can tell me about that. What about Emily and…well?" His tone instantly shifted to a serious, if not somber one. "You're still having a tough time with all of this? You know you are entitled to, this is not easy. Last time we talked, you told me you resent her. Is it because she is sick, or…can't have more children?"

Dedrick remained silent for a moment or so. Even in his slightly intoxicated state, it was difficult to break through his wall of introversion. Only on rare occasions did he reveal deep, personal feelings, yet the weight of his sorrows had left him near collapse. "Yes," he replied simply.

Pieter nodded his head as though his suspicions were confirmed. "Empathy, Dedrick—be her. Live her life and see how you are acting toward her. Understand her perspective and her experiences, and maybe you will see you are not being the partner she needs right now. I love you, you are my brother, yet I know your flaws. I'm not trying to preach or beat you down, but I will be honest. Really, she was inflicted twice, once with smallpox, and then with a husband who will not say it, but blames her for contracting it—I'm sorry, but I think you need to hear this."

Dedrick turned toward the window and peered without expression or thought. It was as though his friend cut through the cocoon of denial and self-pity in which he wrapped himself. "It bothers me only that you're right," muttered Dedrick. "There is no need to apologize for being honest. You know I talk to you because I know you will not simply tell me what I want to hear, or at least avoid what I don't want to hear. Would be a pointless conversation otherwise. Of course, it is not her fault, obviously. There is no blame, and yet, I can't help but find blame in her. I see her suffering every day, I see her doing all she can to keep her anguish hidden from me."

He lowered his head and continued as though his emotions had been allowed free of a leash. It was as though fresh oxygen was filling his lungs as the frustration and personal angst he'd harbored within was allowed to exhale. By now, he was no longer talking to Pieter, but to himself. "I see her skin corroding around her, and I've calloused myself to the point where not only does it not sadden me, it irritates me. Instead of compassion, I feel annoyance. Maybe there are other things too, I can't say for sure. She gets on my nerves. For no reason, for nothing in the least, she irritates me. And the more she tries not to, the more she does. It's not her fault. She has done nothing, not one thing, wrong. She tries, she genuinely tries to be…fun and funny, and she cares and—what happened? What sin did she commit for me to find her so irksome when I never have before? Have I built a wall to protect myself from sorrow or grief? Maybe you're dead-on, maybe I have fought not to reveal itself as though I'm a cold-hearted shit. Maybe I internalize my dalliances by creating a sense of entitlement for bearing her presence. Or maybe she has committed the unforgivable act of becoming familiar."

"It could be all of those things," replied Pieter. "And I think it is because she loves you, and she knows you, as not many do. As long as we have been friends, I cannot truly say that I know you. You keep everyone at an arm's reach, yet Emily knows you. She knows what you think, how you feel—she knows you on a level nobody ever has, and I think it bothers you, even if you don't feel it does. I think it propels you from her. I respect your boundaries, and I think this has enabled our friendship to continue for all these years. Most of our discussions, almost all we talk about is me, or neither me nor you, but hardly ever you. Well…she has you figured out, and that scares you and forces you to drive her away."

Before he could finish his diatribe, Pieter noticed several of the patrons had hustled toward the westernmost windows and peered out with apparent interest or concern. Several others were drawn to them as well, until a good number had gathered. They were all intent, and some struggled to shift to nearly lean over those blocking their view. "Well, I'll be…" cried an elderly gentleman who caught near the middle of the congregation.

Pieter raised his head and looked over them the best he could. "Come on," he said to Dedrick, and the two barely sober men stumbled as they stormed out the back entrance to witness the apparent commotion directly.

From the northern path of Post Road, a large parade of men, carriages, and horses rumbled slowly southward. They were escorted by whirling clouds of dust, drifting leaves, and the thunderous claps of hooves and boots against the dry roadway. At the head was a four-wheeled wagon, which sat several blue-clad soldiers who faced rearward. Without urgency, their muskets leaned against the carriage boards and their feet hung from the base of the cabin bed as they casually observed the column of visibly fatigued Redcoats who marched behind. The Continentals appeared nearly gleeful and quite relaxed as their feet dangled lazily from the open wagon gate. One gnawed his way through a pale green apple until he flung it carelessly off the pathway.

The British columns were without weapons and lined four long, stretching nearly two hundred feet. The procession seemed to include close to three hundred men, if not more. Not one appeared to be anything other than weary and broken; this was no glorious parade. They marched in unison with heads held low, and their stomps thumped to a slow, rhythmic beat. American cavalrymen strode along either side of the lines spaced several lengths apart, and the mounted soldiers watched over their bested counterparts with diligence and delight. The colonial cavalrymen were poor actors if their aim was to hide the look of utter contempt upon their faces. By the decree of their superiors, they were to conduct themselves befitting the honor of respectable soldiers, yet their unpolished nature refused to shine. Notwithstanding the command, the British were often offered insults and intermittent sneering grins.

Dedrick, Pieter, and a host of others lined the road and watched as the procession marched northward. Some of the spectators cheered and clapped in approval, and a young man bellowed, "Our George will trounce your George," and another hollered, "Get this shit back to London." Most, however, were awestruck and observed the passing cavalcade silently. It was a rather shocking sight for Dedrick in particular. Hitherto, he was of the impression the rebellion was on the verge of collapse. The war had fostered mostly apathetic, yet mixed emotions, and now the revelation of an American victory forced him to fully consider the outcome of independence. He glanced over to Pieter, whose expression suggested he was harboring the same reservations.

At the head of the line was Major Andre Morris. His left arm hung in a sling of tattered cotton linens, his face was bruised, his uniform was ragged, and a number of his adornments and decorations were noticeably missing. Morris's expression was solemn and, in a sense, calm. He peered forward and refused to acknowledge the calls and heckles. Occasionally, he would fight himself to mask the winces of pain that shot through his shoulder. Each stride brought his commission in America one step closer to its end. Morris was as valued as any soldier in all the colonies. He broke from the Long Island shore to slaughter unwary Continentals by the regiment. His grenadiers sliced through the valley to sweep the undermanned

American unit from Ticonderoga. In so doing, he conceived nearly an entire generation of widows. The major fought for his country as bravely and tenaciously as one could, yet his charge would conclude inevitably with failure.

Colonel Bell was spared the indignity of being part of the public spectacle. The American commander, General Horatio Gates, extended Bell the courtesy of recognition for his service in the war with the French and Indians. Bell was not part of the slog along Post Road, past jeering colonials under the supervision of crude, green Continental troopers. In accordance with the capitulation terms, Colonel Oliver Bell was sent to Quebec, where he was to join Lieutenant General John Burgoyne's army, while the bulk of his contingent, including the major, was sent to New York Island. Bell chose to press on, to take advantage of the second opportunity afforded to kill Americans. He believed it to be a dishonor to scurry home as a vanquished warrior. Yet, his fate included the scorn of his comrades, who saw him as weak-willed for freely abandoning his position and company.

Bell pushed hard to quell his fledgling reputation and to reclaim the honorable nature of his character. His gallantry drove him to foolish imprudence and unnecessary risks. He fell on the field of battle at Bemis Heights when he refused to yield to the overpowering Americans. A three-pound cannon ball bounded along the dry grassland wildly until it was fired into his right thigh, just above the knee. His bone snapped, and his leg was thrown behind him to lie pinned under his back when he hit the ground. For hours, he agonized while lying in the field, under the beams of the autumnal sun. When General Gates had come to gather the wounded and bury the fallen, he knelt before the remains of Bell, removed the colonel's cockade from his tri-cornered hat, and included it within the routine dispatches to General George Washington.

Morris and the others were escorted all the way to the harbor, where they boarded the HMS *Elizabeth* and were sent back to Britain for the duration of the conflict. Ticonderoga had fallen. The Americans had captured the fortress, seized all the guns, and appeared emboldened by the victory. The tides of war had swayed, and the rebels were gathering in force, to march south and recapture New York City.

"The actions of men [is] the best interpreter of their thought."—
John Locke

Six

October 1777.

The faint glow of the harvest moon and the struggling starlight could hardly penetrate the deep darkness within the stone cave. Whispering winds shuddered the autumnal leaves, and the crackle of crickets echoed throughout the night. Captain Pearson may have heard each and every one of their songs. Not a single minute had passed when Pearson had not tossed himself about or shifted his weight from one side to the other. These last few hours had been, with certainty, the longest of his entire life. At points, before the lamp had given, he did his best to lose himself within Shakespeare's prose, yet the darkness and obvious angst refused to allow such an escape from reality. The shackles at his ankles masticated his flesh as much as the specter of his imminent death did his soul. It was a night wholly unfree of fear, without a semblance of rest, repressed by unrelenting, stomach-churning distress and none but dire thoughts. Though his warm breath was cast in mist, he never felt the bitter chill of the cool air.

He closed his eyes and tried, desperately, to clear his mind from thought. Yet, Elizabeth's face would appear to look upon him from within. The realization he would never again see her had begun to sink into his heavy heart. His eyes were glossed with a layer of tears, and his throat was knotted in strands of sorrow. Without determination to do so, he convinced himself she was far better without him in her life than with him in it. At his best, he was patronizing, and at his worst, unbearable. Mercifully, he had begun to consent to his fate and found a modicum of comfort when he accepted the notion his captors were gentlemen. Evidently, his imprisoners were disloyal to the king, yet loyal to the code of a soldier in the king's command. Pearson believed Bowman had no desire to see him suffer an agonizing end.

From the distance, within the long, tomb-like chamber, the echo of soft and hurried footsteps sounded as though they were rapidly nearing. The voice within Pearson's head warned him, "this is it," and he sat up, tensely, to accept his executioner. Despite it all, Pearson assured himself his last moments of life would be lived with all the pride and dignity his troubled soul could muster.

"Don't make a sound," said the blackness with an abrupt whisper. The figure neared, yet could hardly be seen. The hooded character appeared as the dark angel of death, concealed nearly fully by shadows. He snatched Pearson near his ankles and the shackles which bound them. "Stay silent—move your feet, sir. I cannot get to the clasp."

Pearson was perplexed, yet frozen with disbelief. He was unaware who this man was and completely ignorant to what he was intending to do. "Hurry, roll your feet over, for shit's sake, sir," he once again commanded under his breath. Pearson complied as his eyes peered over the shadowy figure. Lieutenant Shaw unlocked each of the shackles to free the captain of his bondage. Then, he hurriedly shoved the loose key into his boot and removed the captain's crafted soft, leather pouch, which he wore over his shoulder, and thrust it into Pearson's chest. "Take it," he told Pearson. "It is all of your papers and such. There are too provisions, flint, balls and powder, and a map revealing our location—come, with haste."

Pearson clung to his pouch about his chest, yet appeared to show no urgency. He grimaced with pain when his agitated shoulder once again stung him with the reminder of his wound. "What is happening? Where are you taking me?" he asked through an anxious whisper. Shaw's head fell into his chest as he was overcome with frustration. After he flipped the hood from his head and peered directly into Pearson's eyes, he spoke directly as to not repeat himself. "You are leaving here. I'm taking you nowhere beyond that egress, and if we hurry the fuck up, you may just make it without being killed. Now, let's go, sir, before we are both strung from a tree."

Pearson scurried to cram the Duval pistol into his pouch and leaped to his feet. His weary legs were too numb to offer more than the slightest stability. Shaw led him toward the large aperture a dozen or so yards from the passageway. The soft glow of the late evening full moon was cast upon their backs and against the jagged rocks that surrounded them. Both men scaled the large boulders along the chamber wall and hoisted themselves through to the grassy surface of the ground and the open air. Shaw landed first and turned to lift Pearson, who was struggling. "Come the fuck on," he mumbled. Finally, Pearson was lifted from the gap, and Shaw glanced back through. The captain clenched his aching jaw to release the wrenches of pain that shot through his bones. Shaw held his open hand toward Pearson's direction as if urging him to remain silent and still. When he suspected they were, as of yet, unheard, he whispered his instructions to Captain Pearson. "Head this way," he said as he gestured toward the south, then continued at a hurried pace. "Head this way and stay this way. When you reach the tree line, stay this course for two, perhaps three miles. In your path, will be a small, trickling creek running from the northwest to the southeast. If in three miles this creek has not crossed your track, you are lost. Follow the creek to the right and keep following it the same way for however many days it takes you until it intersects with the Quebec Path. That is the first roadway you will meet. Stay south on the Quebec Path, and it will take you all the way to Manhattan Island, this way. Keep the creek to your left, follow it all the way to the path. Head south. Eat only when you must eat and take as little rest as you can bear—eat and sleep all you want when you are home. You must tell your commanders who we are, where we are, and that we have the Kahontsi Ehnita. I don't know who knows what by now. Some in the Ministry have ideas to the occurrences of our disappearance. We have a royal seal and I've sealed the contents. Do your best to protect them, sir."

"Let me take it. I will deliver it to the general," replied Pearson.

"No," said Shaw.

"You do not trust me with it?"

"It is not that I distrust your character, sir," replied Shaw. "I do not trust your resourcefulness; I do not trust you will make it to New York alive. You seem soft and pampered, ill fit for the wilderness. You've only stumbled here by the grace of your incompetence. If I give it to you, I have no control over what can happen to it. I cannot simply hope you will make it. Yet, as of now, this is the best course of action, the only course. Regardless, I would not be able to lift it from Bowman if I tried. He'd snap my hand clean from my wrist in his sleep."

"Inspiring confidence does not seem to be a strength," grumbled Pearson.

Shaw had no interest in the sarcasm, nor in prolonging the discussion. "Fuck your confidence. You may be better to have none anyway. I would wager Wilkinson has heard us and awoken by now. Run—fly south with all your swiftness. Do not stop, do not look back, but run as if being chased by wolves. If Stone tracks you, your death will be far more torturous than your sore muscles or strained lungs, far worse than you can possibly imagine."

"You need to say nothing more, for I can imagine many things," remarked Pearson as he set forth. He began to take a quick step, then turned back toward Shaw. "Thank you, sir," he said.

Shaw simply shook his head, then waved him to hustle along. "Go…" The gap in the cave was amid a flat, open field of tall grass surrounded by dense woodlands of one hundred-plus paces in all directions. Bowman and his company had cleared the trees, so they would be able to see any intruders from a distance.

Pearson burst from the scene at a large, flat patch of grass facing the southern woodlands. His lungs pumped the crisp air wildly, and his weak knees wobbled as though they were threatening to give. The dew-covered, tall blades whipped against his thighs with each of his hard strides. He turned back to see Shaw standing, watching from afar and growing smaller until he was lost in the shadows. Forward, the trees appeared as an onrushing tide moving to engulf him. The amber moon peered from above, and its radiance guided him until he was swallowed by the heavy thicket of pines and brush. He burst into the woods a dozen paces until he stumbled on a thick root and was thrown forward to crash against the hardened soil. An electric burst of pain shot through his shoulder, and he could not help but groan loudly. Instinctively, he thrust his head back to see only night beyond the trees, sprang back to his feet, and scampered farther into the forest.

From his position, Shaw watched the captain leave a wake of turned grass until his moon-cast shadow was consumed by the woodland. The captain's purpose was now far greater than it had been when he broke from Ticonderoga. Shaw accepted the price for his desperate act would be his life and could not help but to presume the unmistakable likelihood of Pearson's failure to be a certainty. Wilkinson could hear a snake slither a mile away, and Stone's determination was matched only by his talents at taking lives. The Fourth Order of Aquitaine Knights were unlike any force on all the battlefields of Europe. They had, by their hands, singularly won wars. Now, they were hunting an injured, weak, and aimless prey who was as familiar with the forest as a saint was to a brothel. Pearson would need God's hand to make it more than a mile. All the same, Shaw was at peace with his decision. It was a resolution he made from the regret fostered by remaining idle in conflict and absent of duty for years. Shaw remained still for the moment, until he heard the inevitable clamoring of agitated steps and grumbling voices from within the cave.

Bowman and Stone reached the empty shackles and stood motionless and in disbelief. Stone knelt to closer examine them as the flickering lantern he held cast its light against his mechanical headwear. He snatched one of the clasps to see it was undamaged and unlocked, then turned toward Bowman. The colonel's face was drawn with a vexed expression, as he knew Pearson did not escape but was set free. Instinctively, his eyes followed the large hollow above them, the likely path in which Pearson fled. There, he saw Lieutenant Shaw, standing, peering back at him to confirm Bowman's suspicion. The colonel lowered himself to clench Pearson's copy of *King Lear*, then, with a quick swipe, clenched it into his hand. "Get Otaktay and hunt down the pompous ass. Try to bring him back to me…somewhat alive. This is my mistake; I should have known better. I'll deal with this here," he said. Stone scuttled back along the pathway. Bowman's eyes were filled with fury as he fixed them on Shaw above the gap at the surface. Slowly, he crumpled the booklet within his fist and lurched toward the large opening atop the cave.

* * *

Where Wall Street and Dock Street meet on the eastern end of Manhattan Island was the *Dea's Francis Bare*, or as it was more commonly known: *Deas's House*. Irving Deas had given his marketplace a name he felt befit the elegance of landed gentry. In truth, he had no idea what the words meant, and those who knew him believed he simply thought of two that sounded nice when spoken. Deas's trade post was a dowry by his young bride, and at the time of marriage, it was no more than an unfinished shed, a few planks, and a splintery pier. In short time and with devious means, Deas turned his modest marital grant into a thriving trade post. He fostered unflattering and untrue rumors about his competition, reneged on loans, short paid contractors, and then disputed the quality of their effort. Irving thanked his wife for his good fortune with frequent infidelities and the infliction of venereal diseases he'd caught from many trysts with whores he "auditioned" for one of his whorehouses. Irving Deas surrounded himself only with sycophants who indulged his delusions and stroked his fragile ego. He cared only for those who had something to offer him, and for only as long as they were able to offer it. Through his entire forty-plus years of life, in his view, any misfortune he encountered, had always been the result of another's shortcoming or mistake. Thus, he had not once apologized nor shown regret. Deas was known to barter anything for anything: food, alcohol, tools, stolen goods, any and all manners of illicit and sexual services, and, of course, the most lucrative commodity, slaves.

The Middle Passage had cultivated great prosperity for New York; most of the captives bound for the colonies were routed through the city. Slavers captured their prizes overseas, rammed them into slave ships, and transported the cargo over the Atlantic. Some remained with the West India Company for distribution in the Caribbean, yet most of the freight continued the voyage toward the American colonies. The bulk was once again stowed away and bound northern to cities such as Boston, Philadelphia, and New York, where they were traded or sold among any category of products. Human captives were peddled alongside everything from beautifully hand-crafted furniture to cheap clay chamber pots. The virtuous few find the institution barbaric, while others see it as the rightful will of Christian virtue, as per the Scriptures. In some fashion or another, most had conditioned themselves to believe the trade to be the simple exchange of economic commodities, or at the very worst, a necessary evil. And like a pebble tossed into a calm pond, the slave trade created fortuitous waves for all. A great number of Yankee merchants, lawyers, bankers, blacksmiths, shipbuilders, prostitutes, and sailors relied on the flesh market for continued prosperity.

Like all things in America, the practice would press on, as it offered pragmatic value to the various levels of the colonial ethos. American slavery had a way of altering otherwise crystal-clear perspectives. Black slaves convinced the downtrodden, socially immobile whites to remain merrily oppressed and loyal to the conviction of so-called self-reliance and hard work. Slavery served to weave tightly the social fabric, as the poor rested assured by the notion of "doing much better than those Negroes." Though their arduous labor provided the capital to tighten the belts of the already well-fed, bottom-feeding whites slept comfortably on their broken backs at night. The elites benefited obviously, yet, despite their best interests, the far-from-elite members of society protected the Peculiar Institution as it veiled their lowly standing. All the same, even the most self-righteous, who feigned outrage and called for abolition, wiped the slurps of tobacco-laced saliva with a soft cotton linen as it trickled from their fat fucking faces. Habitual comforts and growing pockets tended to blind the eyes of morality.

Irving Deas was born into poverty, had no formal education, was not in the least well-spoken or refined, and yet was a shrewd and ruthless businessman. Deas had done well enough to have created a near monopoly on slaving in New York and parts of New Jersey, a feat he was not in the least bashful to speak of. To him, slaves were nothing more than capital goods to be bought and sold. They were not human beings with mothers and fathers, sons or daughters. They did not love and were not loved; they had no feelings or thoughts, no concerns, and no dreams.

It may very well have been he was spurred by perpetual greed and insecurity, or it could just as easily have been his simple mind truly believed those with dark skin were not humans and should not be considered as such. As he saw it, his slaves felt no pain or sorrow. Thus, they were never clothed beyond rags, fed more than scraps of edible trash, and were continually bound by chains and packed into small, windowless chambers by the dozen. While confined, their comforts did not extend beyond being covered in their own urine while lying amongst feces, rats, and insects. While there, some would remain for months at a time without breathing clean air or seeing the sun or the stars. As would be expected, a good number died, and corpses remained among the living for weeks at a time. Deas rightfully claimed it was far more economical to "lose inventory here and there," than to care for them with a shred of humanity.

Major Edmund Blackwood and his aide, Lieutenant Clive Dickenson, ascended the long wooden ramp that connected the yard to an elevated pier some twenty feet or so above the eastern river. The two men were adorned with pressed, long, gray cloaks on their shoulders, bright white breeches, and the pristine, unmarked tri-cornered hats of high social order. Their sturdily crafted swords dangled at their hips, casting gleams from the early morning sun. A brisk breeze blew from the harbor, yet the air was unseasonably warm. The sea was deep blue, capped with cascading strips of white that stirred with the wind. The skyline was cluttered with tall masts, rigs, yardarms, and bowsprits of the uncountable number of tall ships that lined the yard. A number of the king's most majestic warships dominated the view. The most notable and grand of them was the HMS *Victory*, which seemed to cast its foreboding shadow from the eastern harbor over all the city. As the gusts flowed from the sea, her bells clanged lazily, and her hull creaked like the knees of an old man settling for bed. The tall and imposing ship-of-the-line dwarfed the typical schooners and clippers the city folk were accustomed to seeing.

The pier stretched thirty yards or so, and lined side by side with their backs to the waterfront, a long row of slaves stood. Grown men and women, young boys and girls, all naked and still but for their nervous shudders. Each of them was shackled to the other at the ankles, with three feet of chain between them. On their right shoulders, near the base of the neck, each has the infamous Deas sigil branded into their skin. The garish and unstylish "D" appeared as a scar blistered into their flesh. The festering stench of bodily odors, dried urine, and human shit polluted the salty air. Blackwood and Dickenson walked past them, and neither turned an inch in their direction and in turn, they offered not a single sound. It was as if they had been conditioned to be as unnoticed as possible.

From the far end, ahead, a rather squat and unkempt gaunt-looking bloke slithered forward to greet them. Given their fine clothing and appearance of good health, he quickly surmised their potential station and worth. He greeted them with an awkward and insincere smirk. "Gentlemen, Gentlemen, good day. Welcome. I assume you are here because you wish to purchase some Mossheads, yes? I must tell you, the auction has not begun yet. I was simply having my wonderful products cleaned for display."

"These are your products, then? You are the slave trader, sir, Irving Deas?" asked Dickenson.

In typical, tactless manner, Deas was hardly able to control his staring, nor mask his revulsion at the sight of the wounds and blemishes that defined Blackwood's face. "I am the finest slaver, my good man, among many other things. I've built up a grand empire. I hear it from so many that I am more successful than any other." Despite the potential for a sale, Deas could not help but be the two-legged walking piece of wet shit that he was. One could not drown themselves in a pool so shallow, nor survive a fall from the height of his inflated ego. "These are not *just* products, people will tell you; these are the most fantastic in the colony, probably the world."

"Yes, very good, sir. We've come to understand you are the man to speak to in regards to the purchase of quality slaves. It sounds as though I have come to understand this correctly."

"That sounds correct, good sir. I make great deals, that I can tell you. If you're interested in acquiring some, however, you will have to wait a bit. The auction does not begin for another hour or so, Mister...?"

Dickenson bowed his head and tipped his cap. "Then we are in the right place, and you are the right man. My...associate and I are not concerned with waiting nor participating in the auction. From what we have learned and from what you claim, you are a man who recognizes a good deal when presented to him. I gather you are also one who appreciates such opportunities and the many reasons one should not allow them to waste away. It's clear you have done quite well for yourself, sir, thus I take this to be accurate. We are not here for the petty purchase of a slave or two, but are here to discuss a much more substantial proposition. A mutually beneficial private transaction, you might say."

Deas rolled his hands together and nearly drooled like a hungry dog presented with a slab of raw meat. "Substantial, you say?"

"Correct," confirmed Dickenson. "Substantial."

Deas snarled and gagged, then spat upon the planks. He was hunched over with lazy posture, and his clothes were tight enough to further degrade his rotund figure, unseemly and mismatched. To cover his balding head, he wore a stained Monmouth hat, which tilted sideways, and his stringy hair fell down his neck like the tail of a rat. "What did you have in mind, good sir? Believe me, I can get a hundred pounds at auction for one sickly, old Thicklip?"

Blackwood had quickly lost his patience. "We are not here now to purchase slaves, necessarily, Mr. Deas, but to discuss a relationship. A relationship in which you will profit exponentially, and for our part— I'll say the deal will be reciprocal, the details are not important in so far as you are concerned. I assumed, based on your…reputation, you are not confined to proper business practices. Before I can proceed, I need your assurance that what is said here today, does not leave this pier. If I am mistaken or you cannot make this assurance, if we have wasted your time, let me know, and we will waste it no further."

"Now, now," sniveled Deas. "I mean no offense, Gentlemen. I simply do not like to sniff my finger after it has been in my ass, yes?"

The two were entirely unsure what Deas meant, and Dickenson stopped himself when he began to ask for clarification. Blackwood was known for his harshness in demeanor, and Dickenson promptly interjected as to ease potential tensions. "That is to say, your time is clearly valuable, Mr. Deas, and we know you are eager to get back to doing what you do so well. For now, we have three barrels of salt, and we want one strong, healthy male for each barrel," he said directly. Blackwood glanced at him with a disapproving stare. They had discussed offering a single barrel for three slaves, yet Dickenson suspected the major spoiled any potential goodwill with his terse nature.

"Salt, you say, three barrels?" said Deas. His expression suddenly became much more animated. "That is a reasonable offer, my friend. It is fair, I will say. You know, I can get much more—you know that. 'Twill not do, it is a fair offer, yet hardly better than what I could do at auction. Disappointing, Gentlemen, as I expected, I believe you said 'substantial.' Three barrels of salt is small potatoes to me; I have built a hugely successful enterprise. This is hardly an appealing arrangement thus far." Deas was a sniveling, greedy shit. He knew the sky-high price of salt, which in this case dictated an offer well above market value. Nonetheless, he was eager to suck every drop of blood from the stone.

"We will not pay more, Mr. Deas, and in all sincerity, I do not wish to cavil or bargain. We all know the offer is generous and profitable on your end," replied Dickenson. "The salt and the slaves are, of course, small potatoes, to a man such as yourself. We only need those to be on our way for the day. We can settle on this and move on to greater matters, shall we?"

"Ah, that is no fun, my friend. You don't prefer foreplay before you stick it in?"

"Perhaps I see the quibbling over a few schillings as an annoyance, or at best, an unnecessary waste of time. You risk agitating me to no end and losing an easy profit.

The offer is quite significant, and should you let me continue, I would have told you, we do not need a bill of sale. We require no paperwork for the transaction," said Dickenson.

Deas pressed his lips as though he was proud of himself as if somehow, he was skilled enough in some manner to have created this fortuitous arrangement. "That is not bad. You don't need paperwork? You will give me the salt. I will give you three of these?"

"That is correct, sir," answered Dickenson. "We are not looking for a proper and legal transaction. We do not need a bill, nor do we need any documentation, thus…the three Negroes you sell us will never have even existed. You keep their papers. There is no shortage of free men being sold into slavery around here. I'm sure you will have no trouble finding…*replacements,* and when you do, it will be an easy task to make them fit the paperwork you already have."

"I can sell each twice is what you are saying?"

"In a matter of speaking, yes. You can sell them to us today, and you can sell…whomever, or whatever you find, as these Negroes here. I am going to assume you will never again find this offer before you," replied Dickenson. "And again, this is not the crux of what we are here to discuss with you. Please accept this, and we will be free to carry on."

Blackwood and Dickenson planned on ensnaring the easily manipulated Deas in a progression of steps. By convincing him to cooperate in a relatively minor wrongdoing, they would be able to simply urge him into increasingly greater misdeeds. Irving Deas's starving ego made their task all too easy.

Deas's deviant mind was abounding with glee. A sliver of drool ran from his lip, and he wiped it with his open hand. "Yes, yes, yes," he whispered, and he coldly smiled to reveal the few teeth he had. Each tooth resembled old corn nibbles, and his tongue sloppily licked his flat, chapped lips. "Some people, many people, have said I'm the shrewdest businessman in the colony. Believe me, this has not happened because I let chances slip me by. Three barrels. Come, come. Let's look over the inventory, shall we? I know you will be pleased with what I have here, all right?" he said and extended his arm to Dickenson's shoulder. The lieutenant could not help but glance at his hand as it touched the upper part of his arm. "These are extraordinary. So many told me, 'Mr. Deas, you should not invest in the slave market, it turns no profit,' but I've made a huge fortune. I believe I know what I am doing. I'm a very smart man, I'll tell you. Very highly educated."

The three men slowly strolled along the line of desperate slaves as Deas prattled on about his good fortune. The pier was filthy with bird droppings, mud, and grime. Some of the products, as they were, were still dripping from the cold buckets of water Deas had poured over them in preparation for their exhibit. Before putting them on display for auction, Deas typically showered them with ice-cold water, then sprinkled wheat flour about their skin. He believed the subtle and familiar scent of bread would somehow entice potential buyers.

Recent days had been the least trying the poor souls had lived through in some time. The Deas' House standard procedure was to 'fatten them up' before auctions, thus these few had managed to enjoy meals prepared with table scraps normally bound for the trash. Despite Dickenson's and Blackwood's outward disinterest, Deas insisted on continuing his manner of friendly small talk. "I'm guessing by your accents you gentlemen are here with the Brits. Be sure to visit the Kit Kat House—mention my name. Of course, I do very well here and can afford top-shelf whores. I've fucked so many gorgeous women, believe me. To be honest, my dick only works when it's inside a beautiful cunt. Kit Kat House is magnificent, but I'm sure they will accept buckets of salt. No shame in digging through the shit, as long as you get your dick wet, right?"

"Uh...yes, Mr. Deas. We know your time is pressed," said Dickenson.

Near the end of the pier stood a mammoth, statuesque figure. He was as solid as an old oak and stout enough the planks beneath him appeared as though they could hardly support his weight. His frame reached well over six feet in height, and his shoulders were as broad as they were bound with muscle. The towering brute was clad in a deep-green jacket with cardinal box strap and trim and tall, rugged leather riding boots. He tipped his black, pompon hat when Deas approached and lowered his head ever so slightly.

"Gentlemen, I still don't think I ever got your names," uttered Deas.

"Right. I'm Major Blackwood, and he is Lieutenant Dickenson," barked the major. He was loathed to be bound to this so-called man, even to the degree of knowing one another's names.

"Ah, so you are officers in the Royal Army, then?" said Deas as he pressed his lips. "Good, good. I suspected as much, all right? I know many British officers, outstanding people. In any event, this is my most trusted associate; you could say my right hand. Unteroffizer, Gebhard Ruehrschnek, of my *Soldatenhandel*, as I have titled it." Ruehrschnek served as Deas's personal guard and ruthless contracted henchman. Often, he traveled aboard slavers to the Gold Coast to claim the most prized of the lot for his master. When not on the sea, he occupied his time by fulfilling numerous underhanded errands.

Mostly, this involved manipulating markets toward Deas's favor, harassing competition, and threatening rivals and inconveniently principled political figures. Only days before had Irving Deas been honored for his incredible philanthropy when he reimbursed a small, local Anglican chapel after its coffer was pilfered by pathetically dissolute thieves. In this case, Ruehrschnek was the culprit, as contracted by Deas, who not only relished the attention, but used it as an opportunity to advertise the opulence of his new whorehouse. Deas simply *donated* the money his manservant had stolen before he was hailed for his selfless generosity.

"He's the finest soldier, all right?" professed Irving Deas. "A lot of people will tell you that. He's fantastic, hand-picked to ensure everything within my great enterprise goes as it should. Ruehrschnek is ruthless, cunning, and to me, blindly loyal. If I told him to glug a tall glass of my warm piss, he'd swallow away."

"He's a Hessian, a war whore," said Blackwood. "He sells his gun like a wench sells her cunt. You are a fool to trust in his loyalty. For a man who boasts to be so shrewd, this is quite naïve. This German fuck is loyal only to whoever can fatten his fucking pockets. He is as loyal as your wealth allows, and when the well runs dry, so too will his use for you."

Ruehrschnek simply sneered as though he found Blackwood's frustration amusing.

"He's a magnificent soldier. He's cunning and ruthless, all right? Believe me, he is loyal," assured Deas. "And he's pleased to meet you, right, Gerhardt?"

"Unt ju gif a vuck about dee Amedicans, do ju? Ju are a whore vor da king. Ju sell jor soul for dis vukink cause. Ju have no vill," said Ruehrschnek.

Dickenson positioned himself toward the center of the company of men and promptly threw his hand to an arm's reach to create physical distance between them. "Gentlemen, there really is no need for hostilities. We offered our swords to the Empire, he offers his to whoever can afford it—who is to say which is honorable and which is imprudent? Debating these matters is trivial and serves only to get in the way. The fact remains, the reason we are here can serve your pockets as well as our Empire, thus our purpose is one and the same.

Is it not?" For the moment, the lieutenant seemed to quell the escalating tension as he further piqued Deas's curiosity.

"I cannot say," replied Deas. "You have suggested as such, but I have yet to hear your proposition."

"Very good," said Dickenson. "For starters, we need to settle on three strong young males. When we can do this, I will propose to you the opportunity for more inventory than you can possibly imagine. Young Negroes, old Negroes, females, males, slaves to sell to brothels and slaves to sell to farmers. Slaves of all type, to fit all demands. Enough inventory to scuttle the largest slaver, enough inventory to be free from the frustration of waste, to corner the slave market in the entire colony, if not all the north. More slaves than you have ever had, and the king will see to this. The Empire will ensure the continuous replenishment of supply for as long as the Africans continue to have little Africans."

An uneven, yellow-toothed grin festered on Deas's face as he nearly drooled at the thought. Ruehrschnek furrowed his brows and glanced toward his master in nervous anticipation. "The king will see to this?" snarled Deas. "How can this be, and why do I deserve such...charity?"

"'Tis not charity, slaver," barked Blackwood.

"Of course, not exactly," chimed Dickenson, who was, once again, looking to temper potential hostility. "Formally, the Empire shuns the institution as American barbarism, inhumane practice. Though these Negroes have worth in purpose to our cause. From time to time, you will be visited by our comrades, who will require the use of some from your inventory. All you are needed to do is comply and give them what they need. The rest, are all yours. In a matter of speaking, you are simply storing our slaves, and as rent, we will allow you the entire balance of the shipload. Though it should go without saying, I feel it better not to rely on the assumption. This is a clandestine endeavor, Mr. Deas. Being free with your words will, to be sure, result in quite drastic measures."

Blackwood interjected, "He is saying, this fucking Hessian ogre won't be able to save you if you cannot keep your filthy, shit-eating mouth closed about all of this."

Deas cast his eyes toward Blackwood, yet dared not defend whatever honor he may have believed he had. "I know how to stay quiet, all right? Trust me, nobody keeps secrets better than I do. You will be sending ships filled with slaves to me?" Deas confirmed. "And all I have to do is let you have a few of them, and I can keep the rest? This is what you are saying, yes?"

"Basically, yes. Correct, sir," replied Dickenson.

"I am not as successful as I am without being informed of the details, all right? How can this be…how will this happen?"

Dickenson began to feel Blackwood's impatience, yet was better at concealing it. "High-ranking officials in the Admiralty, as well as in the King's Army, will intercept slavers, eradicate the crew, and witnesses, then divert them to New York Harbor, specifically your wharf. If need be, His Majesty will dispatch warships to the African Coast to ensnare Negroes directly—time will tell. These are not your concerns. Your concerns are to accept them, process their paperwork, and remain as silent as a dead man."

Once again, Deas turned toward Ruehrschnek as the gears within his depraved mind began to churn. "Hmmm," he groaned. "You know, I've heard people say discretion has a cost unto itself. I don't know how endless the treasury is in London. I don't know if I should charge for this service, but maybe some would, right?"

"*Dis costs money not to schpeek about zees dings,*" added Ruehrschnek.

"He has a point," confirmed Deas. "It seems to me there will be various inconveniences on my end. Somehow I should account for this bounty of smelly Negroes. And, well, you know the smelliest shits attract the most flies."

"You are a unbelievable fucking prick," mumbled Blackwood. "The treasury is endless; on this you are correct. The treasury is as impressive as the number of troopers in George's Army. Yet, my tolerance for this…negotiation has reached an end, Mr. Deas. We are offering you barrels of salt in good faith. We are going to take whichever three we so choose. You and your slut know we can take whatever we need from you without your permission. Reality had become bitter for you the moment we presented our proposition. Since you were told of our intentions, you now have no choice but to cooperate. You will do this or I will have both of you killed before the nightfall. I have decided now, this is no longer a negotiation, but a demand. Work with the Empire or neither of you will see the sunrise. And you know this will happen, Hessian. You will get nothing more from us, not a pence nor polite handshake. This relationship will see no exchanges, and leave no traces. Your choice is to accept a monopoly on the slave trade, or to lie under a blanket of dirt."

Deas was as thin-skinned as any, yet submissive and not looking to challenge Blackwood's hand. Awkwardly and obviously, he tried to seem assured, as though he was deciding to cooperate. "I must tell you," he said. Then he paused and resigned to not continue his thought. "Yes, yes, very well. Now then, I know you insisted on strapping young males, for now, but perhaps I can entice you with this one, since you, after all, are men and far from home," said Deas as they reached the very first in the column. "She'll do for a quick fuck or two or three, then…do whatever you wish with her. Dump her into the harbor if you want." Her face was drawn with dread and sadness; she was naked and too terrified to be ashamed or self-conscious. "Look at those lips, fine sirs," he continued as he squeezed the sides of her mouth together tightly and repulsively inserted his filthy, blemished, crud-encrusted thumb between her lips. "Can you feel them around the shaft of your cock? Ahh, yes, you are naughty, ain't you, eh?" He removed his appendage and slowly and disturbingly licked it with his saliva-glazed tongue with some manner of twisted delight. "Yes, believe me, she can lick your pole clean to a shine—he-he." He slapped her in the thigh with his open hand.

"We are interested only in three strong men, Mr. Deas," replied Dickenson in a stern and irritated tone. "It is best if we continue on. I cannot say if your time will be better served without us, yet I can say for sure, ours will."

"That's a foolish decision, good sir, one I know you will regret. Let's proceed."

The three continued down the line once again, and without pause, Deas stopped at the next figure in the column. He was a fairly young boy, perhaps no more than ten years of age. He clung to his mother, the unfortunate soul Deas had disgustingly offered to Dickenson and Blackwood. "Step out, boy!" barked Deas, and the youngster strode forward. "This one might do, though I am not really sure what you are looking for. Jump up, jump, little Mosshead," commanded Deas. Without hesitation or thought, the boy leaped up and down a few times, each time scraping the shackle from the shins of the two aside him to which he was bound. "See this, Gentlemen? He is going to grow strong soon—already, he can carry twenty pounds for a mile." Deas clutched his arm at the wrist and jerked it upward. "Look at that frame. He is well-built, this one. He can serve you for a very long time. He is worth more than a barrel of salt, quite a deal for this one."

"No! No, please, sir! No," cried his mother. "Please don't take my child from me. He's all I got—please, sir."

Immediately, Deas released the boy's hand and thrust his face, nose-to-nose to the mother's. "Excuse me? I know you didn't just tell me what to do, you African bitch. You want a Deas's Dose, is that it? You're hungry? I didn't feed you enough, is that what you are trying to tell me?" Deas employed in numerous odious and barbaric punishments to manage his inventory. The most common being was what he proudly referred to as Deas's Dose, which involved pouring feces down the throats of any who spoke without permission to do so. "You're hungry, is that it? Or are you stupid, which is it?"

"Is this necessary, Mr. Deas?" Dickenson demanded. "Does accosting a woman looking to protect her child make you feel worthy? This is how you conduct yourself here—have you no sense of courtly decorum or tact in the company of gentlemen? Mind you, I am not here to tell you how to conduct your business, as it is apparent you have been doing quite well, but while we are here, we will not tolerate such boorish behavior, even to a Negro. Should you insist on continuing these despicable habits, please do them another time, when we are not present to witness."

"They do not care about their brood as we do, good man. Believe me, she is only looking to protect herself. She wants sympathy and mercy for her, not this little one," claimed Deas.

Blackwood was uncharacteristically aggravated and impatient. "That is patently false. Do you lie so blatantly and clearly because you have no regard for my intellect or conviction to tell you personally and plainly, you are a fucking liar?"

"Forgive me, Colonel, or Major. I'm sorry, Major. No offense was intended. I've heard this from many people. Nonetheless, obvious lies have their value. The point of an obvious lie is to render truth as being meaningless. Usually I'm able to make this work for me. However, it is clear you are much more intuitive than those I usually do business with."

Blackwood was not amused. "An obvious lie is also useful at rooting out whoever has the audacity to demonstrate insubordination by calling you on it. Regardless, I gather you try not to surround yourself with such persons." He offered a quick glance toward Ruehrschnek, who could not help but awkwardly shift his body and turn away.

"That aside," grumbled Deas. "It sounds as though I've offended your sensibilities, my good sirs. You have the self-righteous condemnation to pass judgment on me as you are purchasing human property…interesting. I am to assume you are liberating these Negroes, then? You are fulfilling some philanthropic fantasies. Do you abhor slavery and all of those who profit from the institution? You wish to see these gorillas as our equals?" Deas snidely replied.

"Slavery is an institution of mankind," sniped Dickenson. "'The worst form of inequality is trying to make unequal things equal.' Thus, I will never profess to extend you the courtesy or respect I demand you extend me. We wish to hasten the time spent in your company, and clearly, you are rushed to proceed with your Negro fetishes. Now, without further ado, can we please carry on?"

The slaves within the immediate area could scarcely contain their shock, and for them, it was a rare moment of satisfaction. Though they could hardly understand what was being said, the antagonistic tone was quite clear. Deas, of course, sensed the bit of delight which seemed to run along his line of slaves. "*Ju shoot be careful,*" warned Ruehrschnek.

When Deas realized Ruehrschnek expressed a willingness to resist Dickenson's enmity, he was infused with an uncharacteristic glimpse of courage. "How dare you, sir? My business is my own, and I will not stand here, on my property, and allow you to insult my honor, in front of these animals no less. These are rightful grounds for a duel, all right? If I must challenge you, believe me, you will lose."

Dickenson had become impatient and tired of the discussion. Coldly, he looked to end it and continue with the transaction. "Mr. Deas, do you have any idea who we are or what we are capable of?"

"I...Listen, I know a lot of people, all right? Trust me, but you know we have just made our acquaintances moments ago—"

"Precisely," replied Dickenson. "I say with earnest, sir, it would be wise to proceed with caution. He will not say as such, yet your loyal Hessian knows you are speaking foolishly and dangerously. You would sooner fill your trousers with shit before you met me on the field to duel. In the interest of moving this along, I'm going to ignore the suggestion, and we will press forward as though it was not uttered."

Deas had become nervous and unsure. He was torn between defending his delicate self-worth by telling Dickenson to fuck off and closing an obviously profitable deal. His simplistic mind conjured up some balance between the two, in that he could fend off the insult, yet continue the business transaction. "I am no stranger to philosophy, sirs. Despite your obviously inaccurate presumptions, I am a very smart man, all right, very smart. There is nobody more well-read than I. Slavery as an institution of mankind. Many people tell me how wise I am. Now, are we going to continue with your proposed arrangement, or do you want to read these monkeys some more Socrates?"

Blackwood and Dickenson looked at one another, stunned any man could be so crude and bankrupt of character. Blackwood was particularly satisfied as he realized Deas was so weak in nature it would require little effort to manipulate him. Irving Deas relied on bravado to mask his lack of pride. He was driven by gluttony alone and clearly eager to suckle the teat of the Empire to fatten his already corpulent gut. Both soldiers knew they would be able to continue freely insulting this man without jeopardizing the arrangement. It was apparent, Deas's insecurity and lust for material wealth allowed him to eat innumerable personal slights without a trace of indigestion. The satisfaction to do so would have been rewarding, yet both were disciplined in nature and content to simply dislike Irving Deas, especially given their dealings with him, personally, would be infrequent. Deas's pseudo outrage did nothing to sway them, and they were firmly convinced it was safe to move forward with the scheme. Deas's disconnected relationship with the truth and inclination to lie so freely rendered all words that fell from his mouth as unreliable. Clearly, this was a man with no credibility, and in the event he decided to discuss their arrangement, chances were he would not be taken with a grain of seriousness. Without much hesitation, Blackwood peered directly into Deas's eyes and coldly replied, "It's Aristotle, fucking moron."

* * *

North.

Another sunset as another day had passed with Shaw bound at the ankles, naked, and strung with his hands behind his back and his head below his feet. The lieutenant was suspended, limply, as though he were a slain buck waiting to be flayed. His feet felt as though they were on fire, and his lungs struggled to inhale fresh gasps as they were nearly flooded with blood. The volume of blood pooled within his head was threatening to cause a cerebral stroke. From time to time one of Bowman's lieutenants would lift Shaw upright to offer a semblance of relief. For now, Bowman had required the traitor to remain alive, and he was as adept at preserving lives as he was at taking them.

Without resistance, Shaw yielded to Bowman, fully prepared to accept whatever correction his commander had to offer. For days, he had remained as such, lashed to the low branch of a mighty northeastern birch some twenty yards or so from the cave-like quarters Bowman's cult had created. Shaw had been fed and given water, though never once had he been whipped, beaten, or sliced as he had fully expected. Not one time had Bowman come to interrogate or harass. He has simply dangled from the tree by his ankles, inches above a puddle of his shit and piss, which had seeped down his nude body.

Otaktay and Stone had been unable to track Captain Pearson, and this further threatened to unleash Bowman's repressed rage. Over the past days and for the moment, the colonel was unsure exactly what to do with his treasonous lieutenant. On this night, Bowman chose to let thoughtless reaction guide his course. At dawn, when the tip of the autumnal sun had set behind the trees, Bowman approached Shaw, unsure himself what he was going to do. He sidled deliberately and with procrastination, with a blank mind and a desperate soul. In his heart, Bowman knew his obligations and the appropriate responses to mutiny. He was more ashamed to confront the disloyal Aquitaine Knight than he was anything. Shaw had managed to do what was seldom done, and that was to catch Bowman by surprise.

When he reached him, Bowman stood mere inches from Lieutenant Shaw and peered down into his eyes as he waited over him. Shaw returned the look with a despairing expression. It was a struggle for him to catch the breath to speak. "Colonel," he said with a meek, yet respectful tone.

Bowman mostly considered manners to be an inefficient waste of time, yet now, he absolutely had no interest in formalities or consideration for respect. "You are a traitor. You are disloyal to our traditions and our country, and you know you are to be treated as such," he groaned.

Shaw contorted his body a bit and pressed for air. "Who is...the traitor?" he struggled to ask. "You profess to be the beacon of loyalty and dedication to our tradition, our principled compass? A traitor disobeys the will of his king to take matters into his own hands, and no matter if his will is just, his actions are treason." He continued through toiled gasps. "You are bound to honor our call, yet you dishonored it. We were charged to retrieve the *Kahontsi Ehnita* for His Majesty, not for our or more so, *your* personal ownership. Your compunction to protect the country from an unsuitable ruler, is nothing but a pretense to hide your corruption and lust for power. For years, I did nothing but mire in timidity as a willing accomplice, and for that, I deserve justice. Yet, make no mistake, Colonel Bowman, *you* are the traitor."

"You are a fucking, naïve fool, Lieutenant," grumbled Bowman as he circled Shaw in slow steps. "We honor our call by serving our country and countrymen, by protecting them from a centuries-long reign of an ill-fit, ill-minded king. A king who was born from the blood of a corrupt and ineffective dynasty; a lineage which is gradually seeing to the fall of our Empire. We are bound to protect the Kingdom from all enemies, foreign and domestic alike. You believe loyalty compels you to protect the rule of a man who repeats his words mindlessly and pisses blue piss? You believe the fate of our country is best to be dictated by the whims of such a man? His father was bleeding the Empire to a slow death, and now his son is seeing fit to strip it of all signs of life. When George dies, the *Kahontsi Ehnita* will find another to serve, one who will properly defend our faith and our empire."

"You have no right to make such decisions. Tell me, will it uphold your standard of fit?" replied Shaw.

"And you had no right to make yours. Perhaps the truth lies somewhere between us," exclaimed Bowman.

"With respect, Colonel, you are incorrect. There are only right and wrong, and there is no area between," said Shaw.

"Perhaps," said Bowman. "Or perhaps that is too simplistic. These matters are beyond our understanding. My lead brought us to the *Kahontsi Ehnita*. It was entrusted to me, and I will hold it until it finds another. Regardless, it wouldn't matter even if I cared to give the matter any thought. We are all forced to confront the consequences of our actions. We cannot run from them, for running would be the consequence. Then, we will all be purified in death. Sooner for you than for me, it would seem."

Shaw groaned and once again shifted his body about. His legs had become as numb as though they were frozen through, and his skull was flushed with blood. Bowman watched him struggle until he was convinced the mutineer had endured enough. "I deserve justice, but not by your hand. This is not justice. This is murder, Colonel. Be sure that—"

Before another utterance could leave his mouth, Bowman clasped the long dagger he wore at his left hip, gliding it from its scabbard, and forcefully slashed it across Shaw's neck, just below the chin. "You are going to eat those words as your final meal." A deep cascade of cardinal red gushed from the wound, as Shaw thrashed about wildly. Splatters of blood were launched in every direction. Shaw growled a curdled gasp, then gagged and pressed his jaw as wide open as he could in a desperate attempt to swallow some air. Bowman remained sober and unmoved as the blood splattered about his face and deerskin cloak. Without turning away, he leisurely slid his blade back into the scabbard. After a trice, Bowman turned and slinked into the darkness. Shaw would struggle for several minutes until he bled out and the last sign of life gave way to his demise. His remains hung from the birch tree as a warm, inviting slab, ready to be picked apart by the crows and mauled by the wolves.

* * *

North, near the Quebec Path.

The air was brisk, the breeze was biting, and the ground had become almost frozen. The trees had been stripped of all but a few stubborn leaves, and the mid-afternoon sky was already turning dark. It had been seven days since Pearson was freed from Bowman's grasp and thirty-two more since he and his company broke from Ticonderoga. His once-vibrant red officer's coat was now matted, drab brownish, and filthy, and his usually clean-shaven chin was now covered with gruff, uneven stubble. His mature, dark, walnut-shaped eyes were sunken into his loose, dull skin. Each step was heavier than the one before, his right arm dangled nearly lifelessly, and his jaw had swollen to make him nearly unrecognizable. Although he carefully rationed his foodstuffs, only allowing himself a few scraps each day, he was once again hunched over and staggering from the pain of malnourishment. His bowels had come to stream a flow of blood from his ass when he shat. After arduously hiking southward, for what seemed to be an eternity, Captain Pearson once more found his body on the verge of collapse.

He managed to stick to the creek for some time, until it eventually reached a very rudimentary wooden step bridge along a narrow footpath within the woods. A tinge of vigor momentarily pulsed through Pearson's veins as he realized, for better or worse, he had finally made it somewhere. The path weaved through the barren trees to ascend a rather steep foothill. The trail was mostly covered with leaves; here and there, large boulders seemed to have been pushed aside. Pearson's vision was blurring, and his head was becoming light.

He staggered over the footbridge and ambled forward along the trail as it climbed the knoll. With all wits about him nearly lost, he teetered for a minute or two until the last of his strength gave out. Pearson stumbled a few steps onward and held his arms outward as he tried to find his balance. He threw his hands frontward to brace himself, as he expected to be within a foot or two of the nearest tree, though it was well beyond a dozen yards. He collapsed forward and crashed to the ground. His head struck a large, smooth stone as he landed, and for an instant, his feet were lifted and then flopped suddenly to the ground. The violent collision between his skull and the boulder sent a shockwave through his bones. His head resting on its side and the rock's cool, hard surface was a modest relief from his feverish temperateness and clammy flesh. With his lids slit open, his blurred vision remained fixed on the tall weeds in which he lay until they were lost within his blindness. Pearson's body shut down. He rested awkwardly with his arms pinned between his chest and the ground and his legs twisted oddly. In no more than a few seconds, a stream of damp, blood-steeped shit quickly filled his already fouled breeches.

The height of the hill overlooked a community of a few modest buildings. The structures sat side by side; some were brick, others stone, most built of Dutch-style construction. Each seemed to be hiding within the foothills along the river valley, just north of Fishkill. The captain lay on his stomach in the brush just off the trail to the small farming and fishing village. His body refused to press on. The lack of food and sleep had gotten the better of his determination to continue. With his jaw hung low and without consciousness, he wheezed with breath. He was faced with death, alone and helplessly frail. And yet, despite the morbid conditions, his body and soul had found a state of relaxation.

* * *

The Trails—Evolution XIII

Carso Wick, North Ronaldsay of the Orkney Islands of Scotland.

Bleats from the thinly scattered flock of sheep were carried along the bitterly crisp and cool ocean breeze from the North Sea. The winds whispered of the coming storm, and the waves crashed against the shore as though the ocean was clawing to drag the land into the deep. A mile south of the shadows, Citadel North waited for the site of the next evolution. Placed within a field of uneven grass and weeds, a rudimentarily constructed wood platform stood within a series of dirt and weed-matted tracks. The tracks lined in opposing directions, all starting near the splintery log and plank stand. Working within each of the tracks, a man struggled to drive stakes into the unyielding, rocky soil.

The six Saplings were fully nude, other than an iron and wood grate that bent beneath their jaws, behind their necks, and atop their shaven skulls. Their eyes were blocked with a heavy, metal plate fixed tightly by the wiry, demonic-mechanical contraption. The iron masks were so crudely crafted, with exposed jagged edges and prickly shards throughout, they regularly chafed and scraped their skin. Weighing some five pounds, the blinding device strained their upper ends of their spine to a point of near numbness. At the base of their necks along the backbone dangled a sturdy lock binding their blinding device about their heads. Chirurgeon Alard held the only key. Each man was lean and muscular, suggesting a youthful and powerful physique. Aside from unique abrasions and bruises, they were nearly indistinguishable from one another, but for a colored band that dangled along the back of each of their heads. Each wore a red, yellow, green, blue, brown, or white cotton strip, which flapped within the breeze as they toiled away. Their warm breath became mist the moment it hit the bitter air to suggest the chill about them, yet their bodies glistened with perspiration all the same.

The Saplings had all been given a set of twenty-three to four-foot wooden spikes, a heavy stone hammer, and instructions to drive each of them into the ground within a narrow pathway, no less than five feet in distance to any other. Each man struggled to pound the long stakes into his pathway blindly, often crashing the hefty and sturdy hammerhead against his wrist. White landed his stone hammer so hard against his forearm he nearly broke it in two. His bone had been fractured to the point of eliminating him from advancement. His counterparts were slightly less unfortunate as to only suffer varying degrees of bruises and scrapes. The task took the whole of them several hours to complete, the issue not only being their inability to forcefully drive the picket into the dense soil but to comply with the direction each post be less than five feet from all others. Precise measurements taken under Alard's supervision disqualified more placements than not.

After Red, Yellow, Green, Brown, and Blue had completed their respective tasks, each could wander his pathway for as long as it took a captured lamb to collapse after her neck had been pierced with a small puncture. The pathways were all in the same dimension; precisely twenty-one feet wide and one hundred one feet in length. Each of the pathways began at a center point marked with a wood-planked scaffold. The respective tracks extended in opposing directions, creating a star-like configuration. Running along both outer edges were picket and roped railings standing three to four feet in height. Each man was advised to learn to the best of his perceptions and abilities the nature of his path, in particular, the relation to the spikes he had hammered into the earth. When the animal fell, they were escorted from their lanes.

Individually, each Sapling was ushered to a starting point at the base of his corresponding track. Flanking him on either side was a royal mounted cavalryman. Their horses grumbled and flailed about impatiently, and the Redcoats who rode them wore the same childish look of joyful anticipation. Attached to a metallic bolt near the rear of the saddle was a chain stretched between to link both riders. The Saplings stood ahead of the horses and chained some ten feet, wholly unaware of the challenge before them, or the peril behind them.

After Alard positioned himself atop the wood plank to stand between a pair of statuesque infantrymen, the troopers held their Brown Bess firearms at shoulder mount position formally. Strong gusts from the sea whipped about the Chiurgeon's gray cloak, and the set of keys he wore around his neck chimed like distant bells. He turned and, with his old, but keenly perceptive eyes, surveyed the fields in which he was surrounded. The Saplings were each only advised to exhaust all their effort to sprint with the greatest of his swiftness within the boundaries of his path. Announced with the fire of muskets, the Sapling was to dash with unrelenting speed until he reached the end of the track. After a brief head start, the riders would follow behind, galloping on either side of the track, and when the Sapling slowed, he was overrun by the taut iron chain. One by one, each of them, Red, Green, Blue, Brown, and Yellow burst from his position at the thunderous clap of the muskets.

After two or three seconds the heavy thuds from the horses' hooves followed. Yellow was the first to fall. By chance, he passed the first spike, though without much distance. As he raced ahead, he turned as though he anticipated crashing against another, and in mid-stride, his right knee slammed against one of the posts. The rigid spike was scoured against his fibula. The skin along his shin was peeled away as though it was shucked from an ear of corn. His tibialis anterior was torn, and his bone, just below the knee, was badly fractured. With a violent thud, his body crashed against the ground. The tightened chain passed over him as he clutched his leg and writhed about with unimaginable agony.

From the start, Green fared better. He zigged and zagged, nearly stumbling a few times, yet, by chance, he managed to avoid all the spikes before him and stay on his feet. He burst like a bolt of lightning until the naked sole of his foot landed on a raised patch of soil and twisted at the ankle. A jolt of pain was fired into his leg, and he staggered when his body could not move to press any weight on his left foot. For a step or maybe two he hobbled forward, until he was overtaken by the thunderous roar of the warhorses. The taut iron links of the chain lashed against him to ensnare his head at the iron mask. He was pulled from his feet and dragged along the ground wildly. As his body became twisted and contorted, his exposed skin was grated against the ridged soil and small rocks. Nearly twenty feet from the end of the track a stake was hooked into Green's body just below the ribs on his right side. As he was unrelentingly yanked forward, the spike was driven into his diaphragm fully through, to slice his kidney. He was caught as the spike violently wedged against the direction in which he was being pulled, and in an instant, his flesh gave to the pressure. A squelchy burst of meaty pink and brown splotches of the recesses of his stomach were flushed from a gash that was torn above his side below the rib. As he was heaved along the ground, he left behind a wake of moist bile and innards as they drained from his wound.

Witnessing from aloft the raised platform, Alard shook his head with silent disappointment. Only three of his Saplings now remained. Blue, Brown, and Red had managed to finish without incident, though none were particularly impressive. The Trials were not progressing as swimmingly as he had anticipated, and by this point, he was unsure it would even yield a harvest.

It had been some time since the Trials had borne a barren return. The Chiurgeon was overcome with self-doubt and nearly destitute of optimism. To have lost three Saplings in such short order did not bode well for the prospects of this crop. In all his years, Alard had never offered discouraging prospects, and on this day, he was determined to continue with conviction. Despite the bleak outlook before him, Chirurgeon Alard refused to confront Major Blackwood without presenting to him, his new Mole Rat.

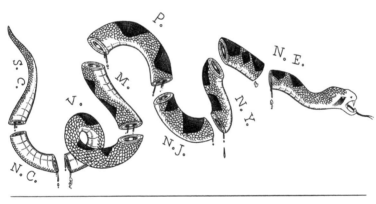

JOIN, or SHE DIES.

"Every man desires to live long, but no man wishes to be old."—
Jonathan Swift, *Gulliver's Travels*

Seven

Late October 1777.

Captain Pearson woke, slowly opened and closed his eyes and
reflexively cricked his neck to the left, then to the right. He winced as
he tightened then loosened the fingers in his right hand. He found
himself, somehow, in a rather unpresumptuous bedchamber,
confined within dull stone walls and inferior quality fixtures. The
ceiling was unusually low, and the heavy beams that ran across it
seemed as wretched outstretched fingers reaching to snatch him. The
rough stone and dry oak walls were confined to the point of
suffocation. Sunlight struggled through the only cracked and dirty
window at the head of the bed in which he lay. The four glass panels
met at a cross that stood before the glaring beams. For a moment, he
was not completely unsure he had not found himself to be in the
afterlife. As his wits and senses found him, his immediate inclination
was to search for his belongings and, in particular, the pouch he was
directed to protect and deliver. He pulled himself upright and
realized he was fully unclothed and restrained by heavy cotton strips
at the wrists and ankles. The force of his strain sent a jolt through his
shoulder, and he groaned with pain.

"Oh, go easy, sweetie," the gentle voice of a rather aged-looking
woman who sat beyond the foot of the bed said. Her thick gray hair
trickled from beneath her paint-stained mob cap, to frame the pruned
skin of her face. She rested at a rickety, wooden easel spotted with
colorful drips, drabs, and strokes of paint. Her plain white frock was
speckled with varied paint smudges, and her bony, liver-plagued hand
quivered as she swept the brush along the palette. "Needn't hurt
yourself," she continued in passing.

The captain was so emaciated he appeared as a skeleton draped lazily with a thin layer of skin. Sharp joints jutted from his shoulders, and his chest was rippled with the bones about his rib cage. As he lay flat on his back, his stomach was pressed within him, seeming no thicker than the bound parchment pages of a short story. The many scrapes, cuts, and bruises about his ghoulishly pale skin were the mementos of his punishing, exhausting, nightmare of a trek he had set out to endure. "What, where am I? What is happening?" he asked in a shaking voice. His head was throbbing; his shoulder stung with pain, and his muscles were sore and weak. Instinctively, his eyes scoured the room, until he saw his leather pouch, resting beneath the windowsill within a scattering of poorly crafted clay jars and jugs. The assurance offered him just enough relief to focus on his latest predicament. "What happened? I can remember staggering about… Where are my clothes? Where am I? Who are you?"

From beyond the closed doorway at the head of the room, Pearson heard the scampering of footsteps against a dry wood door. The old tin door handle rattled and shook as whoever was on the other side struggled to make it work. After a few frustrated jiggles, the door swung open. "Yews awake?" From the doorway emerged Wouter Behrendt, an old Dutch laborer who arrived in the colony from the Netherlands with his wife some thirty-plus years prior.

Their passage was financed with indentured servitude, and when free of his obligation, Wouter hardly managed to ascend beyond a slave's station. He was capable enough, not particularly lazy, though not particularly hard-working. Wouter's apathetic disposition followed him across the ocean, and the new world of opportunities apparently opened no doors for the Behrendts. The same man arrived in America who set forth from the Netherlands.

Wouter had thin, gray hair, horrible posture, several missing teeth, wrinkled skin, and dreary, tired eyes. His words whistled through his lips with the most irritating lisp. He was simple in thought, short on manners, deprived of charm, yet seemingly kind in heart. "I found yah out by da pathway there. Was riding along. Sometimes I head that way cuz it's shorter, but I got to go up the hill there—you seen that big hill? Well, maybe you didn't, I don't know. My old mare ain't good at pullin' up too many hills no more. 'Course she used to haul us around with a full carriage, up all hills when it was we bought her. You remember that, Rosalie? She'd pull our asses up a mountain, right?"

With her attention still fixed on her artwork, she simply replied, "Yes, I remember. She would, dear."

"Yeah," continued Wouter. "She's an old one, she is. The horse, not my wife. But she's got some years behind her too, he-he. So, I been told to feed her greener grass. Something about the old horses eating green grass, but I don't know. Makes her shit stink something awful. Not Rosalie, but I can't say I love sniffing her shit none either. Anyhow, step in that shit…That horse shit, supposed to bring good luck, you know? But I ain't seen no luck. Look who I married?" He finished with a frail chuckle. His wife did nothing more than roll her eyes and continue painting.

Though awake, Pearson was still mostly in a daze. "I see. I collapsed. You found me and brought me here—this is your home, then?"

"Was headin' over to the post to get some eggs and whatnot. You were out cold, young man, right there in the dirt. Saw that red coat of yours. I got me good eyesight. She thinks I should wear those spectacles, but I told her, I got the eyes of an owl. Don't need to wear them things. I can see real good. Can't move like I used to, but can see as good as any young lad you want to show. So, got you in the cart and took you here, put you up nice and snug like. She wanted to tie you up and paint you. Well, not paint *you* like, but paint you, not paint *on* you, like you was a barn or fence or nothing, but oh—paint your picture. I said only you paint trees and things, hills and such, you never painted no man before. But she insisted, and she's the boss. So here you is, naked and being painted."

With his eyes closed, the captain collected himself to process his current predicament. All told, he was fortunate as it happened and despite the unusual situation he now found himself in, he owed Wouter, at the very least, a debt of gratitude. "*A* man." In passing, he corrected, "She never painted *a* man, not *no* man." Wouter removed his drab cotton cap to scratch the top of his head. A perplexed look was drawn upon his crinkly, aged face. Pearson could not help but notice the dried flakes of dust and dead skin that were kicked into the air from his tangled nest of gray atop his head.

"Right, she ain't ever painted a man before," replied Wouter. "I believe that is what I said, Mister."

Pearson simply rolled his eyes and was content to move on. "Yes. If you will, sir," he said. "Would you please untie me? And...my clothes?"

Wouter seemed to snap into action. "Ah!" he exclaimed. He looked about, then fumbled through the top drawer of the most dilapidated, old cabinet adjacent to his wife's art stand. The dry wicker basket and tin pot that rested on its surface rumbled about as he hurriedly ruffled through the mess within the drawer. The loud clangs and bangs rang through Pearson's ears, and he pressed his lids closed. It was difficult for Pearson to maintain his patience as he was latched to a flimsy, soiled bed fully in the nude. It seemed as though hours were passing before Wouter finally seemed to find what he was looking for. "Here!" bellowed Wouter, and he removed an old pitted blade from within the drawer. "Here we go, Mister." He wobbled his way toward the headstand with an uneven limp and struggled to slice the heavy cotton rags that bound Pearson's wrists. Pearson grimaced and turned his head away when the waft of cheap rum from Wouter's breath reached his nose. "Hang in there, Mister, we're almost there. Yeah, she likes to paint and such. Keeps her busy, which be just fine with me cause as long as she is busy, she ain't in my hair. Hey...if you, uh, don't mind me saying so, eh, Mister, you are pretty lucky fellow. Down there, you know? Right, Mister? You know what I am saying?"

"I don't, how is that?" asked Pearson.

"Well, down there, Mister," replied Wouter. "You got yourself a pretty gigantic-sized wiener, must say. Bet you could make my old mare happy if you wanted. My compliments, hmm." From where she sat, Rosalie pressed her lips and silently nodded in agreement. For his part, Pearson was too numbed to give the matter any thought or concern and was becoming frustrated in anticipation of being freed from the binds. After Wouter cut through the second knot around his wrist, he sat upright, groaned, and surveyed the room, hoping to spot his uniform.

Pearson was entirely bewildered. His reflex was to be appalled, yet considering the nature of his host, resigned to accept the compliment and move along as hastily as possible. "Well, I suppose, that is kind of you to say. Since we broached the topic, good sir, may I ask about my uniform?" With his tongue pressed between his teeth, Wouter sliced through the rags at Pearson's ankles and offered no response. "I beg your pardon, sir. My uniform?"

"Just a minute now, Mister," replied Wouter as he cut away the band, then continued to Pearson's right leg to do the same. After toiling for a minute or more, both ankles were finally free, and Pearson clenched his toes, stretched his arms, arched his back, and clicked his neck from one side to the other. His right shoulder stung him back, to remind him of the injury. He tugged at the patterned linen blanket beneath him and covered the personal parts of his body. "There you go, Mister, all free," blurted Wouter. "Sorry, Pumpkin, but we can't keep the man bound to the bed forever. Yeah, she loves her painting, her little busy work and hobbies and such. Keeps her outta my hair, right? Me? I'm too old for such horseshit things—my hobbies be sleeping, eating, and shitting. Or eating, then sleeping, then shitting, or eating as I'm shitting—why not, right, Mister? What is that, uh, you kill two birds in the bush, or some such. Eat as you shit. You ever eat while you're shitting? I ate a whole bushel of berries on the pot. Went right from the plate into—"

Pearson's forbearance quickly expired, and he bluntly interrupted, "Sir. Sir, please. My intentions are certainly not to appear rude or ill-mannered as a guest in your home. Let me first introduce myself to you and your adoring wife. Rosalie, yes? I am Captain Isaac Pearson of the Twenty-First Queen's Royal Artillery in His Majesty's command. Evidently, I owe you a personal debt for your conviction and, as it is, hospitality. More importantly, the Crown is, as well, indebted to you, and I will personally see to it that you are compensated fittingly. On this, you have my word as a man of honor. Until then, I do have a matter of some urgency and must immediately excuse myself from further…pleasantries and take my leave, madam and my good sir."

Wouter rubbed the prickly fingers with muck caked under his nails, along his gray, scruffy chin. He was not quite sure what Pearson was suggesting, other than he wished to offer some form of reward and immediately be on his way. In his own simplistic manner he attempted to verbally, subtly, surmise what Pearson was specifically trying to say. Specifically, what the compensation would be. "Debt, you say? Are my ears right, 'cause I thought I heard you say you owe me, uh, a debt, Mr. Isaac?" was the extent of his diplomatic endeavor. Once again, Wouter found himself lost within the forest of his incoherent digressions. "Isaac—Isaac? Huh, that's a funny-sounding name. *Isaac.* Not sure I care for it, maybe. Isaac, yeah, I'm good with the names. I see a face one time and there it is. I'll never forget your name. 'Cept that one fellow—who the hell...?" Wouter furrowed his brows and snapped his fingers. "Pumpkin, what's the name of that big old, fat tub youngster boy works at the mill, funny-looking bastard. Big fat-looking boy. The one with the shit on his face—what in shit's sake is that boy's name?"

"Tim?" she offered.

"That's it!" he cried and snapped his fingers and pointed directly at Pearson's face. "Tim! That fat fucking, yeah, Tim. That boy is a dumb little shit too, not just fat. God sure done fuck that one up. You can't tell me He ain't make mistakes, 'cause that fat ass Tim ain't right, let me tell you, Mister. You know this dumb shit told me kidnapping was when children sleep? I'll tell you, I saw this boy eat a bag of hair. I can't say where he got himself a big bag of hair, but he was tossing those clumps of hair in his fat face and chewing on it like my old mare chomps on grass. I'd love to be there when he shit—"

"I'm sorry, sir. I've been impolite and not asked for your name. How should I address you, sir?" Pearson blurted.

Wouter took a few seconds to shift his thoughts. "Ah, yes...yes. Well, sir, my name is Wouter Behrendt, and the missus is Rosalie, yes, my pumpkin."

"Wouter, Rosalie," said Pearson, before Wouter could journey into another maze of mindless rantings. "Wouter and Rosalie Behrendt, I am pleased to make your acquaintances. I have not met a more charming couple and one with such an adorable...quaint, home." Pearson turned his head toward the paint-smudged palette and feigned an interest in Rosalie's horribly childish depiction. "This is interesting, an interesting likeness, flattering, really. I see an influence of William Blake, though I am hardly a devotee of fine art, by any means. I digress." She smiled as though William Blake was worthy of comparison and understood his flattery to be genuine. "Well now, Wouter," he continued. "I see you were diligent enough to bring along my belongings, so may I ask if I may have my uniform as well? I'm obviously indecent at the moment."

"Isaac?" asked Wouter.

"Yes, yes, sir, Isaac is my name," said Pearson.

"Isaac…Isaac, fun to say. What kind of name is Isaac, Mister?"

"That is a bit off-putting, Wouter. Nonetheless, it is a respectable English name, one I am quite proud of. I was named after Sir Isaac Newton. For me, it is an honor to share the name with such an important, distinguished, and genteel figure, and, really, I thank you for offering me the opportunity to share that with you."

"Isaac Newton? Who is Isaac Newton? Rosy, you ever hear of any Isaac Newton?" asked Wouter.

"Never heard of the man," replied Rosalie with her attention once again fixed on her cartoonish portrait. She felt a surge of pride, pressing her to finish her perceived masterpiece.

"Well, we don't know the man, Mister," continued Wouter.

Pearson paused for a moment to consider how to proceed. His reflex was to belittle the Behrendts, yet he was sure they would not grasp his condemnation. Still, he struggled to continue without opening a trap for Wouter's endless diatribes. "Sir Isaac Newton, *The Principia*. He is the foremost mathematician—it's inconsequential, sir. He is, ummm, he's long been deceased."

Wouter lowered his head a bit. "Well, I'm sorry to hear that, Mister. Sounds like he was a good man."

"That is, uh, kind of you to say," replied Pearson. "Now then, we were discussing my uniform, my clothing."

"Ah, yes, about the uniform," sighed Wouter. "It is burnt. I burnt it—set it on fire. So your uniform, Mister, is no more. It's burnt. Was soiled with all kind of filthy muck and mud, and you shit it something awful. All kinds of bugs. You know those things spread and get all over ya, and well, I had no choice but to burn it. I suppose we could have tried to ring it through with some soap and fresh water and whatnot, but we didn't. You really shat that thing up, Mister... Isaac."

Pearson was crestfallen as his head collapsed into his chest and he groaned with frustrated disbelief. It was difficult for him to remain composed and courteous, yet the realization Wouter had, for all purposes, saved his life extended the limits of his tolerance. He peered through the window, and for a moment was devoid of thought or expression. The weeks-long venture had afforded Pearson no rest, in physical nor cerebral regard. His mind and spirit were as tired as his bones. His state of numbness was a welcome break from the unrelenting bane of anxiety. For a moment, he remained silent and vacuous, until Wouter disturbed his somewhat tranquil trance. "We got some attires for you, Mister, you can wear my old frock—breeches, old hunting shirt I'll give you. May fit, may be tight on you—you're looking a bit puny, so maybe not. 'Course, I'm not as lean as I used to be, right, Pumpkin? Yeah, as these bones get even older, I eat more and work less. Keep needing bigger and bigger belts. I stopped growing up and started growing out—"

"That is fine," interrupted Pearson. He was instantly bitter and believed he had little more use for Wouter and his wife. "You know brevity is the soul of wit?" he asked despondently, knowing full well Wouter would have absolutely no idea what he meant.

As expected, Wouter looked perplexed and tapped his index finger against his lips. "You know, I ain't considered that, but thank you, Mister. Very kind of you, very, uh, picturesque of you to say."

By this point, Captain Pearson was simply too dejected to care about much, including what he was set to wear. "I see my satchel, and once again, express my gratitude and will speak on behalf of the Empire to express the same. You've provided a valuable service to His Majesty. Now, I do not see, however, an officer's pistol I had worn at my hip. Please tell me you did not burn it as well. Please tell me it was among the pieces you salvaged."

Wouter raised his head and squinted as to reveal his contemplation. He glanced over to Rosalie, who quietly shrugged her shoulders. His fingers stroked the base of a narrow chin, and he groaned with consideration. "Hmmm." Pearson instantly thrust his eyelids shut and refused to open them. Immediately, his concern was ratified by Wouter's hesitation. "I don't recall, Mister, seeing no pistol on you. 'Course, it looked like you been out for some time. I'd bet one of those Wilson boys found you first—they're no good, not a one of them. Always making trouble around here. I'll tell you, if I saw that pistol of yours, I'd use it to shoot at them, the little shit heels. Right, Rosy? They're shit heels. I would hope they cross me; it'd be worth it to shoot at them little loiter sacks, little cow nugget sons of shits."

Pearson remained with his eyes closed as Wouter prattled along a verbal path that seemed to have no end. After a minute or so, he cut him off and with a crestfallen tone, asked, "You have not seen my pistol? That is what you are saying?"

"No," replied Wouter. "No, sir, haven't seen no pistol on you. Think it was those Wilson boys who snatched it off—wouldn't put that past them. They snatched it off you and ran away like the wind. I can give you their whereabouts if you like. They're no good, I'm saying to you, those boys are nothing but no good. I knew they was no good as soon as I seen them, right, Pumpkin? Saw it right away. Soon as I saw those boys, I said it, I said, 'Those boys is shit heels.' I told her, 'Pumpkin, these boys ain't nothing but shit heels,' and she said some nonsense." Once again, Pearson closed his eyes and sought the comfort to be absent of thought. Wouter's rhythmic blathering, oddly calmed the captain's nerves enough to prevent a breakdown of sanity

Pearson was nearly beaten and nearly at the edge of the lengths of his composure and sobriety. He was nude and exposed, amongst the company of strangers. These were strangers far below his level of intellectual understanding and station, and certainly unworthy of his time. He had seen his comrades mangled and mauled, a blameless young boy robbed of his life before it really began, was shackled within the bowels of a dark, musty cave, where he waited to face his executioner, and he had traipsed aimlessly throughout an unknown wilderness in an unknown land, where he knew himself to be an intruder. His body was broken and spirit was threatening to follow. The loss of his reliable heirloom was the loss of the only semblance of identity, title, and family to remain in America. The currency of his father's reluctant affection and approval was lost with lives of those he was bound to use it to protect. With his eyes still closed, he hung his head with only the irrational hope when he opened them again, somehow what was, would no longer be.

Doleful and somber, Pearson pressed to move on. "Very good, Mr. Behrendt. I believe I have extended your courtesy far enough, and at this point would very much like to be on my way."

* * *

Tarry Town.

Inside the manor's main parlor, Emily rested her chin against the delicate wood violin chin rest. The instrument was finely crafted with intricate features and a beautifully varnished finish. Its body was made of light spruce and the neck hardened maple. She wore her most elegant scarlet-red brocaded silk set back gown and embroidered petticoat. The gown was cut low at the shoulders, and this was the first time, in some time, she had ventured to wear it. Her insecurities had been checking the better of her of late. The unrelenting plague of smallpox continued to crawl from her shoulders to her neck. Her otherwise fair and soft skin was infected by the blight of unsightly blisters and lesions as it spread like moss on a tree. The midday sun shone through the large windows, as though it was intented to cast her with an angelic glow. Her delicate, cinnamon hair was tied with a floral lace behind her neck, her face was flushed with warmth, and her eyes sparkled.

She sighed, took a quick breath, and slowly brought the bow toward the instrument. At once, she began, and the gentle hum of Mozart's Symphony Number Twenty-One filled the manor house. Every note was flawless and powerful. Her tempo remained steady, and she played with an elegant flair and poise. As it seemed to be with everything she did, she moved with a graceful disposition. Her fingers danced along the neck with conviction and emotional vibrato. She had a stylish elegance to each movement up-bow and down-bow. It had taken her some time to master the piece, yet it was not in any way apparent with the ease and comfort in which she performed.

The siren calls of the violin strings lured the attention of her wide-eyed daughters. From separate rooms and without uttering a word, they met at the far doorway, under the staircase. Their young minds were yet unable to grasp the sense of pride they felt, yet it warmed their hearts just the same. Perhaps the most finely crafted wooden doll in the valley had been imported from Britain, to find its way to Eliza's tender grasp. She caressed it in her arms, against her chest, as she leaned into her older sister, who rested her hand on Lizzy's shoulder. Their petty bickering and childish antagonisms were washed away by the wave of beautiful music. From the pantry, Vesta wandered toward the entryway to the parlor and, from a distance, looked on to allow herself to bask in the restful composition. Emily's eyes remained closed as she played, and she was unaware of her appreciative audience.

A floor above, Dedrick was at rest, and as per usual, his head was buried in the large, billowy feather pillow. The bright sun filled his bedchamber but did little to disrupt his slumber. Intent on blanketing himself with cool air, he tugged and kicked his feet within the soft wool cover. As with most nights, last night, he had been unable to find comfort, nor remain asleep. Frustrated, he turned to lie from one side to the other and flipped the pillow over his face to rest the un-warmed side against it. He closed his eyes, yet his frustration would not allow rest. "Fuck," he grumbled, then tossed his pillow aside and ripped the wool cover from his body.

He stamped his stocking-covered feet against the stiff, cold oak floor and stomped across the room, toward the near staircase. His long, thick hair was tangled behind his back, and thin slivers were lined along his skin, pressed by the folds within the pillow against his face. He moved with the delicacy of an angry rhinoceros, each step landing so forcefully it seemed he intended to fill the halls with echoes. As he descended the main staircase, near the center of the parlor, loyal Caesar charged from the other room upon recognizing the plodding footsteps of his master. In passing, Dedrick offered him a half-hearted pet atop his head, then pressed on. The mostly reflexive, insincere gesture was more than enough to propel his pet to follow alongside Dedrick, down the stairs.

Emily was fully immersed in her performance. Each stroke of the bow was increasingly more natural than the one before. Her heart warmed at the confirmation her patience and practice had led her to a near proficiency. Without animation, she swayed with rhythm and subtly and elegantly strode with tiny steps in an effortless, nuanced dance. Though her daughters' attention typically spanned no longer than between blinks of an eye, Emily had them engaged and enthralled. "Em!" barked Dedrick when he stopped a few steps in the parlor room. She was startled and jolted free of her reposed state. In an instant, the bow screeched across the strings with an ear-piercing screech. "The fuck?" he added after Emily turned her attention toward him. "I was trying to sleep," he said with a bitter tone. Caesar remained at Dedrick's hip, still yet, with his pink tongue dangling from his jowl.

For her part, Emily was as perplexed and astounded as she was offended. With the violin still resting about her shoulder, she hardly moved, other than to flip the bow uncaringly into the air, toward the near wall. It landed against the wood, just under the south-facing window, then fell to the floor to roll a foot or more. Dedrick's eyes followed it along its path until he shifted them back to connect with Emily's angry green eyes. His frustration flowed from him as though it was lake water, running through a collapsed dam. The barren lakebed was quickly immersed with a sense of guilt and remorse. From the far end of the parlor, he caught a glimpse of his daughters, Sarah and Eliza. They peered back at him as though he was an ogre, yet all the same, he appeared apathetic. "Thank you," he grumbled, then plodded back up the staircase and into his bedchamber.

* * *

North of Tarry Town.

The Quebec Path to New York was as unused as would be expected; no more than the very occasional horse and rider, wagon, or wanderer would pass Captain Pearson as he trudged along. Merchants and travelers generally avoided Quebec Path, or as it was known to some, The Path to Quebec. The pass mostly carried traffic of those who wished to go unnoticed. Some of the travelers along the road relied on the assumption the reputation of the pathway would keep it clear of interested wanderers. Locals were moved by talk of the horrific ends they believed would likely meet them should they venture along the Quebec Path.

Fear of smugglers, who transported kidnapped freemen or contraband to French Canadians, spurred honest traders to travel alternate routes. Quebec Path was infested with the vile characters of the underworld, the unseemly who were bound by no cause other than individual gain. The locals were not concerning, as they were as easily spooked by outsiders as they were by one another. Disturbing fables and questionable accounts grew more frightening as they passed from one mouth to the next ear. All the same, on occasion, corpses had been found within the bush and tall grass aside the pathway. Bodies with heads pulped into a bloody stew would seem to confirm the rumors about the notorious Head Vise. A device commonly used by passing deviants as a method to deter doubt and curiosity. A device in which the victim's head is placed between a bar at the chin and a solid, iron bowl at the skull. As the bolt is tightened, the cap is pressed to meet the bar, causing the skull to crack with earsplitting snaps. When the skull gives, the bones collapse into the cranium. These smugglers were sure to leave what was left of the body in clear view, so it could be found. Still, a small number of ignorant travelers and stubbornly defiant traders ventured the pathway until the sunset.

The muddy track cut through the woodlands southward, past the village of King's Bridge. On either side of the narrow trail, the trees, nearly naked of leaves, were twisted, gray-brown fractures against the dull gray sky. Pearson had become so guarded as to flinch at the birds' chirps and the wind's whistle. He held the leather pouch tightly and kept his head down, watching his feet as he continued along the Quebec Path toward the southern line of Sleepy Hollow. The stretch of the pathway bent perilously near the outskirts of the small village. The residents of the humble Dutch community were withdrawn, guarded, and unwelcoming of outsiders. As such, smuggling runners tended to give the pass no mind. The people of Sleepy Hollow lived simple lifestyles and clung to old traditions and conservative values.

Though they saw the Rebellion as an affront to such tenets, they were not Tory, nor necessarily loyal. There was little talk of politics or the world beyond the thicket of heavy woodlands in which Sleepy Hollow was engulfed. Here, things tended to be as they always had been.

Along the western flank of the trail was a clear field of a grassy common. A few tall green pines stood guard from the west of the meadow, and behind them, oaks and maples reached the bank of the Hudson. The grass was exhausted of green life and left pale brown and dry. A smattering of four or five farmers oversaw the few workhorses who grazed carelessly. They paid Pearson no mind, if any managed to even notice him at all. Yet, each of the strangers' eyes appeared fixed as beams to meticulously inspect Pearson as he walked. In his bones, he was assured everyone knew who he was and what he carried. Continually, he rehearsed within his mind possible answers for prying inquiries. He was so desperate to seem at ease, he may have actually looked anything but. Although he didn't appear as such, Pearson felt as out of place as a black raven amongst a gaggle of geese. Windows from the distant stone folk houses peered through him as intrusive, disapproving eyes. He felt the entwined, jagged fingers of the leafless branches snatching at him as beastly claws. The muddy path seemed to grab his feet and refuse to allow his step without a fight. His heightened awareness portrayed each of the infrequent passersby as meddlers, intent on snatching his leather pouch.

Pearson was more than twenty pounds lighter than when he arrived in America and was yet unable to properly fit into his clothing. Wouter's constricted, snug, poorly made and moth-eaten clothes made him feel yet more out of sorts and out of character. The sleeves of his brown, drab waistcoat reached well short of his wrists, his breeches were given to split with each stride, and his mud-caked, leather-buckled shoes bound his feet so tightly he could hardly feel them.

Ahead some fifty paces or so, the captain noted a small fieldstone cabin just off the pathway, where several blue-clad soldiers stood casually talking to one another. Their posture and manner did not portray a single bit of urgency. In a sense, they looked to be much more relaxed than alert. Pearson immediately stopped in his steps, looked behind, and saw no others. Perhaps they would have no interest in him; he could walk beyond while hardly noticed. Yet, he was unreasonably guarded, nervous and incredibly unsure. Anxiety pumped a rush of adrenaline through his veins and clouded his reason. He struggled to breathe and felt as though the world was closing in to smother him. Good judgment was nearly overtaken by his fight-or-flight impulses. For a second, he considered racing northward, away from the Continental soldiers. Panic nearly got the better of him, yet he concluded the foolishness of such an effort and quickly assessed his best course would be to simply pass them imperturbably. Of course, he knew any verbal exchanges would immediately prompt interrogation, at the very least. Pearson's heavy accent was an unmistakable tell he was not a local, yet any awkward attempts to remain unspoken would be just as, if not more, suspicious. Before he took his next stride, one of the American sentries called out to him from afar, and Pearson was unable to process any decision. He stood, as motionless as one eager to invite birds to perch on his shoulders.

"You there!" the sentry bellowed. "Come forward, sir." He waved Pearson onward in his direction. Still, Pearson was frozen in his tracks. "Come forward, sir!" he repeated in an agitated tone. He was an assiduous bastard, at least he did not seem to be one who was given to let up easily. Captain Pearson appeared to pose no threat, yet any man traveling the path was, by default, suspicious.

The captain felt overwhelmed by panic; a hot sensation of nerves rushed him through as he knew he would not be able to mask his obvious anxiety. His mind was blank, deprived of consideration and given to primal instinct. Without further hesitation, he dashed northward. The five Blue Coats immediately darted after him, each with his long musket clasped in his grip. Splatters of mud were tossed into the air behind them as they furiously charged. Not one of the troopers knew why they were chasing him, yet he was running and so, they chased. With all his might, Pearson pushed his legs until his breath became so heavy he could hardly gasp. Desperately, he cut to the left and leaped into the thick woodlands off the pathway. The band of Continentals flew into the brush and were closing quickly.

The nearest of them was some yards away, yet Pearson felt his grip tear at his neck. He threw aside the low branches and thick brush and pushed along as ferociously as he could. He raced a few dozen yards into the forest until he heard thunderous blasts behind.

"Halt!" hollered one of the American soldiers, yet Pearson continued to throw himself forward as twigs whipped against his face. The Continentals fired another blast, and a musket ball bounded off the very top of Pearson's right shoulder. It was as though a mallet was struck against him. He was thrust leftward violently. Nearly paralyzed by terror, Pearson's legs were twisted beneath him, and the top of his head rammed into the trunk of an unflinching pine tree. All his furious energy was met with the solid, rigid, unforgiving wood and an abrupt thud. The violent crash knocked his vision to a blur and split his ears with an uneven hum. Collapsed to the ground, for an instant, through his haze, he believed he had been struck with a mortal wound. He felt the flow of blood stream from his shoulder, draining his body of warmth and life. All the tensions from his muscles subsided, and he let himself melt into the soil on which he lay. He was strangely content, as though he accepted the covenant this was simply his turn.

The distorted perception of time had Pearson feeling as though he was on the ground for hours, though it was hardly more than a few seconds. His thoughts were composed with no words. Wyandot Panther's warnings told him to flee from the spirit-catching demons who were bound to enslave him for all eternity. Pearson was not surprised to share the afterlife with the savage Mohawk scout. His indecision and miscalculation had cost young men their lives. He was as guilty of taking for granted the consequences of his unpreparedness and indifference as Panther was to have slain the young boy. The Panther spoke to him with a breath of winter's air. When a gust of cold wind blew against Pearson's skin, he was quickly moved to the world of his current reality as he gained consciousness.

The captain was struck by a glancing blow, still, he was dazed just the same. His already tender chin crashed against the tree and was soft and inflated. He was dizzy and nearly overcome by nausea and still felt the onrushing Americans as they neared. The crunching of dry leaves and heavy thuds grew louder as the five troopers stormed toward Pearson's direction. Desperately, the captain struggled to unclip the straps from his pouch and grabbed for the documents within. Just as the first of the soldiers reached Pearson, who was lying on the ground, he jammed a handful of the papers into a cavity within a stretch of large, twisted roots at his side. Hurriedly, he swept a pile of fallen, brown leaves atop of them. The moment the documents were plowed over by foliage was the same moment the first of the soldiers reached him.

"Halt, I say! Don't move!" yelled Corporal Michael Mathews through his winded lungs. He held his musket low, with the bayonet inches from Pearson's ribs. The captain was weary and his vision blurred, yet he was able to see the fear on the young soldier's face. Pearson closed his eyes, then slowly held out his open hands as to surrender. The anticipation of being fired on stiffened his muscles. Mathews's nerves were shaken by the blast of feverish energy that had propelled him through the chase. He stomped his boot on Pearson's ankle with a swift blow. And with gritted teeth grunted, "You fucking...fuck."

Though it was a significantly forceful kick, Pearson hardly felt it. "I have him!" bellowed the corporal. His eyes remained locked on the weary captain. "Come. Hurry the fuck up!" The four remaining American soldiers swarmed toward Mathews's position. All of them held their weapons high and wore the same anxious expression on their boyish faces.

Based on their demeanor and age, Pearson quickly surmised they were as green as April leaves and probably more afraid of him than he was of them. "I'm not running," he said through a panting breath. "I submit to your capture. I am unarmed and will offer no resistance."

The intention behind his words was lost. "Who are you, sir? State your name and your business," ordered Mathews. "Why did you run from us?"

Pearson knew the rules of proper warfare should ensure his safety, yet feared the uneasy nature of the untested soldiers about him. Uniformed soldiers were bound to strict military conduct. Both American and British ranks suffered severe corrections when operating outside the traditions of gentlemanly warfare. He was offered a semblance of ease, given the reality he was at the mercy of Continental soldiers as opposed to the colonial militia who neglected to uphold such honor. Perhaps rumor, perhaps reality, the collective British perception of American militia portrayed them as marginally less savage and uncivilized than Indians. However, these young troopers were more like bungling fawns who were frightened enough to run from the falling acorns. With his heart still racing and his lungs pumping vigorously, he said, "I don't know. I cannot say. I am Captain Isaac Pearson of the Queen's Twenty-First Artillery Battery of the King's Army." He grimaced and reflexively reached his hand to his chin. The rebel soldiers reacted by pulling their muskets close, as though they were ready to fire. Pearson again held his hands high, and open.

"I yield, I am unarmed, and will not resist," he assured. Still panting heavily, he tried to make the case for his safe capture. "I should not have run. You are soldiers. My business is my concern, and as I am sure you gentlemen are aware, I am obliged to tell you no more than what I have. I trust I do not need to explain to you the ramifications of my mistreatment." He was desperate to hide his uncertainty by acting uncharacteristically stern and resolute.

Mathews looked at the others, who all seemed a bit perplexed. "You are in the King's Army, then?" he asked.

"Yes. Yes. That is what I have been saying, good sir. I am surrendering myself to your good graces," answered Pearson.

Mathews didn't seem particularly moved by Pearson's explanations and assertions. He held his weapon with no less caution and looked over the captain with a curious and unsure eye. He flinched his weapon upward and ordered, "Get up...to your feet, sir."

"Thank you, Corporal." said Pearson with a sigh. He sat up, groaning and moaning as the various ailments about his battered body pricked at him. It felt as though his head was trembling, as if it had been placed on his body too loosely as he tried to casually peek to his side, for any sign of what he had hidden beneath the leaves. With ten nervous eyes peering him over so intently it was if it meant their lives, Pearson subtly flapped his injured right arm as to wave a few more leaves onto what he had concealed, just as he rose to his feet. As his nerves settled, the burn of throbbing pain rushed through his jaw. He scowled and looked to draw as much attention from the ground about him as possible, by insulting and agitating the Americans. In truth, this was not all too unnatural for Pearson. As he stood near the center of a semicircle of anxious, musket-wielding soldiers, he ranted, "What are we doing, lads? Forgive me, as I am unfamiliar with your customs. This is what American simpletons do to pass time? You wish to break from the Empire, as to have the independence to stand within the sticks and exchange dimwitted looks? How does this work exactly, help me out? Do we do nothing, do we throw our shit around like monkeys, or…what happens now?"

The ruse cost Pearson a firm belt in the rib as Mathews whipped him with the barrel of his musket, yet it did seem to refocus their attention. Pearson fell forward away from where he had them stashed. "Keep up with the jokes and I will have a reason to break your ribs. Let's go," barked Mathews as he waved his musket toward the direction of the road. With their weapons fixed on Captain Pearson, the Blue Jackets followed behind, nudging him along as he trudged back toward the Quebec Path. He stumbled over the roots and rocks at his feet. Pink lines along his neck were drawn from the twigs and small branches that had whipped into his skin when he ran, and the remains of a few small leaves and bits of debris fell from his chest and shoulders as he moved. Pearson's heart was still beating briskly, and he began to contemplate possible questions and reasonable answers. He could not help but conjure visions of his wife, Elizabeth, and this made him shudder with nerves and dread. Though his captors were several feet behind, Pearson could nearly feel their muzzles pressed against his back.

Within a split second upon reaching the muddy pathway, Mathews pressed Pearson for clarification. The corporal was an exceptionally upstanding and diligent character who was destined for leadership. He was as dedicated to the patriot's cause as any and enlisted into the Continental Army, where he had served consecutive tours, both without pay. The corporal was not a rube farmer who joined the Rebellion because it was the thing to do. He was a veteran of several battles and familiar with military protocol and tradition. He could accurately recite every detail of every article in the code of warfare. "Captain? In the King's Army…?

"Yes, that is what I said, Corporal," snapped Pearson.

"I know what you said, *Captain*, but, I'm a bit confused. Why are you wearing the clothing of common folk?"

Pearson was taken back and paused. He instantaneously was flushed with concern, caught completely unaware. His mind raced as to lose any focus or ability to clearly think. As each second passed, he realized the longer he paused, the guiltier he would seem. With little composure, he blurted whatever words managed to escape his mouth. "Common? How dare you, sir. I'm not a commoner. My uniform is—I don't have my uniform." He was only able to offer no better than reflexive denial. "You're a good soldier, very clever. I'm an artillery officer in His Majesty's Army. I serve under the command of Colonel Oliver Bell. I am *not* common folk, Corporal, this is assured. Forgive my candor but really, only common folk would not realize I am not a commoner. Once again, it seems necessary to remind you of the proper procedures in these matters, particularly as it pertains to officers. From what I understand of your General Washington, he prides himself on upholding the gentleman's traditions of war. I hear he has no reservations about putting improper Continentals in front of firing squads."

Mathews appeared unfazed. "Please, continue to share with me your understanding. Would a gentleman burn a city or ambush a pack of drunken fucks on Christmas? General Washington seeks to win the war, not set an example on how to fight it. You should ask yourself if your kind care to uphold such traditions after you paid the Indians to pillage our folk. Spare your lectures, sir. I know well the proper procedures in these matters. I am not planning on killing you, if this is your fear. Really, I am not sure what you think will happen. There is nothing you can say for me to release you to be on your merry way, this you can be sure. You are an artillery officer, strolling along a smuggler's path in common clothing. Yet, I am not to believe this to be peculiar? I have to be blunt, it seems: either you will hang as a spy or you will hang as an unfit soldier."

Pearson was plainly aware he had no basis for argument. Desperately and pathetically he had hoped to tie what he believed to be the simple-minded American into verbal knots. He pressed his lips together and peered down the muddy pathway, sneered at the irony, and replied, "Because I am not in the garb of a soldier, does not mean I am a not soldier. Soldiers are not defined by the cloth on their back. My affairs are just that: My affairs. As per my obligation, I offered to you all you are entitled to know. It would be dangerous to treat me unjustly.

"You are willing to risk severe punishment because of semantics or hints at impropriety? Should it be the milieu is rather meaningless, it will serve no purpose. I suppose I understand your misgivings, yet the consequence of my uniform is immaterial. It's ironic, really. I've heard the Americans are crude, slightly more civilized than the Natives. For my part, I have refused to accept your reputation as no more than bigoted nonsense. Yet, here we are, and you are treading dangerously close to overstepping the bounds of dishonor, Corporal. Was I wrong?"

The corporal was still unmoved. Pearson's rambling was quickly lost to incoherent mumbling, and Mathews was simply, politely waiting for Pearson to shut his fucking mouth. He was patient and collected, though unsympathetic. "Perhaps. Or perhaps not, Captain, or whoever the fuck you are. Either way, you will be coming with us," he replied. Mathews was eager to proceed in the dealings with Captain Pearson. His post was abandoned, and though unlikely, he was concerned loyalist activity may escape his awareness as he was jostling needlessly with Pearson, or worse still, he'd be away from his post during an unannounced visit from a superior.

Corporal Mathews lowered his weapon and moved to inspect Pearson closely. "If he tries to get away, or annoys the shit from you, don't wait for my command. Just shoot him," he ordered.

Distraught, Pearson held his hands out and uttered through a tone of anxiety, "I'm sorry. I'm sorry. What are you saying? You think it is wise to be flippant about this? Please, explain your sarcasm, as one may believe you to be sincere."

Mathews peered into the woods for a moment, then shifted his hat about his head. "Right, right. Good thought, sir. We are all dimwitted idiots here in the colonies. We sit when we piss and stand when we shit because we are just that stupid."

Pearson sighed with slight relief and continued, "Please... respectfully, Soldier, can you be clear with them?"

The young corporal looked about his company to see each of their faces displaying some degree of amusement. He shook his head, as he could not truly believe the silliness. "Shoot him whenever the fuck you want," he sniped, and jerked the leather strap and pouch from Pearson's shoulders. The others began to remove the few pouches and sacks the captain had with him. Pearson stood still and lifted his arms high above his head as a gesture of cooperation. His shoulder rang with pain, yet he dared not lower it. Occasionally, Mathews gazed up and down the pathway as to offer it some of his attention.

As he shifted through Pearson's belongings, the diligent soldier dropped each item to the ground, one by one. Mathews found nothing worthy of note; the remains of Rosalie's stale bread, a water pouch, assorted tools, and utensils. He was beginning to presume Pearson was perhaps who he claimed, if not unimportant. Then he began to riffle through Pearson's muck-covered soft leather pouch, expecting to find nothing of significance, yet quickly noticed a few documents tucked into a flat, bound pocket within. Mathews's interest was instantaneously piqued as he slid them free.

With the parchment sheets clutched in his free hand, he offered Pearson a satisfied glance. He could not resist jabbing the condescending captain. "Could this be something I need to see? Actually, don't even answer that, just remain silent." He handed his musket to the nearest soldier and scoured the dried sheets of wool paper. His expression appeared increasingly more interested as he flipped through the various pages. Methodically and carefully, Corporal Mathews combed through the set of documents meticulously. For his part, Pearson was as staggered and, in some sense, as curious as Mathews. In his panicked state, he had not considered having left any of his communiqué in his pouch. Without thought, his presumption was all the contents were stashed within the leaves. He did all he could to present himself as being disinterested, yet his heart raced and eyes pored over the corporal's hands as he thumbed through them.

The typically dutiful soldier was especially diligent given the circumstances. The suspense stirred by Mathews's gradual progress nearly caused Pearson to burst. Captain Pearson had no idea which documents were buried in the leaves and which were now in the hands of an enemy soldier. His thoughts scrambled, yet he had no recollection of separating any papers from any of the other papers. As he concluded Mathews appeared to have no more than a few sheets, his hopeful postulation was that not one of them was of Shaw's map.

The corporal flipped through a few pages until he reached an envelope nestled within them. It was sealed with what appeared to be a stamp of official royal offices, and the corporal glanced toward Pearson as he began to open it. Mathews stopped himself when he concluded it to be improper to break the seal. As he was concerned, these matters were beyond his domain. Nonetheless, Pearson's face was awash with the pale stain of dread.

"Interesting, this looks to be the King's Royal hallmark. Things are not looking promising for you, you dorbel, shit-eating fuck. You are a messenger for the British Army?" asked Mathews. "And if this is so, you were trying to slip past us while wearing the clothing of a noncombatant. You silly, silly bitch."

With a jittery and meek voice, Pearson was moved by nerves and could not conjure a thought to help his cause. The words simply fell from his lips, "The Royal seal? I don't...lend these matters any thought. We know this is a soldier's life to be nothing more than pawns on the chessboards of larger men. As you, I am dutiful, though in an unthinking way, not suggesting we are careless. Poor phrasing. I'm...we are dedicated and loyal not to ask about the whys or the details. We may say, this makes us quality soldiers, as we follow our commands without hesitation or contemplation. You wear blue, I, well, usually wear red, yet in this realm, we are comrades, really. Yes? As it turns out, my uniform was destroyed when it was infested with—it was infested."

Mathews lifted his eyes toward Pearson's. "What are you talking about? Please...will you please just stop fucking talking, please? I shouldn't have asked." A collective chuckle echoed throughout the company. Along with dismay and anxiety, Pearson was overcome with humility. At this moment, in Wouter's clothing, he felt as though he fully embodied his pompous perception of Wouter Behrendt. He felt submissive, as though he fully transformed himself into the character befitting his costume. Pearson's unnerved state drove Mathews's curiosity to nearly get the better of his good judgment. The corporal was moved to open the seal. As best he could conclude, Pearson believed the balance of the sheets of text were Bell's dispatch to Howe and not Shaw's scribblings.

"Do not open your mouth; just stand there and listen. You've been stopped with possession of Royal military records. Normally, I would presume you to be a messenger, yet because you are dressed in the clothing of common folk and have attempted to go unnoticed, this makes you a spy. A king's soldier would know this," Mathews warned sarcastically. "And a king's soldier would know the just and suitable punishment for espionage."

Pearson's heart thumped as though it was pressing to burst from his chest. The air was quite cool, yet his sweat gleamed in the muted sun. His limbs were weak, wobbly, and on the verge of giving out. Despite his obvious peril and immersion within a sea of angst, he still felt the bitter sting of dishonor. Pearson could not bear to be insulted by a man of such low stature, particularly an American. Regardless of the circumstance, Captain Pearson was certainly not going to afford Mathews a sense of satisfaction or superiority, despite his predicament. Pearson refused to grovel.

"I am not a spy, Corporal. The suggestion is laughable. I carry a military correspondence, one which I was charged with relaying to the command office in New York. These records confirm my position within the King's Army. My action is within the conduct of formal procedure, and I will presume to caution you, mistreatment of prisoners, officers, especially, is subject to the strictest limits of justice. I am executing a legitimate charge. Now, I have capitulated and accepted my capture. I am prepared to cooperate with the correct measures of a captured officer."

"Executing," replied Mathews. "Perfect choice of words." The young soldier was not the type to yield to vague threats, nor would he have simply accepted the captain at his word. He quickly looked through the pouch further, yet found nothing more than scraps of papers with inconsequential scribbling; none of which confirmed Pearson's claims. By this point, he was fostering a personal dislike for Captain Pearson and recognized it was in his best interest to proceed without prompting Pearson to agitate him into inappropriate behavior. He ordered two of the Continentals to subdue Pearson, and each grabbed one of his arms about the shoulder. Pearson released an anguished groan as the wound in his right side nipped at him. The two free troopers fixed their muskets on Pearson and jabbed at him to move forward.

The troop walked back along the path toward the stone cabin that overlooked the pathway. The building was a humble structure constructed of loose stone and mortar. Tall weeds and ivy crawled up the walls, and the thatch roof was giving to collapse. It had been built as a toll collection point, yet had not collected a single schilling from the travelers on this path for some years. During the war, it had been converted to a small colonial guard post. Although doubtful, some American officers had suspected the British of using the Quebec Path to transport men and material northward. Because those who were familiar with the Path were so because they were operating beyond the bounds of the law, or trying to avoid particular taxation, the regards of the Quebec Path were not amplified to meet the level of concern. Mathews and his modest contingent represented a compromise between those who believed the path to be a vital artery and the ones who saw no value in securing it. The corporal and his small unit were hardly equipped to deal with a British force of size, yet their presence appeased the concerned parties.

Corporal Mathews's dedication to the cause was not lost by his superiors. Afterword of his commitment to the Revolution reached the desk of Colonel Brandt, an aide to General Richard Lee, it was returned to the corporal with an agreeable reassignment. Mathews understood the relative unimportance of his position and managed to stay vigilant enough to still reap its benefits. He, and the sentries he directed, all enjoyed preferential status via various political or moneyed connections. They and Mathews did not hesitate to take full advantage of their post by enjoying the company of whores and the taste of old whiskey. Mathews claimed any day that ended without a raggerbrash, yoltson's mother swallowing his pearly cream, was a bad one. From time to time a suspicious traveler would call them to attention, and seldom were they concerned with thwarting enemy activity. Now, Mathews and his contingent may have very well bought themselves a pass to lick dry the gash between Abigail Adams's legs, if they so choose. Captain Pearson's capture and the seizure of British intelligence would ensure the corporal's good standing for the foreseeable future, despite any effort he may endeavor to sully it.

Tarry Town.

Smoke rises from the chimney of the Hereensburg manor house. The sun is surrounded by a deep-blue cloudless sky to cast its gleam off the flowing Mill River. The white fieldstone house rests on a sea of green grassy pastures.It is a sturdy, yet modest building; one without the trappings to note the affluence of those who live within. The true beauty of the Hereensburg manor house is its simplicity.

Dedrick's Grandfather Jonas Hereen settled the one-hundred-and-fifty-acre Dutch patroon and made use of African slave labor to build the manor's centerpiece. Some, as young as ten years old, laid heavy bricks and stones under the blistering Hudson Valley summer sun to erect a home befitting Jonas' perceived stature and standing among the gentry. Two governors, an Anglican minister, in numerous lawyers, merchants, constables, influential figures of all ilk have dined and slept within its walls. The house has hosted five weddings, any number of dinners and balls, survived two wars and countless cruel winters.

From the south, a small wooden carriage lumbers forward as it nears the house. The weary gray mare follows the footpath lazily as she hauls forward the old open carriage. She is tired and old. Her coat is shaggy and thin and she requires an abusive whip every so often to prod her along. From inside, Dedrick hears the uneven plodding and approaches the window in the parlor, nervously pulls the curtain back and peers through the glass. Within the sun's glare emerges the enigmatic Doctor Cornelius Van Leeuwen sitting atop the carriage bench. The doctor is a very lean and gangly looking figure who sat with his back straight as he held the reins. From a mile, even the least perceptive of folks would detect the plainly discordant look he wore upon his face. It would seem Dedrick and the doctor shared the same sense of displeasure. From Dedrick's perspective,

Van Leeuwen's visit was fortuitous and expected, all the same he was not particularly excited to see him near.

The doctor's skin is pale and wrinkled; his eyes are slim, dark baleful with thin raised brows, narrow of nose and jagged and crooked at the chin. Despite the unseasonable warmth, he wore a heavy black roquelaires cloak and dark brown beaver skin hat with broad brims pinned upwards atop his sinewy white hair. The garb was as black as it was foreboding and only penetrated by a cardinal red ribbon pinned about his chest.

Pales has been Dedrick's hard-working slave horse hand for as long as both men had first noticed pricks of hair around his balls. He is obedient, reliable and respectful and this earns him frequent gratuities such as the leftover pastries deemed too stale as to be consumed by the residents of the manor. Dutifully, Pales stands a dozen yards from the house-porch to greet the doctor and his tired old horse. With each of the soft claps of the hoofs patting the earth his anxious nerves tremble a bit more. Pales is intellectually ignorant to the doctor's reputation, yet his sense of unease has been projected by Dedrick's recent and obvious anxieties in relation to the topic of Van Leeuwen's visit. The site of the doctor's ethereal figure accords his reputation.

Nightmare-inducing tales of the doctor's dealings with various manner of illnesses have reached as far north as Hereensbugh. As travelers and merchants weave their way through the valley along its water and pathways they infect the region's simple innocence with unseemly city manners and torment its untroubled soul with dreadful gossip. The least informed inhabitants of the north claim the doctor to be some breed of sinister wizard and use words such as "witchcraft" and "magic" to describe his methods. How else could such simple minds grasp their belief the doctor has, time and again, defied the will of the Lord? Fear and ignorance are inseparable and human nature tends to create explanations when one does not exist. Superficially, such gossip is harmless as it wanders from the mouths and to the ears of the mostly powerless members of the region. However, from time to time these fears managed to incite unreasonable actions by those who are not powerless within the region.

While fighting to stave off jitters, Pales offers Van Leeuwen with an unsure wave. The doctor coldly peers through the helpful servant and offers the expression as though he was not even there. Dedrick released the curtain allowing it to fall back to place and turns to his family who were at the opposite end of the room, all sharing the same long elegant hickory bench and the same nervous angst. Sarah does her best to appear to be at ease while she offers reassurance to her younger sister by holding her hand tightly. Though well intended the out-of-character gesture does more to further unnerve Liz than it does to comfort her. The young girls are not entirely sure of what awaits them, and their ignorance stirs their nerves and feeds their active imaginations.

Dedrick's understanding of the doctor suggests he is fit only to assist the prestigious and dignified few. Van Leeuwen is fully aware of the value of his time and services and is normally driven more by enmity than any altruistic pursuits to help those who need his help. With that, Dedrick made sure his family was presentable. Emily and their two daughters are dressed in some of their finest attire in anticipation of the doctor's call. Emily wore not one of her favorites; an elegant petticoat and skirt adorned with a floral motif with long white silk gloves which nearly reached her elbows. Her blouse as with most in her wardrobe could not fully conceal the unsightly blisters and lesions on her upper shoulder and neck. Sarah's silk gown is a bright rose and Eliza's a deep blue. From the window, Dedrick was for a moment, lost in his daughters' childlike purity and beauty. Nearly half a smile grew upon his face while his heart was yet filled without much happiness.

For her part, Emily has not presented herself with such stunning splendor for a time she can recall. Dedrick's seen his wife nearly every day for nearly twenty years, yet this is the first time in some time he has noticed her. Her beauty was a flickering candle within the darkness of despair. Feeling a need to be near, to touch her skin he drifted toward her and clutches her hand as though she was threatening to blow away. She welcomed his touch and felt his love and tenderness as though it was passed between them. As of late she has become famished for his affection and the subtle gesture was more than enough to warm her delicate soul. The love shared within the family at that moment was strong enough to radiate the entire grim and cold chamber. These were troubling times, yet all four of the Hereen's felt in their heart, they were not alone.

The brief escape into transcendence was abruptly halted by the carriage's clanking and horse's strides as they grew louder. From outside they heard a shrieking whinny and the doctor fiddled about for a few moments. He exchanged inaudible conversation with Pales, who was setting to prepare his horse. Vesta strolled from the kitchen as she was wiping her hands on her apron and scurried toward the door. She glanced at Eliza and Sarah and smiled assuredly as she passed from one end of the house to the other, toward the door; a rare moment of good nature from the normally hardhearted nanny.

Vesta opened the door, leaned against it and as she peeked outside and asked, "You must be the doctor?"

"And you must be the dim-witted, negro house servant," he said dryly with his back turned to her as he collected his things. He moved slowly, resembling some manner of tall bird, a crane or stork perhaps and his strides were heavier than his appearance would suggest. The doctor held a brown leather medical case low at his left while moving with the aid of a finely crafted walking stick. Each of his steps landed loudly on the wooden porch. Vesta stood at the doorway and though in her own way she was affronted, she welcomed him as she would any guest. In a most nonchalant manner he casually removed his hat and held it and his ornate walking stick at her face, without uttering a sound or hardly glancing in her direction. The reliably sensible Vesta was unmoved by the rumors and wives' tales which portray Van Leeuwen as demon of sorts and simply found him to be as charming as a warm piece of shit. She sighed and took the doctor's belongings from him before he continued into the entryway.

Although typically reserved, Dedrick tried to awkwardly present an outgoing demeanor and greeted the doctor with insincere cheerfulness, "Cornelius...Doctor. You're a welcome sight. I hope your trip was comfortable and without incident...I know the road from the city is long and can be, at times, grueling, if not boring." Van Leeuwen grumbled inaudibly under his breath, but otherwise hardly acknowledged his host's greeting. Despite his charms, Dedrick quickly finds himself lost within awkwardness. He struggled to find something to say and uneasily continued, "I um…Well, from what I've heard you are a talented man. I know the governor thinks highly of you…as do others…Your work with medicines and whatnot…It's not lost on me that this is a great inconvenience to you and your times is valuable, sir. I am truly grateful…*we* are truly grateful, and I never let gestures of good will go unreturned."

Dedrick extends his arm firmly and poignantly as an affable gesture. Van Leeuwen simply looks at his open hand and groans, "You and I know I am not here as a gesture of good will, Dedrick." He peered his dark eyes toward Emily and the girls. "I should say *Mr. Hereen* may be more fitting it would seem…I understand you are a man of means and with many friends, regardless the best you can offer me in return may just be to let me get on with this. You can assume this an altruistic gesture if you wish, yet make no mistake I would not be here had it not been for the people you know and the connections you have, presumably governor Tryon…I'll let others speculate on that. Please, if you are intent to offer me a favor than do so by sparing the charade."

Dedrick kept his arm extended, closed his fist abruptly and replied "I see…You're cranky. I would be too, long trip, it gets a little tiresome ten miles or so north of the Island. What did it take you, twenty, twenty-five hours? I'd be a bit irritable myself."

The doctor was aloof and made no efforts to hide his impatience and discontent for having been there. "You are right about my time; it is quite pressed…and from what I understand yours is as well." Van Leeuwen did not wait for an invitation to continue into the manor house and began walking toward the main dining table outside the upper kitchen area. Dedrick strode alongside and once again struggled to break the awkward tension. "Indeed, it is, and I know you are eager to return home, good sir."

Still, the doctor had no interest in any conversation beyond which was necessary, "I am going to assume, since she has been stricken with the virus you have been intimate with your wife…No need to elaborate. Her condition is transmitted through fluids. Ostensibly, since you have not gotten the virus by now you should be safe… however I cannot say the same holds true for these two," he said as he gestured toward the girls.

"You mean our daughters…Sarah and Eliza," chided Emily from the parlor some twenty feet away. Emily's abrupt sarcasm triggered Van Leeuwen's natural inclination to foster an ill-mannered condescending retort. Untrue to his nature, he responded only with a silent look. His predisposition to take offense was overcome by his admiration for her stunning beauty. Emily's deep blue eyes pierced the doctor's hardened temperament moving him to place he had not come to know; Van Leeuwen was instantly smitten.

Careful not to succumb to, or at least present a sense of capitulation to his infatuation, the doctor now had to work at his inherently cold disposition. "…Yes, of course, your daughters," he replied. "I have had some encouraging outcomes at times, yet I cannot assure you *Sarah and Eliza…*" he said mockingly, "…will not be stricken with the pox. They are more vulnerable than your husband, and in truth, my inclination is this could be a waste of my time…Nonetheless, I have made the tiresome slog from the city, so if you please, I will continue."

Dedrick jumped into the exchange, "Well, *encouraging results* is a better prospect than the one we now face. We all understand you are not here to offer assurances, yet when you have nothing to lose, you have nothing to lose."

"Perhaps," replied Van Leeuwen. "What I *can* assure you is this procedure will be unpleasant, and, you can expect the two of them to become stricken with a mild strain within some days, perhaps a week. In all probability, it will pass and I would expect both to then be immune to the virus moving forward."

"*In all probability* it will pass?" asked Emily.

"Yes, Mrs. Hereen," sneered the doctor. "'In all probability.' This is a fledgling science which, to date does not offer reliable assurances. Some patient's antimicrobials are unable to overcome the smallpox virus, even a mild strain. I may just as soon infect them as easily as I immunize them."

Emily rose to her feet and approached with her stare fixed on Dedrick. The two silently waited for the other to express caution or doubt. "Well…" Emily chided, struggling to maintain composure, "With all due respect, I cannot risk the lives of my daughters on the hopes they will not be the *same.*"

Van Leeuwen had become visibly impatient and made no effort to hide this. "I see, it seems this has been an incredible waste of my time," he said as he looked to regather his belongings and be on his way.

Emily and Dedrick remained hushed as she expected his inclination would have him overrule her perceived decision and he was as unsure as she appeared to be. In his heart, Dedrick recognized the obligation to do so and Emily was torn between guilt and fear. She had always felt guilty as per the burden she had imparted to her family. Even though she was entirely not at fault, it would be a natural inclination to feel responsible for introducing a toxic virus into her home. At times, the cold nature of her husband has done well to amplify such misgivings. Dedrick's occasional implications during moments of frustration were not lost on her. To her, this episode was yet one more in which she brought misfortune to her family. By now, her realization was when no clear option is present, the best course is to choose none of them. Her resolution at this point, was for Dedrick to make such a decision.

"Hold on...Can we take a deep breath for a second Em?" said Dedrick as he rested his palm on Van Leeuwen's hand as to offer him to stop packing his things. "You're so quick to shoo this man away after he traveled a hundred miles to help us...He wouldn't even be here...well, regardless, we are more than lucky he has taken the time to help us...for whatever reason he is helping us. I didn't expect all this to be without risk...Would you rather do nothing, but pray? Let me ask you this, doctor: If this were you...Would you give the inoculation to your child?"

Van Leeuwen looked about the house silently, inspecting and assessing the splendor of their properties and the quality of their taste. He wondered how select his company was if they were worthy of his continued time and effort, The Inn's request notwithstanding. His lack of empathy had become apparent, "I don't have any children Mr. Hereen...At least to my knowledge I don't. Typically, I believe it is unwise to make such decisions guided by our emotions. I will say, the odds are in your favor."

Emily and Dedrick once again locked eyes and exchanged somber expressions. "Would you give it anybody you loved?" Pleaded Emily.

"Whomever it is you care for…would you give them the inoculation?"

Doctor Van Leeuwen paused for a moment and gave the matter a bit of thought, "The miserable have no other medicine but only hope."

With a smug tone Emily gaped directly into his shadowy eyes leaned forward and replied, "Yes doctor. Be absolute for death: either death or life."

The doctor was staggered. Whether it be her gentle, seductive tone or breath of confidence, Van Leeuwen was nearly overcome by her grace and gorgeousness. A rare smile polluted his typically dower expression and he found an inkling libidinous. Without trying, Emily's charisma had pierced the cock sucker's buttress of arrogance, apathy and abject scorn which surrounds his infinitesimal, wintery-cold heart. Though her husband had apparently grown immune to her magnetism, their guest felt a surge run through the insipid, wrinkled, pale-gray pickle which dangled between his twisted, bony legs. "Brava, Mrs. Hereen,"

"*Emily* is fine, Doctor. I won't make you say you are impressed or just maybe you are not entirely regretful to have taken the time to journey north to visit our home, but I know you are and don't," chided Emily. "We are not all the bumpkins I assume you assume us to be." She concluded as she offered him a gentle poke to his stomach with her soft cotton gloved finger.

Dedrick abruptly and dismissively interrupted, "Are we done or…? You want to keep going with this banter or leave him to treat our children? Perhaps it would be wise to move this along as to not prolong the torment our young daughters are, at this moment, torn-up over. Or no? You want to keep going with the small talk?" Emily was filled with contempt as she knew she had gotten under Dedrick's thick skin. As for the doctor, he was lost within himself and not fully aware of how he fit into the triangular dynamic. Though he was aware enough to have felt a twinge of uncharacteristic sympathy and empathy toward her as manifested as agitation toward Dedrick. The sarcastic scolding seemed to reveal a lack of appreciation for how fortunate Dedrick was to be married to such a stunning woman. Gradually, the doctor's eye slyly surveyed Dedrick's face as if he was assessing the man's character. He caught himself and groaned subtly, tried to once again find his coarsened nature and said, "It appears as though we are moving forward…I'm going to work over there," then headed toward the parlor table.

He opened his case and removed several instruments one at a time then placed each side-by-side atop the table. Still near the doorway, Vesta fiddled with the doctor's hat as she clutched it in her hands nervously and could not contain her restraint any longer.

"This going to hurt them girls Mister doctor?" she asked in an uneasy manner.

"Excuse me?" he replied as he crossly looked toward Dedrick. Doctor Van Leeuwen refuses to be addressed by a slave and was immediately insulted by the gall for her to dare to do so. "Perhaps I am ignorant to the manner of etiquette in these parts north… Though, I would be embarrassed to remind you a gentleman does not allow his help…especially a Negro, to speak unless spoken to."

Dedrick replied as he glanced toward Vesta with a penetrating look, "No need for embarrassment. You would be correct to do so. At times, we can be a bit spoiled in these parts, doctor. Vesta is sorry, and she will be reminded about her place. For now, she was actually on her way back into the kitchen to prepare tea, which I am sure you will enjoy…" To which she bowed her head and scurried toward the upper kitchen area.

The house was quiet, other than the floor which creaked as the doctor moved about as he placed his instruments on the dining table before him. Dedrick sauntered back toward the girls and sat upon a rather impressively crafted oak trunk in front of them. He stroked his scruffy chin, as he often does, and tilted his head toward his oldest daughter. "How are you doing?" he asked.

"I will be better when this man leaves our house," she whispered.

He offered a half-hearted grin and said, "You too, huh? He will be gone soon enough." With a grave tone, he continued, "I know you are worried and I cannot say this will be fun. Regardless, you need to trust your mother and I when we tell you this is necessary to protect you. We take no joy in subjecting you to being upset. You're a big girl and smart enough to understand this will help you and your sister."

Without turning to face him, Sarah replied with a tone of indifference, "Daddy...please. I'm not a baby, I understand why he is here. Can you just let me be nervous? Please stop trying to make me feel better."

The doctor slowly removed his cape, folded it over and rested it on the chair at the head position. He snatched an instrument from his bag then turned toward the family from the parlor some twenty-five feet away. He held a long, thin metal blade and rotated it back and forth as he inspected it closely as its glare danced over his leathery skinned face. While fixed on the instrument he softly addressed the Hereens with his typical lack of emotional understanding, "I am going out to my cart for perhaps a moment. Leave the door open, do not close it behind me and when I return I expect one of those two to be seated in that chair...at the opposite end of the table. Do not make me wait for her to find her seat, have her in it." He places the blade and a few other implements back into his case then snapped it shut.

Though he wore fashionable, low heeled soft leather shoes, his strides echoed throughout the entire house. He lurched the door open then disappeared outside. The sunlight cast itself upon the girls' faces as their eyes curiously watched him leave. "Where'd he go... where did the doctor go?" asked Eliza. "He went home?"

"I'm sure he is going to get medicine," replied Sarah. Her voice was mixed with concern, annoyance and reassurance. "Right, mom?"

Becoming slightly more concerned Eliza continued, "You think the medicine will taste bad?"

"Yes, it will, it will taste very bad. Have you ever eaten medicine that tasted good, Liz? They make it taste bad on purpose so people won't eat all of it and they can save it for sick people," said Sarah.

Eliza's anxiety drifted toward bewilderment until Dedrick demanded, "Alright, enough about the taste of medicine. You're not going to be eating any medicine...so some good news there. Lizzy, let's go." He rose to his feet and offered his hand as to help Eliza.

"No, Daddy, it's alright," snapped Sarah. "I'll go first."

Dedrick furrowed his brows, partially annoyed, yet mostly confused, "Thank you, Sarah that is nice of you to offer. Eliza is going to go first. You agree it will be better for her to have this behind her sooner rather than later? Right?"

"I want to go first so she can see that it won't be so bad."

Though he rolled his eyes, Dedrick understood his daughter's point and admired her bravery. "Fair enough," he said and directed her toward the parlor. "You're a good sister, Sarah. We are very proud of you," he concluded as he gently stroked the top of her head.

Outside Doctor Van Leeuwen approached the back end of his open carriage. Pales harnessed the horse to the post firmly and took it upon himself to attach a floppy canvas feedback around her mouth. He rubbed the worn-down beast's neck and shoulders affectionately and sympathetically. The doctor quickly noticed Pales and waved him away and without hesitation the slave happily disappeared. Van Leeuwen covered his long prickly nose and slim-lipped mouth as he neared the back end of the wagon. Inside the carriage bed a sickly young man, appearing just old enough to shave his chin, lies on a loose bale of hay which has been scattered about. He was on his back with his head pressed against the wagon board so tightly it looked to be forced into his chest. His clothing was tattered and stained and his skin was so balmy the gleams of sweat were nearly blinding. The left side of his face is rotted with bubbly red and black blisters and his left eye is swollen as to be fully closed. The unfortunate soul's mouth is open only so slightly as to allow slow, painfully desperate gasps for breath.

The doctor brushes aside a few hay straws then rests his instrument case on the carriage bed where he pops it open. He places his scalpel, a pair of rough, iron tweezers and a thin glass tray on the base of the wagon's bed. In systematic fashion, he works as if the young man was as feeling as one of the stones at his feet. Casually, he clutches the sickly man's left arm and rolls back the ragged sleeve toward his elbow. In so doing, strands of mucous are stretched from the lumps and scars along his arm to the fabric of his shirt. With some strength, Doctor Van Leeuwen presses the victim's limb to rest flatly and firmly against the carriage boards. He holds it tightly against the base of the carriage bed with one hand and with the other carefully reaches for the scalpel. Slowly he picks at one of the lumps with the blade's cutting edge. He slices at the lesion in a sawing motion until it is carved from the ailing man's flesh. With careful deliberation, the doctor scrapes the scalpel against a shallow glass tray, removing the bit of flesh from the blade. He repeats the gruesome process several times more and throughout the young man does not flinch nor make a sound.

Inside the house Sarah is seated at the head of the parlor table. Her slight frame is virtually lost in the grand cherry-wood chair in which only the adults have sat. Her wide eyes seemed to have grown as they are varnished by the tears she tries so desperately to keep. With her stomach tied and knots and her flush with nervous tensions, she does her best to appear relaxed. Her father was at her side, yet she felt as alone as ship lost at sea. "I'm scared Daddy. I have to do this right?" she whispers nervously. "We have to do this so we will not be sick, like Mommy?"

Dedrick moved to consider her massive, blue eyes and was overcome as it for a second, he believed to have been looking into Emily's. "I know…I know…I know you're scared Little Levana. There is no shame in being afraid. You cannot be courageous if you are not afraid. Your mother and I would not have you do this unless we knew it would keep you safe from this sickness. This will only help you. I told you before, and I said it because I meant it; we are all part of this and you are not alone."

Quickly she peeped toward her younger sister who wore a look of near terror. She gave the matter only some thought and once again whispered to her father, "Can I sit on your lap? Please, Daddy. Let me sit on your lap when he does this."

He could not help but sigh as Dedrick realized he was essentially called to act upon his claim. He glanced toward Emily as though he was seeking her assistance and she responded only with a silent look as to suggest he was on his own. "Sarah, that's really…I can't say that is a good idea. The doctor was pretty clear with his instructions. What happened to all of the courage for your little sister' talk?"

With sorrow in her eyes, Sarah's pleading had shifted to astonishment, "I'm sorry. I sorry I want my father to care about me when I'm scared…and I'm sorry I asked."

Disappointed, Emily saw Dedrick's warmth expire rather quickly and scolded him, "Dedrick, your daughter is frightened and wants to sit on your lap. You can't be serious, right now." He allowed his head to fall into his chest as though he was crestfallen and sighed, "Evidently not."

Perhaps not fully in tune with the sarcasm, Sarah felt a tinge of relief which nearly brought a smile onto her face. Dedrick brushed her aside, "Move it kid," he jibed. With new-found energy, she leaped to her feet almost gleefully. Sarah was charged with a sense of reassurance and a pinch of gratification as to winning the subtle competition with her father. As she lowered her weight onto his lap, Dedrick could not help but to give her a hard time. "Pfft," as he forced a few puffs from his mouth as to blow away the stands of her hair from his face. Sarah giggled and re-positioned herself and snapped her wrist at the shoulder brushing more of her soft hair to tickle his chin. "So that's funny, then?" he said as he tipped her toward her side, threatening her to fall from the chair. He tickled her ribs which prompted outward and infectious laughter as little Eliza began to chuckle as she observed the exchange. The two chuckled and for a moment and were totally at ease, nearly forgetting what was happening or what was about to happen.

Doctor Van Leeuwen slowly thumped across the porch with each step a bit more strident than the one before it. Sarah's giggles instantly turned to cold silence when his looming shadow was cast from the doorway. He lowered his head and groaned, "It seems we are unable to properly follow simple instructions. I thought I was clear one of them is to be in the chair."

"And one of them is," quipped Dedrick. Clearly his family's fate was in his hands, yet It was not easy for Dedrick to curb his disdain for Doctor Van Leeuwen.

"Are you trying to waste more of my time with verbal games or are you truly dense? I am looking for a reason to be on my way back to New York as soon as possible. It seems I just may have found one."

Dedrick continued, "Right. New York, where you can tell Caldweller, or whomever sent you, you did not do what you tasked to do because you insisted I tell my seven-year old daughter she cannot sit on my lap? You know the governor has three young daughters I'm sure."

The doctor was backed into a corner as Dedrick played his hand. There was no pragmatic reason for his instruction, yet he was driven by stubbornness not to yield. The reality being Van Leeuwen was afforded no options here. The Inn had sent him to Tarry Town with the charge to treat Dedrick's daughters with a smallpox vaccination. Returning to New York without having done so, barring the most extreme of mitigating circumstances, would find the doctor in a potentially deadly position. As it is, Van Leeuwen needed Dedrick as much as Dedrick needed him. "Very well," grumbled the doctor. He began by placing his medical bag on the parlor table and rested a glass vile beside it. In the small glass plate was the ooze and scabs from the doomed smallpox victim within Van Leeuwen's wagon. The doctor shuffled through his case and removed a wooden-handled instrument with a small blunt knob on its end. With it he pressed the blunt end into the dish and twisted as if removing a cork from an old bottle of wine as he navigated himself around the table toward Sarah and Dedrick. It made a most unpleasant shrieking shill until he finally stopped just as he reached the two of them.

"This inoculation will be uncomfortable and I will tell you, the more you resist, the more difficult it will be for the two of us," he said. He shifted his attention toward Dedrick, "Exposure to Cow Pox is presumably the culprit. The pathogen spreads with the exchange of fluids...your wife's symptoms...the vomiting and blisters...are the result of the virus trying to spread to other hosts. We have performed this procedure on six prisoners and none of the six had become infected when exposed. Granted, they were older and presumably better able to stave off the virus."

"Thank you. I trust we are in good hands Dr. Van Leeuwen," replied Dedrick.

"Yes...I need her to roll back her sleeve if you will," instructed the Doctor. He then rested the glass dish on the table and removed short, thin blade from his case.

Dr. Van Leeuwen made a small incision on Sarah's left forearm. She groaned in pain as he slowly sliced the skin and blood trickled around her wrist. Sarah forced her eyes closed and although she remained as still as she was able; her trembling was uncontrollable. Both her and her father sensed her jitters beginning to irritate Van

Leeuwen, yet for the time being he appeared unusually tolerant. With wire tweezers Van Leeuwen dabbed a few drops of the mucous into the open abrasion and pressed firmly with his thumb. Sarah could not help but look, then quickly looked away in disgust. Dedrick leaned his head aside hers while whispering assurances into her ear. The doctor noticed his consoling gestures and suddenly felt to be an intruder into their lives.

The procedure was not as dreadful as expected, yet enough to creep into the dreams of both young girls for some time. Both Sarah and Eliza took to the comfort of their beds as Emily and loyal Vesta remained at their sides through most of the night. Downstairs, Dedrick did his best to present himself to be a grateful host as he and the doctor finished a pot of tea and a small number of pastries. The two struggled to find an area of discussion and mostly prattled mindlessly about the weather and their anticipation of a harsh or not-so-harsh winter. From time to time, Dedrick would flip a scrap under the table to his loving hound who was bundled at his feet. Van Leeuwen caught Dedrick sneaking crumbs from the table to Caesar every time felt the same condescending revolution. While he was mostly grateful for Dedrick's plainly insincere gesture of hospitality, Van Leeuwen was quite aware he was not particularly welcome by this point. In turn, he was more than eager to be on his way and the late day sun was threatening to turn into early evening darkness. With a few sips of lukewarm tea and a bite or two of Vesta's apple tart left in front of him on the parlor table, Van Leeuwen decided it best to push past wasteful pleasantries and mindless talk. "Mr. Hereen... Dedrick, "he said. "I'm going to make you a proposition, and regardless of your interest, it will not leave this table, and should it, I will be forced with no other choice than to deny it while attacking your honor."

Peaked in curiosity of course, Dedrick quickly veered from tired banalities requiring less than half of his concentration to an arousal of full attention. "Curious," he replied. "I wasn't interested in mindless small talk either. You do realize you cannot leave the table without telling me what you are thinking." His words were true as the doctor, perhaps with a demonstration of atypical miscalculation, virtually tipped whatever hand he may have been playing by inferring the profound nature of his thoughts. Yet, it was more that the doctor shred himself of doubt when he moved to put himself in the position where he was essentially given little choice but to offer his proposal.

"Very clever, Dedrick. Clever indeed," snarled Van Leeuwen. "As we sit here, it is a certainty your wife will succumb to her illness. To be clear, her condition is terminal and offers little time. You can rely on hope, or faith, if you value such things, to pacify your soul as your mind comprehends the inevitable. I will not begrudge you this as I have seen better men than you convince themselves irrational superstition will triumph over natural science…regardless. I loathe to repeat myself, yet will say this again as to ensure my clarity and your understanding: What I am about to offer is for your ears and your ears only. This is beyond the likes of The Inn, the governor or any such influential acquaintances you may have the good fortune to call friends. I can tell you my associates, as they are, serve to protect me and my interests and I can also assure you they will abide by no code of honor to ensure I am protected. The Keepers and governor himself would not be able to protect you from such men. The fact remains, under any circumstances, my word will always trump your word in minds to those who matter. And if you speak of such things, you can be certain, you will be killed. All this being said, shall I proceed?"

Moved and puzzled, Dedrick agreed if for no other reason than to satisfy his intense curiosity. "I don't think there is any way I would consider telling you not to proceed, Cornelius."

"Good," replied the doctor. "Very good. Now then, I believe interesting developments, may provide you and your wife with greater prospects than prayer and common medicines. The details are not necessary for our purposes…What you need to know is there is a way to save her life. A native artifact holds medicinal promises far beyond my skills or studies. Far beyond any known scientific medicines in fact, and as you can gather, the knowledge of such a… uh…prescription, is closely guarded by a powerful and very few."

Dedrick furrowed his brows and was clearly perplexed and more than a little cynical. "A native medicine, is that what you said? What does this mean? Drinking deer piss or eating wild mushrooms? I'm sorry, this sounds like fairy tale. I would be killed for speaking about Indian fantasy?

I must say I'm surprised you would…well, put any stock in such notions."

Van Leeuwen was not in the least surprised by Dedrick's reaction. He sipped the final drops of tea from the delicately crafted teacup as though he was preparing to set out back to New York. "If you are surprised then perhaps your perception of who I am and what I am capable of should hold more weight than your immediate dismissal of what you do not understand. You are traveled enough to know I am wholly unmoved by gossip or fantastic tales of the extraordinary. My reputation is valuable and I work to keep it this way. That means I don't take stock in fairy tales. I know, you know I only react to evidence and sound reason…As this case may be, I will remind you: because something does not sound correct does not uphold that it is incorrect. This is not a native medicine; it is medicine which has been in the custody of natives. I would gather their primitive minds have no understanding of its value. As a physician and a man of science, I can promise you, it can save your wife's life.

"It is with immense gravity I share this with you. I know the risk, we are mutually bound by the restrictions of the Inn. The Keepers will have my head on a pike if you chose to, rightfully, tell them I am in violation of the code."

Dedrick was moved as to rest back into the chair and draw a bewildered look upon his face. He believed Van Leeuwen, yet was not entirely sure why he believed him. His mind conjured the many aspects to suspend his disbelief. Perhaps he was so desperate to trust the doctor to be true he shut down his better judgment. "And why are you telling me this, Cornelius? You are right, I am traveled enough to know the devices of your intellect, yet I also understand the nature of your heart. What do you want from me? What is the balance of the proposition you eluded to? You have wealth and connections, I can't imagine what I have to cause you to take such a chance in telling me all of this, should it be true or not. I believed you when you said I have nothing to fucking offer."

A partial smile cracked along Van Leeuwen's sinister expression as he blurted his request so bluntly it was as though he could no longer wait to keep it to himself, as though the mere sound of hearing him saying it was sufficient compensation, "I want to fuck your wife."

As the words reached Dedrick's ears he was instantly aghast and speechless. Despite his horror, he was not entirely shocked as a hunch, buried within him suggested this was what Doctor Van Leeuwen had required all along. All the same, he diligent mind required further exposition as he sought to process all that had been presented before him. "I beg your pardon...what?"

"Eh, you heard what I said, Dedrick. I will not repeat it. You have two very clear options, and really, I cannot understand how you would consider one of them. For a man who loves the mother of his two young daughters, I cannot see how this would require any consideration. I will arrange for Emily's exposure to the healing apparatus when my price is met. She will live and you will all be afforded the lives you were meant to have before she became stricken with the virus."

Habitually, Dedrick stroked the scruff about his chin as he peered through the southern window. With his gaze fixed on the sun's warm glow and the stray leaves drifting along the faded green grass the vision of the ghoulish fuck contaminating the purity of her tenderness and tainting their connection consumed him. He was not inclined to assume anything other than deadly seriousness given Van Leeuwen's humorless nature. All the same, he was having trouble processing what was evidently obvious, "I...I'm sorry. This is not happening...are you really asking me this?"

"Believe your ears, Dedrick," snarled Van Leeuwen. "I am free of tricks, riddles, subtext, nuance or hidden agendas. My proposition is as apparent as it seems. This is not a negotiation yet a dualistic choice between only A and only B. I want to fuck her, and when if this is the route you so choose, I will make all the necessary arraignments to save her life. Now, to be a fair man I will disclose to you the details which involve your participation in this. I would not expect you to simply rely on my word."

Overcome with disgust Dedrick shook his head decisively, "Fuck off Cornelius, there is no way in fucking hell we are going to include you in some perverted three-way sex orgy. Not in a thousand years is that going to happen. There is not a single thing you can offer me to convince me otherwise. We'll take our chances with fate."

Van Leeuwen narrowed his eyes in mild confusion and gave the thought a minute to marinate within his mind, "Sex orgy? I have no interest in involving you in the act of intercourse, sir. You misunderstood my direction. I wish to fuck, only Emily. I am making it clear to you, you will need to involve yourself in this war for me to negotiate the particulars. In simple terms, the Empire is, shall we say, cautious in this way. Even I cannot arrange for such drastic measures for a neutral party...no matter how well-connected her husband may be. Now, if he offered his services and arms for the King, I will have no trouble making such accommodations. Furthermore, I have suspicions of foul play...Regardless. I would need to position you within the expedition to retrieve the healing artifact."

"Hold on...You don't even have this fucking thing?" asked Dedrick.

"Details," mumbled the doctor. "Please do not concern yourself with the details and please do not allow your ignorance to them influence your reasoned verdict. You will be required to fight for the King, and from what I understand, you are benevolent to his cause, thus it would be an honorable gesture. I'm offering you the opportunity to subdue the upheaval and save the life of the woman you love. I invite you to make every precaution, to turn over every stone and do all the diligence you deem necessary. Do not to presume I have not gotten where I am by riding the tide of empty promises. My word is as strong as the stone walls of this fine structure in which we sit. You know me not to be a charlatan, and we both know the powerful men who live in the shadows would ensure neither you or I find harm in the other. Consider this and consider your family. I believe you said you have reached the point of having nothing to lose, yes? Forgive me, I thought I heard you say your oldest daughter to be seven. Am I mistaken or is she nine?"

The delicate teacup which Dedrick hand been fiddling with was nearly tipped over as he reacted to Van Leeuwen's assertion. Dedrick raced to consider if he had misspoken as was not wholly sure he had not. Telling regardless was his realization it would not have been entirely unusual had he confused her age. Sarah and Eliza needed a mother more than he needed a wife. His mind was virtually set as to what he was going to proclaim, yet Dedrick held off for if he could to not actually say the words of agreeing to this sordid arrangement. He could not help but to conjure the specifics, the actualities in bitter and repulsive detail. The image of his gentle bride gagging on Van Leeuwen's prickly, pink cock until she gargles his warm, slimy cum was making his stomach curl. His dick has been in every hole in Sally's body and between the teeth of so many whores, he couldn't possibly remember them all if he had uninterrupted days to recall. Yet the darker the voices within his head assured him penetrating another is a rather tolerable misdemeanor, whereas allowing oneself to be penetrated is nothing short of vile. Dedrick knew of the doctor, yet did not know who he was, as such was completely unenlightened to his preferences in such affairs. He struggled to bargain with his sense of disgust and reach an acceptable conclusion in that he could bear to put his dick only where Van Leeuwen's had not been. Thus, he considered to suggest the doctor only stick his cock into her bum, yet even such discussion did nothing other than to make Dedrick, yet more disgusted. He resigned to accept the sacrifice of his dignity and her purity for the greater good on the condition to himself which is he would remain completely in the dark in regard to particulars.

Dedrick rested his elbows on the parlor table's surface and buried his face into his hands. For a few moments, he massaged his eyes as though somehow, he could cleanse the filth from his thoughts. "She is nine, yes," he grumbled. "This is not a decision I am going to make for my wife, yet I will talk to her."

With a glow about his insipid face, Doctor Van Leeuwen straightened his back and looked directly at Dedrick, "You have made a wise decision, my good man."

CPSIA information can be obtained
at www.ICGtesting.com
Printed in the USA
BVHW08s0444130618
518918BV00001B/4/P

9 781939 665515